THE CHARADE

EDEN FALLS ACADEMY

the *charade*

JUDY CORRY

ALSO BY JUDY CORRY

<u>Eden Falls Academy Series:</u>

The Charade (Ava and Carter)

The Facade (Cambrielle and Mack)

The Ruse (Elyse and Asher)

The Confidant (Scarlett and Hunter)

The Confession (Kiara and Nash)

<u>Kings of Eden Falls:</u>

Hide Away With You (Addie and Evan)

Say You Remember Me (Maddie and Ian)

Wish You Were Mine (Lucy and Owen)

<u>Rich and Famous Series:</u>

Assisting My Brother's Best Friend (Kate and Drew)

Hollywood and Ivy (Ivy and Justin)

Her Football Star Ex (Emerson and Vincent)

Friend Zone to End Zone (Arianna and Cole)

Stolen Kisses from a Rock Star (Maya and Landon)

<u>Ridgewater High Series:</u>

When We Began (Cassie and Liam)

Meet Me There (Ashlyn and Luke)

Don't Forget Me (Eliana and Jess)

It Was Always You (Lexi and Noah)

My Second Chance (Juliette and Easton)

My Mistletoe Mix-Up (Raven and Logan)

Forever Yours (Alyssa and Jace)

<u>Standalones:</u>

Protect My Heart (Emma and Arie)

Kissing The Boy Next Door (Lauren and Wes)

For my husband, Jared.
Thank you for going on this crazy journey with me and for all your support as I chase after my dreams.
Some people have comfort animals. You are my comfort human.

PLAYLIST

"Timebomb" by Tove Lo
"Sometimes" by Ben Rector
"Ross and Rachel" by Jake Miller
"Good for Somebody" by Kaitlyn Bristowe
"Lose Somebody" by Kygo & OneRepublic
"Cop Car" by Sam Hunt
"Into You" by Ariana Grande
"The Other Side" by Jason Derulo
"Control" by Zoe Wees
"Always" by Sofia Carson
"Anyone" by Justin Bieber
"Ocean Away" by Barlow & Bear
"In My Blood/Swan Lake" by The Piano Guys

AVA

"I'M GOING to miss you girls so much," my mom said, gathering my twin sister, Elyse, and me into her arms for one last hug before she left us at the entrance of our new private boarding school.

My sister and I hugged our petite mother, our five-foot-nine-inch frames towering over her barely five-foot one.

"Sure you can't just take us with you?" Elyse asked our mother when we pulled away from the hug, the look of apprehension in her expression mirroring how I felt.

"Yeah," I said. "I mean, isn't online schooling all the rage these days?"

Mom shook her head as she gazed at my sister and then at me. "I won't have you miss the last opportunity to be kids." But even as she said it, the tears at the corners of her dark-brown eyes told me she hated saying goodbye as much as we did. "You're going to love it here. Some of my best memories were made at this school when I was your age."

I looked behind us again, feeling so small next to the

hundred-year-old castle-like building that would be my home for the next nine months.

I'd been so on board with the dream of my mom finally making it big in the fashion world, since I loved fashion and couture almost as much as she did. But if I'd known that getting her own fashion show in New York this past year would soon lead to her traveling the world—necessitating that Elyse and I attend a boarding school to finish our senior year—I would have told her to hold off on that dream a little longer. Because I wasn't ready for the *three amigos* to be separated.

But ready or not, my mom's dreams had finally come true and now we were starting our last year of high school on the outskirts of Eden Falls, Connecticut—a world away from the tiny house in Ridgewater, New York where we grew up.

My mom had attended Eden Falls Academy when she was our age—her family being wealthy property developers in Israel and wanting to give her the study-abroad experience.

So now that she could afford to send us here, there were apparently no other options worth considering. After all, if her strict Jewish parents had felt safe sending their only daughter half a world away to school here, then it was most certainly good enough for us.

So here we were with our suitcases already delivered to our room, ready to start our senior year at a high school whose tuition and board for a year cost more than my mom used to make annually.

I was thankful my mom cared about us so much that she would do anything to give us all the things she felt we'd lacked the first seventeen years of our lives. But as a rabble of butterflies fluttered around in my ribcage when I looked up at the huge iron doors surrounded by vines with pink flowers, I couldn't help but think that staying at Grandma Cohen's home in Israel would have been a much less daunting prospect. At least I'd been there before, so it was somewhat familiar.

What if no one liked me here?

What if all the social groups were already so tightly knit that there wasn't extra room for new faces?

But since I knew this was already a hard enough goodbye, I forced myself to stand up straighter, pulled my shoulders back, and said, "I'm sure once we're settled, we'll like it." I looked at my sister, whose golden-brown eyes were the same color and shape as mine. "Elyse and I will watch out for each other."

"Yes, I'll make sure Ava gets at least some of her homework done in between flirting with all the guys," Elyse said, shooting me a smirk.

"And I'll make sure Elyse has a little fun as she's maintaining her 4.0 GPA," I countered back with a wink.

"Just look out for each other and everything will be fine." My mom glanced at Elyse and me. "And remember, I'm only a phone call away if you need me."

She gave us each one last hug, and before we could shed too many more tears, she waved goodbye and climbed into the black car waiting for her on the cobblestone drive.

And there she went, the great Miriam Cohen, the woman who had clawed her way back up to the top after her father had disinherited her when she had Elyse and me out of wedlock.

I hoped that someday I could be half as strong of a woman as my mom was.

Which meant that I needed to practice being strong now, even though I was afraid.

Elyse and I linked arms and waved as we watched the car holding our mother drive away, a cool fall breeze causing the leaves of the towering trees nearby to rustle.

Once the black car disappeared down the tree-shrouded path and through the tall iron gates, Elyse turned to me and asked, "Ready to go back inside for our tour?"

"I guess."

And so, instead of putting off the inevitable, we walked side by side up the few steps that led to the entrance of our new school.

A GIRL WEARING one of the school's blue blazers and plaid skirts was waiting for Elyse and me when we made it back into the school's lobby. She had long, dark auburn hair and looked so much like a younger Lily Collins that I couldn't help but wonder if they were related.

"Ready for the grand tour?" she asked us when we got closer.

"I, um..." I glanced over to Elyse briefly, then returned my attention to the girl ahead of us. "Sure. That would be great."

"Perfect." She beamed. "My name is Scarlett, by the way." Scarlett held her hand out for me to shake. "I'm one of the captains for our house."

"I'm Ava." I shook her hand.

"And I'm Elyse." Elyse did the same.

Scarlett narrowed her brown eyes for a moment, looking us up and down and side to side.

"Trying to figure out how you're going to tell us apart?" I guessed, knowing the look in her eyes well enough.

Scarlett pursed her deep pink lips. "Usually, when I meet twins, I can tell them apart because they do their hair or makeup differently from one another. But you two are obviously the kind of twins who like keeping people on their toes."

"Why have an identical twin if you can't have a little fun tricking your friends and family every once in a while?" I said, proud of the certain mystique Elyse and I took with us wherever we went.

"Just give me a few days." Scarlett's lips curved up into a slow smile, like she thrived on the idea of a challenge. "I'll figure it out."

I shrugged. "We'll see."

Elyse and I *had* cultivated our own looks through the years with our own fashion styles and beauty preferences— me taking after our mother more when it came to dressing up and Elyse going for the more natural and casual look. But if we wanted to do the twin switch here and there, even our own mother had a hard time discerning who was who.

So if we could still trick our mom on a weekly basis, I didn't see this new acquaintance deciphering the tiny differences that made us unique anytime soon.

Scarlett guided us around the main section of the school first, showing us the various classrooms, the auditorium, and the gym. And despite the actual school building being over a hundred years old, everything inside was state-of-the art—the school and its grounds breathtaking, actually. According to Scarlett, the school sat on ten acres. It had the usual football, baseball, and other sports fields, which she pointed out from the doors near the swimming pool. But it also had lush gardens with a walking/running/bike path that reminded me of the beautiful gardens from the rich estates in the regency romance movies my mom sometimes watched.

It actually kind of felt like a real castle. Only that instead of royalty living within the walls with servants helping to run the place, there were teachers and students milling around, chatting among their peers about their plans and hopes for the new school year.

"Do either of you play sports?" Scarlett asked Elyse and me after we'd walked around the girls' locker room, which displayed the school colors of maroon and silver everywhere.

"Definitely not," Elyse said, a hint of amusement in her voice, like the thought of anyone even asking if she was athletic was comical. "I think all the athletic genes went to Ava when the egg split. But I'll be first in line for this year's theater productions."

"Oh cool. I'll have to introduce you to Nash and Cambrielle then. They're in our house, too, and know all about that." Scarlett turned to me next, an expectant look on her face. "So if you're the sporty one, does that mean you're going out for any of the girls' teams this year?"

"I'm hoping to try out for the girls' basketball team this winter," I said with a shrug, trying to seem like I didn't care too much if I made the team.

"Nice!" Scarlett said. "I'm on the girls' volleyball team right now, but basketball is my first love."

"Oh fun." My cheeks warmed at the prospect of already

getting to know someone who had similar interests as me. "What position do you play?"

"I was the forward last year, so I'm hoping Coach will put me there again," Scarlett said. "What about you?"

"I was the point guard at our last school, but I know that coming in when there's already an established team, I'll be lucky just to get a spot on the roster."

"Our point guard actually graduated last spring," Scarlett said. "So I'm sure Coach Jenkins will be excited to have you try out."

"That would be awesome."

You know, as long as I earned grades high enough to even try out in the first place.

When my mom had applied for us to come to her alma mater, I almost didn't get accepted because my GPA was lower than they'd like for such a prestigious school.

Eden Falls Academy was serious about their students' education and only wanted to accept those who would fit into their high academic standards—they wanted to make sure they could continue to boast a ninety-percent acceptance rate to all the Ivy League schools in the New England area.

But after a lot of back and forth between my mom and the headmistress, they came to the agreement that if I put extra effort into my math class this year—meaning, I met with a tutor twice a week to keep my grade up—then I could join Elyse at the academy.

It was embarrassing that I hadn't even started the school year and was already set up for extra help with math. But if Elyse could say that I got the athletic genes when our egg split, I could also say that Elyse had gotten the math genes.

So humiliating or not, I was already set up to meet with my new math tutor in the library after school tomorrow.

I just hoped it wasn't some hoity-toity rich snob who'd make me feel dumber than I already did.

Scarlett led us out of the girls' locker room, through the gym and across the hall, to a long room with weight-lifting machines and free weights lined up along the walls. When we stepped onto the padded black floor, I saw there were already a few guys who looked about our age at the other end of the room lifting weights.

"This is the weight room, obviously." Scarlett gestured at the various black-and-white machines beside us. "We have PE every day, but if you want to get some strength training in during your free time, this is open from six in the morning until nine at night for you to use."

I looked around at the various machines, not having the slightest idea of what I would even begin to do in here. I'd never taken a weights class at my old school and definitely never had a pass to a gym before, but I was intrigued and would probably try to find a time to sneak down here when there weren't other people to watch me fumble my way around the machines.

"Scarlett Caldwell?" A deep voice sounded from across the room, taking my attention. "Is that you?"

"Mack!" Scarlett turned her gaze to the owner of the voice, a huge grin lifting her cheeks. And in the next second she was bounding toward a tall guy with rich brown skin, wearing a maroon stringer tank top that showed off his well-defined biceps.

"Do you think that's her boyfriend?" I whispered to Elyse

as Scarlett enthusiastically hugged the guy she'd called Mack.

"I don't know," Elyse said, eyeing Mack's toned arms. "But if that's what all the guys at this school look like, I don't think I'll be complaining too much about transferring here."

"Me neither." I looked Mack over again. He was so tall, at least six-foot five from the looks of how he towered over Scarlett. And yes, he was super cute.

"Ava and Elyse," Scarlett said, turning back to my sister and me after pulling away from the giant beside her. "This is Mack."

I stepped forward, holding my hand out to him. "Hi Mack, I'm Ava."

"Ava?" He shook my hand, his large one engulfing mine. "Nice to meet you."

Elyse introduced herself next, and then Mack narrowed his dark brown eyes at us both. "So, do you two always dress alike?"

"Not all the time," I said, looking down at my pink T-shirt with the graphic of a blue whale on it that matched Elyse's. "Just whenever we want to make a statement."

"I like it." Mack's big lips lifted into a crooked grin. "Though, hate to break it to you, but everyone at this school dresses alike. So you might need to find a new way to make a statement." He winked, and I knew immediately that I was going to like this Mack guy. He seemed to be the kind of guy who could joke around with anybody.

"I guess we'll just have to find another way to stand out then," Elyse said, and I didn't miss the sparkle in her eyes as she looked up at the handsome stranger.

Mack turned his gaze to my sister, looking her over from

head to toe. "Somehow I don't think you standing out is going to be a problem."

And in that moment, I really hoped, for my sister's sake, that Scarlett and Mack were just friends because I really didn't want Scarlett to hate us after seeing the sparks between him and my twin.

When I glanced over at Scarlett to make sure she wasn't staring daggers at us, I was relieved to see that she had turned her focus instead to the two guys racking their weights behind Mack.

"Carter. Hunter," she called, waving her hand. "Come meet my new friends before you start your next set."

A guy with dirty-blond hair turned to look at us over his shoulder, and when our gazes met, my heart did a little flip-flop because...wow. He was gorgeous. Totally my type: Tall. Aqua-blue eyes. Square jawline. An athletic build. Warm tan skin.

Yeah, he might even be cuter than the male model I'd been crushing on since my mom's fashion show.

I drew in a quick breath, hoping no one had noticed how I'd stopped breathing for a second, and then made my gaze move to the other guy with chestnut-colored hair approaching us.

But as the two guys moved closer, all I could think about was how maybe Elyse was right after all. Maybe transferring to a school full of extremely good-looking guys might just be the best thing that ever happened to us.

The guy with short chestnut hair held his hand out to Elyse first. "Hi, I'm Hunter," he said in a deep voice. "Welcome to Eden Falls."

She shook his hand and told him her name, and then he shook my hand next.

"I'm Ava," I said. "It's great to meet you."

"Likewise." He nodded. "It's been a while since we've gotten new seniors to our house, so I'm sure everyone will be excited to meet you when school starts tomorrow."

I smiled, grateful for the positive comments. "I'm excited to get to know everyone."

Especially the tall, deliciously handsome guy behind you.

As if reading my mind, Hunter turned and gestured to Mr. Hottie McHot-Hot behind him. "And this is Carter. He's a senior, too."

"Nice to meet you, Carter," I said, feeling all jittery with nerves.

But instead of offering his hand to shake in greeting like the other guys had, Carter simply folded his arms across his defined chest and gave us a quick nod. "Good to meet you." Then turning to look back at his friends, he said, "Ready for the next set?"

Okaaaay, I thought, rocking back on my heels at his immediate dismissal.

So maybe not all the people at this school would be as welcoming as Scarlett, Mack, and Hunter.

Mack must have noticed my discomfort because when Carter and Hunter went back to their weights and Scarlett and Elyse walked over to look at the dance studio, he put a hand on my shoulder and said, "Don't take Carter's one-track mind personally. He's just the kind of person who likes to focus on one thing at a time."

I furrowed my brow, not understanding. "What do you mean?"

Mack lifted one of his broad shoulders. "Let me just put it this way. If he's marked a workout in his planner from 3:30 to 4:15, you can bet that he will work out from exactly 3:30 to 4:15 with only thirty seconds to a minute break between each set."

"So he's very regimented and likes to stick to a specific routine?" I asked.

"Precisely," Mack said, his big lips forming into a smile. "But he makes time for socializing, too."

"As in he probably wrote, 'Work out with Mack and Hunter' into this planner of his and considered it bro-bonding time?"

Mack lifted his ball cap from his head, rubbed his hand across his short, curly hair, and said, "I mean, I didn't look at his schedule for today or anything, but yeah, knowing him, that's probably what he wrote."

"Well, maybe we'll have to teach him to add a few minutes of wiggle room into his calendar here and there so he can make a better first impression when he's meeting new strangers."

Mack looked back to where Hunter was spotting Carter as he started a rep using the bench press. "I'll make sure to tell him that one of the cute new girls says he needs to be more flexible." And when he shot me a flirtatious wink, my cheeks heated.

Had this tall, dark, and handsome hottie just said I was cute?

And then winked at me?

I was just trying to think of a witty response to his comments when Scarlett and Elyse returned.

"Ready to see the girls' dormitory?" Scarlett asked.

"Um, sure." I tucked a lock of my light-brown hair behind my ear. "That would be great."

"Great," Scarlett said before turning to head out of the door we'd come through with Elyse trailing behind her.

Before I followed them, I turned back to Mack who still hadn't returned to his friends and said, "It was great to meet you, Mack. I'm sure I'll be seeing you around."

"I'll make sure to save a spot for you and your sister at my table tonight." He winked again.

"Thanks." My cheeks flushed even deeper at his offer. "I guess I'll see you later."

Deciding to end on that high note, I made myself walk away from probably one of the most welcoming and cutest guys I'd ever met before and went to find Scarlett and Elyse.

2

AVA

"THIS IS OUR COMMON ROOM," Scarlett said when we walked through oak doors that led into a gorgeous room with a wall of windows framed by dark wood. A large gas fireplace was the focal point, with several couches and chairs set in groupings around the room. There was a flat-screen TV in one corner and a kitchenette in another with a fridge, microwave, and a tea-and-coffee station.

I glanced around at the traditional decor. "This is beautiful," I said. It was exactly how you'd picture a grand living area to be like at a private boarding school. Everything was so rich and vibrant. The traditional vibe made me immediately feel at home.

"It's one of my favorite places to spend my downtime," Scarlett said.

Elyse and I walked around the room, taking it in. I smoothed my hand along the back of a brown leather couch, loving the texture of it beneath my fingertips.

"I think I've found my study spot." I plopped myself down on the couch.

"You sure you don't mean your make-out spot?" Elyse turned back to me with a teasing smile on her lips.

I ran my fingers along the cushion and bit my lip as I considered kissing in here with a guy we'd already met today. Mack had such an enigmatic energy to him that I had no doubt he'd be a lot of fun to kiss—probably a lot of fun to date, too.

And he was tall.

Mmmm. I loved tall guys. There was just something so nice about feeling petite and small next to a guy. Being five-foot-nine myself, there weren't many guys at my last school who had been tall enough to do that for me.

But then there was also Carter. He wasn't as tall as Mack, probably more like six-foot two or three. But that was still a great height. And dang, he was attractive.

That jawline.

Those tightly corded muscles that had been visible under his tight blue T-shirt.

And those striking eyes against his warm tan skin.

Sigh.

Even if he had barely given me the time of day when we were introduced, I had a shallow enough side to me that I knew I'd still totally kiss him if the opportunity arose.

And since my imagination was really great with things like that, I found myself picturing what it would be like to kiss Carter. To have those aqua-blue eyes of his focused only on me. Have him scoot close enough on this couch that I could run my fingers through his dirty-blond hair. Have him tilt his face toward mine so I could see if he tasted as good as he looked.

Being as regimented as he was, he was probably a fantastic kisser. People who were perfectionists usually had the determination to excel at everything.

"Are you coming?" Scarlett's expectant voice broke into my thoughts.

"Earth to Ava," Elyse added.

I startled and looked behind me to find Elyse and Scarlett waiting at the bottom of a wide staircase, their expressions concerned.

Had I totally just zoned out?

Yikes, one look at a super cute guy and I was already fantasizing about making out with him.

I shook my head, realizing just how ridiculous my daydreaming had been.

Obviously, I was feeling deprived when it came to my love life.

How long had it been since I'd even kissed a guy?

Probably since last winter when my ex-boyfriend, Jameson, and I had made out in the library stacks when we were supposed to be studying for a math test.

Yeah, no wonder my math grade had suffered so much.

But our fling fizzled out once winter break came, and he started dating someone else. And sadly for my bruised ego, no one had even interested me since then.

Until now, apparently.

"Sorry. I'm coming." I stood up, deciding that maybe studying wouldn't work so well on this couch if my mind was already drifting away to other places.

When I reached them, Scarlett led us up the long staircase. "I should have warned you before you sat down that that couch is famous for way more kissing sessions than the headmistress would ever want our parents to know about."

"It is?" Elyse asked, peeking over at me. "Does that mean you and one of those guys we met in the weight room have put it to good use?"

Scarlett's cheeks colored. "Maybe once or twice."

"You and Mack?" I guessed.

"No!" Her jaw dropped and she shook her head vigorously. "Ah, no. Definitely not."

"Really?" I frowned, surprised by the insistence in her tone. "You guys seemed close from what I saw."

Scarlett shook her head again. "Mack and I have only ever been friends."

"Was it Carter?" I asked, a hint of envy filling my stomach at the thought of them being together.

Scarlett laughed. "Yeah, no. Carter only dates supermodels."

Of course he does.

My chest fell at the thought. I mean, of course I didn't even really know the guy and we probably weren't even compatible at all, but did Scarlett have to ruin my daydreams already?

"So, is he dating a supermodel right now?" I asked.

"He was dating Sofia Cardoso until last summer when she started dating an older guy."

"*The* Sofia Cardoso?" My jaw dropped. "As in, the Brazilian supermodel who just did the cover of Teen Vogue this summer?"

"Yeah, that would be the one."

"And they know each other how?" I asked. I assumed it

was probably because rich people all knew each other—something I was only getting my first taste of since my mom had just joined the millionaire club only recently.

"She goes here."

I stopped on the step I was on. "Sofia Cardoso goes to school here?"

"Yeah." Scarlett tossed some of her auburn hair over her shoulder with a shrug, like having a famous supermodel at our school was no biggie. "She's in a different house but she's a senior like us, and I'm pretty sure her dad is still insisting she finishes high school here instead of going online."

What?

"A-are there a lot of other people whose names we'd recognize that go to this school?" Elyse asked, on the same wavelength as me since that would have been my next question.

"You'd probably recognize some of their parents' names." Scarlett leaned against the banister. "But Sofia definitely has the most social media followers out of any of the students going here."

Which was probably in the millions.

And though the common room had made me feel so at home earlier that I'd easily slipped into a daydream, the high ceilings and ornate paintings suddenly made me feel incredibly insignificant.

Was I going to even have a chance at fitting in at this school where everyone had known each other for years? With a bunch of people whose families had always run in the same circles?

Elyse and I were probably the only ones who had never even met a famous person until the movie star Justin Banks introduced himself to us after my mom's fashion show this summer. He had asked if my mom would consider designing his fiancée's wedding gown.

I glanced around the landing that Scarlett was on, half expecting to see a famous parent walking toward us after dropping off their teen at school for the year. But I only saw a few younger girls chatting outside a door, looking like they were catching up from the summer away.

Scarlett gestured at Elyse and me to follow her toward the door where the girls were chatting.

"The headmistress is a stickler about keeping the boys from sneaking into the girls' dormitory at night and vice versa, so this security code is private to just the girls in our house." Scarlett punched in a code to unlock the door that I now realized led to our rooms.

"So boys aren't allowed in our dorm rooms?" I asked.

Scarlett opened the heavy oak door. "They're allowed in here before curfew. They have to check in with our room mom, Heather, and the door has to stay open the whole time they're in there so she can make sure everyone's behaving. But once ten o'clock rolls around, they need to be back in their dorms, which are on the other side of the common room."

"Has anyone ever broken the rules?" I asked, curious how a simple code could really keep the hormones at bay if a girl was to give the code to her boyfriend.

"People have tried." Scarlett led us down a long corridor with a dozen doors, one of which I assumed led to the room Elyse and I would be sharing. "But an alarm goes off on the dorm parents' phones if the door is open after curfew, so not many people dare attempt anything anymore."

"Modern technology for the win, huh?" Elyse said.

"I guess." Scarlett shrugged. "It keeps the teen pregnancy rate down, at least. Which our parents always appreciate."

"I bet," I said. Elyse met my gaze with wide eyes. We were both still virgins and planned to keep it that way for a while, since being raised by a single mom had taught us how difficult that path could be. It was interesting how matter-of-factly Scarlett talked about it.

We passed a few rooms, some with decorative letters or name signs on the doors that their residents must have placed there to make the space more their own. As we walked past one with the name Emmaline in vinyl letters, I realized that I still didn't know where Scarlett came from and how famous her parents might be. I asked, "Are your mom and dad someone we should know?"

She shook her head as we passed a door with a big S wrapped in green foliage. "Not unless you've been talking to wealth management consultants lately or attended a recent sermon in the heart of New York City."

I furrowed my brow, wondering if she was joking.

She smiled. "My mom's an investment banker, and my dad's a pastor of a big church in Manhattan."

"Oh, wow. That's cool." I nodded.

"Yeah." Scarlett hesitated. "I had an interesting childhood, at least."

The way she said it made me wonder what she might be referring to.

I guess it would be different to be the daughter of a pastor. Where I hadn't had a father figure in my life to make sure I was staying on the straight and narrow, as a religious leader's daughter she probably had a whole congregation of people watching her every move to make sure she didn't do anything that would go against her father's teachings.

Talk about pressure.

"Anyway, this is your room." Scarlett pointed to a dark-brown door with the number seven in the middle. "I guess you two chose to have a double?"

"Yep," I said. "Can't split the Cohen twins apart."

"That's good that you two are so close. I'm an only child, so I can't say I know what that's like." Scarlett shrugged. "Anyway, your ID cards should open the door for you."

I started digging into my back pocket to retrieve the card I'd been given when we met with the headmistress earlier. But Elyse was quicker and had swiped hers through the card reader before I could.

The light on the card reader blinked green, and after turning the knob, the door opened.

The room was a little bigger than the one we'd shared in our home growing up with two large windows to help it feel even more open. Twin beds sat on opposite ends of the room. There were two small desks where we could do our homework, a small table with two chairs for if we decided to eat in our room, and separate closets. Our suitcases were sitting next to the beds, which had been brought up for us when we'd first arrived with our mom.

"I'll let you two make yourselves at home," Scarlett said, still standing in the doorway. "Dinner's at six. The headmistress likes us to wear our uniforms to our meals, so make sure to change into your Monday uniforms before heading down. It's the one with the blue blazer and blue skirt." She gestured at what she was wearing.

Elyse and I both nodded.

Content that we knew what we were supposed to do next, Scarlett pushed away from the door frame. Before leaving us, she said, "I'm just next door in room five, so if you need anything don't hesitate to knock."

"Hey, Scarlett," Elyse said before Scarlett got two steps out the door. "From what you said earlier, it sounds like Hunter is the guy you kissed, right?"

"He is." Scarlett's cheeks colored at the mention of the guy with short chestnut hair whom we'd met in the weight room. "W-why do you ask?"

Elyse twisted some of her long brown hair around her pointer finger. "I want to make sure I know which guys are off-limits, so I don't accidentally make things weird. You seem cool, and I think we could all turn out to be great friends. I just want to make sure Ava and I don't step on anyone else's toes."

"That's thoughtful of you." Scarlett smiled. "Hunter and I dated for a few weeks last spring. But, um...we just had a lot going on at the time and decided we're better off as friends."

Elyse nodded.

"So to cut to the chase," I interrupted, since I too was interested in the subject. "Are there any guys who are, like, off-limits? You know, it's been a while since I've been on a date and from what I've seen so far, this school is like a breeding ground for really attractive guys."

"Eden Falls is kind of like the Garden of Eden when it comes to beautiful humans, isn't it?" Scarlett smirked, like she knew exactly what I was talking about.

"Not just humans," I said. "From what I've seen so far, the buildings and grounds are gorgeous as well. Like a scene straight out of a fairytale."

"It is beautiful," Scarlett said. "But to answer your question. Regarding me specifically, I've dated a few guys here, but since we're such a condensed school and we're around the same people basically all the time, it wouldn't be right for me to tell you that anyone is off-limits. Sure, it might make things a little awkward for a while if you were to date someone seriously and then break up, only to end up having to be around them for the rest of the year. But that's just life at a boarding school. We do have some day students, like Mack and Carter, who are only here during school or for extracurricular activities and at meals if they want, so they're a safer bet. Plus, it gives you a good excuse to leave campus if you're dating someone who lives in town.

"My only real advice is to just enjoy your time here. If you feel like dating, that's great. But what's awesome about Eden Falls Academy is that the friendships you make here are the kind that can last your whole life. So just try to enjoy everything while you're here and I think you'll have a great year."

The kind of friendships that would last a lifetime?

Hmm, interesting. My mom had gone here, but she never talked about it. Elyse and I actually didn't even know this school existed until our mom suddenly sprang the idea on us a few months ago.

But my mom didn't talk to us much about her past life anyway, so it was probably just her personality.

The idea of making lifelong friends while I was here was definitely an appealing idea to me. Which was why I asked Scarlett my next question.

"So, are you saying that you'd be totally cool if I go up to Hunter at dinner tonight and ask him out?" I raised an eyebrow, figuring the direct approach would give me and Elyse the real answer we were looking for.

From the way Scarlett's eyes narrowed and her expression darkened, I knew I had my answer.

"That's what I thought." I laughed.

Scarlett shook her head and sighed. "So maybe things are just a little complicated."

"It's totally understandable. But for the record, I think Mack and maybe Carter are more my speed."

Scarlett let out a relieved laugh. "Well, Mack would be a great choice."

"But not Carter?" I asked, curious why she only said Mack's name.

"Well, Carter is just Carter. He's on an entire plane of his own." She shrugged. "Basically, every girl at this school would sell their soul to be in his field of vision, but so far, the only girl he's ever dated from here is Sofia. Like I said, he only dates supermodels."

Elyse and I might have been able to walk the runway at our mom's fashion show this summer, but yeah, supermodel was definitely not something I could put on my résumé.

Scarlett appraised me with her eyes. "You're really pretty, though. I guess it'll be fun to see if anything changes this year."

"Yeah," I said. Then, not wanting her to think I was already all gung-ho about a guy I'd barely said more than a few words to, I added, "But of course there are many more guys to meet before school starts tomorrow morning. Who knows, maybe there'll be other new guys to kick Carter off that pedestal it sounds like everyone has put him on."

"Maybe," Scarlett said, though it didn't seem like she thought such a thing was possible.

Which I guess said something for what an enigma Carter was at Eden Falls Academy.

"Anyway, I guess we'll see you when it's time for dinner," Elyse said, seeming ready to unpack her things and turn this room into our home.

Scarlett nodded. "Just knock on my door when you've unpacked and changed into your uniforms, and we can go down together."

3

CARTER

THE GREAT HALL—A huge room with stone walls and tall pillars that connected in arches to the rafters above—was bursting with students when my buddy Mack and I sat at our usual table in the back corner of the room.

"So those new twins are pretty hot, right?" Mack arched an eyebrow as he sat beside me on the bench.

"I guess." I gave him a non-committal shrug, briefly glancing up at the large chandeliers that hung from the two-story vaulted ceiling. "If you're into that kind of thing."

"If I'm into that kind of thing?" Mack gave me a sideways glance that told me he couldn't fathom anyone *not* being into identical twins who—sure, if pressed—I'd admit were prettier than the average high school girl.

"They're pretty," was all I said, since I had to stick to my new goal of staying uninterested when it came to the female population.

I couldn't have another disaster like last summer on my hands.

This year was the year of redemption.

The year where I went back to my old cold-hearted ways and didn't let stupid things like *feelings* and *emotions* get in the way of logic when it came to the opposite sex.

Girls were a distraction, and I had the title of valedictorian to secure after all. You didn't get straight A's in advanced courses if you were busy chasing skirts.

"I think I'll stick with hot." Mack smirked, liking his verbiage more than mine as usual.

"Does that mean one of them will be your next victim?" I shot him a half-smile, knowing how he'd react to my word choice.

"Victim?" Mack scoffed. "More like one of the luckiest girls in the world."

"I guess the *lucky* girl will have to decide whether they're a victim or not then," I said dryly, picking up my fork.

"Whatever." He ran a hand across his short black hair. "Now I just need to decide which one to ask out first."

I pursed my lips and dabbed my broccoli in the Alfredo sauce that had pooled around my pasta. "Maybe you should try to get to know their personalities before you make that decision."

"Personalities?" Mack asked. "But you know all I care about are looks, right?"

"Pretty sure that's obvious."

"Says the guy who's so picky that he would rather stay single than date anyone who isn't a supermodel."

I scowled at my friend. "It wasn't just about her looks," I muttered.

No, if dating Sofia had only been about her looks, it

would have been much easier to scrape my heart off the ground when she dumped me for Simon Bailey.

My family came from old money, which was what all girls saw when they looked at me—the empire the Hastings family had increased ever since my great-great-great grandfather John Hastings had made his fortune in the railroad and shipping business.

With Sofia having a similar background as me for the first several years of our lives, I'd assumed she'd be different.

But when she tossed me aside for Simon, who was eleventh in line for the British throne, I realized she was like every other girl I knew.

She'd just been better at hiding it than the rest.

Apparently, the way we'd connected so well over our pasts could never compete with the chance of becoming entwined with the royal family.

Mack must have sensed that he'd hit a nerve because he held up his hands and said, "Sorry. I shouldn't have brought Sofia up."

"It's fine." I lifted a shoulder and plopped the steamed broccoli into my mouth, hoping to exude the uncaring vibe I'd been working so hard to maintain.

"Is she still dating that prince? Or, uh, duke?" He furrowed his dark, thick eyebrows like he was trying to remember Simon's title.

"The viscount?" I filled in for him.

"Yeah."

"I don't know. Probably." I glanced over my shoulder to make sure no one was listening to our conversation. "I unfollowed her last month so I wouldn't have to see their photos anymore."

"Smart."

I guess. Though, if I'd really been smart, I would have stuck to my original plan of never getting serious with anyone in the first place.

Surface-level relationships were the only way to go in high school. Getting emotionally invested in someone was not something I had time for.

Hunter took a seat across from Mack and me with a tray of food, along with my half-siblings Nash and Cambrielle.

After scooting into his spot next to Hunter, Nash asked, "Any guesses on whether we get any new girls in our house this year?"

"New girls?" Mack asked. "I'm guessing Hunter hasn't told you about them yet?"

"Them?" Nash frowned, looking between Hunter, Mack, and me. "As in, we have multiple girls joining our house?"

"Yes." Mack uncapped his water bottle, a glimmer of mischief in his brown eyes.

"Are they hot?" Nash leaned forward, seeming to be almost as excited as Mack was at the prospect of new females joining the small pool of girls in our house.

"Let's just say they caught my attention." Mack pressed his lips together, obviously fighting a grin. "But if you haven't seen them yet, I won't spoil it for you."

Almost as if on cue, the doors to the great hall opened and Scarlett walked into the room with a twin on each side.

The whole room went quiet and multiple sets of eyes followed the girls as they strode down the aisle that led to the cafeteria line where they could grab their tray of food for this evening's meal.

When I looked at Nash, his reaction to seeing double didn't disappoint.

His mouth hung open, his blue eyes blinking rapidly as if not sure they were seeing correctly. Only when the girls stepped behind a large pillar and out of our view did Nash turn back to the rest of us with an almost dazed look in his eyes. "Am I in heaven?" he asked in the overdramatic tone he used when practicing for the school's theater productions. "Because I think I may have just seen identical angels."

Did I mention that Nash and I are only half-siblings? Because, yeah, I really hoped I didn't have that kind of idiocy in my genetic makeup.

"Heaven on earth as far as I'm concerned," Mack agreed, sounding like he'd gotten the same genetic mutation as Nash. "But if you're interested, you'll have to get in line, buddy."

"You're calling dibs on them?" Cambrielle stared at our brother and Mack with a look of disgust on her heart-shaped face. "Are they property? Did we go back in time to the eighteen-hundreds or something?"

Mack gave Cambrielle one of his easy smiles. "You know you'd love to be my property if your big brothers let you."

"As if!" Her jaw dropped and she tossed a piece of broccoli at his face, missing of course and hitting his shoulder instead. "And even if I was interested, I certainly wouldn't need my brothers' permission!"

"What do you think, guys?" Mack looked at Nash and then at me. "Think you'll let me take your little sis out on a date sometime?"

"Sure." Nash glanced at our sister and winked, knowing his answer would only rile her up further. "If that keeps you distracted from those twins, then please, take care of my sister for me."

Cambrielle smacked Nash on the arm, and even though she was tiny, it looked like she hit him hard enough to leave a bruise.

"So what do you say, Carter?" Mack waggled his eyebrows at me. "Mind if I take Cambrielle to visit the falls this weekend?"

The falls—as in the waterfall which our town was named after—was also the spot that could be renamed as *hookup point*.

Yeah, Mack would *not* be taking Cambrielle to the falls.

I shook my head. "Apparently, I'm the only brother who actually cares about Cambrielle's well-being. So no, Mack, even though Cambrielle can date whoever she wants, I would most definitely pull the 'older brother' card and forbid *you* from touching my sweet, innocent little sister."

Cambrielle stuck her tongue out at me, apparently not liking my answer, either.

But then, Cambrielle looked at me with her light blue eyes and asked, "I take it you're not interested in the new girls then?" She must have noticed how Mack and Nash were already scanning the cafeteria for the twins but I wasn't.

"Nope."

"Still going strong on that girl cleanse of yours?" She arched a dark eyebrow.

"I'm focusing on my studies."

"Well, I'm sure Dad would appreciate that."

"I'm sure he would." Being an heir to the Hastings' fortune did come with its responsibilities. "Which is why Nash should probably spend more time focusing on school instead of girls, so he won't be useless when it comes time for us to help Dad manage everything. Pretty sure Dad expects us to help out more once we're through here."

Some upper-class families let kids take a year off after high school, give them a gap year to go off and see the world.

Not the Hastings, though. Not only were we expected to be accepted into Yale, which was about thirty minutes from our small town of Eden Falls, but we were also expected to intern at Hastings Industries as we did so.

A "where much is given, much is required" sort of thing.

"I don't know." Cambrielle tossed our distracted brother a look. "Maybe we should let him run amok like Ian. One less brother to split Dad's billions with doesn't sound too bad."

I laughed. "True." But really, once you were working with billions, did it even make a difference? I spun my fork in my Alfredo noodles. "I don't know, I think I'd rather have Nash earn his keep instead of begging off his more responsible brother and sister."

"You have a point." Cambrielle elbowed Nash in the back. "He should have to work for his inheritance, too."

"They're headed this way." Nash turned to Mack, anticipation filling his face, clearly oblivious to my conversation with Cambrielle. "Scarlett is leading the twins to our table."

"Of course she is," Mack said, like he hadn't just been holding his breath as he waited for the new girls to reappear from the cafeteria line. "I told Ava I'd save her a seat at our table."

"Ava?" Nash asked, grasping onto this new information like an alcoholic licking the last drop of vodka from his shot glass. "And what's the other one's name?"

Mack pursed his lips as if trying to remember. Then he

glanced between Hunter and me. "Do you remember her name?"

Hunter was so focused on the messages blowing up his phone that he didn't hear the question. Even though I knew I shouldn't have stored their names in my memory from the brief interaction I'd had with them, my brain recalled them anyway. "Their names are Ava and Elyse."

"Yes, that's right." Mack snapped his fingers. "Can't tell you who is who, but those names sound right."

"Ava and Elyse..." Nash spoke their names slowly, like he was savoring them on his tongue as he watched the girls approach. "I love those names."

Of course he did.

"Hot, right?" Mack cocked an eyebrow.

"Definitely," Nash agreed.

I just rolled my eyes at my best friend and brother. It was like they hadn't seen a single female since school let out last June and were parched from the thirst.

I didn't get it. Sure, the new girls were nice to look at, but they weren't any prettier than, say, Scarlett, or even Cambrielle.

And before you could think it, no, I didn't have the hots for my sister. *Never have, never will.*

We might be an interesting family, but we were not *that* interesting.

"Hey guys," Scarlett said when she got to our table, a big smile on her lips. "Any room for me and my new friends?"

"Sure." Hunter slipped his phone into his pocket, Scarlett's presence taking his attention from his screen for the first time since he'd sat down. He made space between him and Nash. "You can sit here."

Mack scooted closer to me so that there would be room on his other side. "One of you can sit here." He patted the bench, looking at the twins in earnest.

"Yeah." Nash not so gently nudged Cambrielle in the arm with his elbow to get her to budge. "There's room here, too."

Cambrielle rolled her eyes at Nash. But being the wing-sister that she was, she obliged him.

Scarlett slipped onto the bench beside Hunter. After having some sort of twin-telepathic conversation, one twin sat next to Mack with flushed cheeks while the other set her tray on the table between Nash and Cambrielle to sit in the spot across from me.

Before the girl in front of me could even take a breath, Nash eagerly asked, "So what's your name?"

"I-I'm Ava," the girl said, tucking some of her long, nut-brown hair behind her ear nervously. "Ava Cohen. What's your name?"

"I'm Nash Hastings." Nash held his hand out for Ava.

"Nice to meet you, Nash." Ava shook his hand and seemed to appraise my brother. Nash, at six-foot even, was a few inches shorter than me. But since Ava was on the taller side for a girl, they were almost eye level with one another.

Taking more after his mom than our dad, Nash always joked that what he lacked for in height compared to me, he made up for with his charm. Which was definitely some-thing he had a lot more of than I did.

Being charming took too much energy.

Cambrielle introduced herself next. "I'm Cambrielle Hastings."

"Hastings?" Ava asked, looking between Nash and Cambrielle. "Are you twins, too?"

"Definitely not." Nash shook his head. "I'm clearly the more mature sibling."

Cambrielle snorted. "More like Mother Nature knew Nash would need the head start to keep up."

"So you're younger?" Ava asked my sister, trying to piece things together.

"Yes," Cambrielle said. "I'm a junior. Both my brothers are seniors."

"Both your brothers?" Ava furrowed her brow and glanced around the table as if looking for a Nash look-alike.

Before Ava could look confused for too long, I cleared my throat, held up my hand, and said, "I'm the other brother."

The small pucker line that had formed between her eyebrows deepened as she looked at me and then at Nash. We both had the same Hastings' blond hair and blue eyes, but beyond that, the family resemblance wasn't as strong. "Fraternal twins?"

I shook my head. "Different moms."

Nash was the purebred. I was the illegitimate son my dad had sired on a trip to Guatemala eight months before he and Dawn had gotten back together.

"Oh." She nodded, understanding seeming to fill her amber-colored eyes. "That makes more sense."

"I bet you were wondering how I was lucky enough to score all the looks," Nash said with a wink.

"Um..." Ava pursed her lips, and after flicking her gaze toward me for a split second, she said, "O-of course."

The flush that filled her cheeks may have been caused by the fact that she was being asked to judge my looks compared to my brother, and that made her uncomfortable. But it wasn't the first time a girl had blushed when studying my unusual features.

Cambrielle always told me I was too arrogant for my own good, but it just came with the territory. I knew I was good looking—a half-Latino, half-Caucasian mix that got the best of my parents' features: my mom's perfectly smooth, light bronze skin, and my dad's aqua-blue eyes and square jawline.

But what did that matter, anyway?

I'd had dozens of girls flinging themselves at me on our trip to the Hamptons this past summer. So what?

I wasn't like my brother Ian. I didn't care about finding my next plaything. And I wasn't like Nash either—eager to have anyone want me.

Being disciplined was what really mattered when it came to being successful in life, and if anything, girls were just a distraction.

A distraction I wanted nothing to do with this year.

4

AVA

"SO, TELL US ALL ABOUT YOU," Cambrielle said after I'd officially been introduced to her and her brothers.

I usually did okay talking to new people, being the more outgoing twin, but for some reason, I was flustered sitting at this table full of new, beautiful people.

The fact that her brother Carter—the guy who'd basically ignored me when we'd met earlier—was sitting across from me and judging my every move didn't help, either.

But even though he was probably the least welcoming person I'd met today, he was still gorgeous. His pale blue eyes against his light tan skin reminded me of that famous National Geographic photo of the "Afghan Girl."

While his brother and sister had been giving me a more-than-friendly welcome, it was Carter whom I was hyper-aware of. So aware that my face burned every time I looked in his direction and caught him studying me.

But Cambrielle had just asked me a question, right?

I racked my brain, trying to remember what she'd asked. She wanted me to tell her about myself?

"What do you want to know?" I asked, hoping I'd guessed right.

"Where are you from? What grade are you in?"

Easy questions.

Good.

I might be able to handle those.

"I'm from Ridgewater, New York," I said, unscrewing the lid of my water bottle and taking a quick sip to moisten my dry mouth. "And I'm a senior."

"Cool," Cambrielle said. "So you're not too far from home."

"Nope. It only took about four and a half hours to drive here." I set my water bottle back on my tray. "What about you guys? Where are you from?"

"We're actually from here," Cambrielle said. "Our estate is just on the other side of Eden Falls."

Estate.

As in, not just a house but a place with a big ol' plot of land and probably a castle to go along with it.

I swallowed, realizing that most people at this school probably grew up in places you didn't call home but rather "the estate," "the penthouse," or "the mansion."

Sure, in Ridgewater we had families like the Carmichaels, Perkins, and the Brooks who were wealthy, but their homes could still technically be called homes.

I was so out of my element here.

"I'm guessing you're day students then?" I asked, hoping my face didn't give away how out of place I felt.

"We are," Cambrielle said, "But it almost feels like we live here sometimes since we're here so much."

"Are you involved in extracurricular activities?" I asked.

She nodded. "I'm in the drama club with Nash. I'm not a spotlight hog like him and so I've mostly just been part of the crew, but I'm thinking about auditioning for a part in the winter musical this year."

"I'm not a spotlight hog," Nash said. Then tossing his head dramatically, he said, "It's not my fault that the crowd adores me."

I couldn't help but smile at the dynamic between these two. They were hilarious.

"Elyse was hoping to get involved in the drama program, so I'll have to tell her to talk to you two about it."

Nash seemed to perk up at my mention of my sister having similar interests. "I'd love to show her the ropes." And when he looked at my sister with sudden interest, I had a feeling she was going to be receiving a similarly warm welcome from him.

"I think warning her about Nash may be a better way to go." Cambrielle grinned as she glanced over to my sister who was in the middle of a conversation with Mack, Hunter, and Scarlett. "But it'll be fun to have her join us. My best friend was in the drama club with me last year, but she transferred to a school in London. So, I'd love to have a new friend in there with me."

"I'm sure Elyse would love a friend in there, too. While I can be amazing when it comes to pretending to be my sister when we feel like tricking our mother, beyond that my acting skills die. I'm actually hoping to play basketball this winter."

You know, if I get the right grades.

"Basketball?" Nash pulled his attention from my sister at my mention of the sport. "If you're into basketball, you've sat at the right table. Mack, Carter, and Hunter are all on the boys' team and Scarlett plays like a banshee on the girls' team."

"Really?" I asked, though I guess I shouldn't be too surprised. Mack was basically a giant and Carter was really tall, too.

"Yeah, they practice on the court at our house all the time," Nash said. "I'll be too busy with the winter musical to play for the school's team this year, but I could totally put together a scrimmage game or two at our court sometime, if you want to practice before the tryouts in November."

"S-sure," I tried to say, caught completely off guard at his offer. "That would be fun."

"Actually," Nash said, his eyes lighting up. "We're having a back-to-school barbecue at our place this weekend. You should come."

I was being invited to a party?

Already?

"Th-that sounds fun." Social circles were decided quickly at schools like this, and I'd better jump into the social scene while the invitation was there.

Cambrielle sat a little taller. "If you don't have anything going on before the party, you could come early and hang out. I've been stuck in the Hamptons with my brothers all summer, so it would be nice to have some girl time."

"You wouldn't mind?"

"Mind?" Cambrielle asked. "Definitely not. In fact, if your sister and Scarlett want to come, we can just call it our pre-party."

"Hey, wait a minute," Nash said, setting his hands on the table. "Don't tell me you're going to try to steal Ava from me. I thought Carter and Mack would be my biggest competition, not my baby sister."

He thought Carter and Mack would be competing for me?

I was flattered by the sentiment, but Mack seemed to be dazzled by my sister at the moment, and Carter was currently reaching into a charcoal-colored backpack beside him, having ducked out of the conversation minutes ago.

I looked at Nash and Cambrielle, wondering what was going on. Was this just some kind of game they played with each other? See who could make the most friends the first week of school?

I'd been worried that everyone would already be settled into their friend groups and wouldn't want to make room for Elyse and me, but were the Hastings siblings actually fighting over me?

Well, two of the Hastings siblings, that is. Carter was currently opening what seemed to be a non-fiction book—written in Spanish from the looks of the title I couldn't translate—and his attention to it was intense, as if he was planning to escape into its pages while he finished his meal.

Who was this guy?

I could understand the compulsion to read an addictive romance novel in order to find out how the couple got together in the end, but a Spanish self-help book at dinner? I didn't understand the pull for something like that.

Unless it was, of course, scheduled into that planner of his that Mack mentioned earlier.

I pushed away my curiosity over what made Carter

Hastings tick and focused back on Nash and Cambrielle who were now apparently deciding who got to drive Elyse, Scarlett, and me to their house on Saturday afternoon.

No bother over the fact that Elyse probably didn't even know about the party, let alone a pre-party, and therefore couldn't be counted on attending for sure yet.

I was about to suggest that since most vehicles had five seats, we could all just drive in the same vehicle when Carter's deep voice cut into the air. With a hint of annoyance, he said, "You two are going to scare Ava and her sister away before the end of the night, if you don't stop arguing."

From his tone, I expected him to be glaring at his siblings. But when I glanced across the table at him, he was still focused on his book, casually turning a page. As if breaking up his siblings' fights while reading came as naturally to him as breathing.

"Oh, just read your book, Carter," Cambrielle said, waving her hand at her aloof brother. She turned to me and said, "How about this: Nash can drive you to our house and I can drive you back since we all know how Nash loses track of time during his parties."

"Good thinking." Nash held a finger in the air. Then looking at me, he asked, "How does that sound? I'll drive you to our place, and my responsible little sis will bring you back to the school afterward."

"I, uh—" I swallowed, not used to this kind of attention. "I guess that sounds good."

"Perfect," Cambrielle said, beaming that her plan had won out over her brother's.

A moment later, the headmistress, Mrs. Sutton—a spindly woman with dramatic features wearing a white ruffled blouse and a black pencil skirt—stood at the podium in the front of the room to welcome us to a brand-new school year at Eden Falls Academy. While everyone's attention was turned to Mrs. Sutton, I glanced at my sister to see how she was faring so far.

When she looked my way, she mouthed, "Doing good?"

I nodded and then mouthed, "You?" To which she gave me a thumbs-up sign.

So far, so good.

5

AVA

THE FIRST DAY of classes began the next morning. I wore
uniform number two since it was Tuesday—a cream-colored
blazer, white button-down shirt, pink-and-burgundy plaid
skirt, a necktie, and burgundy socks. It was my favorite of the
uniforms we'd had to buy for the school year since the lighter
colors went well with my skin tone.

But with the colors being more feminine, I wondered if
the boys would be wearing the same color palette. My question was answered when I went to breakfast in the great hall
and saw that while the boys' ties were made from the same
pink-and-burgundy plaid material, their blazer and slacks
were navy blue—which actually went together nicely. My
mom would be proud of whoever chose the school uniforms
because they clearly had an eye for fashion.

I ate breakfast with Scarlett, Hunter, and Elyse. Mack
and the Hastings crew were all day students, so Scarlett told
us that they rarely ever had breakfast at the school.

My first class of the day was AP English. Unlike math, I

actually did quite well with the subject. When the teacher, Mr. Brown, went over the syllabus for this year, thankfully it wasn't too overwhelming. We were to read a few classics on our own and as a class, do some reports and group projects, and when it came time to take the AP test at the end of the year, we'd hopefully have learned enough to pass the test and have some college credit before graduation.

Elyse and Scarlett were in my class, along with Mack and Nash, so it was nice to see some friendly faces among the new ones.

"Which class do you have next?" Elyse asked me as we walked down the student-crowded hall after English.

I glanced at the schedule that I'd printed out and slipped into the front cover of my floral binder.

"I have Statistics." I groaned. "Talk about ruining the day before it really got started."

Elyse chuckled, knowing well how much I loathed math. "At least you'll get it over with, right?"

"For the morning portion, anyway."

"Do you start your tutoring right after school then?"

I nodded. "As per my agreement with the headmistress."

"Who knows, maybe your tutor will be really cute," Elyse offered, like working with a cute guy would make the tutoring sessions less torturous.

"If only I could be so lucky." I sighed, hugging my books to my chest. "Pretty sure Mom knows all about my study sessions with Jameson last year and knows better than to let me be set up with someone like that again."

Elyse laughed. "For your grade's sake, I suppose I should hope that your tutor is a middle-aged woman so you're not caught making out in the library stacks instead of studying."

"Yep," I said.

We came to the end of the hall where Elyse would go one way to her next class, and I would go the other.

"Good luck with math," Elyse said, turning to look at me before separating. "Who knows, maybe it'll be your favorite class this year."

I resisted the urge to roll my eyes. Elyse had been on this positive psychology kick recently and seemed determined to make it rub off on me.

"I'll see you at lunch," I said.

"See you then."

I watched Elyse disappear into the crowd of students wearing cream and blue blazers. And then, deciding not to put off the inevitable, I headed toward the A hall where Mrs. Simmons's class was.

I walked into the room, which had large east-facing windows and posters with various inspirational quotes. There was a handful of students already seated at the tables, chatting among themselves.

There was a middle-aged woman with red, shoulder-length curly hair standing at a whiteboard writing notes for today's class. When she noticed me out of the corner of her eye, she stopped writing.

"Oh hello," she said, placing the cap on the black dry erase marker she'd been using. "You must be Ava."

"Um, yeah, that's me," I said, surprised she knew my name even though we'd never met before. But in a school with less than five hundred students, it shouldn't really surprise me. They probably didn't get much turnaround at a place like this.

"It's so great to have you at our school," she said, her smile wide on her burgundy-colored lips. "I'm Mrs. Simmons."

I just nodded, not sure what I should say since saying I was excited to meet my new math teacher would be a lie. Math was a torture device invented by disturbed humans, and math teachers who *chose* to immerse themselves in the subject had to be possessed by a math demon to willingly spend multiple hours of their day surrounded by the subject.

So I went with a simple, "I love your shoes."

My mom had taught me that the best way to get on someone's good side was to give them an honest compliment. And since I needed to get in Mrs. Simmons's good graces more than anyone else's at this school, I planned to give her a compliment each day I had her class.

Because surely she wouldn't fail someone who was always looking for the best in her...right?

It was the best plan I'd come up with so far, at least.

She looked down at her black peep-toe wedges briefly, a smile slipping onto her face. "Thank you. They were a birthday present from my husband."

"He has good taste." I smiled earnestly because I truly did like her shoes. In fact, for a teacher in her early forties, she actually had a great sense of style.

A few more students walked into the classroom, which brought Mrs. Simmons back to whatever she'd meant to tell me. "I've already spoken with Headmistress Sutton about your situation." She cleared her throat before ducking her head closer and continuing in a hushed tone. "And we thought the best way for you to excel in my class this year would be for us to do something we've had success with in the past years."

Great.

Apparently, my case was special enough that the teachers had already been warned about me.

A deep feeling of shame seeped into my chest, spreading throughout my whole body and making me feel hot in my blazer.

I tugged on my necktie and quickly glanced behind me to make sure the students already seated weren't eavesdropping on this possibly humiliating conversation.

Thankfully, they were all either busy chatting with each other like long-lost friends or staring into their phones.

Mrs. Simmons continued, "I always try my best to cater to the needs of each of my students, but since it can sometimes be helpful to have things explained in different ways, we have arranged for your peer tutor to attend during this same hour so you can sit together. This way he can help answer any questions you may have during my lectures."

He? My tutor was a guy?

"Okay." I nodded and then breathed in through my nose, telling myself that if I remained calm, none of the students behind me would guess that Mrs. Simmons was doing anything other than welcoming a new student to her class.

My teacher's attention caught on something behind me, and then she smiled again. "Looks like your tablemate has just arrived."

I glanced behind me and found a tall guy with dirty-blond hair and piercing blue eyes that only appeared even more blue next to his navy blazer.

Yes, I was looking at Carter Hastings.

Oh no, oh no, oh no. Please don't let him be my tutor.

Carter nodded in our direction before taking a seat at a

table in the center of the second row, leaning back and stretching his long legs. He lazily draped his arm across the back of the chair beside him. And when his gaze lifted to mine, looking at me through eyelashes that were surprisingly dark for his lighter hair, my face burned hot with embarrassment.

Had he known yesterday when we met that he'd be helping me this year?

Was that why he'd barely given me the time of day? Because he already knew I was beneath him?

Ugh!

Of all the people at this school I could have been partnered with to help me with math, why did it have to be *him*?

I turned away from Carter and focused back on my teacher. "I have to work with Carter?" I asked, my throat dry.

"Oh, so you're already acquainted with Mr. Hastings?" Mrs. Simmons's eyes lit up, obviously not sensing how unenthusiastic I was at this pairing. "He's one of my brightest students and has proven to be a great tutor in previous years."

So he did tutoring on the regular. Was that, like, his charity project? Rich people always liked being seen as charitable, right?

The bell rang.

"I, um, guess I better take my seat," I said, even though the thought of sitting next to Carter and officially outing myself to the whole class as the girl who needed Carter's benevolent help this year was about the last thing I wanted to do.

But since I didn't want to draw any more attention to myself by standing next to the teacher after the bell had already rung, I walked the few feet to where Carter was and set my binder on the table. And then, after waiting for Carter to remove his arm from the back of my chair, I sat down and scooted in.

"Good morning," I said to him. I decided that if I didn't make the first move to break the ice, based on our previous interactions, he might just ignore me altogether.

He took his time to turn in my direction, and before he said anything, he looked me over from head to toe. His gaze seemed to linger on the burgundy-colored socks that hit just below my knee, but then he finally lifted his gaze up to mine and said, "Hi."

I furrowed my brow together, confused at why he'd eyed my socks for so long. Had I worn them wrong or something?

I'd never had to wear a uniform to school before, but I was pretty sure it was customary to have the socks pulled up instead of folded over.

I was just about to glance around and make sure the other girls were wearing their socks the same way when Carter's deep voice sounded again and he asked, "You're Ava, right?"

"Yes." I cleared my throat, and with a shaky hand, I pointed at the gold letter A that I'd pinned to the end of my necktie. "The A is for Ava."

He nodded. "I figured as much. I noticed you and your sister's pins yesterday at dinner."

"You noticed our pins?"

Wow, way to state the obvious, Ava.

A slight smirk lifted his lips. "I'm quite observant."

And because I seemed to be on a quest to make Carter Hastings think I was truly an idiot, I said, "You were so enamored with your book during dinner yesterday that I wouldn't blame you if you forgot we were even at your table."

A hint of a smile graced his soft pink lips. "Looks like I wasn't the only observant person at the table yesterday."

And when he winked at me, my heart had the gall to skip a beat.

But I told it to stop because my heart was just being stupid, fluttering over someone like Carter. Just because he may be the world's most beautiful human being didn't mean I needed to care about him. I was pretty sure he already cared about himself enough from his all-too arrogant vibe.

Deciding to get down to business, I glanced around me to make sure no one was listening. "I assume you know why our teacher had me sit by you?"

He shrugged his broad shoulders. "Because you and math aren't exactly on the best of terms at the moment?" he said in a low voice so others wouldn't overhear.

"I guess that's one way to put it," I said, even though admitting my flaw to this guy who had an air of perfection about him wasn't exactly doing my pride any favors.

Just then, a girl I'd never seen in person before but knew more about than I'd care to admit walked into the room. The girl who Scarlett had warned me would be coming to this school.

"Ah, Miss Cardoso," Mrs. Simmons said when the super-model strolled in. "So glad you could join us."

Sofia Cardoso, who somehow made the same exact uniform I was wearing look like it belonged on the runway, tipped her head to our instructor and said, "Sorry I'm late. I had my schedule mixed up."

"Just take your seat next to Miss McCall." Mrs. Simmons

nodded to a girl with curly blonde hair on the front row. "We were just about to get started, so you haven't missed anything important yet."

Sofia moved to take the seat the teacher had indicated, but before sitting, her gaze dropped down to Carter for a long moment.

Carter sat up a little straighter. But as I watched the two, I noticed that he seemed to refuse to look in the Brazilian beauty's direction. Instead, his blue-eyed gaze was intent on the whiteboard ahead, as if the notes our teacher had written up there were suddenly the most interesting things in the world.

As if she understood that Carter was refusing to give her the time of day, Sofia shrugged as she sat next to the girl our teacher had called Miss McCall.

As Mrs. Simmons welcomed the rest of the class back for the new year, my mind drifted off to wonder what exactly had happened between Carter and Sofia. Because whatever it was, he clearly wasn't ready to be friends with his ex-girl-friend yet.

6

CARTER

OKAY. *So far, so good.*

Just two minutes left and I'll have successfully made it through my first class with Sofia.

She'd walked into our math class after the bell, which wasn't typical for her. Back when we were dating last year, she, like me, had always liked to be on time for things.

But something had seemed off when she came in this morning. She still looked as put-together and beautiful as she always did—her uniform freshly pressed, her dark hair slicked back into the high ponytail that showed off her elegant neck.

I couldn't put my finger on what was different exactly, but there just was a different energy about her when she walked in.

Less confidence, maybe?

Though I wouldn't know why. She was more famous than my dad was—and my dad was the seventh richest person in the United States.

And she was dating a viscount the last time I checked.

Was it wrong of me to hope that she'd walked into our class with her tail between her legs because she regretted the way she'd dumped me?

That maybe seeing me again face to face for the first time since our breakup was as uncomfortable for her as it was for me?

Either way, I needed to figure out how to avoid speaking to Sofia today. Because from the way she kept glancing in my direction from her seat adjacent to mine, I knew it was coming.

Though I'd rehearsed our initial post-breakup meeting several times in my head while preparing for this school year, I still wasn't ready to have a conversation with her. Even three months later, everything was still too fresh. My heart was still raw from the wire brush she'd scraped across it.

I glanced at the clock above Mrs. Simmons's red hair.

One more minute.

One minute to think of how to avoid the inevitable.

I looked out of the corner of my eye at Sofia. Her thin shoulders rose and fell, like she was taking deep breaths. Her right leg bounced under the table. Her long, delicate fingers flexed and contracted on her lap against the pleats of her skirt.

"Since we just did a quick overview of our class today," Mrs. Simmons voice cut through my thoughts. "Your home-work for today's class is to find twenty minutes or so where you can get together with your tablemate and fill out the questionnaire that I have up on our class website."

A few groans sounded around me.

Mrs. Simmons gave her head a quick shake, clucking her

tongue. "I suppose I could assign a page of math problems for you to review instead, if the interview isn't to your liking." She ran her gaze over my fellow classmates and me. Then, with a half-smile, she said, "Okay, so the getting-to-know-you interviews, it is. I know a lot of you have been together at this school for several years and feel you know each other pretty well, but I have a feeling that these questions will bring out some things that may surprise you."

The bell rang then, and several students darted out of the classroom like they couldn't get to lunch fast enough.

"Well, I guess today's homework should be simple enough," Ava said from beside me.

"Sounds like it," I agreed, setting my iPad on top of the Statistics textbook Mrs. Simmons had handed out today.

"So should we—" Ava started to say before her attention caught on something beside me that made her eyes go wide.

My heart instantly took off to the races when I realized what, or rather, *who* had most likely startled her.

And sure enough, when I craned my neck to the side, I found Sofia standing at the end of our table with her designer backpack slung over her shoulder, her signature perfume filling the air around her.

"Hi Carter," Sofia said in her raspy, alto voice, her cheeks pinker than usual.

"Hello." I swallowed and sat up straighter. "Uh, long time no see."

Long time no see?

Wow, I'd had three months to figure out what I'd say to her when we came face to face and I'd said that?

"Yes, it's been too long." She twisted her gold charm bracelet on her wrist, a nervous tick of hers.

Well, good. I was glad she was nervous.

She continued, "I was wondering if you wanted to have lunch together. Maybe catch up on what's happened since we last saw each other." She cast Ava a quick glance before meeting my gaze again with her dark brown eyes.

"Oh, um—" I gulped, my face suddenly hot as I shifted uncomfortably in my chair.

Don't do it, Carter.

Don't do what she wants.

When Ava shifted in her seat beside me, an idea came to mind. "Actually, I already have plans for lunch with Ava today." I gestured at Ava, hoping she'd go along with my lie.

Ava turned to me with a small frown, clearly surprised by these plans I was making for us without her consent.

I widened my eyes at her, hoping to communicate that I really needed her to go along with this plan.

After a few heart-pounding seconds, she pursed her lips together and said, "Yeah, Carter was so sweet to invite me to lunch today since I'm new here. I think it was his way of apologizing for basically ignoring me yesterday when Scarlett introduced us."

So apparently, Ava hadn't appreciated how aloof I'd been yesterday.

For which I couldn't really blame her. I wasn't exactly known for my welcoming nature. That was what Mack and Nash were for.

But despite all that, she'd just come to my rescue, so the girl deserved some props.

I looked back at Sofia. "So as you can see, today isn't going to work." Hopefully, she'd not only buy the excuse but would also take the hint that I wasn't interested in making whatever amends she was trying to make.

"Oh. I—" Sofia bit her plump bottom lip. "I didn't realize..." She drifted off, and I almost felt bad for how obviously I was avoiding her.

She glanced at Ava and slipped what looked like a forced smile onto her face. "It's nice to meet you, Ava." She held her hand out to the girl seated beside me. "I'm Sofia, one of Carter's, um..." She pinched her lips together and her gaze rested on me as if to ask what previous relationship she could claim we had. But I was interested in hearing the answer myself, so I just waited. After a beat, she said, "I'm one of Carter's old friends."

Friends.

The word hit me like a punch to the gut.

Two years of shared memories and a connection I'd never experienced with someone before was now reduced to "just friends."

Huh.

I pressed my eyes shut as pain hit my chest.

For some reason, I'd rather have her tell this near stranger that we'd been lovers instead, then at least it would make all the pain I'd felt these past few months seem valid.

But who knew, maybe she'd always seen our relationship differently than I had. She'd been the one to break up with me out of the blue just when I'd been considering inviting her to spend the summer in the Hamptons with my family.

"It's great to meet you, Sofia." Ava shook Sofia's hand, oblivious to the knife twisting in my chest. "But I'd be lying if I pretended not to know who you are."

Sofia nodded, looking down at her black Jimmy Choos. "I'm still not used to that, I guess."

"I imagine you're not," Ava said. "But if it makes it less weird, my mom's also in the fashion world, so we've made it our business to know who's who in the modeling world."

"Who's your mom? Would I know her?" Sofia asked, perking up a little.

"Her name's Miriam Cohen. She's a designer. She just had her first fashion show this past year so it's all new for us."

Sofia's eyes lit up, like she recognized the name. "I totally went to her show this summer with Sim—" She caught herself before finishing the name of my replacement. She gave me an apologetic glance and said, "I was there with a friend."

So maybe "friends" was the term Sofia favored when talking about the guys whose hearts she'd enjoyed stringing along.

Maybe I should warn poor Simon he might be headed toward a similar fate as me.

"It was an amazing show," Sofia continued. "I loved the purple off-the-shoulder dress. I think it was called The Vienna?"

"That's my favorite of hers, too." Ava smiled. "I actually helped my mom come up with the concept for that one."

"So you're a prodigy?" Sofia asked, showing how personable she could be. It was something that had drawn me to her in the first place. Being uncomfortable meeting new people myself, it was always nice to be around someone who could become instant friends with anyone.

But she stabbed you in the back with a smile on her face, I reminded myself before I could start remembering too many of Sofia's better qualities.

"Oh, I don't know about that." Ava's fair cheeks flushed at Sofia's compliment. "My mom's the real deal, but I like being part of the process."

"That's cool." Sofia gave Ava a genuine smile. "Someday I hope to get into design as well."

There was a long pause where it seemed like the two girls had run out of things to say. After a beat, Sofia cleared her throat and said, "I guess I'll let you two get to your lunch." She adjusted the strap of her bag and looked at me. "It was good to see you again, Carter. We'll have to catch up some other time."

"Sure." I swallowed the lump that formed in my throat. "Some other time."

Unless I can come up with another excuse to get me out of it next time.

Sofia turned on her heel, the back of her skirt swishing with the movement and drawing my eyes to her long, toned legs.

I used to love that her skirts hit higher on her legs than the other girls at school since she was five-foot ten and her legs were so long.

But now they just taunted me.

I tore my gaze away from her legs and focused back on Ava.

"Ex-girlfriend?" Ava asked, a knowing look on her face.

"Yeah."

And if I was the type of person who shared his personal details with people he barely knew, I might even admit that

Sofia had been the one to dump me, in order to explain my agitated behavior.

But since that wasn't me, I simply left it at that. There was no need to let Ava know just how weak I could be.

7

———

AVA

"I GUESS I better get to lunch," I said to Carter as I gathered my notebook and textbook into my arms, figuring it would be weird to stay any longer now that it was just us and our teacher left in the classroom.

"Wait." He reached over and touched my arm. "Where are you going?"

"Huh?" I stared at his hand for a moment, surprised at the warmth that glowed down my arm from his simple touch.

"Uh, I..." He cleared his throat and removed his hand after noticing my blush. "We told Sofia we were having lunch together to work on our interviews. So, I'd kind of like to follow through with that."

"I thought that was just an excuse," I said, surprised that he'd actually been planning on it. "I didn't think you actually meant we'd have lunch together."

"Well, we do have that interview to start." He cocked his head to the side, the gesture making him seem more boyish and less severe somehow. "And since I assume you probably eat meals here and there, I was thinking we could go to this restaurant just off campus whose food I'm craving."

"We're allowed to eat off campus?" I asked.

He nodded. "As long as we aren't tardy for next period, the headmistress doesn't mind."

I bit my lip, trying to decide what to do.

It was the first day of school. Elyse had seemed to hit it off with Scarlett and her crew yesterday, and then again this morning at breakfast. Would she be okay without me for lunch?

"We wouldn't want Sofia to think you lied to her, right?" Carter asked.

Pretty sure he was the one who had started the lie.

But when I looked at his aqua-blue eyes, I suddenly didn't want to give him a reason to scowl at me again like he did yesterday.

Especially if he was going to be my tutor this year.

"Okay." I let out a low breath. "But since I'm the one doing you a favor, by making Sofia think you're cool enough to hang out with someone like me, you have to buy my lunch while we're at it."

His family lived on an estate. Surely he could afford to buy me lunch.

I raised my eyebrows, waiting to see if he'd go along with my conditions.

He studied me with narrowed eyes, as if trying to piece my personality together with the few short interactions we'd had so far.

Then, seeming to understand that I was the one helping him and not the other way around, he sighed and said, "Fine."

"WHAT ARE YOU DOING?" I asked Carter when he pulled out a dark blue bullet journal and started writing in it instead of leaving the classroom.

He peeked up from his writing. "I'm just updating my planner." He drew a line through something on the page after writing *Lunch with Ava off campus* in blocky handwriting.

I frowned. "Don't people usually put things in their planner so they can remember them?"

Mack had hinted about Carter's love for keeping to a set schedule, but did he actually document every single thing he did throughout the day?

"That's one use." He shut the silky, faux leather cover, his long fingers wrapping the black elastic around the edge to hold it closed. "But I'd written *lunch in the great hall* in that spot, and since I'm going with you off campus instead, I needed to correct it. I like to make sure my planner is accurate."

I nodded slowly, not used to someone being so meticulous about their schedule. I mean, Elyse was really into bullet journaling too, and the way she made her daily to-do lists was borderline obsessive. But even she didn't take her planning to this extreme.

Carter slipped his bullet journal into his bag, along with his textbook and iPad.

"Ready to head out?" He slung his backpack over a shoulder.

"Sure." I hugged my books to my chest, and then we left the math classroom that I'd been inside for way too long.

It was sunny when we walked out the front iron doors of the school, the weather still warm this early in September.

I loved when summer came to the New England area since the afternoon rain showers were my favorite. But I also enjoyed that we had all four seasons and looked forward to autumn and the vibrant leaves that gave new color to the overall green appearance of the lush geography.

"My truck is this way." Carter gestured to the right when we made it to the parking lot at the east side of the school.

"This is the student parking lot?" I asked Carter as we walked past a Lamborghini, followed by an Audi, and then a Range Rover.

He gave a sideways glance to the expensive vehicles I was eyeing. "The faculty parking lot is on the other side of the school."

"So all of these vehicles belong to kids who go here?" I tried to clarify.

He nodded, unfazed at the fact that the contents of this parking lot alone were worth a couple million dollars. "That's Nash's car." He pointed to a lime-green BMW Convertible. "This one is Cambrielle's." He patted the hood of a shiny red car with a Mercedes symbol on it. "And this is mine." He pulled a key fob from the pocket of his slacks and pressed a button to unlock a black Ford F-150 Raptor.

"Wow." I blinked, not believing that kids my age drove these kinds of cars. In Ridgewater, the Carmichael twins and Chance Clemont had driven super fancy cars like this. But most of the student parking lot had been full of hand-me-down cars that made sense for newly licensed teens to drive.

Carter climbed into the driver's side, so I got in and settled onto the passenger seat.

I didn't know what exactly I'd expected once I was in his vehicle. With what I knew about him so far, I didn't expect it to be littered with takeout wrappers, or stinky gym clothes like the stereotypical teen boy, but I also hadn't expected to be greeted with the most delicious-smelling cologne I'd ever breathed in my entire life.

I'd been sitting by the guy all throughout the past hour, but how had I not known that he smelled like this?

Dang.

I drew in a deep breath, trying to be discreet about it so Carter's ego wouldn't know that I thought he smelled like heaven.

"Sorry about the smell," Carter said, apparently noticing me sniffing the air despite my best effort to hide it. "My cologne bottle broke in my gym bag yesterday and soaked the backseat. I hope it's not too strong."

"It's fine." I schooled my face into a neutral expression, hoping that he wouldn't pick up on just how obsessed I could become with it. "I don't mind."

I mean, what teenage girl didn't want to suffocate from a scent that could be put in a bottle with the label advertising it as "Hot Guy Ambrosia?"

"Well, I guess that's good because I have a feeling the smell may stick around for a few days since the guy who details our vehicles is on vacation until next week."

"You have a guy who details your family's vehicles for a living?" I asked, my eyes going wide.

Carter lifted a broad shoulder, like it was completely normal. "We have a lot of cars. It takes a lot of time."

When he saw what was probably an astonished look on my face, he just chuckled and said, "I'm guessing from what you said to Sofia about your mom's success being recent, you didn't grow up with a trust fund like most people at our school?"

Would admitting that I was different from everyone else be a bad thing?

"I still don't have a trust fund," I said, deciding to just be honest about how new my mom's money was since it was probably obvious, anyway. "And yeah, if our mom wanted her car cleaned, when we were growing up, Elyse and I had to use the hose and a sponge to do it ourselves."

"Sounds fun."

"Not really, but I guess it taught us about manual labor."

"Ah yes, manual labor." He strummed his long fingers on the black steering wheel as he pulled onto the cobblestone path that led toward the gates at the front of the school. "Now that's something I'm familiar with."

"*You're* familiar with manual labor?" I asked before I could stop myself.

He narrowed his eyes, as if offended by my question. "You don't think people who have a staff that take care of their vehicles have ever had to work with their hands?"

I pressed my lips together, wondering how to backtrack so the next forty-five minutes with him wouldn't be completely awkward. "I didn't mean to say it like that."

"Then, what did you mean?" He cocked an eyebrow.

"Um..." I tried to think, but the way he was looking at me like he was ready to dissect every word I said in order to point out my flawed thinking was making it hard to concentrate.

When I didn't say anything, he said, "I may not have had the same car-washing and Saturday-chores experience as you did growing up, but just because my last name is Hastings doesn't mean I was born with a silver spoon in my mouth."

"Your parents liked using gold silverware instead?" I asked, mostly joking because I didn't really know what else to say after apparently offending the guy.

I'd hoped he'd laugh at my joke, but instead he just said, "I have a lot of nice things in my life right now, sure, but that has definitely not always been the case."

I waited for him to continue, to explain what he meant since none of it made much sense to me at the moment. But he didn't.

So I tried to focus on the soft, pop music playing on the radio instead and told myself not to assume I knew anything about this obviously very touchy guy.

It took about five minutes for us to drive from the school's grounds to the sign that said, *Welcome to Eden Falls, Connecticut. Population 29,000.*

My mom had driven us straight from home to the school the day before, so I hadn't seen any part of the town yet.

There were rows and rows of trees along the road as we entered the city limits, and then various buildings started popping up here and there.

"Do you like Italian or Mexican food?" Carter broke the silence that had fallen over us after we'd passed by a few streets lined with colorfully painted houses that looked like they'd been built in the early 1900's.

"I'm good with either," I said.

"Good."

And then we were quiet again.

Why had I agreed to come to lunch with Carter? This was sooo awkward.

We drove a little farther down the main road until Carter switched on the blinker and pulled along the curb in front of a weathered brick building with a big sign that read, The Italian Amigos, in red and green lettering.

I did a double take at the sign, wondering if I'd read the restaurant name correctly the first time. "Is this place actually called, The Italian Amigos?"

"It is," he said, a slow smile lifting his lips as he put his truck in park, like he knew exactly what I was thinking.

"But *amigos* is a Spanish word, isn't it?"

"*Sí, señorita,*" he said, apparently deciding to answer me in Spanish.

"So the name of the restaurant translates into The Italian Friends?" I asked, confused.

Did the owners think *amigos* was an Italian word and not Spanish?

The building looked old enough to have been around way before the Internet had made translating words in other languages as easy as a simple Google search, but surely someone would have told the owners about the naming mistake before they'd done everything to set it up.

"Just come inside," Carter said, unbuckling his seatbelt and opening his door. "You'll understand it better once you see the menu."

I climbed out of Carter's truck, my math notebook in tow, and followed him into the restaurant.

8

AVA

CARTER HELD the door open so I could walk in first—a surprisingly thoughtful gesture from such a self-absorbed guy—and when I stepped inside, I was met with the most interesting mishmash of decorations I'd ever seen.

A miniature version of Michelangelo's *David* statue stood beside a bench in the waiting area. But this wasn't just any regular *David* statue. No, this one was wearing a sombrero on its head, and covering his nether regions were swim trunks with little Mexican flags.

What the heck?

I pulled my gaze from the strangely decorated figurine to find that in another corner, there was another *David* replica —only this one wore a colorful fiesta serape and had a black mustache attached above his lip. And sitting on the sling over his shoulder was a plate with a wood-fired pizza.

I furrowed my brow and looked up at Carter. "So...it's an Italian *and* Mexican restaurant?"

"It's a diamond in the rough, for sure," he said, amusement in his expression.

A middle-aged waitress with dark hair, wearing a completely normal polo shirt and jeans, noticed we'd come into the restaurant. When she saw Carter, a huge smile lifted her cheeks.

"Carter Hastings." She held her arms open to the tall boy beside me. "I was wondering when I'd see you again."

"Hi Rosa," Carter said, rolling the "r" in her name, with a rare smile on his face as he bent over to hug the petite woman. "It's good to see you, too."

They held each other for a moment before Rosa stepped away. "Did you grow over the summer?" she asked, looking Carter up and down. "You're getting so tall these days."

"Maybe another inch." Carter shrugged his broad shoulders, seeming more at ease with this woman than I'd ever seen him since meeting him yesterday. "But then again, it's not too hard to be taller than you." He shot Rosa a teasing smile.

"Some of us only need to grow so much until we reach perfection, *cariño*." She patted his arm. "Apparently, it's just taking you longer than most."

"Hopefully, I'll make it there before too long." Carter laughed, a deep relaxed sound that surprised me. Then, as if he'd just remembered me, he said, "This is Ava, by the way. She and her sister just started at my school today."

"So nice to meet you, Ava." Rosa gave me a smile, her dark brown eyes warm. "Welcome to Eden Falls."

"Thanks," I said. "It's nice to be here."

"Well, since I know you probably have classes to get back

to," Rosa said, grabbing two menus from the hostess's podium. "Let me get you seated so you're not late."

She showed us to a booth in a corner with a painting of a Tuscan landscape on the wall beside it. The tabletop was lined with Mexican tiles, but the salt and pepper shakers were in the shape of the Leaning Tower of Pisa.

I couldn't help but smile when I took in the eclectic decor. If the food was good here, this might just be the coolest restaurant I'd ever been to.

After setting the homemade menus in front of us, Rosa asked, "Would you like me to start you off with something to drink?"

"Just water for me," Carter said.

"I'll take a Dr. Pepper," I said.

"Great, I'll be right back with those."

After Rosa left, I took the time to glance over the menu. And sure enough, when I turned through the pages, I found that there was a full lineup of Italian-style dishes on the first two pages, and then Mexican cuisine on the last two.

"When you asked if I liked Italian or Mexican food," I said. "I thought you were planning to narrow the options down." I glanced around the room again. "I didn't expect *this*."

"They don't have places like this where you're from?" Carter raised an eyebrow.

"Apparently, we're a lot more boring in central New York."

"Eden Falls definitely has its own special charm," Carter said.

"Do you know the story behind this place?" I asked, hoping to keep up the more relaxed vibe Rosa had seemed to bring to Carter so we didn't have to go back to the awkwardness that had been in the truck.

"Yeah, Rosa is actually one of the owners." He leaned his elbows on the table and pointed in the direction Rosa had gone. "She came to the United States with her parents when she was a lot younger but grew up making traditional Mexican cuisine. She enjoyed cooking enough that she went to culinary school, and while there, she ended up dating a guy named Lucca who was originally from Italy and had just moved to the U.S. for school.

"Anyway, they got married and soon after, they moved to Eden Falls and started a restaurant together. And since they were blending two cultures into one with their family, they decided to do the same with their restaurant."

"And so, The Italian Amigos was born," I guessed.

He nodded. "That's the story Rosa told me, anyway."

"You and Rosa seem close. Do you come here a lot then? Or is she just like that with everyone she knows?"

From our minimal interactions, I already guessed that Carter wasn't so friendly with everyone he knew.

"A little of both, I suppose." He shrugged out of his blazer, setting it on the booth beside him. "But I did come here a lot when I first moved here." He pulled on the long white sleeves of his button-up that had ridden up his forearms, which was kind of a shame because the guy had amazing forearms—all veiny and muscular with just the right amount of golden arm hair.

Rosa brought us our drinks. She had two other glasses on her tray and said she'd be right back to take our orders.

"You said you came here after you moved here. Does that mean your family isn't from Eden Falls?" I asked, picking up where we'd left off. For some reason, I'd assumed the Hastings family was like a founding family of this small town. Something to do with them having an estate and all.

Carter fiddled with a small gold chain bracelet around his wrist. "My great-great-great-grandfather Hastings actually settled the town. But, um, I lived in Guatemala until I was eight."

"Your family lived in Guatemala? That's cool."

"No." He shook his head, letting go of his bracelet and reaching for his glass of water. "That was just me."

"Oh." He had lived separate from his family for the first half of his life? He'd said he and his siblings had different moms.

My mom had told me about a documentary she'd seen one time about a pilot who had two separate families who didn't know about each other. Was this something like that? Had Carter's father kept him a secret for the first eight years in Guatemala and brought him to the U.S. only when his other family found out?

And if so, what did that mean for Carter's mom? Was she still in Guatemala or had she moved to the U.S. with him?

I wanted to ask questions, to see if it was something similar or something completely different, but before I could, he continued by saying, "Anyway, I didn't speak English when my dad found me, so I ended up hanging out here with Rosa a lot those first few years since she was the easiest person to talk to."

Which explained the Spanish book he'd been reading at dinner yesterday and the slight accent I detected when he said Rosa's name. I was vaguely wondering if he spoke more Spanish than English when my mind picked up on the other thing Carter had said. That his dad had *found* him in Guatemala.

Had Carter been kidnapped then?

All kinds of new scenarios started forming in my mind until Rosa came back with her notepad in hand. "Are you ready to order?" she asked.

"Um, almost." I looked down at the menu, realizing I'd barely even glanced at the food since I'd been so caught up in the conversation with Carter. But knowing we were short on time, I said, "Actually, do you have chicken enchiladas?"

"Of course," she said, followed by something in Spanish that I didn't understand.

When I just looked blankly at her, Carter said, "She says she doesn't like to brag but her enchiladas de mole are the best you'll ever have."

Rosa's jaw dropped. "Now you make me look like I'm bragging." Rosa tsked at Carter, making a show of being embarrassed that he'd revealed what she'd really said.

"Well, I guess I better try them and see if they really are the best." I smiled at Rosa, enjoying the playful energy she and Carter had together.

"Good choice." Carter folded his menu up and handed it to Rosa. "I'll have the same thing."

"Two enchiladas de mole coming up," Rosa said in her accented voice before heading toward the kitchen again.

"Should we get started on those questions for class?" Carter asked, pulling out the notebook he'd brought in with him along with his phone.

"Sure." I opened my math notebook, and when Carter noticed the cover, the biggest smile I'd seen from him so far stretched across his face.

And man, he really was gorgeous when he smiled like that.

Which I guess was probably why he kept the smile mostly to himself. He'd never escape the throngs of hormonal girls from our school if he handed smiles like that out like candy.

"You pick that notebook out especially for Stats?" he asked, eyeing the skull-and-crossbones pattern on a light pink background.

"I thought it went well with the subject matter," I said lightly, not letting on that I was happy he'd made the connection.

He chuckled. "You really don't like math, do you?"

"I don't like things I'm not good at." I shrugged.

"Well," he said. "Hopefully, I can help you change your opinion on the subject before too long."

"So you're one of those math tutors who actually likes math?" I narrowed my eyes so he'd know I was judging him big time for that.

It was his turn to shrug. "Math works the same in English and Spanish, so yeah, it's the one subject I didn't suck at when I moved here."

"I guess I never thought about it that way." I found myself even more intrigued by his background and hoped he'd tell me more.

"But I totally get why you don't like it." He rolled up the sleeves of his button-up and it was a treat to see his forearms again. "I felt the same way about a lot of things until my tutors explained them in a way that made sense to me."

So my tutor had had tutors before?

"Is that why you're a math tutor, then?" I asked, because

from what I knew about him so far, I really doubted he needed the money he'd earn from working with me.

He shrugged, the fabric of his white button-up stretching across his broad shoulders with the movement. "I guess I like the challenge of taking someone who sees math as an enemy to seeing it on friendlier terms by the time we're done with our tutoring sessions."

"Do you tutor lots of people from school?" I asked, a weird sensation of jealousy forming in my stomach at the thought of him spending one-on-one time with multiple math-challenged people from school.

Which is ridiculous, I know.

Never thought I'd feel possessive over my math tutor... whom I'd just met, by the way.

And yet, here we were.

"I usually tutor a few people at a time, depending on how long my services are needed," he said. "But since I'm enrolled in more advanced courses this year, I told Mrs. Simmons I only had time for one."

"So should I feel special?" I asked. "Or embarrassed that I'm a bad-enough case that I'm the only one to make the cut this year?"

"Let's go with special." He looked down at the notebook he'd brought in with him and pulled a sheet of paper from the front. "Actually, that reminds me. I have a contract that I'll need you to sign before we get started." He slid the piece of paper across the tile tabletop so I could read it. "It's just something I have everyone I work with sign so we can make the most of our time together."

I frowned as I looked at the words printed on the page.

Carter cleared his throat and pointed to the paragraphs

he had printed there. "So, it basically just goes over some of the expectations that I have for our tutoring sessions."

"Are you going to grade me, too?" I asked, the whine in my tone coming out more prevalently than it probably should have.

But he shook his head and said, "No, nothing like that." He leaned over the table and pointed to the bullet points about a third of the way down the page.

He had really nice hands for a guy. Long fingers. His nails short and clean. And the veins crawling up from his knuckles and disappearing into the sleeves of his white shirt were very nice to look at, too.

Okay, focus, Ava.

"The first bullet point talks about how I expect you to come to our sessions willing to work hard and learn," Carter said. "Basically, to make the most of our time together, I need you to be cooperative. I don't like wasting people's money, and I don't like having my time wasted, either."

He lifted his gaze to mine, as if waiting for a verbal agreement. But with him leaning forward with his gaze intent on me, I suddenly found it hard to breathe, because having his face only a foot and a half away was kind of overwhelming.

I'd thought his eyes were just plain aqua-blue before, but now I could see little flecks of turquoise in them, too.

"Do you think you can agree to that first expectation?" he prodded when I didn't say anything.

"Um, yes." I cleared my throat, hoping it would also help me clear my head of the impulse I had to agree to anything he said if he would promise to keep looking at me like that forever. "I can try to do that."

"Good."

If he noticed how much his close proximity dazzled me, he didn't show any signs of it.

His index finger pointed to the next bullet on the list. "The second item says that I expect you to be on time to our tutoring sessions. I have my own classes to study for, along with some other obligations. So if you're late, it just means we'll have a shorter session because I won't be able to change my schedule around it."

"Sounds fair enough," I said.

Mack had warned me about how anal Carter was about his schedule.

His finger moved down to the next and final bullet point on the list. And when my gaze ran across the words he had typed there, I wondered if I was seeing things because I couldn't believe what I was reading.

I looked up at him with wide eyes. "You have a rule about not dating the people you tutor?"

He frowned momentarily as he read over the last rule, as if he couldn't remember what he'd written.

After a short pause, he pressed his lips together and tilted his head back up to look me in the eyes. "Ah yes, the most important rule of all."

"The most important rule?" I furrowed my brow, so confused why such a rule was even necessary in the first place. "Is this your way of saying you'd never deign to fraternize with people who need tutoring?"

Was his talk about understanding what it was like to struggle with something all just an act, and he was actually silently judging me for my stupidity?

Were people who admitted that they actually needed help somehow inferior to this "Mr. You Can't Date Me?"

And to think I'd just thought he was as dazzling as Edward Cullen a minute ago.

Ugh. Looks could be so deceiving sometimes.

The arrogance that it would take for someone to actually write that rule down was mind-boggling to me.

"I can see you think I'm a pompous jerk for even listing that last rule," he said, picking up on the shift in my mood. "But..." He paused, seeming to think. Then as if remembering something, he continued, "I can't tell you how many girls have pretended to be bad at math just to work one on one with me."

Seriously?

Sure, he was obviously hot. But who in their right mind would *choose* to do more math if they didn't have to?

Even *I* wasn't that dumb.

I shook my head. "Well, lucky for you and unluckily for me, I actually am terrible at math," I said. "I mean, they only let me come to this school if I promised to have tutoring right from the start."

"So...you're not going to try to date me?" He arched an eyebrow, as if he was actually worried I wanted to jump his bones.

And sure, maybe I'd gotten lost in his eyes for a few seconds here and there. But that was just because his eyes were interesting: light against his tan skin and full of secrets.

I definitely didn't want to drown in them or anything.

I sat up straighter, and in the most indifferent tone I could muster, I said, "I'm not interested in dating you. I'm just using you to keep my grades up."

"You're sure about that?" He narrowed his gaze, clearly not believing the words I'd just spoken. "Because we'll be spending a lot of time with each other and I don't want this to become an issue."

Okay, wow. He certainly had a high opinion of himself.

Did he really think he was so amazing that girls couldn't help but fawn all over him like they were Cinderella's stepsisters and he was the prince?

Sure, I'd been thinking that the definition of his forearms deserved to be immortalized in marble just like the *David* statues in the corner, but that was only because I appreciated art.

Instead of answering his question, I folded my arms across my chest and said, "Who's to say it shouldn't be the other way around?" I arched an eyebrow for effect. "Maybe *I* should be the one with the contract that says *you* aren't allowed to fall in love with *me*."

Take that, you egotistical narcissist.

He didn't respond at first—just stared at me unblinking, like he couldn't believe what I'd just said.

Then, after looking me up and down with an appraising eye that made me feel like he was seeing and weighing my every flaw, he leaned back against his cushioned seat and said, "I don't think that will be an issue."

Okay.

Ouch. Talk about a slap to the ego.

But I wasn't about to let him know how much his words stung, so I uncapped my pen and said, "Well, it looks like we're on the same page with things then."

It took everything in me to keep my hand steady as I signed his stupid contract when all I wanted to do was climb under the table and hide.

After signing my name and taking a deep calming

breath, I decided to drive the point home that I was not the one who'd be left wanting in this arrangement of ours. So, at the bottom of the contract, I added in purple ink the words:

I, Carter Hastings, vow that I won't fall in love with the beautiful and alluring Ava Cohen, even though she is a Goddess on earth. I will be on my best behavior during our tutoring sessions and not let her enchanting personality, charming wit, or captivating eyes distract me from doing my job.

And just below that, I drew a line where he could sign his name.

I slid the paper back to him. "I'm going to need you to sign my little addition," I said, capping my pen.

A half-smile formed on his lips as he read my amendment to his contract. But then he signed his name in a nice, flowing scrawl.

"Looks like we've come to an agreement," he said, tucking the contract back into the front folder of his notebook. "How about we get to those questions now."

9

———

CARTER

"WE MISSED YOU DURING LUNCH," Mack said, finding me in the hall as I walked toward Mrs. Johnson's room for my last class of the day. "Where were you?"

"I took Ava to The Italian Amigos."

"What?" Mack asked, his thick eyebrows knitting together. "And here I thought you said you weren't interested in the Cohen twins."

"I'm not."

He shot me a disbelieving look. "Then why take Ava to lunch?"

"We had a math assignment we needed to work on." An assignment that we'd only made a small dent in since we'd spent too much time chatting and going over my tutoring contract.

When I'd pulled out the contract for her to sign and she'd questioned me about my no-dating rule, I had to think fast for an excuse as to why that last rule was there in the first place.

My experience with my older brother Ian had come in handy as I'd played the part of a self-absorbed player who thought he was king of the world.

And from how riled up Ava had gotten after I'd basically implied that I was up to my eyeballs in propositions from girls, I figured I'd played the part well enough.

Which was great. I hadn't wanted to waste time with the female population this year, anyway. So even though I was pretty sure Nash must have hacked into my computer and changed my contract as some sort of prank, he had actually done me a favor.

At least, I'd stopped any chance of Ava ever being interested in me romantically. And if she did what I suspected she might and tell all the other girls about how full of myself I'd been during our lunch, it wouldn't be long before I had my weekends all to myself.

"Since when do you work on math assignments during lunch?" Mack asked.

We met a roadblock in the hall where it came to an intersection. As students shuffled past us, most of their heads several inches below ours since we were so tall, I said, "Ever since I needed an excuse to avoid Sofia."

"Ah, gotcha," Mack said. "I guess I'd probably want to avoid that conversation too, if I were you."

"Hopefully, she got the message that she doesn't have to try to be my friend just because she feels guilty."

The roadblock full of beige and navy-blue jackets cleared so we continued toward the B hall.

Mrs. Johnson's classroom for Adult Roles was at the end of the hall. She taught all of the family and consumer science classes so her classroom block was one of the biggest, with the cooking and sewing rooms attached just off of her instruction room.

When Mack and I walked inside, there were already quite a few seniors sitting at their tables. Scarlett and Hunter sat at the table that was front and center—Scarlett sitting up straight with her notebook and pen ready like she couldn't wait to ace this class. She was my biggest competition for valedictorian, so her eagerness didn't surprise me at all. Hunter, on the other hand, was slouched on his desk, his tie already loose around his neck like he just couldn't wait to get the first day of classes over with.

Just behind them was Ava and her twin sister Elyse. I was pretty sure Elyse had been in my last class and knew she was the twin with her hair straight and down while Ava's was curled with the top half pulled back and pinned with a sparkly barrette.

When our gazes met, Ava leaned over to her sister to whisper something. From the annoyed expression on her face, I figured she was probably informing Elyse about the stupid contract Nash had messed with and warned her about my jackhole tendencies.

And as she eyed me, I just shot her a smile so she'd know I knew she was talking about me.

That was what conceited people did, right? Assume the world revolved around them.

Maybe I should thank Ava for spreading the good word.

Sometimes you have to act like a jerk to keep away from unwanted drama.

"Let's sit there," Mack said from beside me, bringing my attention back to him. He pointed to the table behind the twins.

"Sure," I said. I was about to take the seat behind Elyse when I noticed that Sofia and Nash were sitting at the table just to the left of it.

Yeah, I'm not going there.

Sofia was right next to the aisle and I wasn't about to leave myself open to any sort of interaction.

Before Mack could take the spot behind Ava, I asked him if we could switch places.

Mack shrugged before shuffling around me to get to his seat.

I set my backpack on the floor, and before I could even scoot my chair in under the table, Ava was twisting around in her seat and saying, "Couldn't stay away from me, could you?"

I maneuvered my chair in and leaned over my desk so our faces were only a foot apart, before sending her my best smoldering gaze and saying in a low voice, "Apparently, I have a weakness for goddesses."

When her cheeks glowed a nice shade of pink at my flirtatious comment, I couldn't help but shoot her a wink as well.

I expected her to turn around, but instead, she scooted her chair back until it rested against my table. And then, after shooting her gaze toward Sofia for a split second and then back at me again—in a way that told me she was trying to communicate something unspoken to me—she said, "Are we still on for after school?" She bit her lip and looked at me like I was a chocolate tuxedo cake and she was a chocoholic.

And I had to give it to her, the girl had the sexy pout down to an art.

If she hadn't been so annoyed at me during lunch, I'd almost believe she was interested in me.

Even though I knew she was only referring to the study session we'd already arranged to have in the library after school to finish our math assignment, I couldn't help but wonder for a crazy second what it would be like to do exactly what her body language was telling Sofia and everyone around us that we might be doing after school.

I looked at her pink lips. They were just the right size and shape for her face. And yeah, kissing them would probably be a great way to spend an afternoon.

But before I could wonder too much about how soft they'd feel pressed against mine, I noticed that we now had several heads turned in our direction, watching us. So I went along with the production Ava had decided we should both star in and said, "I'm counting down the minutes to our *study* session." I emphasized the word *study* to imply to all the onlookers that we would be doing anything but studying.

Ava's eyebrows shot up in surprise, like she couldn't believe I was actually going along with whatever she was doing. But she quickly regained composure again, and without missing a beat, she took my hand in hers and turned it so my palm faced the ceiling. With the same purple felt tip pen that she'd used on my contract earlier, she wrote the words, *Back corner of library. 3:00 pm.*

Using her other hand, she folded my fingers over my palm to show me and everyone around us that what she'd just written there was of utmost importance.

Then, with the confidence of someone who knew exactly how to get what she wanted where guys were concerned, she gave my hand a long, meaningful squeeze before saying, "Don't be late."

Even though I knew this was all just a show, my arm lit up with electricity that seemed to shoot all the way to my cold, dead heart.

When her amber eyes looked coyly up at me, I was almost convinced that this was real.

Almost.

But fake or not, I knew one thing: Ava Cohen was trouble.

And tutoring her this year might just be a lot more fun than I'd originally thought.

10

CARTER

THE NEXT HOUR was spent listening to our teacher, Mrs. Johnson, as she went over the course curriculum. The class seemed interesting enough. The Adult Roles class was only offered to seniors at our school—a class that was supposed to prepare us to go out into the world and act like upstanding, responsible citizens.

I'd mostly signed up for this class because I wanted an easy A to buffer the rest of my intense schedule. But who knows, maybe learning more about building healthy romantic attachments, and the responsibility of raising children later, might come in handy a few years down the road when I would be settled into my future position at Hastings Industries and would have more time to think about these things.

After the final bell of the day rang, Ava turned around in her seat and slid a folded-up piece of lined paper across my table. "This is for you," she said with a wink. "Wait until I leave to read it."

Before I could even open the note, she left the room with her skirt swishing around her long legs.

When I looked sideways at Mack to see what he was thinking about Ava's shenanigans, he had a stunned expression on his face. "Now, what exactly did you two do at lunch?" The way he swallowed told me that he too had noticed the sexy way Ava's hips had swung as she'd walked away.

"We just ate enchiladas and worked on our assignment," I said, knowing I probably looked as stunned as he did.

"Well, either you're remembering it very wrong, or she just interpreted things differently because that girl's not being subtle at all."

"Yeah." I blinked as I flicked the edge of the note she'd given me. "I think she's just trying to help me out with Sofia. But who knows, maybe she's crazy."

I really didn't know the girl yet.

Mack chuckled. "Well, if that's the kind of crazy the new girls are bringing with them, sign me up."

I shook my head and decided I might as well satiate my curiosity by reading what she'd written in her note.

Inside, in the same flowing cursive that she'd used on my hand and on my contract, was a note that read:

To Mr. Haughty McHot-Hot,
Pretty sure Sofia was trying to burn a hole in the back of my head all throughout class with her death glare. So...you're welcome. We'll talk more about how I want you to return the favor in the library.
xoxo,
Ava

And in a smaller script with an arrow pointing to the word "haughty" was a note that said: *Yes, I spelled that right.*

Oh Ava. You're going to be quite the handful, aren't you?

I MADE it to the library first.

Apparently, for all of Ava's antics in front of our class, she hadn't actually been as excited to meet up with me as she'd pretended.

While I waited for her to show up, I pulled out my AP Psychology textbook to get started on the reading assignment my teacher had given us for chapter one.

I had only made it through the first page before I noticed Ava appear at the entrance to the library with Nash at her side.

She laughed at something Nash said to her, and then after another short exchange where they smiled more than I ever could without it tiring my underused smile muscles, she handed him her phone to type what I assumed must be his phone number. And then she waved goodbye to him.

I set my psychology text aside and opened my math notebook to the page I'd written the answers to our interview questions earlier as she walked toward me in the back corner of the room.

"Looks like Nash didn't buy your little production from last period," I commented when she took her seat in the chair beside me at the small round table.

"I think it was more your side of it that he didn't buy." She shrugged. "He knows all about the no-dating clause in your contract and somehow figured out that you'd only flirt back with me if it was already known that nothing would ever happen between us."

"Huh," was all I could say in response. I guess Nash was more observant than I'd thought.

And apparently, I'd also been correct when I suspected that he'd been the one to mess with my contract in the first place.

"So, from the way you just got his number, I'm assuming that you have a favorite Hastings brother already."

"I don't know... You both have provided a lot of fun entertainment for me so far," she said with a sly look on her face. "But it's refreshing to be around a Hastings boy who is actually socially capable and genuinely good-natured."

I had to chuckle at her ripping me a new one. "Being pleasant all the time takes too much energy."

"Maybe you should try drinking some coffee for an energy boost," she said. And then I thought I heard her mutter under her breath, *"Being hot can only get you so far,"* as she dug into her bag for the skull-and-crossbones notebook she'd used earlier.

I couldn't help the smirk that lifted my face after hearing her disgruntled words. "So you find me attractive?" I asked.

She looked up from her bag, her face going pale as she realized she'd spoken the words loud enough for me to hear. "I-I didn't say that."

"Yes, you did."

"No, I didn't," she insisted, even though we both knew that she had.

"Ava," I said in a chiding tone. "Didn't your parents ever teach you it's not okay to lie?"

"Fine." She let out an aggravated sigh. "So you're hot. You

obviously already know that, so I shouldn't be ashamed for thinking so."

"Thanks for the compliment." I shot her a smile. "I mean, your 'Haughty McHot-Hot' compliment was nice earlier. But it's always great to hear how good-looking I am in person."

Her eyes widened and she sat up straighter with a hmph. "I wasn't compli—"

"It's nothing to be embarrassed about," I cut her off. "In fact, I was about to say that you yourself have the most captivating eyes."

Which, despite my teasing tone, was actually true.

In fact, they were really pretty—a lighter amber color that kind of surprised you.

And as I studied the flecks of gold in her irises, I could tell the moment she realized I'd just complimented her because her eyes went wide with shock.

She blinked a few times, like she was having to switch gears with whatever retort she'd planned to say and instead said, "Th-th-thank you?"

I shrugged. "Of course." Then leaning closer so our faces were mere inches apart and her sweet perfume filled my nose, I decided to see how far I could take things by tucking a loose strand of hair behind her ear. In a voice just above a whisper, I said, "Not only are your eyes captivating, but I also find your personality enchanting and your wit positively charming."

She swallowed and just stared at me, probably completely stunned by my words and the intimate way I'd just traced my fingertip across her smooth skin.

As her questioning gaze studied my face for signs that I

was being facetious, I worked hard to maintain a straight face. But not nearly the actor my brother was, I was only able to keep in character for another second before the corners of my lips betrayed me and the smile I'd been fighting forced its way across my lips.

It only took another second for her eyes to narrow and her jaw to drop as she realized that I'd just complimented her with all the qualities she'd listed at the bottom of our contract.

"Ugh." She pushed her hand against my shoulder, forcing more distance between us. "You think you're so funny, don't you?"

I shrugged. "Sorry, I'm really great at reaching for the low hanging fruit."

I mean, how could you not when it was just sitting there?

But though I'd only done it just to get a reaction from her, it was strange how my fingertips still burned a little from touching her cheek. It had been a long time since I'd had any sort of reaction like that with a girl.

Ava shook her head, her silky brown curls bouncing slightly with the movement. "Anyway, since I know how anal you are about your schedule and that we only have forty-five minutes before you probably have a workout or something else planned, I wanted to briefly talk to you about what I hinted at in my note."

I leaned back in my seat, resting one arm across the table in a relaxed pose. "I'm listening."

"Okay," she said. "So I'm guessing that you might be a little curious about why I decided to put on that whole charade during our last class after we'd just gone through that whole contract thing during lunch."

"Just a little curious." I drummed my fingers on the wooden tabletop. "You might say that you totally flirting with me after signing a paper saying that you wouldn't try to date me was kind of the opposite behavior that I expected."

"So I may have had a little fun." A little smirk lifted her lips, like the memory of the whole debacle was hilarious to her. "But I guess after everything today, it got me thinking that maybe we could make an arrangement that's mutually beneficial." She studied me, and for the briefest moment there was a glimmer of vulnerability that showed through the mask of confidence she'd been wearing all day. She looked down as she smoothed her hands along her pleated skirt. After releasing a heavy breath, she met my gaze again and said, "I know that during lunch I joked a little over the fact that I needed a tutor in order to even attend this school in the first place, but—" She shifted in her seat and tossed her long hair over her shoulder, as if trying to get more comfortable for an uncomfortable conversation. "—it's actually something that I'm really embarrassed about."

She trained her gaze to the side, as if admitting her weakness took a lot of bravery. Then she said, "And I guess that since I really don't want everyone at school to know that I need help with math and you seem eager enough to make Sofia regret breaking up with you, then maybe we could kill two birds with one stone and pretend like we're spending our afternoons together for less scholarly reasons."

"You want people to think we're romantically entangled?" I asked, not sure I was understanding her correctly.

"Well, maybe not exclusively," she said. "I'd still like to have a fun senior year with guys."

"Like my brother Nash," I offered since she'd just been with him.

"Sure, him and others." She shrugged. "It's my first day, there are still a lot of guys to meet."

I knew it was insane to feel the least bit possessive of this girl whom I'd just met twenty-four hours ago, but for some strange reason, her talk of dating *lots* of other guys caused an unusual jolt of jealousy to rise in me.

But I pushed the feeling away since caring about who or how many guys Ava spent her time with really shouldn't affect me at all.

"So anyway," she continued, "I was just thinking that while neither one of us is officially dating anyone else, it would be a nice arrangement for me to save face and for you to get back a little at Sofia."

I strummed my fingers on the table as I thought over what Ava was proposing.

I hadn't exactly wanted to mess with the drama that dating and girls brought with them this year, so pretending to flirt with Ava wouldn't hinder any of that—in fact, it might even help fend off other girls who might otherwise try to flirt with me. And then, of course, making Sofia believe I'd moved on and was completely over her was also a very appealing idea—especially since I could do that without the less desirable side effects of having to actually be invested in a new relationship.

Plus, this plan of hers wouldn't even add an extra time constraint into my schedule since I'd already planned on our Tuesday and Thursday tutoring sessions for the rest of the school year.

The only thing I'd really need to do differently was more

of what we'd done during last period, which—when I thought about it—had actually been kind of fun.

Maybe Nash and Cambrielle weren't the only Hastings siblings with a future in the theater?

"So, what do you think?" Ava asked.

"You think it'll actually work?" I pressed my lips together as I looked at her.

"I think so," Ava said with a shrug. "I mean, I guess I've heard that you only date supermodels, which yeah, obviously I'm not one, so maybe that simple fact will make it unbeliev-able to anyone who knows you. But if you're not too worried about looking like you're slumming it with the new girl, I think it could help us both in our own ways."

"I don't think anyone would think I was slumming it," I said, not wanting her to think that my lack of interest in dating her had anything to do with the way she looked.

"Why, Carter Hastings!" Ava put a hand to her chest in a show of surprise. "I think that may be the nicest thing you've said to me yet."

"Well, I do what I can." Then after thinking about it for a moment longer, I said, "How about we nail down a few particulars for how this would even work, and then maybe I can give you a better answer?"

11

———

AVA

CARTER and I spent the next few minutes going over the details of our little arrangement. Since this was all pretend, and definitely not an exclusive sort of thing, it was pretty simple. Basically, we would just be extra flirty in the classes we had together so Sofia would have a front-row seat to it all, and then we'd just make it seem like our study sessions were more of a social thing instead of an actual requirement for me to pass math.

It was kind of a great situation, actually.

I was still allowed to flirt with other guys and go on dates if I wanted while he would, in his own words, continue to ignore everyone else like he usually did.

Man, my math tutor sure was a catch, wasn't he? The kind of hot that could make me forget my own name, but severely lacking in social skills.

But if publicly flirting with him kept my secret safe while I earned my first ever A's in math, I could put up with Mr. Grumpy Pants.

Carter pulled out his phone once we were ready to get back into the interview questions Mrs. Simmons had assigned us. "I think what's next is whether we'd like to be famous or not, and if so, in what way?"

"I'll go first on that one," I offered. I liked that the questions so far were pretty non-invasive, even though our teacher had suggested that these might bring out some things we didn't already know about our classmates. "I think it would be fun to be famous." It would mean that I'd probably not have to worry about money since hopefully, I'd be a rich famous person and not famous for something bad. "And as for what way, I'd love to follow in my mom's footsteps and make a name for myself in the fashion world."

Carter nodded as he wrote down my answer in his notebook. I smiled when I saw the words *Ava wants a fashion empire* in his blocky handwriting, because the word *empire* had so much power in it.

When he was done jotting my answer down, I asked, "And what about you? Do you want to be famous?"

"Nope."

The way he said it was so final, like he didn't even care to entertain for one minute the idea of what it would be like to be famous.

"Why not?" I asked, so curious since I figured most everyone I knew would want to be famous in one way or another. If not famous themselves, then at least have something they created become famous.

"I'm already critical enough of myself that I don't need random strangers nitpicking at my flaws," he said matter-of-factly. "When you're famous, people strangely think that you somehow owe them the nitty gritty details of your life: who you're dating, who you went on vacation with, what kind of toothpaste you prefer. I've seen my dad and Dawn deal with enough crap—and they're only famous in the business world. I just don't need to live under a microscope. I like my privacy too much."

"I must seem really naive to you then," I said, suddenly regretting what I said about wanting to be famous.

And to think I'd just been thinking that these questions were tame a second ago.

When he gave a non-committal shrug in reply, I knew he had to be totally judging me.

Ugh. So much for being on equal ground with this guy for once.

Carter cleared his throat. "Ready for the next question?"

I quickly jotted Carter's answer down in my notebook. "Sure."

Hopefully, I could answer this one without seeming stupid to him.

"Okay, this one's interesting," he said. "It asks if you ever rehearse what you're going to say before making a phone call."

I squished my eyebrows together, wondering how this was even a question. "Is that actually a thing?" I asked at the same time Carter said, "I do. What about you?"

"Wait— You rehearse your conversations beforehand?" I asked, realizing what he'd just said.

"If I can send a text, I'll choose to do that instead," he said. "But sometimes, when I'm making calls for my dad's company, I'll run through what I need to say ahead of time so I don't mess it up."

"Interesting."

"Not all of us are the social butterfly that you seem to be," he said. "I'm guessing from your reaction that you don't do this."

"Can't say that I do."

Was it possible that my math tutor sometimes came off as unapproachable not because he thought he was above everyone, but because he had some social anxiety?

The next few questions were pretty easy, asking us things like what our favorite color was, favorite thing to do during our free time, and our favorite food.

Our answers were the following:

Me: Pink, hanging out with Elyse and our friends, and pizza.

Him: Blue, reading, and his family chef's famous strawberries and cream crepes.

Apparently, he was a lot fancier than I was.

"The next question asks what your favorite place in the whole world is," I said, after reading from the list. After thinking about all the places I'd ever been in the world, which granted probably wasn't many compared to a lot of the kids at this school, I said, "I guess my favorite place that I've ever been to would have to be Habonim-Dor Beach near my grandma and grandpa's home in Israel."

"Your grandparents are from Israel?" Carter asked. "Does that mean you lived there?"

"No," I said. "My mom came to this school when she was in high school and loved the United States, so she came back again to stay after college. I've only ever lived in Ridgewater until now. But we've visited my grandparents a few times when they offered to fly us over."

Things had been pretty strained between my mom and

grandpa for a while there. Having him disinherit her when she'd told him she was pregnant hadn't exactly put them on the best of terms. But he'd come around a few years later with the help of my grandma and a huge change of heart, and eventually, they were able to patch things up and have a relationship again.

"Cool," he said. "Is your dad from the United States, too? Or did he and your mom meet in Israel?"

"Oh, um—" I looked down at my notebook, feeling my cheeks heat up. "I actually don't have a father."

"You don't?" He frowned.

"Well, I mean," I said after realizing how that had sounded. "I obviously have a biological father out there somewhere since that's how science works and all, but um, yeah, I just don't know who he is..." I let my words taper off at the end, wishing for about the thousandth time that I had at least a name or photo or something...anything to give me a clue.

But sadly, my mom was really, *really* good at keeping secrets.

"Oh, sorry." Carter swallowed, looking uncomfortable. Then after seeming like he was trying to decide whether to say something or not, he said, "I can kind of relate. I, uh, I didn't know who my dad was until I was eight."

"You didn't?" I met his gaze again, surprised that we would have something that was so rare in common.

He gave his head a slight shake, his expression somewhat cautious as he said, "All my mom ever told me when I asked about him was that my father was a *gringo* who'd only been in Guatemala for a short time."

"Yeah?" Then, after hesitating for a moment, I asked,

"Since you're here now, I'm guessing you eventually found out who he was."

"Yeah." He sighed and shifted in his seat. "Anyway, um, my dad came to work at one of the orphanages he sponsors when I was eight and after putting two and two together—Nash and I could have passed for twins when we were younger and blue eyes aren't exactly common among Guatemalans—he had a DNA test done and found out that he had a son he'd never known about."

Wait. What?

Carter had lived in an orphanage?

"W-what were you doing in an orphanage?" I asked before realizing it was probably the stupidest question for me to ask right then.

People usually only ended up in orphanages for one reason.

Which meant Carter's mom had probably died sometime before he was eight.

I was about to tell him that it was none of my business and I probably shouldn't have even asked the question in the first place when a range of emotions crossed his face and he said, "My, um—" He sighed heavily before meeting my gaze. His eyes showed a hint of pain when he looked at me. "My mom left me at a childcare one day when I was five and never came back."

My heart stuttered to a stop.

Carter hadn't been orphaned.

He'd been abandoned.

By his own mother.

And lived in an orphanage for three years before his dad had found him.

Suddenly, never knowing who my dad was sounded way easier than him being abandoned by the only parent he'd known at such a young age.

"I'm sorry to hear that. That must have been so hard," I said lamely. What else could I say?

Based on his mention of his family having an employee who cleaned all of their fancy vehicles, and knowing he'd dated a supermodel in the past, I'd assumed he had always lived in the lap of luxury. But from just those few details he'd shared with me, it sounded like the first few years of his life had been more difficult than I could have ever imagined.

Geez.

He'd lived in an orphanage in a third-world country.

My mom, sister, and I might not have had the nicest house growing up, but we'd never gone without.

"Anyway," Carter said, drawing in a deep breath. He chuckled awkwardly. "How's that for a getting-to-know-you game?"

I shook my head slowly from side to side. "Definitely a bit deeper than I thought we'd get."

That was for sure.

"I promise I'll try not to make all of our study sessions so heavy," he said.

"I'm the one who started us off by saying the whole thing about not having a dad," I said with a shrug, hoping to lighten the mood.

"True." Then shooting me a half-smile, he said, "But then I had to one up you with my whole sob story of living in an orphanage, since I'm competitive like that."

"I guess I'll try to be less of an underachiever in the future," I said in a joking tone.

When he smiled at my comment, I was relieved to see that it actually reached his eyes this time.

And it was kind of the most beautiful thing I'd ever seen in the world.

Dang. For all the range of emotions this guy had put me through in the past twenty-four hours, from lust to hate and everything in between, he really was different from anyone I'd ever met before.

And I had the feeling that if I wasn't careful and constantly reminding myself that any flirtations we shared over the next few weeks were purely fake, I might just be in danger of getting the hugest crush on my math tutor.

A crush so big my heart might not survive it.

12

———

AVA

THE REST of the school week went by quickly and as the days passed, I felt more and more settled in at my new school.

I hadn't thought that I would like *living* at my school very much, but it was turning out to be pretty fun sharing my mealtimes and daily routines with my new friends and just getting to know everyone better. Elyse and I were getting more and more settled in with Scarlett and the friends she'd introduced us to on that first day.

"How long do you think you and Carter will keep up this fake flirtation thing you have going on?" Elyse asked me Saturday afternoon as we waited in the common room for Nash to come pick us up for their back-to-school barbecue.

We'd invited Scarlett to join us for the pre-party with Nash and Cambrielle, but since she'd been so busy with volleyball throughout the week, she'd chosen to stay behind to catch up on her homework, saying that she'd just hitch a ride later with Hunter.

"I'm not sure how long we'll keep it up." I glanced around to make sure we were still alone in the large common room. "I guess it just depends on however long it takes for either of us to get more interested in actually dating someone else."

Which was still an up-in-the-air thing for me. A few guys had piqued my interest this week. Mack, for one, was probably one of the hottest guys at our school—right alongside Carter—and had been super fun to joke around with. But even though we flirted here and there, I got the vibe that he was more interested in Elyse. It could be because she was more shy and he preferred someone who was a contrast to his vivacious personality. Or it was possible Carter hadn't told his friends that our flirting was purely for show, and so Mack was trying to respect the bro code or something. But either way, he'd focused more of his attention on Elyse the past few days, so I knew better than to try and be anything more than friends.

Nash was also fun to hang out with, and he'd gone out of his way to make sure I was included anytime he and the group had plans to study together or go to one of Scarlett's volleyball games, or something like that. But even though we had a lot of fun together, and he was super cute and sweet, I also saw him as more of a friend.

And then Hunter was just off-limits because he and Scarlett had whatever they had going on. So, until I branched out and tried to get to know other guys outside of my current circle, I was fine keeping up this charade Carter and I had going for the foreseeable future.

Unless he decided to go with one of the offers he had from the throngs of girls who apparently bowed down at his Italian-loafer-wearing feet.

"It's a pretty clever idea you came up with," Elyse said. "Taking the guy who made you sign a contract about not dating him, and then turning things around on him so that instead of trying to date him you just get to flirt with him instead."

"It's been fun," I admitted. "I can be as over the top as I want, and he can just throw it all right back because we know there's no chance either of us will get confused by it and try to make something else happen."

"You're basically a genius." Elyse chuckled. "All the perks of having a boyfriend, without any of the responsibility."

"I don't know if I'd say I'm getting *all* the perks." I arched an eyebrow. "I haven't exactly figured out how to convince Carter that we need fake make-out sessions or anything." Though, I'd be lying if I didn't admit that I had wondered a time or two what it might be like to kiss my math tutor. He did have those amazing lips.

And the fact that he was gorgeous didn't hurt, either.

"Fake make-out sessions?" Elyse laughed. "Yeah, now if you figure out how to do *that,* let me know. I haven't kissed a guy in way too long."

"Same." I sighed. "Maybe we can convince everyone to play Truth or Dare or Spin the Bottle at the party tonight. You can always count on a good make-out session with those kinds of games."

Did kids at private schools play games like that at parties? I mean, those kinds of games provided great entertainment in Ridgewater, but we were about to go to a party at an *estate.* They probably had much more refined activities, like watching a firework show from a balcony or promenading around their extensive gardens.

Why was I suddenly picturing a regency ball with girls in fancy dresses and guys in suits with elegantly tied cravats?

Oh that's right, because I've only ever heard of people having estates in my mom's regency-era movies.

And because I had no idea what to expect from tonight, I might have packed a few different outfit options since I wasn't sure if the T-shirt and jeans I currently wore were fancy enough for a party at the Hastings'.

I was probably overthinking it but having grown up with a mom who taught me that the way we dress impacts the first impression we give to the world, I didn't want to give anyone the impression that I had no idea what the heck I was doing with all these rich kids.

My phone buzzed, interrupting my anxiety session. It was a text from Cambrielle.

> Cambrielle: Nash wanted me to tell you that we're about five minutes away. He says he'd come to the common room to get you, but since Bree Peterson gave him her cheek when he was trying to kiss her at the end of their date last night, he wants to avoid running into her.

A second text came through a second later.

> Cambrielle: And now he's mad that I told you that because he wanted you to think he's this big time Casanova.

"What's so funny?" Elyse asked when I laughed out loud. She looked over my shoulder at the texts. Then after reading them, she laughed too and said, "Well, if our Spin-the-Bottle idea doesn't work tonight, we might at least be able to count on Nash for some action."

"True." I laughed. "Though I'm sure you'd rather make out with Mack." I winked.

When Elyse's cheeks darkened, I knew it was true.

I shot Cambrielle back a text saying that we'd meet them out front. With our backpacks full of everything we'd need to get ready for tonight's party, Elyse and I headed down to meet our ride.

NASH'S LIME-GREEN convertible was waiting on the cobblestone drive at the front of the school when Elyse and I made it to the front steps.

Cambrielle climbed out of the passenger side once she saw us and said, "One of you can sit up front with Nash. He's annoyed at me for texting you about his kissing fail." Then with a smirk on her lips, she said, "Apparently, he's trying to impress the new girls." She shot Elyse and me a wink.

I gave Cambrielle a look that said, *I've got this.* Then I stepped closer to Nash's BMW and said, "Wow, this is an amazing car. Almost as awesome as the guy driving it. I totally call shotgun!"

"See, Cambrielle," Nash replied in a loud, overly exaggerated voice that I could imagine him using on the stage. "I told you the ladies are always fighting over me."

To which Cambrielle responded in an equally exaggerated tone, "Oh, yes, my dear brother. They're practically fawning all over you. How ever will you make it through the party tonight with so many girls begging for your attention?"

Nash put a hand to his chest, and this time he slipped a British accent in as he said, "'Tis a hard job. But I'll do my best to rise to the occasion."

Okay, these two were a riot.

After the spur-of-the-moment theatrical production had ended, Cambrielle and Elyse slid into the backseat and I took the spot beside Nash up front.

It was a beautiful fall day, sunny and warm, as we drove to the other end of the small town. I'd never ridden in a convertible before but as we drove and the wind whipped at my hair, I was thankful that I'd decided to wait and curl it while getting ready with Cambrielle.

We pulled off the main road about fifteen minutes later. After driving down a long residential road where the houses just seemed to get bigger and bigger the farther down we got, we took a right turn onto a private drive lined with pleached linden trees.

When we came to a large, wrought-iron gate, Nash pushed a button on his car's visor and the gate started opening.

I turned back to Elyse, wondering if she was as curious as I was about what we were about to see. She just looked back at me with wide eyes and mouthed the word, *Wow*.

Yeah, my thoughts exactly, sister.

The asphalt road we'd been driving on turned into a Belgian block driveway, and after another thirty seconds, we finally emerged from the tree-shrouded path until we reached the terrace of the biggest house I'd ever seen in my life.

"Here we are," Nash said, putting his car into park in front of a huge stone country house. "Home sweet home."

Home sweet home?

More like mansion sweet mansion.

I blinked a few times. The gigantic house was so tall and wide that I had to turn my head up and down and side to side to take it all in.

And as I looked at the beautiful gray stone exterior, the dozens of windows with white shutters, and the tall white columns of the portico, I couldn't help but think that wondering over whether tonight's barbecue would be like a nineteenth-century ball might not have been too far off, because this was exactly the kind of house that belonged in a Jane Austen novel.

Nash must have noticed the way I was gaping at the house because he reached across the center console and nudged my jaw shut with his finger. "Don't look impressed yet," he said with amusement in his voice. "You still haven't seen the inside."

"Well, if the inside is even half as impressive as the outside, I may need to rethink my wardrobe choices for tonight because I forgot to bring my prom dress."

Nash chuckled as he climbed out of his side of the car and came around to open my door. "Seeing as how I forgot to have the maid take my tuxedo to the cleaners after our family dinner last night, I'm sure whatever you brought is perfect."

I paused, glancing at Nash and then at Cambrielle behind me. "You wear a tuxedo to your family dinners?"

"Maybe we should call Scarlett and ask her to bring something else for us to change into," Elyse said at the same time.

The siblings both laughed. Nash said, "I was joking. If we haven't already changed out of our school uniforms before dinner, we're lucky to wear anything fancier than a T-shirt and sweatpants."

"So you guys aren't like one of those crazy, weird, super rich families?" I asked.

"We're as normal as any other family," Cambrielle answered.

But as we got out of the car and walked through the huge double doors and into a foyer with white marble floors, a huge chandelier, and a grand staircase with the most intricately designed handrail I'd ever seen, I couldn't help but think that the Hastings family's definition of "normal" was a lot different from my definition of the word.

"DO you want a tour of the place before we get all dressed up for the party?" Cambrielle turned to look at Elyse and me.

"Um, of course," Elyse said. "That would be awesome."

"How about we start upstairs so you can leave your backpacks in my room?" Cambrielle suggested.

"Sounds good to me." From the size of the house, I had a feeling the tour might take a while and my backpack was already heavy with all the things I'd packed in it.

"How about I catch you guys after the tour?" Nash asked as Cambrielle started leading Elyse and me up the stairs. "The guys said they were going to start their basketball game around four, so I'm gonna join them."

"Sure," Cambrielle said with a shrug. "I can take it from here."

Nash, who was already wearing gym shorts and a T-shirt, disappeared around the corner and the three of us girls went upstairs.

"So, this is where all of our bedrooms are," Cambrielle

said at the top of the stairs. "My parents' suite is that way." She pointed to the left toward large, white double doors that were closed. "And mine and my brothers' rooms are this way." She led us to the right, down a long hall where gigantic family photos hung on the wall space that was separated every so often with a door.

I glanced at the family portraits, curious what the rest of the Hastings family looked like. The first portrait we came to looked like it must have been taken fairly recently based on the fact that Nash, Cambrielle, and Carter all looked pretty similar to what they looked like now. The photo had been taken outside, with a beautiful purple and pink sky behind them. And despite what Nash had said about them wearing loungewear to dinner, the boys were all dressed in designer suits while Cambrielle and her mother—a beautiful woman with dark-brown hair, green eyes, tan skin, and an hourglass shape similar to Cambrielle's—wore designer gowns.

"Is that your older brother?" I asked Cambrielle, pointing to the guy in the photo beside Carter whom I hadn't seen before. He had darker hair than his brothers—closer to the same color as Mrs. Hastings and Cambrielle's hair. And instead of the bright blue eyes that the younger three siblings must have gotten from Mr. Hastings—a tall man with light blond hair and aqua-blue eyes himself—the older boy's eyes were brown.

"Yeah, that's Ian," she said. "He just graduated from Yale last spring."

If he'd recently graduated from college, then he must be at least four or five years older than us.

Did that mean Mr. Hastings had already been married to Mrs. Hastings when he'd had his relationship with Carter's mom in Guatemala? Because that probably would have caused a lot of drama if she hadn't known about the affair and Mr. Hastings suddenly came home from a later trip with an eight-year-old he'd fathered.

Cambrielle must have seen the confusion on my face because she said, "Ian is from my mom's first marriage. She and Dad met when he was, like, five."

"So Nash is your only full-blooded sibling?" Elyse asked, as if trying to piece everything together.

"Technically, yes," Cambrielle said. "But we don't call each other half siblings or anything like that. We're just brother and sister. And even though my mom isn't Carter's biological mom, and my dad isn't Ian's biological dad, they still just call them Mom and Dad."

"That's cool," I said.

I studied the family in the photo for a moment longer, interested in the family dynamic that they had. I knew a photo was just a snapshot of one moment in time, but in this one at least, they seemed like they were a happy family. And from the few interactions I'd had with Carter, Nash, and Cambrielle so far at school, they seemed like they were each other's best friends.

I loved that Elyse and I were so close, and that we shared a special bond with our mother. But as someone who'd always dreamed of what it would be like to have a bigger family with a dad and maybe another sibling or two, I couldn't help but feel envious of this picture-perfect family in front of me. As I studied the way Mr. Hastings had his arm around his wife and the other around Cambrielle, the longing for a father figure burned stronger in my chest than usual.

But like I did every time I came across a big family, I pushed the longing away because it didn't do any good to wish for something that I'd never have.

My mom might not have told Elyse and me very much about our bio father, but she had said that we were better off without him, so I just had to trust that she was right.

"Anyway, this is my room," Cambrielle said, moving away from the portrait of her family and to a door on the opposite side of the hall. "You can just put your things in here."

She led us into a gorgeous bedroom with pale pink walls and tall windows surrounded by long, shimmery gold curtains.

"Your bedroom is amazing," Elyse commented, setting her backpack on the floor just inside the door.

"Thanks," Cambrielle said as she ushered us farther in. "My mom let me redecorate it this summer, so I'm glad you like it."

"'Like it' would be an understatement," I said as I took in the queen-sized four-poster bed with white-and-gold bedding and so many throw pillows that it would probably take at least ten minutes to make the bed. "This is, like, my dream room."

"Really?" Cambrielle asked.

"Yeah, mine too," Elyse added.

"Well, thanks." Cambrielle smiled, genuinely happy that we liked her interior design. "It was fun to put together."

I noticed that while there was a nightstand on either side of the bed, a super cute, comfy-looking chair in one corner, and even a gas fireplace beside the chair, there was no dresser.

"Do you not have a dresser?" I asked.

A half-smile slipped onto Cambrielle's lips and she walked toward a door that led to what must be a closet. "I keep all my clothes in here," she said.

Only when she opened the door, it wasn't a closet but a bathroom with a huge mirror, a nice big soaker tub, a shower, and a little toilet room off to the side.

Dang, her bathroom was the size of Elyse's and my bedroom at home.

"The closet is just through here." Cambrielle walked toward a door next to the vanity, but then she stopped, grabbing what looked like an Old Spice deodorant and a blue toothbrush from off the countertop and quickly shoving them into a drawer.

"Sorry about that." She glanced back to Elyse and me with flushed cheeks. "I forgot to put those away earlier." She cleared her throat. "Anyway, this is my closet."

I briefly wondered why she seemed embarrassed that we'd see she preferred Old Spice to Secret deodorant, but my attention was instantly drawn away from that thought when she opened the door to her closet and turned on the light to reveal the most gorgeous space I'd ever seen.

The ceiling was painted pink to match the color of her room, with white crown molding. There were white built-in cabinets with open shelving on top with racks upon racks of blouses and designer jeans that could have come straight from one of my mom's fashion shows.

There were shelves of designer shoes. Shelves of jewelry and bags. Several racks of cocktail dresses and evening gowns. Fancy coats. Beautiful hats.

Hiding off to the side in the back corner, I spotted a rack of our school-approved uniforms.

And as I took in what just might be the most magical room in the whole world, I realized that with a fashion sense and a closet like this, wearing the school's uniforms every day must be even more painful for Cambrielle than it was for me.

"I know it's kind of a lot," Cambrielle said, noticing the look of awe on our faces. "But, um, if you ever need to borrow anything, I'm your girl." She gestured at the haute couture around her. "I know the school doesn't provide much space for clothes, so I'm totally happy to let you borrow anything you like."

I looked at Cambrielle. She was probably barely five feet, so I doubted much of what she had in here would even fit us and our five-foot-nine frames. But it was super sweet of her to offer, so I said, "I may take you up on that some time because this is amazing. Even our mom would be jealous."

A little while later, Cambrielle continued the tour by showing us the rest of the second floor. While Elyse was drooling over the movie collection in the theater room, I decided that I might need to take a bathroom break before we continued since there was still a lot of the house to see. "Do you have a guest bathroom up here that I can use?"

"Oh, sure." Cambrielle looked away from what she was showing Elyse. "It's just down that hall. Three doors down and on the left."

"Thanks."

I hurried down the hall in the direction she'd pointed and after counting three doors, I opened what I assumed was a bathroom.

Only, I didn't see a bathroom at all.

Instead, the door opened to a bedroom about the same size as Cambrielle's. Rather than pink walls and gold curtains, the room had a much more masculine vibe with lots of blues, whites, and grays. The focal point of the room was a king-sized bed with a gray, modern-style headboard. And behind the bed was a wall painted to look like the night sky with various constellations that covered the entire space and all across the ceiling.

I was tempted to step inside for a moment to see if I could figure out whether the room belonged to Nash or Carter, when suddenly, a bare-chested Carter walked out from what could be his bathroom with a gray T-shirt in his hand.

14

———

CARTER

"S-SORRY," one of the Cohen twins yelped when I walked out from my closet to see who had come into my room while I was changing into my basketball clothes. "Cambrielle said it was the third door on the left, and so I opened it and I..." The girl—who I still wasn't sure was Ava or Elyse—rambled on anxiously, a vein in her forehead becoming more and more pronounced the longer she talked. "And I didn't realize anyone would be in here. And...I...um..." Her gaze traveled from my face and panned down my torso and arms, and when it seemed like she was having a difficult time finishing her sentence, I realized that I was still holding my shirt in my hand.

She was totally raking me in.

"Uh, sorry, I didn't know..." I started to apologize about my current state of undress before realizing I shouldn't be the one apologizing, since technically, I'd been changing in my own room and had shut the door before doing so. So, I'd just let her finish her apology.

But instead of picking up from where her words had trailed off, her eyes narrowed as she looked at me. Her lips moved like she was counting under her breath, and then she suddenly blurted out, "You have an eight-pack?"

And with that one sentence, the mystery of which twin had barged into my room unannounced was solved.

Because from what I knew of the Cohen twins, only Ava would say something like that.

Deciding to test my assumption, I said, "Yes, Ava, I have an eight-pack." I pulled my shirt over my head since obviously my body was more of a distraction than I'd thought. "Is that the real reason you barged into my room just now? Because you wanted to practice your math skills by adding up my abs?"

"What?" Her jaw dropped, and then she added, "How did you know it was me and not Elyse?"

I tugged on my sleeves so they rested more comfortably on my shoulders. "Elyse doesn't exactly seem the type to blurt out questions like that."

Or the type to blatantly count a guy's abs in the first place.

"What's that supposed to mean?" Ava put her hands on her hips. And when she did that, I couldn't help but give her an inspection of my own.

Aside from the day she'd arrived at our school, I'd only seen her in her school uniforms. So seeing her in her jeans and a T-shirt was different. And while I may have admired her long legs in those plaid skirts she somehow looked better in than all the other girls at school did, Ava in her jeans just might rival even that.

But since she didn't need to know that I too found her

appearance distracting, I lifted my gaze back to her eyes and answered her question. "I just meant that Elyse is more reserved while you're significantly less so."

I mean, she had signed a contract that said she wouldn't try to date me...only to immediately turn around a couple of hours later and convince me to fake a flirtation with her.

If that wasn't the work of a master manipulator, I didn't know what was.

I still couldn't believe that whole thing had happened, actually.

One minute I was planning to ignore the entire female population at our school, and then before I knew it, I was purposely faking a romance with this girl I barely knew just to make Sofia think I'd moved on.

Insane, right?

And yet, I was still doing it.

I was even enjoying it a little because Sofia seemed to believe it all and hadn't tried to approach me since the first day.

"Well, I may be the more impulsive twin," Ava admitted. "But I promise I didn't just pretend to get turned around in your family's massive mansion just so I could catch you without your shirt on. I really thought this was the bathroom."

"So let me guess." I cocked an eyebrow. "You were just counting my abs for research purposes?"

"For research?" She furrowed her brow.

"Well, yeah." I grabbed my basketball shoes from the loveseat in front of my bed and sat down to start putting them on. "If we keep pretending like we're doing less schol-arly activities during our tutoring sessions, it makes sense that you would want to know something like that to make our little charade more believable."

I tied my right shoe, but when Ava didn't make a sound, I looked up to see if I'd said something wrong. Her eyes were wide and her mouth had gone slack as if I'd just made her speechless.

"W-why would us dating have anything to do with me knowing how many ab muscles you have?" she asked after regaining her composure.

My eyebrows knitted together, and I was legitimately confused at how she couldn't see the correlation between the two things.

"You've had a boyfriend before, right?" I asked, slipping on my left shoe and tying it. Because there was no way in the world that this girl didn't have experience playing with guys' minds.

"Well, yeah." She shrugged. "I mean, I've dated a few guys. But, um, it wasn't ever serious. And it's not like we went hot tubbing or swimming all the time."

Okay, so maybe she really didn't know what I was getting at. Maybe she was less experienced with guys than I'd assumed.

Which was totally fine. Not all people my age took their romantic relationships to a more physical level.

And now that I was on this side of my relationship with Sofia, our breakup probably would have been a lot easier on me if we hadn't ever brought sex into the equation. I didn't necessarily regret it since we'd dated for two years and at that time, I'd thought I loved her. But it did add some complications and a bigger sense of betrayal when she left me for another guy.

So, instead of pushing the topic with Ava, I just said, "Yeah, I don't go hot tubbing on all my dates, either."

I finished tying my shoes and stood up, ready to get downstairs to the basketball court. But just as I was about to walk past Ava and through the doorway, she grabbed my forearm. "Wait, were you just hinting that people at our school—" She shook her head before staring at me with her big, golden-brown eyes. "T-that Sofia's going to think that we're...that we're hooking up during our tutoring sessions?"

And the look of shock and terror on her face at the thought told me that what I'd assumed about her dating life was probably right.

Spending the night with guys wasn't an extracurricular activity for Ava.

But since I couldn't resist being the one to keep her on her toes for a change, I stepped closer. She retreated. With her back pressed against the wall, I bent down so my lips were next to her ear and whispered, "With two people as hot as we are, I would almost bet on it."

Her whole body went still—her breath seeming to catch as she took in what I'd just said. Then after a moment, she asked, "Y-you think I'm hot?"

I couldn't help but chuckle at the way this girl's mind worked. Because even though it was apparent that she was also overwhelmed by my close proximity and the thought of people assuming we were hooking up bothered her...my saying she was hot was the thing she wanted to address first.

In a low voice, I said, "I guess I did say that."

Which was true. I liked what I saw whenever she was in my view.

Probably liked it a little too much, considering I was her

math tutor and the only kind of relationship we'd be having this year was of the professional...or fake kind.

She braced her hands on my chest. Even though I'd just reminded myself of the boundaries our relationship would have, my heart didn't seem to get the memo since it pounded against my ribs at her touch, my whole body acutely aware of just how close we stood.

Crazy as it was, I had the strange urge to close the rest of the distance between us—to do something so impulsive and so out of character for me—and just kiss her right then and there so I could find out if she tasted as good as she looked.

My gaze fell to her mouth which was parted slightly, so soft and supple-looking.

She pressed her lips together. When I lifted my gaze back up to her amber eyes, I imagined there was some sort of anticipation in them—like she was as curious as I was about what it would be like to kiss each other.

I could imagine worse ways to spend an afternoon.

I was about to slide my hand up to cradle her neck when Nash's voice suddenly sounded from my Apple watch. "Carter, are you coming?"

And just like that, I was jolted back to reality.

Ava jumped at the sound of Nash's voice as well and immediately removed her palms from my chest, as if we'd just been caught in a compromising position.

Which yeah, it would have seemed compromising...if anyone was actually around to see it.

After taking one last look at Ava, I pushed the button on my watch to respond to Nash. "I'm on my way." Then after standing straighter, I cleared my throat and said to Ava,

"Sorry. I, uh, forgot what I was doing for a minute." I stepped back to give us both some much-needed space.

"Yeah, I did, too." Ava tucked some of her long hair behind her ear. "I was trying to find the bathroom."

"The bathroom is right there." I pointed to the door straight across from my room, fighting the urge to run my fingers through her hair so I could discover if it was as silky as it looked. "Cambrielle is always getting her directions mixed up."

Ava stepped out of the doorway, and it might have just been me projecting my own feelings onto her, but I imagined she didn't seem in any hurry to leave quite yet.

But since I had people waiting for me downstairs, I came out of my room, closing the door behind me, and said, "I'll see you later, Ava."

"Yeah, see you, Carter."

And then I hurried down to the basketball court, wondering what in the world had just happened.

15

———

AVA

I WAS DISTRACTED for the next hour as Cambrielle showed Elyse and me the rest of her house.

I barely saw the various rooms we walked through. Barely noted all the people buzzing around on the main floor as they prepared food for the back-to-school barbecue that Cambrielle said about fifty of our classmates had been invited to attend. Barely heard the music the hired DJ played as he set up and tested his sound system.

I barely registered anything Cambrielle and Elyse chatted about as we moved from gorgeous room to gorgeous room, because all I could think about was the way my heart still felt like it was going to beat right out of my chest a full fifty-five minutes after standing with Carter in his doorway.

It was crazy. I knew it'd all just been his way of playing with me, and yet, my whole nervous system had gone haywire from our brief encounter.

I flexed my hands as Cambrielle showed us a library on the main floor that looked just like the one from the movie

Beauty and the Beast, with floor-to-ceiling bookshelves and a wooden ladder attached to a metal bar at the top to access the high shelves.

And even though I'd flexed my hand several times, I still remembered the way the thin fabric of Carter's T-shirt had felt against my palms and how his heart had pounded when I'd touched him.

I couldn't have imagined how fast his heart had been beating, could I?

We finished our tour of the upper and main levels, so Cambrielle showed us the way to the basement. After we'd gone down the wide staircase, Cambrielle gestured at the double doors to our right. "We have a workout room right through those doors." Cambrielle turned to me and said, "But you'll probably be interested in this one, Ava, since you said you play basketball."

We followed her to a different door, which had a narrow staircase that led down to the basketball court where Carter and Nash were playing a game with Mack, Mr. Hastings, the older brother Ian I'd seen in the family photos, and another guy I didn't recognize who was probably Ian's age.

The guys continued their scrimmage game as we walked by. From the way the ball was passed between Mr. Hastings, Ian, and his friend, it looked like the teams were separated into older guys versus my schoolmates. Mack jumped up to rebound a missed shot from Mr. Hastings and then made a fast pass to Carter who, currently unguarded, dribbled the ball down to the other end of the court and shot a lay-up. The ball hit against the backboard and then went through the net with a swish to score two points for his team.

Nash and Mack cheered and gave Carter a high five.

"Okay, guys," Mr. Hastings said, his hands on his knees as he tried to catch his breath. "I need to call it quits for the day. I can only keep up with you young bucks for so long."

"Oh, come on, Mr. Hastings," Mack called to the middle-aged man, spinning the ball on his middle finger. "You sure you don't have time for a game of Knockout?"

Mr. Hastings shook his head, sweat dripping down from his blond hairline. "If I were twenty years younger, I might say yes, but since I'd like to walk up and down the stairs tomorrow, I'll have to pass."

"Anyway, this is the sports court." Cambrielle gestured to our surroundings as we walked across the floor toward the guys. "We mostly play basketball in here, but we're also set up for racquetball, volleyball, and basically whatever game you can think of."

"The twins are here. Nice." I heard Mack say to Nash as we approached, like he'd been too involved in the game to notice our entrance earlier.

"I picked them up before the game," Nash said before stealing the ball from Mack and dribbling it over to where Ian and the other guy stood under one of the baskets, waiting to shoot more hoops.

"So, what do you think of the Hastings mansion?" Mack asked, leaning an elbow on Carter's shoulder after he took a pull from a gray water bottle. "I'm guessing Cambrielle has been giving you a grand tour?"

"It's beautiful," Elyse said, her cheeks glowing as she looked up at Mack.

"I've never seen anything like it," I added.

Which was true. Even though I'd been walking around in somewhat of a daze, I had caught enough of my surroundings to know that this was probably the nicest house I'd ever step foot in.

"Yeah." Mack shrugged, looking up at the windows at the top of the court that let in the afternoon sunlight. "My dad's only a neurosurgeon, so our house looks like a shack compared to this."

Everyone laughed at Mack's joke, and I had to assume that his house was probably super nice as well.

Carter looked like he was about to say something about Mack living in a shack when Mr. Hastings joined us after getting a drink at the water fountain in the corner.

"Hi, I don't think we've been acquainted yet," he said, holding out his hand to me. "I'm Joel Hastings, Cambrielle, Nash, and Carter's dad. It's nice to meet you."

"Nice to meet you, I'm Ava." I shook his hand briefly, and then pointed beside me. "And this is my sister Elyse. We're Ava and Elyse Cohen."

"Cohen?" Mr. Hastings' eyebrows shot up, like he recognized our last name for some reason.

"Yeah, our mom is the fashion designer, Miriam Cohen," I said. His wife and daughter wore designer dresses, so maybe that was why our last name sounded familiar to him?

"Miriam Cohen is your mom?" Mr. Hastings' blue eyes went wide, and his expression was one of surprise. "Now that's a name I haven't heard in a long time."

"You know our mom?" Elyse asked.

Mr. Hastings rubbed the back of his neck with his towel. "If she's the same Miriam Cohen who went to the academy back in the day, then I'd have to say that your mother and I were very good friends."

"You were friends with their mom?" Carter asked, mirroring my thoughts. "Now that's a coincidence."

Mr. Hastings nodded. "I know it's probably difficult to imagine that an old fart like me could be the same age as your beautiful mother. But yeah, we go way back." He shook his head contemplatively, as if taking a stroll down memory lane in his mind. "I didn't realize she had kids the same age as mine. We lost touch through the years, but I hadn't heard of her marrying."

"Oh, that's because she didn't," I said. As far as she'd told us, our mom had a one-time, one-night stand with my mystery father and ended up with two miracles—Elyse and me—because of it.

"Of course," Mr. Hastings hurried to say. "I certainly didn't mean anything by it. I mean, I of all people should know you don't need to be married in order to have children."

He was probably referring to how Carter had been born to his mother and not known his dad for the first eight years of his life.

"You say your mom's a fashion designer now?" Mr. Hastings narrowed his eyes and seemed to take in Elyse's and my appearance, like he was comparing us to the memory he must have had of our mother.

"She's just getting ready for Milan's Fashion Week," Elyse said, a smile stretching across her lips. "She's been getting a lot of notice lately, which has been really exciting for our family."

"That's so good to hear. I always knew Miriam was going to do great things one day." The look of pride in his eyes told me that he really must have been a good friend to our mom.

"We're really proud of her." I smiled.

"I bet. And are you two juniors like Cambrielle?"

"No, we're seniors."

"Seniors?" Mr. Hastings' eyebrows shot up. "So you're Carter's, and Nash's age?"

Had he assumed that we were Cambrielle's age since we'd walked in with her?

"Yeah, we're seniors," I said, not used to my friend's parents asking so many questions. Usually, a quick *hi* and *what's your name* was all they ever cared about.

Maybe he was showing more interest since he'd been such good friends with our mother?

Though, apparently, not good enough of friends for her to ever mention him to us. But my mom didn't really talk about anyone from high school.

Mr. Hastings glanced at his watch. "Ah, it's already five o'clock. Looks like I better hit the showers so I'm ready for my hot date with my girlfriend."

His girlfriend?

But wasn't he married?

Seeming to notice my shock, Carter laughed and said, "He's talking about his wife, Dawn. They're weird, though, and like to call each other girlfriend and boyfriend."

Mr. Hastings patted Carter on the shoulder. "Gotta keep the romance alive somehow, bud."

"Whatever," Carter said, but when his gaze briefly met mine, a bunch of butterflies swarmed my stomach as I remembered standing close to him in his room.

Pretty sure Carter didn't need any tips from his dad about keeping romance alive, because just one look from him had me swooning all over again.

But I tried to push those thoughts away because he didn't need to know this.

"It was great to meet you," Mr. Hastings said, looking at Elyse and me again. "You'll have to tell your mother I said hi the next time you talk to her."

"Will do," Elyse said, smiling at Mr. Hastings.

Mr. Hastings left, and it looked like Carter was going to say something to Elyse and me when Cambrielle came back over to us after shooting a few hoops with Nash and the other guys.

She put her hands together. "So, now that you've met the old guy at our house, would you like to see the pool and the pool house?"

Glancing at Carter briefly and wondering what he'd been about to say, I said, "Um, yes."

"Why didn't you show us those when we first got here?" Elyse added.

Cambrielle laughed. "I figured I'd save the best for last."

And then we were all off again.

16

CARTER

I WAS JUST ABOUT to head downstairs for the party my siblings were making me throw with them when Nash knocked on my door.

"Hey." He leaned against the door frame. "I just wanted to let you know that the first people have arrived for the party."

"Okay." I slipped my phone into the back pocket of my jeans. "Let's go be social."

But as I started to move to follow him down to the main floor where the party would be taking place, Nash set a hand on my chest to stop me. "Hold on," he said. "The reason why I actually came up here was to give you a heads up."

"A heads up?" I frowned. Needing a heads up was never a good sign.

"Yeah, I figured you'd want to know who just arrived so that you're prepared."

A feeling of dread filled my chest because I knew who he was talking about.

"Sofia?" I asked.

"Yeah." He nodded. "And Simon."

Simon?

What the heck was he doing here?

Didn't he have some royal duties to take care of across the pond?

"Well..." I stepped back and grabbed the edge of my door, making ready to shut it. "I hope you enjoy the barbecue."

I hadn't really wanted to be social tonight, anyway.

I was about to retreat into the solitude of my room when Nash followed me inside.

"Don't let her ruin your night," he said, slipping his hands into his pockets.

"I'm trying not to," I said. "Hence the reason why I'm going to stay up here."

"That's not what I mean. Just..." He paused, seeming to think for a moment. "She knows you live here. So if you're not downstairs, she'll know that you're avoiding her. And she knows you well enough to understand that the only reason why you wouldn't attend a party at your own house was if you were avoiding someone."

"Just tell her I got a sudden case of food poisoning." I shrugged.

"You really want to pull the sick card?" Nash shook his head. "Why not get a little revenge of your own? Why not show her you've moved on, too? With someone more interesting and fun."

"Someone more interesting and fun?" I asked, because there was no one else coming tonight who I found interesting enough to be interested in.

Nash just looked at me like I was dumb. "Do I really have

to spell this out for you? Didn't you just set up something with Ava to take care of this very thing?"

"Oh..."

"Yeah, *oh*." Nash shook his head. "I know I'll probably regret even encouraging you to keep up that thing you started with her last week since I was hoping to ask her out sometime myself, but she offered to help you out with Sofia. You might as well take her up on it."

"I don't know," I said, glancing around my room and liking how much quieter it was than the noise coming from downstairs. "I kind of think I'd rather stay up here than fake something with Ava tonight."

After our little interaction in my room this afternoon, it would probably be wise to put some distance between us so my body could get unconfused about how it should react to her.

"How could you prefer sitting in here alone to having fun with Ava?" Nash asked, like he couldn't understand it at all.

Which made sense. Nash was a natural extrovert. He thrived on other people's energy, loved being the center of attention.

I was the opposite. Flirting with people drained me. Heck, just being around people for extended periods of time drained me.

When I sat on the loveseat in front of my bed, Nash furrowed his brow and said, "This is our last year of high school." He shook his head slowly. "You have the rest of your life to be all brooding and crap in your room. Don't miss out on making good memories just because a girl stomped all over your heart."

"All over my heart in front of her millions of Instagram followers."

My brother had forgotten that Sofia had posted all kinds of photos of us when we'd dated, using the hashtag #lovehim at least once a week so all the guys trying to slide into her DMs would know she was spoken for. But when she got tired of me, she'd replaced photos of me with photos of *him* and continued using the same hashtag.

Which made me wonder what Simon had messaged her to get her to answer his DMs.

I shook my head. I really didn't need to go down that road again.

We were through. I didn't need to know which opener from him had solidified my fate.

For all I knew he'd sent a simple selfie with the words, "Only ten people have to die for me to be a king. Wanna be my queen?" and the rest was history.

"Are you going to come?" Nash asked, the concern in his blue eyes showing.

I drew in a deep breath, hoping it would calm my nerves as I thought about meeting Simon for the first time. "Just give me a few minutes to figure something out and I'll be down."

"Good." He smiled, his whole face brightening. "See you down there."

I SAT in my room for the next five minutes, listening to the doorbell ring followed by laughter and all kinds of happy sounds as more and more people came to enjoy the party.

And as I sat there with my ears perked, I could make out

Sofia's alto voice as she introduced Simon to person after person.

Hi, this is my hot new boyfriend, Simon. Did you know he's a viscount?

Okay, so maybe she wasn't saying that, but it was probably what she was thinking.

Did I really want to do this? I wondered as I continued to listen to the sounds below. Could I really face Sofia and her boyfriend, and put on a face that told them I couldn't care in the least that they were together now?

I sighed and rubbed a hand over my face. I could do this. I might not have ever taken a theater class like my brother and sister, but I had perfected the detached and bored look as good as any guy my age. Surely I could manage to appear unfazed for a few hours.

It wasn't like I had to be downstairs the whole time, anyway. I could make a showing, make Cambrielle and Nash feel I was part of the back-to-school celebration, and then I could sneak back up to my room when everyone was otherwise engaged, and no one would miss me.

"Tonight's going to be amazing," Cambrielle's muffled voice sounded from just up the hall. I assumed she was talking to the Cohen twins since they'd been getting ready for tonight's festivities in her room for the past hour or so.

When I realized they were probably almost to the staircase to head downstairs, I knew I needed to act quick if I was going to have a chance to do what Nash had suggested earlier.

So I dashed forward, threw the door open, and peeked my head out into the hall and called out, "Hey, Ava. Do you have a minute?"

All three girls stopped in their tracks and turned to look at me with curious expressions.

"Did you just say something to me?" A twin wearing skinny jeans and a red top put a hand to her chest.

I assumed it was Ava since I'd addressed her, but I couldn't really be sure since I wasn't close enough to look for the gold necklaces she and Elyse had worn earlier with their names in delicate cursive letters.

"I need to talk to Ava," I said, just in case I was looking at the wrong twin. "It'll just be for a moment." The twin in the red top pouted her lips for a second as if trying to decide whether my request was worth listening to. So I added, "Please," with as much sincerity in my eyes as I could muster.

The please must have done the trick because the twin in the red top glanced back at her sister and Cambrielle. With a shrug, she said, "I guess I'll see you down there."

Once Ava reached me, I gestured for her to come into my room, but she stopped just at the threshold. With an eyebrow arched, she asked, "You're not trying to finish what you started earlier, are you?"

And the memory of standing in this very spot with her back pressed against the wall, with only a few inches between us, jumped to the forefront of my mind.

I still couldn't believe I'd flirted with her like that. I never did that kind of thing. Especially not with girls I barely knew.

So to put Ava at ease, I said, "Sorry to get your hopes up, but I just need to talk this time."

"Good answer." She shot me a half-smile before stepping inside my room.

I shut the door behind her and gestured for her to sit on

the loveseat while I pulled over the chair at my desk for myself.

"Do you remember that little scheme you came up with earlier this week? You know, the one where you help me make Sofia think I've moved on and no one knows we're just doing math homework."

"I remember," she said.

"Okay, so I'm going to have to ask you a huge favor."

She crossed her arms and leaned back against the cushion. "I'm listening."

"So..." I licked my lips, feeling jittery with nerves for some reason. "Nash came up here a few minutes ago to tell me that Sofia came to the party with Simon."

"Simon Bailey?" Ava asked, her mouth falling open. "As in, the 'Simon Bailey who has his afternoon tea with the queen' Simon Bailey?"

"That would be the guy. He's here with Sofia."

"Wow, Simon Bailey is downstairs right now." Ava stood up quickly as if ready to head down this very minute to check him out. "My friends in Ridgewater are never going to believe this. They *adore* him." She patted her back pocket as if checking to make sure her phone was there. "Do you think he'll let me take a selfie with him?"

"What?" I asked, rushing to the door before she could disappear and take my chances of saving face with her. She was just reaching for the knob when I slid into the small space between her and the door. "You said you were going to help me."

"But I need to get a photo with the prince before he leaves," she said.

"He's a viscount. Not a prince."

"Same difference," she said. "Can I go now? I just want to see if he's as hot in person as he is in photos."

Seriously?

Was this really how all girls reacted to Simon Bailey?

I folded my arms across my chest. "I'll let you go down in a minute. But first we need to talk about our little arrangement."

"Okay, yeah." She took a step back, as if only now remembering what I'd been talking about before she'd gotten sidetracked by Simon's name. "So, what were you saying before?"

"I was asking if you'd be fine playing into the little arrangement of ours a little more tonight. Instead of just flirting, I was wondering if you could pretend you're actually my girlfriend," I said. But then, since my ego seemed to require that while I didn't have an English title to my name, I wasn't exactly Freddy Krueger either, I added, "I mean, I just wanted to give you first dibs on being my arm candy for tonight."

"Ohhh." She drew the word out as she gave me an understanding nod. "So let me get this straight. Pretending to be your actual girlfriend and making Sofia think I'm hopelessly infatuated with you would actually be your way of doing *me* a favor?" She gave me an unimpressed look. "Is that what you're trying to say?"

I tilted my head to the side. "Yes?"

"Well, if that's the case, then I think I'll pass." She shrugged. "I mean, I'm sure you have dozens of girls dying to play the part for real downstairs, so who am I to steal such an amazing opportunity from them?"

She made a move to open the door again, and I knew I was about to lose my ticket to an easy night.

"Okay, fine." I grabbed her forearm. "So maybe you'd be doing me the huge favor."

"And?" She looked up at me with her liquid-gold eyes, as if waiting for me to grovel a little more.

She was going to make me beg for this, wasn't she?

I sighed. "And *I* would be the one who would be lucky to spend the evening in the company of a goddess like yourself."

A slow smile lifted her lips. "Keep going..."

What? She wanted even more groveling?

I shook my head, not believing that this was actually happening to me.

Since when did I ever have to beg a girl to give me the time of day?

Since never, that's when.

Well, until I met Ava Cohen, apparently.

But I really didn't want to go downstairs alone and spend more energy flirting with some random girl only to have to tell her afterwards that it meant nothing. "You like shopping, right?"

All girls liked shopping, didn't they? At least Dawn and Cambrielle certainly ran up huge bills on their credit cards whenever they went out for a girls' weekend in New York.

"If I'm the one doing the shopping, then yes, I enjoy it," she said.

"Okay, so how about if you help me put on a show so good that Sofia believes we're actually boyfriend and girlfriend, then I'll take you to any boutique you want in Eden Falls tomorrow and buy you whatever you want for a hundred dollars or less?"

She studied me for a moment, pursing her pink lips like she was thinking things over. After the longest ten seconds of my life, she shrugged and said, "Add in lunch at the nicest restaurant in town and it's a deal."

"Seriously?" I asked. Spending the next two hours by my side was that big of a chore?

"Cambrielle said there would be a lot of cute guys here tonight. And according to our non-exclusive arrangement, I should still be able to go on dates with other guys. So if I'm going to miss out on flirting with them tonight and pretend that we're actually dating, I think I deserve some sort of reward." She folded her arms across her chest and shifted most of her weight to one foot to tell me that was her final offer.

This girl was the one to come up with the whole fake-dating plan in the first place, but now she was expecting a real day date?

But since I didn't want her to add any other requests into the mix, I sighed and said, "Okay, fine. A shopping date and lunch."

"Great. It's a *date*." A satisfied smile lifted her lips before she slid her arm through mine. "I can't wait to see you show everyone what a huge crush you have on me tonight."

The crush *I* had on *her*?

I considered telling her that it should be the other way around—that Ava would be showing Sofia how amazing she thought I was—but decided it was pointless. Ava did things her way and only a fool would mess around with this girl.

17

CARTER

"SHOULD WE GRAB SOME FOOD?" I asked Ava when we walked onto the terrace behind my house. There were about thirty kids from school scattered around the stone patio and on the grassy area below, most with plates of food already made up as they sat and chatted happily with each other.

Our chef, Marie, had done a great job with the menu as always. We had decided on hamburgers and grilled chicken for the main dish, along with vegan burgers for our friends who didn't eat meat, and then there were various side dishes lined out on the banquet-style table to fit anyone's tastes.

"I haven't eaten anything since lunch, so yes, let's get food now," Ava said.

I grabbed two thick plastic plates with a hammered gold design, handing one to Ava. We went down the table, telling the servers which foods to add to our plates.

After Sofia broke up with me, I'd decided to focus on building up my muscle tone as my own little form of revenge

—hoping that when she saw me at school again, she'd regret casting me aside for Simon. So, I asked for extra portions of the grilled chicken because I could always use more protein. And even though Marie's famous strawberry pretzel Jell-O salad was calling my name as I passed it on the table, I had a server put a big helping of the green salad and grilled asparagus on my plate instead.

When our plates were full, I made a quick survey of the area to see where Sofia and Simon were. They must be still inside since I didn't see them anywhere on the terrace or at the grassy area below. I led Ava to a table near the edge of the terrace that overlooked the pool and gardens.

"Do you always eat so healthily?" Ava commented after glancing at my plate once we were seated.

"I try to for most meals," I said. "Why?"

She shrugged and picked up a potato chip from her plate, dipping it in ranch. "It just looks so boring."

Her plate had a hamburger, a helping of fruit and the Jell-O salad, potato chips with dip, and a few cucumber wedges.

"Do you like everything in your life to be exciting?" I arched an eyebrow.

"I just think that since we don't know how long we really have, we might as well make the most of every opportunity."

"Yes," I said, agreeing with her point. "But then, don't you think that eating foods that really nourish your body instead of simply bringing pleasure would count toward longevity?"

"It might help you live longer," she said. "But how boring would life be without a brownie or cheesecake every once in a while?"

"Touché," I said, unable to keep a smile from lifting my lips at her thought process.

I bet Ava had an argument for everything. She could probably have a great career in law if her dream of having a fashion empire didn't work out.

"Mack did warn me about how disciplined you were," Ava said conversationally. "I just didn't realize it went to your food choices, too."

"You talked to Mack about me?"

She shrugged and took a small bite of a cucumber. After swallowing, she said, "It was his excuse for why you were so rude the first day in the weight room. He said you like to stick to your routines."

"That's true." I picked up my fork and knife and cut into my chicken. "Is there anything wrong with sticking to a routine?"

"It's fine. I mean, it gives you a sense of control and helps you know what to expect, but I don't know. I guess it seems like it could also get boring." She cast a glance at my food. "Like your plate."

What she called boring, I called security. And after having so much instability for the first half of my life, I quite liked the safety my routines provided me—even if everyone gave me a hard time about it.

But instead of explaining, I pursed my lips and cut off a small piece of my chicken. "If you knew how good this chicken was, I don't think you'd say it was boring."

She arched an eyebrow, challenging me.

So I speared a piece on my fork and held it up for her. "Try it."

She narrowed her eyes, gauging whether I was serious

about letting her eat some of my food, and then she opened her mouth.

I placed the forkful of chicken in her mouth and then waited.

She chewed slowly, savoring the taste of the meat, and then her eyes widened with surprise. "What kind of chicken is this? It's amazing."

"It's our chef's secret recipe." I smiled and cut another small piece for myself, plopping it into my mouth. "But it's good, right?"

"I'm seriously tempted to throw this plate away and get one that looks like yours now." As if to prove her point, she scooted her chair back, lifted her plate, and stood up. "Actually, I think that I'll—"

But before she could finish her sentence, I reached out and quickly snatched the plate from her hands. "You're not going to throw a whole plate of food away."

She froze in her spot, half-standing, half-sitting, and completely shocked at what I'd just done. After staring at me like I was crazy, she took her plate back from me and said, "No. I was going to grab a piece of that delicious chicken." She glanced around the terrace, an embarrassed expression filling her features. "But now I kind of just want to die."

Her gaze flicked around us, and that was when I realized our sudden movements had brought an audience to our meal.

And I looked like the guy who had issues with the food choices my date was making.

I pinched my eyes shut, wishing I could go back in time about fifteen seconds and smack myself.

But since time travel wasn't invented quite yet, I cleared

my throat, feeling my cheeks burn as I met the curious eyes watching us. In a lowered voice, I mumbled, "Sorry. I, uh, what I should have done was offer to get that chicken for you."

Ava gave me a wary look. But she was better than me at being the center of everyone's attention. She managed to put on a smile that almost seemed real and said, "How gentlemanly of you, Carter." After handing me her plate, she spoke to the crowd still watching us, "Isn't my boyfriend the best?"

With her plate in my hand and everyone's eyes on me, I strode over to the buffet table and added the dumb piece of chicken to it.

I really shouldn't have come down to this stupid party.

I was just trying to figure out how to get myself out of eating my meal beside a girl who probably hated my guts now when I saw that Ava was no longer alone at our table.

Sofia and Simon had joined her.

Man, this night was just getting better and better.

18

CARTER

"THANKS FOR GETTING that chicken for me, babe," Ava said, giving me a quick kiss on the cheek when I reached the table and handed her the plate of food. "You're the best."

"Y-you're welcome," I said stiffly, caught off guard by the kiss on the cheek and term of endearment since last I'd checked, she'd rather die than sit at the table with me after how badly I'd botched our earlier interaction.

But when she turned to my ex-girlfriend and the guy I'd been replaced with and said, "Carter saw me drooling over his plate and was so sweet to get me some of that amazing chicken his chef grilled," I knew that even though she was probably still annoyed at me, she was putting it aside for the moment to continue with the fake boyfriend/girlfriend plan we'd agreed to before coming down here.

Ava had said that her sister was the one who was going out for the school's next theater production, but based on the past few seconds, I couldn't help but feel she had yet another calling in life: a career on the stage.

Apparently, Ava was a girl with a plethora of hidden talents.

"Marie's chicken is my favorite," Sofia said, a broad smile on her lips as she spoke to Ava. "I've tried to copy her recipe so many times, but it never turns out as good. I even tried to get Carter to sneak into Marie's recipe box when she wasn't around, but he never found it."

"I'm ninety-percent sure she burned all the copies of that recipe and just relies on her memory now, so no one can ever steal it," I found myself saying as I sat back down in the chair beside Ava.

"You're probably right," Sofia said, her eyes lighting up. "She knows how addicted your family is to the stuff. She probably keeps the secret locked down tight so that your family has to keep her on forever."

"Marie is crafty like that," I said with a smile.

I glanced back at Ava and noticed a look of surprise on her face. It took me three full seconds to realize why.

I'd just talked to Sofia like we were friends.

So, not wanting to give anyone the wrong impression, I cleared my throat and quickly removed the friendly smile from my face, replacing it with my usual neutral expression.

Sofia must have noticed the shift in my demeanor because her smile disappeared as well.

"Anyway..." Sofia cleared her throat awkwardly. "The reason why I wanted to stop at your table was to introduce Simon to you." She gestured at the tall guy beside her who had short brown hair that curled slightly at the ends, green eyes framed by dark-rim glasses, and a neatly trimmed beard that I knew Sofia must be in love with from how many times she'd tried to get me to grow out my facial hair in just the same way.

"I'm Simon Bailey," Simon said on cue in his British accent, holding his hand out for me to shake. "It's a pleasure to meet you."

I considered ignoring the friendly gesture, but since I didn't want to look like the petty and jealous ex, I introduced myself as well and gave his hand a firm shake—squeezing slightly harder than necessary to prove—what? I didn't know exactly. That I had strong hands?

After giving me a weird look, he shook Ava's hand. "And what's your name?" he asked.

"I'm Ava," she answered, a slight flush filling her cheeks. "Ava Cohen." From her blush and what she'd said in my room earlier, I almost expected her to ask if he'd take a selfie with her right then and there. But she surprised me by returning her hands back to her lap and simply adding, "It's an honor to meet you, Your Highness."

Simon chuckled for a moment before saying, "You can just call me Simon."

"Okay, it's nice to meet you, Simon." Ava giggled, and from the way she ogled him, I got the feeling that if she stayed in his royal highness's presence for much longer, I may not only lose my ex-girlfriend to the dude but also my fake girlfriend.

"So, what brings you all the way over here from London?" I asked Simon in as conversational a tone as I could manage. "Do you have business in the states?"

"I'm not here on business." Simon shook his head and glanced over at Sofia. "I missed seeing my girl, and so I came here as a surprise this weekend."

"That's so sweet," Ava said, her voice slightly higher than usual.

"It is." Sofia looked down at her hands with a slight smile on her full lips, like she was both happy about Simon's thoughtfulness but also uncomfortable that I was witnessing it. "Simon's always surprising me with things like this."

When she lifted her gaze to Simon again, the way she looked at him with her brown eyes was like a knife in my heart. Because she was looking at him like he was the center of the universe and all she wanted was to be in his orbit.

I'd always thought she cared about me as much as I'd cared for her when we were dating, but with that one look, I knew she couldn't have because she'd never looked at me the way she was looking at Simon.

I swallowed the lump in my throat, hoping to keep my disappointment from showing. But I must not have hidden the pain in my expression very well because when I caught a glimpse of Ava out of the corner of my eye, she was watching me with a sad smile on her face. As if she knew exactly how much it hurt for me to come face to face with the reality of how I hadn't measured up to Sofia's expectations and how Simon did.

Ava slid her hand onto my leg and gave me a gentle squeeze just above my knee.

Sofia must have noticed the gesture because she asked, "So, tell me about what's been going on with you two? It seems like you've been inseparable since you met."

"Things are so good," Ava said with the biggest smile on her lips. "When I saw Carter that first day, I thought for sure that he was taken already. I mean, he's just so gorgeous that there was no way he wasn't already dating someone." She glanced over at me and slid a little closer, slipping her hand around my left bicep possessively. "But then I found out he was actually single, and I knew I had to get on his radar fast since guys like him don't stay single for long. I mean, he's so smart and witty and we were able to connect on a different level than I usually do with guys, since we have some things in common." I was guessing she was talking about our common thread of not always knowing who our fathers were. "And I know it probably seems pretty fast since we just met, like, five days ago, but I just think that if you two hadn't gotten together behind Carter's back and he hadn't been available, I never would have had a chance with him. So, thank you."

Did she just diss Sofia and Simon for cheating on me?

Had she just buttered them up over the past few minutes, only to turn the tables and give them the smackdown?

This girl was an evil genius.

When I watched Sofia and Simon for their reactions, the shocked expressions on their faces told me they were as surprised by the sudden turn of events as I was.

"D-did Carter tell you that I cheated on him?" Sofia finally said after processing Ava's words.

"Oh, no." Ava put a hand to her heart all innocently. "Did I assume wrong? I just thought that someone as famous as you probably has all sorts of offers from guys, and so when one from a prince came through you couldn't resist. Was I wrong? Did my sweet Carter dump you?" She squeezed herself closer to my arm. "He's just been such a gentleman so far that I didn't think he would break someone's heart like that."

I watched Simon and Sofia carefully, interested in their answers since I myself had been wondering the very same thing for months. Had they gotten together before she broke up with me?

"I—we—" Simon cleared his throat, fumbling for an answer.

But Sofia put her hand on his to stop him. "You don't need to answer that, honey." Then tilting her head up so she was looking down her nose at Ava, she said, "I don't know what gossip you've heard, but I'd be careful before you start spreading rumors about us." She stood up and said, "Come on, Simon. I think it's time for us to move along, so I can introduce you to some of my *closer* friends."

19

———

AVA

"THANKS FOR SAYING ALL THAT," Carter said, leaning back in his chair after Sofia and Simon had walked down the stone steps from the terrace to talk to her friends below. "It was perfect."

"I've always wanted to do something like that, so it was fun," I said.

It had been fun. I mean, how many girls could say they put a supermodel and her royal boyfriend in their places at a back-to-school barbecue with her hot fake boyfriend by her side?

Not many.

So even though it was highly possible Sofia might take an embarrassing photo of me and post it to her Instagram stories later for revenge, seeing the jealousy on her face as I'd cuddled up to Carter was totally worth it.

That's right. I have a world-famous supermodel jealous of little ol' me.

I was feeling so high on life right then that I almost told

Carter he didn't need to take me shopping for payment since I had so much fun doing it.

But I'd never turn down a free outfit, so I kept that info to myself.

"You sure you're not interested in auditioning for one of the school plays?" Carter asked with a chuckle in his voice. "Because after hearing everything you just said, even I was starting to believe that we might be perfect for each other. And I'm in on the secret."

"I don't know." I leaned closer to him, close enough that I could breathe in the delicious scent of his cologne, which I'd wanted to drown in since that first day in his truck. "Maybe we are."

"You think so?" He narrowed his aqua-blue eyes at me, like he wasn't sure if I was still playing a part or not. But then he sat up straighter, and his tall, muscular physique couldn't help but capture my attention. He said, "Then I guess it's too bad you wrote that little addendum to my contract, forbidding me from falling in love with you, huh?"

And the way he looked at me, like he might have been interested in me for real if I hadn't needed his help with math and we didn't sign that contract, made me wonder if something could have happened on its own even without this fake dating arrangement of ours.

But then I remembered that Carter only dated supermodels, and while I may be tall enough to be one, I most certainly didn't look like one. So I pushed those thoughts away and simply said, "I guess it's something we'll always have to wonder about, isn't it?"

He seemed to study me for a moment before saying, "I guess it is."

CAMBRIELLE, Elyse, and the rest of the crew joined us as we finished the last half of our meal. Nash and Mack decided to recount stories of the various pranks they'd pulled on the headmistress and the drama teacher and soon had us all laughing until we had tears coming out our eyes.

When we'd finished eating, Scarlett challenged us to a game of volleyball on the court below with a few of her volleyball friends. After playing a game where she, Hunter, and Mack basically dominated on the sandy court, I decided to take a breather and explore the little path that led into the gardens Cambrielle had pointed out when she was showing us the pool-house and pool on our tour earlier.

I was just walking onto the stone path lined with bushes and beautiful flowers when Carter jogged up to my side and asked, "Everything okay?" He wiped a bead of sweat from his forehead with the back of his hand, his breathing still hard from the volleyball game. "You're not escaping in here because you're mad that your team lost the game, are you?"

"No, of course not." I shook my head, finding it funny that he would even think of it. "I don't care about the game. The only things I get competitive over are basketball games and when other girls try to steal guys from me."

"Okay, good," he said. And then, with a half-smile slipping up his lips, he added, "But thanks for the heads up on that. I'll have to remember to warn my next fake girlfriend that you could be a little territorial over me." He winked.

I couldn't help but smile at his comment. "Are you planning to make this fake-girlfriend thing a habit?" I asked.

"I don't know, maybe." He shrugged his broad shoulders.

"It's been kind of fun, don't you think? And it certainly seems a lot easier than doing the real thing."

"Has finding a girlfriend been difficult for you in the past?"

Because yeah, I definitely wouldn't believe that. He was hot.

And tall.

And from what I'd seen of his eight-pack abs in his room earlier, he was also in amazing shape—which was another kind of hot on its own.

Not to mention the less shallow attributes of being super smart and fun to talk to as well.

And while Carter wasn't the life of the party like Mack and Nash were, he was still really fun to be around in his own way.

So yeah, him having a hard time finding a girlfriend was not something that could be real.

"Finding a girlfriend isn't the problem," he said, apparently on the same wavelength as me. "I guess it's more the work that's involved in keeping one."

And there it was. This guy, who most girls my age would probably consider a teenage god, was insecure about his ability to keep the interest of a potential girlfriend because his last girlfriend had left him.

It was crazy, right?

Because I was pretty sure that if I hadn't signed a contract saying that I wouldn't catch real feelings for this guy, I might be in real danger of doing exactly just that.

Even with the contract, I had totally imagined what getting tangled in his strong arms and lost in his kiss would be like.

He was the forbidden fruit of Eden Falls Academy, and I was the girl tempted to taste him.

But since I couldn't admit to any of that, I just said, "Yeah, dating someone because you like them and not just because you want to get revenge on your ex is for the birds."

He put his arm around my shoulders and squeezed me against his side for the briefest moment. "See, and this is why our arrangement is so perfect."

He let his arm drop, and even though I'd only been close to him for a few seconds, I felt colder when he stepped away.

We walked down in silence for a moment, just listening to the sounds of laughter and voices from the party growing quieter the farther we got down the path.

I took in the beautiful scenery around me. The path was lined with daisies and hydrangeas, and then just beyond were various shrubbery and trees whose leaves were just beginning to show signs of change.

"How big is your family's property?" I asked. I'd never been to a home with such extensive grounds. They seemed to have everything you'd ever dream of having here. The beautiful home. The pool. The amazing yard.

"All in all, it's about a thousand acres." Carter slipped his hands into his pockets, his elbow bumping against mine as he did so. "But when my great-great-great grandpa first settled the town and bought his property, it was about ten times that."

"Your family lives on a thousand acres?" I stopped in my tracks and didn't even try to hide my shock. "What in the world do you do with that much land?"

"Lots of things." Carter shrugged and continued down the path. "We have a horse stable out that way." He pointed north. "And then the blueberry fields are over there." He pointed to the east. "The golf course is this way." He pointed west. "And then there's just a lot of land that hasn't been developed much, and it's where we ride our ATVs."

"Wow." I shook my head slowly. "I know it's probably something I should know by now, but you're, like, really rich, aren't you?"

Carter chuckled, a deep and vibrant sound that made me happy for some reason. "The only money that's mine aside from my trust fund is the small allowance they give me and the money I make tutoring. My dad and Dawn are the ones who are wealthy."

"I'm not rich, my parents are," I mimicked him, resisting the urge to roll my eyes. "That's just something rich kids say, isn't it?"

Carter laughed again. "I don't know. Is that something *you* say?" He raised an eyebrow. "Your mom's a famous fashion designer. You can't tell me you're not one of us."

One of us.

"I don't know," I said, looking around at the scenery again and feeling like such an insignificant drop in the pool of the rich and famous. "My mom's money is new. Super new. It's different from people who've had decades and decades for their investments to compound into something massive."

"I suppose that's true. Having billions to your name is a lot different than millions."

Billions.

I couldn't even fathom what that much money would look like.

"I'm guessing your dad's one of those people working

with billions then?" I asked since he'd thrown the number out there.

"That's what his financial people tell him, anyway." He narrowed his blue eyes at me, the setting sunlight peeking through the trees making them brighter than usual. "You didn't come up with this scheme to be my fake girlfriend because you heard my dad was the seventh richest guy in the U.S., did you?"

"What?" I choked a little on my own spit and then coughed. "Of course not! I didn't even know your family was that kind of rich until just now when you said it." Sure, when his siblings said they lived on an estate I figured they weren't dirt poor or anything, but yikes, I had no idea they were billionaires. Or the seventh richest family in the United States!

But when he still looked skeptical, I hurried to add, "If I had any ulterior motives for pretending to be with you, it would be because you're hot. Not because of your dad's position on the Forbes list."

He needed to believe me. From my little experience with the rich and famous, I knew they were always on guard for people just trying to use them for some sort of gain. And while I *was* using Carter to help my math grade, I didn't have plans for anything else.

I watched Carter for his reaction to what I'd just said, but then I realized I'd just told him exactly how attractive I found him.

Again.

I internally kicked myself because I'd been trying so hard not to think about how hot he was.

Carter got a mischievous look on his sexy face and said,

"So you really were snooping around my room earlier today with hopes of checking me out, weren't you?" And when he waggled his eyebrows in a suggestive way, I wanted to smack the smug look off his lips.

I settled for shoving his arm instead. "In your dreams."

I must have pushed him harder than I thought because he stumbled to the side with the momentum. And either he had the worst luck or I had the best timing, because just as he was tripping over a rock sitting in the flower bed, the sprinklers turned on.

He ended up catching himself before he could face-plant in the daisies, but by the time he got back up to his feet, the sprinklers had already given him a pretty good shower.

"So now you're trying to see what I look like in a wet T-shirt contest?" Carter asked as he wiped the wet dirt off his hands.

And when I saw the look in his eyes, I knew I needed to run as fast as I could, or I was going to find myself in the wet flower beds and getting way dirtier than him.

"Oh no, you don't, Cohen. You're not getting out of this," Carter called out as I started sprinting away. And a second later, his footsteps were chasing me down the stone path.

I looked over my shoulder when I'd made it past a curve in the path to see if he was still running after me. He was only about five feet away, thanks to those long legs of his.

Crap! I was in trouble!

I came to a part of the garden where the sprinklers hadn't turned on yet, and since there was a break in the flowers, I darted through the opening with hopes of escape.

I rushed through the trees as fast as I could, looking for a place to hide since I knew I couldn't keep up this pace for long. When I found a big fat tree, I ran to the side that wasn't visible from the path and pressed my back against it so I could catch my breath.

I strained my ears to see if I could make out his location, but my heartbeat pounded too loud in my temples for me to hear anything.

I was just about to peek my head around the corner when Carter suddenly jumped around the other side of the tree and said, "You can run, but you can't hide."

And then he pulled me into his arms and pressed me against him, the dirt from his shirt rubbing off on my new, red crop top and getting me all dirty and wet.

"You're going to ruin my new shirt!" I squealed when he hugged me closer to him.

"What?" he asked, clamping his strong arms around my torso, locking me against him. "You don't like this? You don't like it when someone covers you in mud?"

"Carter!" I squealed again. Though this time, it didn't sound nearly as annoyed, because now that I was in his arms, I kind of didn't care what happened to my shirt anymore.

He felt good. Those abs and chest of his that I'd drooled over earlier felt really, really nice against me, and I kind of wanted him to ruin my shirt a little longer.

"You know what I think?" Carter asked, seemingly wrapped up in the moment as well. "I think I might need to throw you in the pool for payback."

I stopped struggling and went still in his arms. "You wouldn't."

He looked me straight in the eyes and said, "I would."

He was just squatting down to throw me over his

shoulder when the silence around us was suddenly filled with two voices coming from the opposite end of the path.

Carter must have recognized the voices because he instantly stopped trying to abduct me. Instead, he pushed me against the tree with his body as if attempting to blend in.

"Who is it?" I whispered into his chest since his tall body was blocking my view of whoever was coming our way.

He narrowed his eyes for a second as he checked the area. Then he whispered breathlessly, "It's Sofia and Simon."

We stood there for a few moments. I tried to get my breathing in control, sure they'd hear my panting since I was still out of breath from my jaunt through the woods, but my breathing wasn't cooperating because I was all too aware of how I was trapped between a tree and Carter.

I guess I wasn't exactly "trapped" trapped; I could probably slide away to freedom if I wanted to.

But as I let myself get drunk on his delicious scent and the feel of his strong body flushed with mine, there was no place on earth I'd rather be.

Carter was breathing hard too, his chest heaving with the movement, but he didn't seem to be nearly as aware of me as I was of him since he was still watching Simon and Sofia's approach.

So, deciding to just make myself comfortable, I turned my head to face the same direction that Carter was looking. He adjusted his footing, stepping so his feet were splitting mine, and then leaned even closer so that my ear was to his chest. I listened to his heartbeat as we waited, liking the sound. It was strong and steady, and thanks to our race through the woods, probably pounding faster than its usual tempo.

Hearing someone's heartbeat was such an intimate thing. I'd maybe only listened to a few heartbeats in my life—like when I played doctor as a little kid—so it was kind of nice to have this little insight into the part of Carter that literally made him tick.

"What are they doing now?" I whispered, so it wouldn't be so obvious how much I liked being so close to him.

"It looks like they were just coming from the pond," he said. After a short pause, he said, "And now they're sitting on the bench over there."

Oh, darn it. Looks like I might be stuck basically hugging Carter for a little longer.

I smiled to myself at the thought.

"I'm sorry I'm so annoyed right now," Sofia's voice traveled over to us. "I just expected tonight—this week—to go differently."

"Yeah?" Simon's deep voice answered.

"I've been trying to fix things with Carter all week to explain everything," Sofia continued. "But every time I try to, he's with that new girl." She paused for a moment, and then added, "And I can't believe they think that we cheated on Carter. I know we got together quickly after I broke things off, but it's not like I knew I was going to meet you at the London fashion show."

"I know, honey," Simon said, and I imagined him rubbing her back in a soothing way. "We did nothing wrong."

I shifted my footing a little, hoping if I just moved a little, I would actually be able to see the couple through the bush blocking them from my view.

"Yeah, and I just—" Sofia started to say before I stepped on a stick, which snapped loudly, startling her.

Carter and I both held our breath, waiting for them to continue their conversation. But then I heard Sofia say, "Someone's spying on us."

I looked up at Carter with wide eyes at the same time he looked at me and whispered, "What do we do?"

He got an anxious look on his face, and after seeming to make a split-second decision, he whispered gruffly, "You're my fake girlfriend, right?"

"Yeah..."

"Good."

Before I could register what was happening, his face dipped closer and his lips pressed against mine, coaxing them in a give-and-take. And I was so overcome with the sensation of it all that my brain seemed to short-circuit itself.

"Carter—" I gasped, pushing against his chest so I could try to figure out what was going on. "What are you—?"

He put a finger on my lips to stop me. "Two hundred dollars at whatever store you want if you go along with this."

He was bribing me to kiss him?

Was he suggesting we make out behind this tree so Sofia wouldn't think we'd just been listening to them?

I must have hesitated too long because he leaned close to my ear, his warm breath sending chills racing up the back of my neck as he mumbled, "Please."

Well, if he was saying please...

Who was I kidding? I'd make out with him for free just to see if he was as good as my daydreams from earlier this week.

So even though I wasn't the type to turn down a free shopping spree, I pushed myself onto my tiptoes, wrapped my arms behind his neck, and said, "You can kiss me for free."

And that was apparently all the okay Carter needed because in the next instant, his soft lips were back on mine and coaxing them into the kind of exchange that might just make me forget my own name.

The kind of kiss that told me Carter could indeed excel at everything he put his mind to.

He slid one hand up my arm, along my bare shoulder, and then let his fingers stroke through the hair at the nape of my neck.

Even though it was a warm September night, I shuddered under the gentle touch because having his fingers against the sensitive spot felt so unbelievably good.

He must have picked up the wrong signal though, because he stopped what he was doing. He rested his forehead against mine, concern etched in his eyes as he asked, "You still okay with this?"

I couldn't exactly speak right then, since his kisses had left me tongue-tied and breathless. So I just nodded and mumbled, "Uh-huh."

I was more than okay with this.

I was pretty sure I might be okay with doing this forever.

To prove he hadn't pushed me too far in the least, I let my hands do some exploring of their own, sliding along the muscular ridges of his sides and rubbing up the damp fabric of his shirt so my palms could smooth over the solid contours of his chest.

And wow, he felt incredible. Every bit as good as I'd imagined.

Based on what I'd seen of his dad and brothers so far, I assumed part of his amazing physique could be attributed to winning the genetic lottery. But judging from how solid he felt against me, I knew he also had to spend at least some of his free time working out to achieve a muscle tone like this.

How was a guy like this even real?

And how in the world had Sofia dumped him?

She must be insane.

A huge part of me wanted to continue exploring more of him—maybe see if his butt felt as tight as it looked in his jeans, but since this make-out was only for show, I kept my hands above the waist in the territory appropriate for a kissing session with a *fake* boyfriend.

Carter's lips traveled away from my mouth as he trailed slow kisses along my jawline. I was vaguely aware of the sound of footsteps approaching—most likely Sofia coming to see who was spying on her.

I should probably care that she was going to witness the hottest make-out session of my life, but I was so beyond caring about anything other than the way Carter was currently making me feel that I sort of blocked everything else around me out.

It was just Carter and me in this stolen moment. The reasons behind its existence didn't even matter to me anymore, because I was currently floating away on cloud nine without another thought other than how I could get more of this.

Carter's mouth worked its way down my throat and then back up again, leaving a trail of fire everywhere his lips touched. And when his lips captured mine again, I instinctively deepened the kiss. I opened my mouth to his, letting it tell him what I'd never dare say.

That I liked this. And wanted more of it.

That I probably never should have signed his contract

because it was going to be impossible not to want a repeat of this moment after today.

And it was glaringly obvious why he'd had that rule in the first place. Because after just one taste of this forbidden fruit, I was hooked. Carter Hastings was my drug and going cold turkey after this might just send me into actual withdrawals.

I let my fingertips graze against his strong jawline before pushing them into his hair and up his scalp. His hair was softer than I'd imagined.

"Ava..." He groaned quietly against my lips, the sound so low and seductive it made my stomach muscles contract. "You... We... We should probably—"

But he didn't finish his thought. Instead, he smoothed his hands along my lower back, flattening them against the skin just below my crop top and sending a heat wave through my system as he pulled me even closer to him.

He was feeling the effects of this fake kiss, too.

Even if he turned around after this and claimed he'd only been playing into this moment for Sofia's benefit, his body language was telling me a whole different story.

Carter liked kissing me.

And the thought of someone like Carter enjoying this moment as much as I did scorched my insides from head to toe.

"Do you think they're gone?" Carter asked a while later, pulling away and scanning the area, his chest heaving from the intensity of the make-out session.

"Yeah," I said, smoothing my hair down with my hands and trying to catch my breath as well. "At least I think so."

I couldn't exactly be sure how long we'd been kissing,

since time had seemed to disappear when I was in Carter's arms, but the sun was nearly set now and I couldn't see nor hear Sofia or Simon anymore. They were probably back to the party by now.

"Think they bought it?" He turned back to face me, and that was when I noticed I'd left lip gloss all over his mouth.

"Maybe," I said, moving to wipe my lip gloss away. While I was at it, I fixed his hair too, adjusting until it looked close to what it'd been like before I'd run my fingers through it.

Carter just watched me as I worked to make him more presentable, and my nervous system was all too aware of how closely he was studying me.

Did he like what he saw when he looked at me? Was he as attracted to me after that kiss as I was to him?

"Thanks for cleaning me up," Carter said when I'd finished with his hair. "I, um, I guess we better plan a time for me to take you shopping now, huh?"

"I do deserve to be rewarded for suffering through the past few minutes, don't I?" I arched a teasing eyebrow.

He smoothed his fingers through my hair to tame it, and even though I'd just been kissing him a minute ago, the sensation of his light touch sent warm tingles from my head to my toes. "If that's what you act like when you're suffering, I can't imagine what you act like when you're kissing a guy you actually like. There must be literal fireworks and rainbows that explode when you're into it."

So apparently, he had caught onto just how much I'd enjoyed it all.

Oh well. It's not like I needed to be ashamed since he seemed to like it just as much.

But to keep up the little game we had going, I shrugged and said, "I'm just really good at this acting gig."

"Really?" He gave me a look that told me he didn't believe I'd hated kissing him for half a second. "Well, I guess it's good we're on the same page then, because kissing you was pretty much the worst."

"Whatever." I gave his shoulder a playful shove. "More like, you're probably going to take your little tutoring contract to your lawyer tomorrow to see if she can find any loopholes because you know you're addicted to me now."

He chuckled. "I was actually planning to email it over to her as soon as we got back to the house."

"I thought so."

We stood there smiling goofily at each other for a moment, and I liked that when I studied his eyes there was a look of wonder in them. Like he didn't know what to make of what was happening between us.

He broke the eye contact after a moment, though, and peered off into the distance. The sun was close to dipping below the horizon. "Should we head back to the party?"

I kind of wanted to stay out here all night to flirt with Carter and see what might happen, but I stood up straighter and said, "Yes, let's go."

The path was less visible in the dim lighting, my footing not as sure. After I stumbled over a few branches, Carter reached for my hand to guide me back to where we'd come from. And as we walked through the trees and bushes with our fingers laced together, sparks of electricity sizzled up my arm. I knew I was going to have a hard time letting go of him when we made it back to reality.

Man, my heart was in trouble.

20

CARTER

AVA and I arranged to go shopping the next day. So after doing my Sunday morning yoga and meditation session with my family—a tradition my dad and Dawn had started after a trip to India a few years back—I showered, grabbed a quick bite to eat, and then headed toward the garage with my jacket in hand.

I was just walking past my dad's office when I overheard his voice coming from inside. He didn't usually take business calls on Sundays since he said if the good Lord got to take one day off a week, he deserved to take a day off, too. So it was rare to hear him on a call at this time, instead of doing his weekly planning sessions with Dawn in the sunroom.

"You tell me not to worry but I did the math," my dad's voice cut through the air as he spoke to the person on the other end of the line. "And I can't help but suspect that you made up the story about the miscarriage."

The what?

I frowned and stopped in my tracks, not used to hearing the word miscarriage in my dad's every-day conversation.

My dad paused for a moment, as if listening to whoever he was talking to. Then he said, "Yes, I understand." Another short pause. "Okay, we'll talk about it when you come to town." He sighed, and I could imagine him running his fingers through his hair. "I know. Things were crazy back then, but you..." His words trailed off like he was flustered and trying to think of how to finish his thought. "I just don't understand how you could keep this to yourself for eighteen years. I mean, do the girls even know?"

The girls?

Who was he talking to?

I inched closer to the door, hoping it would help me figure out what my dad was talking about. But he must have sensed my presence or something because his footsteps came closer and then he shut the door to block me from hearing any more of his conversation.

Weird.

He'd said things had been crazy eighteen years ago—which was about the same time he and Dawn had been separated and I'd been conceived. Was it possible my dad had gotten another woman pregnant at the same time and had assumed until now that it had ended in miscarriage?

He said something about girls knowing something. Did I have sisters I'd never met out there somewhere?

For my dad and Dawn's sake, I really hoped he was talking about something completely different. They'd barely survived the last time he came home with a random child—me—and I didn't know what would happen if history repeated itself.

AVA WAS WAITING in the school's lobby when I made it to the academy. She'd told me to text when I arrived so she could just walk out. But since I had a part to play and I'd always gone inside the school whenever I would pick up Sofia for our dates in the past, I decided to do the same for Ava. For all anyone else knew, I was just taking my girlfriend out for a day date, and so I intended to make it look exactly like that.

"Such a gentleman," Ava commented when I opened the passenger door of my truck to let her in.

She wore a fitted teal V-neck that looked amazing next to her tanned skin and a denim mini skirt that hugged her hips in just the right way.

As she stepped up into my truck, I allowed myself to take her in a little more. I didn't know how she did it, but she seemed to get prettier and prettier every day.

I pushed the thoughts away though, because getting a crush on my fake girlfriend was not part of the plan. And even if I'd relived our kiss in the woods about a million times since last night, it didn't mean that anything would ever happen between us.

Because I didn't have time to date anyone for real this year, and she also deserved to have a math tutor who was more concerned with helping her pass her tests instead of trying to make passes at her.

That would be so unprofessional.

Plus, who was I to assume she'd even be interested in dating me for real, anyway?

I shook my head to push the nonsensical thoughts away.

Once she was seated comfortably and reaching for the seat-belt, I shut the passenger door and walked around to climb in on my side of the truck.

We ended up at a clothing boutique across the street from The Italian Amigos, and it didn't take too long for Ava to find an outfit and boots that she liked enough for me to plop my money down on.

"Isn't my boyfriend the best?" Ava said to the cashier as she rang up the items. "I tried to tell him that he didn't need to get me anything for our one-week anniversary, but he insisted. Didn't you, sweetie?"

I should probably be worried about how easily Ava could spin a story and make it sound authentic, but when the cashier gave me the total, I tapped my debit card against the card reader and said, "Anything for my girl."

If the cashier thought it was strange for me to spend a hundred dollars on my girlfriend after being together for only a week, she didn't mention it. She simply handed Ava her bags and me the receipt and told us to have a fantastic anniversary.

When we made it out of the store and back to my truck, I asked Ava, "So do you usually celebrate each week of your relationship with a guy?"

"No," she said, eyeing me with a mischievous smile on her lips. "But if you want to make it a habit, I think I saw a few more things I wouldn't mind you buying for me next week."

"Nice try," I said, pushing the button to turn on my truck. "But if we're still doing this thing next week, I'll let you take *me* shopping for our two-week anniversary. It can be a trade-off."

"I don't know if I can afford this relationship." Ava chuckled. "You know, since my mom is the one who's rich and not me." She glanced sideways at me and winked, referring to our conversation the day before when I'd told her my dad and Dawn were the ones who were rich.

We ate lunch at my favorite wood fire pizza place called La Piazza since I remembered from our interview session that pizza was Ava's favorite food—yes, I was basically the perfect fake boyfriend to remember such things.

As we ate our pizzas—a pepper jack for me, a margherita pizza for her—we chatted about what she had planned for the rest of the day.

"Scarlett is working on some project for homecoming week and asked if Elyse and I would help her find some photos from the old yearbooks that she can use for it."

"And you couldn't think of a nice way to turn her down?" I asked, folding my slice of pizza in half to take a bite.

"It doesn't sound too bad." She shrugged. "Plus, I thought it might be a chance for me to see if they have yearbooks from the time my mom was here. She never really told Elyse and me very much about going to school here, so it would be interesting to see what clubs or sports she did. Maybe see if she had any old boyfriends she never talked about."

"I guess that could be interesting if you're into that kind of thing," I allowed. "My dad and Mack's dad both graduated together, so I've heard stories here and there. Mostly about how Mack's dad always dominated on the basketball court while my dad was the ladies' man who got voted Most Preferred."

"That's fun." Ava's eyes lit up. "I didn't know Mack's dad was friends with your dad, too."

I leaned back against the booth seat. "They've been best friends since they were kids. Been with each other through everything."

"And they're neighbors now, right?" she asked.

I nodded. "Yep. My dad sold Mack's dad a few acres when he moved back after medical school and he built the house next door."

Ava seemed thoughtful as she sipped her water. When she set the cup back down on the table, she said, "I think that's cool that they've stayed so close through all these years." She picked up the piece of pizza she'd been working on. "I have Elyse who's been like that for me, but I always think it's such a cool thing when I hear about adults who have been friends for decades and have all sorts of shared memories together. My mom wasn't like that. She kind of said something before about having a close-knit group of friends in high school, but it sounds like something happened after high school that caused her to lose touch with them all."

"Didn't my dad say he was good friends with your mom back in the day?" I asked, remembering what my dad had said when he met the twins on Saturday.

"I think so."

"Maybe they just lost touch when they went off to college?" I shrugged. "Or when my dad got married to Dawn. I think it's harder to maintain friendships with the opposite sex when you have to worry about a wife getting jealous of the friendship."

"Are you saying that if I want to have a lifelong friend from Eden Falls, I should probably stick with Scarlett or Cambrielle since your future wives—yours and Mack's,

Hunter's, and Nash's—wouldn't be able to handle you guys being close friends with someone as alluring as me?"

So she wanted to be friends now?

I didn't know whether to be happy that she enjoyed my company enough to want to be friends or worried that I might be on my way to the friend zone.

My subconscious must have been trying to figure out how to get the best of both worlds because I found myself saying, "Or you could just do like Mack's parents. They were friends in high school and managed to stay friends."

"I would hope they were still friends since it sounds like they're married and all," Ava said, a smile in her eyes.

I laughed. "Yes, well, I guess that does make a difference."

"Is this your way of proposing to me, Carter?" Ava raised a teasing eyebrow. "Because we've only been pretending to date for less than a week. I think I might need to get past the two-week anniversary mark before I'm ready to make that kind of commitment."

My cheeks heated with her flirtatious comment, because while I obviously hadn't been proposing anything, the thought of having a relationship for real with Ava wasn't as objectionable to me now as it'd been just a few days ago.

Which couldn't be good because it would complicate everything.

Wouldn't it?

But since acting all flustered and uncomfortable at her assumptions would only make it obvious that I might be getting the tiniest crush on her, I put on my most unaffected expression and said, "I suppose I'll have to hold off on the ring shopping for a little longer then."

AVA

"I GUESS I better let you go now," I said when Carter pulled up to the front of the school to drop me off after lunch. "I wouldn't want to make you late for whatever you have scheduled next in that planner of yours."

"Is this your way of saying that having a routine makes life boring and predictable?" Carter asked from the driver's seat of his truck. "Because I don't know how we'll make it to our two-week anniversary if you're going to make fun of my beloved bullet journal."

"I would never dare make fun of such a thing," I said sarcastically as I unbuckled my seatbelt.

"Sure you wouldn't," he said. "But the jokes on you because I actually let my wild side out on the weekends and try not to schedule anything. Hence the reason why I was able to fit in this spur-of-the-moment shopping trip."

"You wild thing," I said in a joking tone. "Who knew that my math tutor was so good at living life on the edge?"

Carter chuckled, and I liked the way it sounded—deep and

throaty and not anything I would have expected after that first day I met him when I thought for sure he was a hoity-toity arrogant snob who couldn't be bothered by mere mortals like myself.

But here we were, talking and laughing like we'd known each other for far longer than a week.

It was actually strange to think just how much things had changed in a matter of a few days. At the pizzeria, I'd briefly mentioned wanting to make the kind of friends that lasted a lifetime while I was at the academy. But the more time I spent with Carter, the more I was finding that he was getting higher and higher on my list of possible lifelong friends.

Sure we had that other thing going for us, where the slightest touch from him made my body feel like it'd just been touched by a livewire, and which would probably bother his future wife. But the more time I spent with him, the more time I *wanted* to spend with him.

This had never happened to me before with a guy or anyone, for that matter. I'd always assumed it was because Elyse and I had our whole twin thing going, and so no one could ever rival that connection. I knew it seemed strange, but what I had with Carter felt a lot like it. Like we had some sort of intangible connection that just clicked.

I'd thought it had to be a mostly physical attraction, since let's face it, the guy was hot. But it was like our energy fields were the perfect match for each other, and once the initial connection was made, we couldn't be satisfied with being mere acquaintances anymore. We needed more.

Or at least, *I* needed more. I guess I couldn't really speak to how he felt about me since I couldn't read his mind.

Though I couldn't help but think that we were like Bella

and Edward in *Twilight*—just less vampiresque. Where Bella was Edward's exact blood type, Carter was my exact brand of human.

But that was weird, wasn't it?

More likely I was just drawn to the guy because he'd given me the best first kiss of my life yesterday and my mind was trying to think of an explanation for why I couldn't stop thinking about it.

"So, are you going to get out?" Carter said from beside me, and I realized I'd totally just zoned out for a moment.

"Yes, sorry." I reached for the door handle. "I guess you mentioning how you don't follow a strict schedule on the weekends just shocked me so bad that I forgot what I was doing."

He chuckled. "Sure."

He reached behind him to grab the shopping bags from the backseat, the movement causing his T-shirt to slip up at his side and give me a quick view of his tanned abs. And before I knew it, I was saying, "Actually, do you want to come in?"

"What?" He gave me a confused look. "You want me to walk you in?"

"No..." I tucked some hair behind my ear, suddenly worried I may have misread all our interactions from today. Were we not the kind of friends who hung out just for fun? But since I'd already started, I had to finish my invitation. "I, um, I just wondered—since you said you didn't have plans for the rest of the day—if you might want to come scavenge the yearbooks with me." Then just to give him a way out, I added, "But I totally understand if that's not your kind of thing. I'm sure you have better things to do at that mansion of yours."

He handed the shopping bags to me and with a shrug, he said, "I guess I could help out for a little while."

"Yeah?" My body flooded with relief and excitement at the same time.

He wanted to spend time with me.

His blue eyes studied mine for a second before he said, "I mean, it would probably help our little arrangement seem more believable if I spent most of the day with my *girlfriend,* right?"

Oh. So maybe he wasn't agreeing to this because he wanted to spend time with me. Maybe it was just to help with the production we'd been putting on all week.

I tried not to feel too much disappointment with those thoughts.

He put his truck back in gear. "Let me just park this thing in the student parking lot and we can head inside."

***

AFTER TAKING my shopping bags to my room, Carter helped me find the special collections area of the school's library where Scarlett, Elyse, and Hunter were already perusing the yearbooks.

"Sorry I'm late." I pulled out a chair next to my sister and sat down. "It took a while to convince Carter to show some school spirit and help us."

Carter chuckled and took the seat beside me. "More like Ava's late because she had to try on about twenty different outfits at the store before settling on the first ones she'd pulled off the racks."

"Sure." Scarlett nodded, a knowing smile on her face. "I'm sure you were just *shopping*."

Hunter chuckled at her comment, and I had the feeling they may have been talking about Carter and me behind our backs.

They'd given us funny looks when Carter and I had come out of the gardens last night, but was it possible they believed Carter and I were dating for real?

I'd only told Elyse about the deal we'd made, and she knew all about the kiss and the reasons why it had happened in the first place since I'd gushed over it in our room while we got ready for bed last night. But had Carter not told anyone else about it?

He'd at least clue his friends in, wouldn't he?

But since I wasn't sure if we were letting the rest of our friends believe we were dating for real or not, I just said, "Yeah, *shopping* with Carter was better than I thought. Pretty sure we might need to do it again soon."

I looked over at Carter to see his reaction—wondering if he would set the record straight. But he just put his arm around my shoulder, pressed a quick kiss to my cheek, and said, "We can go shopping anytime you want."

Okaaaaaay. My face felt like it might catch on fire from how hot it became after his quick kiss.

Did he have any idea what he was doing to me?

He had to know. A guy like him had to know the effect he had on women.

I sat up a little straighter, hoping it would help me regain my composure. "We'll save the shopping for later. Right now, we're here to help Scarlett."

"If you insist, babe." Carter grabbed a yearbook from the stack that had been placed at the center of the table.

Had he just called me babe?

Eek!

I never thought I'd like that term of endearment before, but having it come from his lips and directed at me might just be the best thing I'd ever heard.

I scanned the yearbooks, checking the years on the sides for one that matched the time my mom had been at the academy. As I sifted through the pages for photos from my mom's past, I couldn't help but wonder if something was really happening between Carter and me and whether I should be reading into it.

Because let's face it, I really, *really* wanted to read into it.

"LOOK AT THIS," Elyse said to me a little while later. "I don't remember Mom ever telling us she was in a school play. Do you?"

"She was in a play?" I leaned over to see and found a spread from the school's production of *Romeo and Juliet*, with a photo of my mom as Juliet at the top. "She was the star?"

"Crazy, right?" Elyse said, as surprised as I was by this fact.

"She looks so young there."

"I know," Elyse said. "She was our age. She looks just like us."

"She was so beautiful," I said, taking in our mom's long, brown hair that cascaded down her back in curls.

I slid the yearbook away from Elyse toward Carter so I could show him. "Doesn't she look just like Elyse and me?"

He studied the photo with narrowed eyes and then moved his gaze to my face, as if comparing the two of us. "You definitely look like you're related. Is she as tall as you two?"

I shook my head. "No, she's only five-foot. She never says much about our bio dad, but she has said that we got our height from him."

"I got my height from my dad, too," Carter said. "I don't think my mom was very tall."

He got a strange look on his face when he mentioned his mother, and I was reminded of what he'd said about how she'd left him at a childcare center when he was little and never returned.

He swallowed and resumed looking at the yearbook as if searching for a distraction. Then he pointed to a photo and said, "Looks like my dad played Romeo."

"He did?" My jaw dropped at the coincidence. Sure enough, a guy with light hair who looked like a younger version of his dad was in a photo with my mom, doing the dramatic double suicide scene at the end. And while I didn't have a thing for older guys, Mr. Hastings had actually been pretty cute in high school.

But I guess that shouldn't surprise me since his son was gorgeous himself.

It made me wonder if my mom ever had a crush on Carter's dad growing up.

"Did you know your dad played Romeo in the school play?" I asked Carter.

He shook his head. "I knew he did a lot of different things in high school—sports, clubs, and whatever interested him. But he never specifically mentioned being in a play."

"Apparently, neither of our parents considered starring in the school's play worth bragging about to their kids."

"I guess not," he said. "But that must be where Nash got his flair for the dramatic from."

"And Elyse from my mom."

It looked like he was going to say something about my acting skills too, but when he glanced over at Scarlett and Hunter who were immersed in yearbooks of their own, he seemed to think better of it. He probably didn't want to clue them in to the fact that everything they'd been seeing from us this week had been an act.

"Do you think this play was how our parents became friends?" I asked Carter, referencing back to what his dad had said the day before about him and my mom going way back.

"Probably." Carter shrugged.

I gave the yearbook back to Elyse and continued searching through the one I'd been working on. When I turned to a page with the title of Sweethearts Ball at the top, I saw a photo of Carter's dad wearing the kind of sash girls wore in beauty pageants, with the words "Most Preferred" in thick black lettering across his chest.

"This must have been from that story you told me, what Mack's dad likes to tease your dad about."

Carter leaned closer to look at the photo I was pointing to, his shoulder pressing against mine. "Yeah, that's my dad."

But then he seemed to notice something else, because he chuckled and pointed to another guy in the photo. "And that's Mack's dad." He shook his head and smiled. "Looks like he took second place. Maybe that's why he always brings that story up. Because he's jealous he didn't win."

The man in the photo looked nothing like what I'd been imagining Mack's dad to look like.

Since Mack was black, I'd assumed his dad must be black, too. The photo was black and white, so it didn't show the exact skin tone, but it was obvious that his skin was closer to Mr. Hastings' coloring than Mack's. But he did have the height that Mack had. Mr. Hastings was probably close to Carter's height, but in this photo, Mack's dad stood a few inches taller than his friend.

"Mack's mom was originally from South Africa," Carter said, seeming to notice that I was trying to figure out how everything worked. "Or at least I think her family is from South Africa. I think she was born in the U.S. And I'm pretty sure she was in the same grade as my dad and Dr. Aarden."

"That's cool," I said.

I was about to turn the page when my eyes caught on a photo at the bottom with the caption that read, *Miriam Cohen and Joel Hastings dance the night away.*

What the—?

I took a second look at the photo. Carter's dad wore the "Most Preferred" sash in the photo and my mom wore a sleeveless dress that while it was probably the height of fashion twenty something years ago, she probably wouldn't be caught dead wearing today now that she was a fashion icon. But what I noticed most was the way they were dancing. It wasn't the awkward, rigid pose where you could fit five

Bibles in between their bodies and still have room. No, they were practically hugging and looked *very* content to be in each other's arms.

I blinked my eyes, not used to seeing my mom being romantic with a guy—for as long as I could remember, she'd never really dated anyone. She'd always claimed she was too busy and that she didn't want her attention taken from raising Elyse and me.

But the way she was resting her head against Mr. Hastings' chest, and the way his chin rested on top of her head with his arms wrapped tightly around her waist, I couldn't help but think they'd been more than the simple "friends" that Mr. Hastings had called them yesterday.

"Um, guys?" I said, looking to my left and then to my right to make sure I had Carter and Elyse's attention.

They looked up from their yearbooks. Scarlett and Hunter looked up as well. With their eyes on me, I pointed to the incriminating photo and said, "So, um...I'm pretty sure our mom and Carter's dad dated back when they were in high school."

WE SEARCHED the rest of the yearbooks from the years that our parents were at the academy, and by the time we were done, Elyse and I figured out that Mack's mom and our mom had been best friends all four years at the academy. Our mom and Carter's dad didn't show up in any photos together until the play *Romeo and Juliet*. And then after that play, which had happened during their junior year, photos of Mom and Carter's dad popped up here and there, and in most of them they stood close enough that I figured it was safe to assume that they had indeed dated—or at the very least had been very close friends.

"That's kind of cute that your parents dated in high school and now you two have your own thing going on," Scarlett gushed as we stood to put the yearbooks back on the shelves where they belonged.

I peeked over at Carter, curious how he felt about the possibility.

Was it weird for him?

Or did he not think much of it since we weren't actually dating?

He picked up a stack of yearbooks from the table and started walking around the table with them, ignoring Scarlett's comment.

So I just smiled at her and said, "Apparently, the Cohen women have a thing for tall guys with blue eyes."

"Is that true for you, too?" Scarlett eyed Elyse. "Do you go after the same type?"

Elyse grimaced, like she wasn't exactly comfortable talking about who she may or may not like. But after tucking some hair behind her ear, she shrugged and said, "Blue eyes are nice. But I don't really have a preference. I, um..." Her cheeks colored. "I guess it's more the inside that counts."

Scarlett smiled. "That's probably a more mature way to go about things."

Elyse shrugged. "And what about you? Do you have a type?" she asked Scarlett.

It was Scarlett's turn to look uncomfortable—her eyes widened briefly and her cheeks got slightly rosier than usual. When she gave Hunter a sideways glance, I remembered what she'd said about things with him being complicated. From what I'd gathered so far, they'd been best friends since their sophomore year and had kept things platonic for most of that time, but then last year they dated for a couple of weeks—only to realize later that they were better off as friends.

They were basically tied at the hip when she wasn't doing volleyball or house-captain stuff, so it seemed like they'd been able to maintain their friendship well enough after everything was said and done. But from the way they glanced at each other at Elyse's question, I couldn't help but wonder if maybe there were still feelings brewing deep down inside.

Scarlett cleared her throat before saying, "I don't have a type. I, um, I don't have time to date right now, anyway."

She busied herself with picking up the stack of photos that she'd copied for the project she was working on. Hunter, looking equally uncomfortable, offered to take the last stack of yearbooks to wherever Carter had disappeared to.

Elyse and I eyed each other briefly, and I could tell she was thinking the same thing I was. That dating at this private school was probably way more complicated than we'd assumed.

A moment later, Carter returned from the library stacks. After seeing that everything had been cleared from the table, he said, "I guess I should probably head home for dinner." Then glancing at our spectators, he seemed to make a split-second decision and quickly pulled me into his arms. After kissing me briefly on the top of my head, he said, "I'll see you at school tomorrow."

And even though it was such a little thing, I kind of loved that he did that because it was such a boyfriend thing to do.

When he pulled away from the hug and ran his thumb across my cheek, I didn't want to let him go because it just felt so nice to be close to him.

But since he wasn't my real boyfriend, I let my hands drop from his waist and said, "I'll see you tomorrow. Have a good night."

He said goodbye to Scarlett and Elyse, and then nodded at Hunter. Then he left us.

As I watched his back get farther and farther away from

me, I couldn't help but think that based on everything he'd done for this charade of ours this past week, he'd probably make an amazing real-life boyfriend.

And I might just need to find a way to make him my real boyfriend.

THE NEXT WEEKS PASSED QUICKLY. Now that we were settled into the new school year, the teachers must have all gotten together and decided it was time for them to take their classes to the next level and start assigning more homework.

So. Much. Homework.

At my last school, I probably would have slacked off and only put in the minimal amount of effort to get a passing grade. But since I was at a prestigious private school where apparently everyone but me was a genius, I had to step up my game if I was going to keep up the grades it would take to play basketball.

But it wasn't so bad. I had Carter helping me with math for our one-on-one tutoring sessions on Tuesday and Thursday. And then in the evenings, Scarlett and Hunter and whoever else decided to stick around at the school after hours got together to study.

It was kind of nice, actually. I'd always studied with Elyse in the past since we often took the same classes, but there was just something about having a bigger group of kids working together that really helped me grasp the various concepts. And for the first time in my life, I actually looked forward to studying, since it was made fun by being with my new friends.

And yeah, on the days that Carter stuck around after hours—which happened on Wednesdays and Thursdays, I was extra invested in those study sessions because it gave me a little extra time to be with him.

Sofia had joined our study sessions a few times, since she and Nash were still good friends. It had been a little awkward at first, but she and Carter seemed to be getting used to being in the same vicinity as each other again. As we all continued to study together, the more normal it became. Sofia and I even chatted about fashion and modeling here and there, and it was interesting to hear what was happening in the modeling part of the industry.

We probably wouldn't ever be super close, since she thought I was dating her ex, but we smiled and said hello when we passed each other in the halls now. So I was confident at least that she wasn't going to blast me on social media for what I'd insinuated about her and Simon at the barbecue.

Carter and I continued with our charade as well, since we didn't want Sofia to know we'd just been faking it and I still wanted an alibi for our one-on-one tutoring sessions. But we didn't do anything over the top like our make-out session in the gardens. We actually kept all PDA very low-key, which was basically sitting beside each other at lunch and during our study sessions and saying a flirtatious comment here and there.

It was kind of like having a boyfriend, just without the cuddle sessions and kissing.

I was trying not to want those too much.

Trying not to let myself think of ways to convince him that we needed to practice those very things just in case.

But it was almost impossible not to think about it when every time he leaned close and I caught a whiff of his faint cologne, I was taken back to that tree in the gardens and wished I could relive that moment in real life instead of just in my daydreams.

"You guys don't have anything planned three Saturdays from now, do you?" Cambrielle asked us one day at lunch.

"I don't know," Mack said, draping his arm around the back of her chair as he sat next to her. "I was hoping to take you on that date I talked to your brothers about. You're not already making other plans, are you?"

"As nice as a date with you sounds—" She nudged her back against his arm, pushing it off her chair. "—I do already have plans."

"What's going on?" Scarlett asked, stabbing some of the kale salad on her plate.

"Well," Cambrielle said, glancing at Nash who was sitting next to Scarlett. "As you know, I've been slightly addicted to *Bridgerton* ever since it came out. And seeing all the fancy parties and balls in the TV series has me wanting to throw a big soirée of my own."

"A *Bridgerton*-style party?" Elyse gasped, her mouth dropping open. "I am so here for this."

Cambrielle smiled at my twin, encouraged by her enthusiasm. "We wouldn't have to wear period clothing or anything." Her eyes brimmed with excitement. "You can wear whatever formal dress you want. But I don't know, I've always wanted to have a fancy party like this with everyone, and since most of you are going to graduate this year, I wanted to have it before you all leave."

"Are you saying I'm going to need a new tux?" Mack asked, a skeptical look in his eyes.

"Your navy-blue suit would be just fine," Cambrielle said to him. Then looking back at the group, she said, "So, do you think you guys can come?"

"I can," Scarlett said.

"I guess," Mack said with a shrug.

Hunter gave a non-committal grunt.

"I'll be there if I can wear a cravat," Nash said, which probably shouldn't have surprised me because he seemed to always want to be in character one way or another.

"You know I'm there," Elyse said, since this was exactly her kind of party. "And I think I might have just the dress for the event."

"I'll be there, too," I said.

"You're coming too, right?" Cambrielle addressed Carter when he didn't say anything.

"Let me check my calendar," he said, pulling out his bullet journal. He counted the weeks and seemed to note the date. "Are you talking about October sixteenth?"

"Um, yes," Cambrielle said, the look in her eyes becoming slightly more anxious at his mention of the date. She adjusted her shoulders in her cream-colored jacket. "I think that sounds right, anyway. I thought it would give us enough time to plan everything while still having good weather in case we wanted to do some things outside."

"That's the only reason why you picked this specific weekend?" Carter studied his sister with narrowed eyes, as if trying to figure something out.

She nodded, her gaze flitting to Nash before she said, "Yes. I don't remember there being anything else going on that weekend, do you?"

Nash made a show of frowning, and then said, "Nope. Nothing special about October at all."

Carter looked at his brother and sister suspiciously for another long moment before finally saying, "I don't have any special plans for that weekend, either. So I guess I can show up."

Relief showed on Cambrielle's face, and after giving Nash a quick glance, she said, "Great. I'll tell my mom that you're all in."

CARTER

"I DON'T KNOW if you'll need a tutor much longer," I told Ava after we finished our math assignment one Thursday afternoon. "I barely feel like you need my help as it is."

When Mrs. Simmons first told me about who I'd be tutoring this year, she'd made it sound like I'd have my work cut out for me.

But so far, Ava had caught onto all the concepts we were learning about in our Statistics class without too much extra help from me, and I wouldn't be surprised if Ava was acing all her tests before long.

"I appreciate the vote of confidence," she said, her cheeks flushing a beautiful pink. "But I think I'll keep you around a little longer."

Was it weird that I actually looked forward to our tutoring sessions?

In previous years, I'd mostly seen tutoring as a way to give back—to help people who struggled with the subject to get on better terms with it.

But it was different with Ava. Sure, I wanted her to get to where she didn't groan every time the word *math* was brought up in a conversation, but I also had more selfish reasons for wanting to keep our tutoring sessions going. I liked having the one-on-one, uninterrupted time with her. I liked the excuse to sit close and accidentally brush arms as we worked side by side. I savored the chances I got to breathe in her delicious shampoo when I leaned close to check her answers.

And I also liked having a reason to keep our fake relationship going. Because while we'd probably already satisfied my need for our arrangement—the need to give Sofia the impression that I had indeed moved on from her—as long as Ava wanted people to believe I was wooing her instead of tutoring her, I had an excuse for why I was always close by her side when we were hanging out with our friends.

I *should* probably remind her that having a math tutor was nothing to be ashamed of in the first place. But the selfish part of me just wanted to keep this thing going for another month, or two...or possibly until we graduated.

Would it be too obvious if I offered to tutor her in college?

"Got any other fun plans for this evening?" Ava slipped her notebook with the pink skulls on it into her backpack.

"Not really." I shrugged. "You?"

"Elyse has a drama club meeting and I think Scarlett said she had a volleyball game tonight, so I was probably just going to watch a movie in my room or something since I finally don't have homework."

Was this her way of hinting that her night was open if I wanted to hang out with her?

I didn't think I had anything other than a workout scheduled for tonight, and since it was just a run, it shouldn't take me very long to do.

I studied her, trying to figure out if I should take a chance and ask her to hang out with me tonight.

Despite spending a lot of time together the past few weeks, we hadn't done anything alone that didn't involve schoolwork. I was pretty sure that we'd gotten to the place where she considered us friends—at least I hoped we were friends now. But were we the kind of friends who could do things without a larger group of friends around?

The kind of friends who didn't need tutoring sessions or fake girlfriend/boyfriend duties to be able to hang out alone?

Deciding that the best way to figure out the answer would be to actually ask her to hang out, I said, "The only thing I have planned so far is a quick run, but after that my schedule is wide open." I fiddled with the chain bracelet on my wrist, running my thumb across the name engraved on the small charm, nervous for some reason. More nervous than I'd been to invite someone to spend time alone with me in a long time. Years maybe.

I cleared my throat and tried to push some confidence into my voice. "Would you want to come hang out at my house after that? I could do my run on one of the trails around the school and we could head to my house after."

"That sounds fun." Her cheeks lifted into a warm smile at my offer, and I released the breath I hadn't realized I'd been holding.

"Great. Meet me in the lobby in about forty minutes?"

"I'll meet you there."

"I'LL JUST TAKE a quick shower and then we can grab some dinner," I told Ava when we got to my house. I hadn't wanted to shower at the school, only to change back into my school uniform again since I hadn't brought an extra change of clothes with me today. So hopefully she wouldn't mind entertaining herself for a few minutes while I got myself unstinkified.

"Should I just wait in the family room at the end of the hall?" she asked, gesturing in the direction of the room my siblings and I usually hung out in the evenings before heading to bed.

"That, or you can wait in my room if you prefer," I offered, since I really wouldn't be that long.

She bit her lip and eyed my room, and I realized how that might have sounded.

After thinking it over, she took a step toward the family room and said, "I'll just wait out here."

I considered teasing her about the first time she'd barged into my room and asking her why she seemed so timid now, but she was likely turning down my offer because she knew just how explosive the fireworks could burn between us and that it was better not to tempt fate. I nodded and said, "I'll be out soon."

I made quick work in the shower and grabbed the first clothes that I saw—a charcoal button-up and dark-wash jeans. Then I headed down the hall to get Ava.

She was texting someone when I walked into the room, so I took the seat beside her and waited for her to finish.

"Sorry, I was just messaging my mom." She set her phone face down on the couch when she'd finished.

"Yeah?" I asked. "And how is she?"

"She's good." Ava smiled. "Her show in Milan went really well and she made it back home yesterday. She said that she wants to come to Eden Falls this weekend so we can spend a couple of days together."

"That sounds like it'll be fun. Do you know if she's spent much time here since she graduated?"

"I don't think so." Ava shook her head. "When she dropped us off for school, I think she said the last time she'd been here was for her five-year high school reunion. So it's been a while."

"That was probably, like, eighteen years ago, wasn't it?" I asked, doing the math quickly in my head based on the year she and my dad had graduated.

"Yeah." Ava nodded. "I think it was the summer before Elyse and I were born."

"Probably wanted to avoid running into her ex." I winked.

She laughed. "If our assumptions about her and your dad dating in high school are even true. You didn't ask your dad about that, did you?"

"No," I said. "I forgot to ask when the teachers decided to dump a buttload of homework on us."

"Yeah, I didn't ask my mom about it, either," Ava said. "But I'll probably ask her more about what she did in high school when she's here this weekend. Maybe she can take me and Elyse to all the places she used to hang out at when she was here."

"Take a stroll down memory lane?"

She nodded.

I was about to suggest we head downstairs to see what Marie had whipped up for dinner when Ava asked, "You don't think it's weird that our parents might have dated, do you?"

Her golden-brown eyes looked at me cautiously. Like our parents' history might somehow impact us and what our relationship might be.

I would have to admit that the thought of my dad dating the mom of the girl I was trying to figure out how to date was slightly weird. But it wasn't like they'd gotten married or anything. And while there was a possibility that they'd also hooked up during that time—since my dad had told me he'd had sex when he was in high school—at least it hadn't ended in a pregnancy. Ava and Elyse were their mom's only children. So it wasn't like Ava and I shared a half sibling or anything.

To answer Ava's question, I just said, "It's a little weird to think about. But it happened so long ago that I don't think it should be anything to worry about. It just shows that our parents had good taste in high school, right?"

Ava nodded slowly, like she still wasn't sure how she felt about the possibility. But then she shrugged and said, "You're probably right. Probably nothing to feel weird about."

CARTER

AVA and I headed down to the kitchen a minute later. Dawn was sitting at the large, white marble counter, eating her steak and Dutch-oven potatoes. My mouth instantly watered because Marie's steak was the best, juiciest steak I'd eaten in my whole life. Not even the five-star restaurants in New York could rival the steak I was about to eat.

"Hey, Carter." Dawn looked up from scrolling through her phone as she ate. "Sorry I didn't realize you were here already. I would have waited for you if I'd known."

"Oh, it's fine." I waved my hand at the woman who'd been my mother since my dad brought me here. "I wasn't sure if I'd be eating at the school tonight, so you're totally fine."

Dawn's eyes went to Ava, a curious expression in them. "And who's your friend?" She arched a dark eyebrow as she looked Ava over from head to toe.

"This is Ava," I said. "She's just started at the academy

this year but is a senior." Then turning to Ava, I said, "And this is my mom, Dawn."

"It's nice to meet you, Mrs. Hastings." Ava stepped forward to shake Dawn's hand.

But since Dawn was Dawn, instead of taking Ava's hand, she stood up and gave Ava a quick hug. "It's so great to meet you, Ava. I think I may have heard a little about you from my kids. You're one of the twins, right?"

Ava nodded, her cheeks flushing at the mention of having been previously discussed at our house. "Yeah, that's me. My sister Elyse and I are twins."

Dawn took a step back and gave Ava a good once-over before smiling. "Well, it was very nice to meet you. Cambrielle, Nash, and Carter have all said very nice things about you."

"They have?" Ava looked at me, her expression full of questions. "Now I'm really curious what they've said."

Dawn laughed. "Well, Cambrielle says she's excited to have new girl friends to hang out with. Nash may have told me all about how beautiful the new girls at school were. And Carter..." Dawn glanced at me, as if trying to remember what I might have said.

Honestly, I couldn't remember what I'd said about Ava. I was sure I hadn't been the one to bring the twins up in conversation, but if my siblings had mentioned them at dinner, I had probably added my two cents.

Then Dawn seemed to remember what I'd said. "Oh, yes. And Carter said something about either your sister or you being a lot to handle."

Ava giggled. "He was probably talking about me then."

She raised her hand. "Let's just say the first day of school was quite the eventful day for us."

I chuckled at the memory. "Yes, let's just say that Ava has a way of keeping me on my toes."

Dawn studied us with the kind of look I only saw from her every once in a while. The kind of look that told me she'd noticed how happy I'd been the past few weeks and was realizing just now that Ava was probably a big part of the reason for it.

She caught herself smiling at us a second later, though, because she cleared her throat. "Anyway, I wasn't sure who'd be coming home for dinner since Nash and Cambrielle had their drama club meeting, so I had Marie put the rest of the food in the fridge for you to heat up later. So go ahead and take as much as you'd like."

"Thank you," Ava said with an appreciative smile. "It smells so good in here."

"Just make yourself at home." Dawn picked up her dishes and started rinsing them off in the sink.

As I was pulling the containers of food from the fridge and setting them on the kitchen island, Dawn spoke again. "Oh, and Carter?"

"Yeah?" I peeked around the stainless-steel fridge to look at her.

She wiped her hands on the towel after putting away the dishes and closing the dishwasher. "Did Cambrielle tell you and your friends about the party three weeks from now?"

"The one on October sixteenth?"

"I think that's the date," she said, and from the hint of anxiousness in her eyes, I couldn't help but wonder if my suspicions from earlier had been founded.

"She mentioned it."

"And did it sound like everyone would be available to attend?" she asked, seeming to be holding her breath as she waited for my answer.

"Yeah, pretty much everyone said they could come." And then to test my theory, I added, "I made plans to visit Yale's campus that weekend, if you remember, so I'll probably have to miss it. But I'm sure everyone will have a great time."

"What?" Dawn said in a louder voice than she'd used before, clearly surprised.

Ava narrowed her eyebrows. She was probably confused about it too, since I'd just said earlier today that my schedule was wide open that weekend.

"W-why did you plan it for that weekend? I, um...I thought you'd be around." Dawn frowned like she was trying to solve some sort of problem in her head. She said, "Would you be able to reschedule your tour? We have just put so much into planning this already, and we'd really like for you to be there."

Of course they would.

Cambrielle might have said it was just for fun and a way to live out her fantasy of dancing with a duke while wearing a fancy ball gown. But the timing was too coincidental for me to believe that they weren't planning exactly what I suspected.

I could probably keep this going on a little longer, but since I loved Dawn and I really didn't want to cause her too much stress even if she was doing the exact thing I'd told them I didn't want, I said, "I was just teasing you. I don't have any plans for that weekend."

Dawn placed a hand to her chest, and then she shook her head and said, "You enjoyed that, didn't you?"

I grinned and shut the refrigerator door. "What's the use of being a teenager if I can't tease my mom every once in a while?"

Dawn rolled her eyes at me, but I could tell she wasn't really mad. "Anyway, I think I'm going to go take Penelope for a ride." Penelope was her Thoroughbred horse. "It's been a few days since she's gotten a good run in." She turned her gaze on Ava. "It was so good to meet you, Ava. I hope we'll be seeing more of you in the future."

"I hope so too." Ava smiled at Dawn. "And it was great to meet you."

"SO, WHAT WAS THAT ALL ABOUT?" Ava asked as we heated up our plates of food in the microwave. "Why did you tease your mom about not going to the party?"

"Oh that?" I raised an eyebrow, leaning back on my palms against the counter. "That was just me testing a theory."

"A theory?"

"Yep."

"And what theory was that?" she asked.

"A theory about why they're really having this party."

"And that theory would be what?" Ava asked, folding her arms across her chest, not seeming to like that I was making her work for the answers.

The microwave beeped, so I opened the door to grab my food, which was steaming hot. I pulled it out carefully. With our plates and glasses of water in hand, I nodded toward the back door, indicating for Ava to follow me out to the terrace where we could eat our meal.

"Are you going to tell me why you think they're really having this party?" Ava asked impatiently as we seated ourselves onto the striped cushions.

I set my dishes on the patio table and started cutting into my steak with the steak knife. "I'm pretty sure they're planning a surprise birthday party for me."

"Really?" Ava's eyes widened, and she started cutting into her steak as well. "Is your birthday October sixteenth then?"

"No, it's the next day." I put a bite of steak in my mouth and had to resist the urge to moan because dang, it was so good. I closed my eyes as I savored the taste for a moment.

"Did you just grunt like a caveman?" Ava asked, amusement in her voice.

I opened my eyes and saw her staring at me open-mouthed. Apparently, I hadn't been able to hide my neanderthal tendencies as much as I'd hoped.

But since I had better manners than a caveman, I made sure to finish chewing my steak before I said, "This is so good."

"Kind of like the chicken at the back-to-school barbecue?"

"Even better."

Deciding to test it herself, Ava put a piece of the steak in her mouth, and when her eyes lit up as she chewed, I knew she was impressed. She swallowed her bite and said, "Um, do you think Marie has time to come cook for the school, too? Because I'm pretty sure this is the kind of steak that they serve in heaven."

I laughed, but since I was a bit territorial when it came to Marie, I said, "Sorry. She only has time for my family."

"Well then, I may just need to invite myself over to dinner every night."

"I think I could get on board with that," I said.

And when our eyes met, I couldn't help the goofy smile that took over my face because I realized that I really did want something like that to happen. I wanted to spend as much time as I could with this vivacious girl who always had me on the edge of my seat.

Ava cut into her steak again. "So how do you feel about this surprise party of yours? Is a soirée the kind of party you had in mind for the big eighteen?"

"Honestly?" I asked.

"Of course."

"Well..." I skewered a potato with my fork. "If it was actually up to me, I wouldn't have a party at all."

"What?" Ava pulled her head back, obviously caught off guard by my answer.

I looked at my plate and swallowed. "I'm just not a huge fan of my birthday."

"What?" she said again, clearly never having met someone who didn't like their birthday before. "Why don't you like your birthday?"

I pressed my lips together, wondering how to explain it. With a sigh, I said, "I guess it's just that the first birthday I remember having ended up being one of my worst memories."

Ava's expression immediately turned somber. "Did something bad happen on your birthday?"

"Well, it wasn't on my actual birthday." I rubbed the back

of my neck, not sure if I really wanted to get into the story tonight. But I was starting to like this girl and knew that if I ever wanted anything to happen with her for real, then it meant I would need to open up to her and show her everything that made up Carter Dominic Hastings. I said, "The bad memories came from what happened the day after my fifth birthday."

CARTER

"SO, I guess I should probably tell you a little about what life was like for me in Guatemala." I set my fork and steak knife down on my plate and leaned back into the patio couch, trying to figure out where to start. I didn't talk about my life before Eden Falls very often. Only a few people knew my story—my family, Mack, Hunter, and then also Sofia after we'd been dating for a few months.

Talking about it made me emotional. And since I didn't like getting emotional in front of others, I just chose to not really talk about it.

Which meant, I also didn't tell people why I didn't like celebrating my birthday. I usually just said I was a private person and parties centered on me made me feel awkward—which was also true—but what I didn't tell them was that my last day with my mom had been the highlight of my child-hood that turned into a nightmare.

But there was something about Ava that told me I could tell her about my past and let her see more of what made me into who I was today. In fact, I kind of *wanted* to tell her about this story.

So I cleared my throat, adjusted the knees of my jeans to get more comfortable, and said, "Growing up in Guatemala was a lot different than growing up in this mansion." I gestured at the house behind us and the grounds in front of us. "I guess after my dad's fling with my mom, he gave her some money before he left. He'd gone there under a different name since he was volunteering at his own orphanage and didn't want the people to know who he was. He went by the name Carter Jones, and he just kind of spent his days painting the walls of the orphanage and getting it ready to open its doors."

"So your mom didn't know that she'd been dating a billionaire?" Ava asked.

I shook my head. "No. She thought he was just a regular Joe who'd come to do some missionary work during his vacation time."

"And she named you Carter because she thought she was naming you after him?"

"Yes." I sighed and continued. "She and my dad had their little thing going for those two weeks, and during that time, my mom became pregnant with me without either of them realizing it." I rubbed my arm, feeling awkward talking about this with the girl I was interested in. I cleared my throat again. "Anyway, when he left, he didn't think there was any possibility that he'd fathered any children while in Guatemala since he'd always used protection, and so he came back to Eden Falls without giving it a second thought. He and Dawn worked things out later on that year and before long, Nash was on his way."

"When was he born?" Ava asked.

"His birthday is May twentieth."

"So I'm older than him." Ava smiled.

"Yeah? When's your birthday?" I asked, curious if I was much older than her.

"Elyse and I were born on April seventeenth."

"You were born on the seventeenth, too?" I asked, somewhat surprised by the number. "That's cool. That means we were born six months apart."

"That is cool." She smiled. Then seeming to remember that she'd interrupted my story, she asked, "So what happened to your mom? Did she find out she was pregnant with you right away?"

"I'm not sure," I said with a shrug. "When I was five, I wasn't exactly interested in asking her about that. And since my dad didn't know about me until I was eight, he didn't know either."

"And you probably didn't have any other relatives in Guatemala who would know about it," Ava assumed.

"Yeah, I ended up in the orphanage because there was no one else to take care of me."

"Of course," Ava said, looking down and acting sorry for bringing the subject up.

But since I didn't want her to feel awkward about asking any questions, I gave her a smile that hopefully told her she hadn't offended me. "It was just my mom and me during the first years. My dad said he gave her some money when he left, and either my mom spent it all quickly or lost it somehow, but I don't remember her having more than a few cents to rub together at a time.

"I vaguely remember how she took me with her to clean

the homes of some wealthy people. I played with a little girl who lived there while my mom worked. But she lost that job somehow, and we really struggled after that."

"Did you have a home? Food?" Ava asked, her eyes looking worried over the wellbeing of my childhood self.

But I shook my head and said, "So, you know how Mack said his house looks like a shack compared to this one?"

"Which means it's actually probably bigger than the house I grew up in," Ava guessed.

I nodded. "I haven't seen your house, but since the Aarden's house is bigger than most of the houses in Eden Falls, I'd guess that it was bigger." I cleared my throat. "Anyway, I brought up the whole shack thing because I actually did live in a shack for a little while, and so I can legitimately roll my eyes every time Mack talks about his shack."

"Did you go hungry, too?"

I nodded, remembering even all these years later how my stomach had always felt hungry. How while we managed to get a small amount of food most days, I didn't know what it felt like to truly satisfy my hunger until I was in my dad's orphanage and they fed me three meals a day.

"We didn't have much," I said, not wanting to go into all the details. "After my mom stopped cleaning houses, she started scavenging the dump for things that she could sell or trade for a little food or money. I went with her a few times when the childcare was full, but on the days they had room, I was able to go there during the day. Those were my favorite days because I actually got rice and beans to eat."

I peeked at Ava to see her reaction, and she had the saddest look in her eyes. She said, "I can't imagine living like that. I'm sorry."

"I didn't really know any different at the time." I shrugged, trying to put off just how hard it had been for my mom and me. "And I was actually luckier than a lot of kids."

Ava shook her head. "But still. It's sad to know that happened and still happens to millions of people all the time."

I sighed and gave her knee a gentle squeeze. "I know what you mean. I always feel a little guilty that I have so much when there are so many people out there with nothing."

"Does your dad still have the orphanage?" Ava asked.

"Yes. He has a few down there now actually, and we're planning to go there over spring break to help build another."

"Really?" Ava's eyes lit up. "That's so cool! I've always thought it would be nice to do something like that."

I nodded. "I'm looking forward to it. I'll probably try to see if the lady who took care of me at the orphanage is still around, so I can catch up and thank her for taking care of me."

"That's so sweet," Ava said, her eyes moist. Seeing her get emotional about this made tears prick at my own eyes because it was something that was so near and dear to me.

I wanted to say that she should join us on the trip, since it would be cool to experience that with her. But we weren't exactly at that level quite yet, so I stopped the words before they could make it out of my mouth.

I wiped at the corners of my eyes, trying to push away the emotions because I knew I'd need to keep them at bay if I was going to make it through the rest of my story.

"I don't remember a ton from back then because I was so little, but I do remember my fifth birthday." It was impossible to forget since it was both my best and worst memory. "Things hadn't been great for us, and even though my mom always tried to be strong, I could tell she wasn't doing well. She was probably only a few years older than we are now, but she seemed so old to me at the time—like her body had aged several years between my fourth and fifth birthdays."

The long days had been hard on her body, and without the proper nutrition, I now understood that her organs had probably been slowly dying. "Anyway, my birthday came, and my mom surprised me by taking me out for a fun day together instead of taking me to the childcare so she could work at the dump."

I swallowed as I remembered how excited I'd been to have the whole day with my mom since that hadn't been happening very much in the days and weeks before.

"We went to this waterfall at the edge of the city, and I had the best time just playing in the water. I remember my mom letting me eat most of the lunch that she'd brought with her since I was the birthday boy." Which meant that she probably didn't eat anything that day—something my egocentric, five-year-old self hadn't even noticed. "She even had a chocolate cupcake for me to eat, which was something I'd begged and begged her for every time we walked past the bakery window to get to the childcare."

She'd probably saved for a long time to buy the special cupcake for me and gone without. And I knew I'd just been an innocent kid and hadn't wanted to make my mom feel bad about not being able to give me all the things I wanted, but still to this day, I couldn't eat chocolate cupcakes. They reminded me of how much my desire for them had probably become a burden placed on my mom's shoulders.

"Anyway, we had a really great day together, just my mom and me. We laughed and played and had cake. And that night when my mom sang me to sleep, I remembered going to bed with a smile on my face and just wishing that every day could be like that perfect day."

"But since you don't like celebrating your birthday, I'm guessing something went wrong," Ava asked in a quiet voice, as if she wasn't sure she really wanted to know what happened next. She knew I'd been in an orphanage for three years, so she probably had a good idea of what came the next day.

My mind went back to that time, to that day when my world dropped out from under me and things never went back to being the same no matter how many times I'd prayed that they would.

"I woke up the next morning—and it was just like most mornings in our little makeshift home. My mom always liked to leave first thing so we could get to the childcare early, so as soon as the sun was up, we packed our few belongings into our tattered bags. I held my mom's hand as she guided me through the streets. My mom seemed more on edge than usual, but I just thought it was because she was in a hurry to get to the dump before it got too crowded. She took me to the front door like she always did and gave me a long hug." My voice wobbled a little as I remembered that last hug from my *mamá*. "Her hug seemed a little different that day, too. I'd been ready to go and play with my friends, not wanting to stand around and hug my mom all day, but she just held onto me a little longer. I thought maybe she just wanted the extra-long hug because we'd had such a good day together the day before and she was going to miss not being with me all day.

"I could still remember how she'd felt. She wasn't quite twice my height—even then I was tall for my age, especially in Guatemala. But as I'd hugged her tiny waist, I noticed just how bone-thin she was. And for the briefest moment I'd thought about how I probably should have given her more of my cupcake."

"Oh Carter..." Ava said, scooting closer and looking like she wanted to hug the five-year-old version of me.

I gave her a faint smile and my eyes pricked with tears again. I drew in a deep breath. After casting Ava a sideways glance, I said, "Anyway, she finally let me go and told me she loved me and that I needed to be a good boy for Señorita Celeste who ran the childcare. I told her I would be a *buen niño* and that I'd see her later. Then just before she left, she pulled me off to the side and told me that she'd forgotten to give me my birthday present. I told her I thought the cupcake was my birthday present, but she said she had a special one. And then she took off the gold chain bracelet that I'd never seen her take off and looped it around my wrist."

Ava gasped, her eyes lighting up as she reached for my right arm where my gold bracelet rested. "Is that why you wear this bracelet all the time?" she asked, running her index finger along the thin metal. "I've always wondered why you wore a woman's bracelet."

"Yes," I said. "This was hers."

"Was her name Astrid?" Ava asked, pointing to the name inscribed on it.

I nodded. "It was. Astrid Garcia Díaz."

"That's such a pretty name."

"I think so, too."

As Ava continued to trace her fingers along my bracelet and the surrounding skin of my wrist, I continued my story. "Like I said, she gave me this bracelet as a birthday present and told me that she loved me so much and that she wanted me to always remember that. And then after another hug and a kiss on the top of my head, she took me back inside the childcare and then went off to work.

"I remember playing with a dinosaur puzzle during quiet time, and how Señorita Celeste read us a story about a boy who helped his *abuela* sell the wall hangings that she weaved at the market. I remember more details about that day than most days I've had since then. But what I remember most was waiting by the window at the front of the childcare after the other parents had picked up their kids and wondering when my mom was going to come.

"Señorita Celeste took my hand and pulled me back to the small kitchen where she had some rice and beans cooked up for dinner. She told me to eat with her and the two other kids who'd been left at the childcare the month before—their mom never came back for them, either.

"I remember going to sleep on the small mattress that night and hugging the thin blanket to myself as I wondered what might have happened to my mom at work that day. Had she gotten hurt? Was she still working? Had she somehow forgotten which childcare she'd left me at?"

I shook my head at the memory of how scared I'd been that night. It was the first time I hadn't slept next to my *mamá*.

"Did you ever find out what happened to her?" Ava asked, her finger stopping its stroke along my arm.

"We're not exactly sure," I said, releasing a shaky breath.

"My dad hired a private investigator after finding me to see if they could dig up some kind of explanation for what happened to my mom that day. But we think she probably died shortly after that. We think she probably knew she couldn't take care of my basic needs any longer, and so she left me where she knew I'd be safe."

"And she did that after giving you one last good memory, one magical day to remember her by."

I nodded and stifled a wave of emotion that threatened to overcome me, knowing that if I spoke, I'd probably just end up crying. "It was her last goodbye to me."

I leaned back against the cushion, feeling spent after telling my story. Ava studied me for a moment before curling up against me and resting her head on my shoulder. "I bet that was really hard for her to do," she said. "Your mom probably put it off for as long as she could."

I draped my arm around Ava's shoulders, needing her beside me more than I'd known. "I guess that could be right. Maybe she'd tried to leave me dozens of times before she finally got up the nerve to do it."

"Are you mad at her?" Ava angled her head up so she could read my expression.

I let out a long breath as I tried to figure out the answer to that question.

"I was really sad and worried for the first month," I said. "I kept waiting for her to show up. And when she never did, I was mad that she could just leave me like that. I was mad for a really long time." I sighed. "But now that I'm older and have a better understanding of how hard it probably was for her, I just feel sad she was even in that situation in the first place."

"Were you ever mad at your dad?" Ava guessed.

"Yeah," I said. "I was pretty mad at him when I came to his house and saw just how much money he had. I was mad that he got to live in a huge house, with people he paid to do everything he wanted done for him and our family. I was mad that while he got to go to Guatemala for two weeks at a time, help a little here and there, write another check to solve a problem, my mom had literally starved to death. I was so mad at him. I hated that he'd had his little two-week fling, gotten her pregnant, and then left without even making sure she was provided for."

"Do you think he would have taken care of her if he'd known about you?"

"He would," I said, not even having to think about it. "He probably would have moved her in to live with him and Dawn in a heartbeat, if he'd known about me."

"Because deep down, he's a good dad," Ava said. "A good person?"

"He is."

We were quiet for a minute, each lost in our thoughts.

After a long moment, Ava said, "I can understand why you would have been mad at him."

"You can?" I looked at her.

She nodded. "You know what kind of resources he has at his fingertips, and so you know that if things had been different and he'd given your mom his real name—if he hadn't been down there all incognito-style—then she could have contacted him and she might still be here today."

"Exactly." It was like Ava could see into my thoughts somehow because I'd thought those very same things so many times before.

She sat up again so she could see my face better. "I've

always been a little frustrated with my mom for a similar reason. I know she's the one who had to do the hard work of raising Elyse and me all by herself—but if she'd just tell us who he is..." Ava shook her head and looked down at her hands that she was wringing in her lap. "If she'd have told him about us, then at least he could've had the choice to be a part of our lives or not."

"He doesn't know about you?"

"No." Ava wiped at the moisture pooling at the corners of her eyes. When she spoke again, her voice wobbled. "She said she never told him about us because it would only bring more drama into our lives and we were better off without him."

"Was he, like, a criminal or something?" I asked, curious about what kind of a guy had given her half of her DNA. "Part of the mafia?"

"I don't think so." She shrugged. "I snuck into my mom's file cabinet when I was younger to see if I could find his name on my birth certificate, but the place for the father's name was left blank. So not even the government knows who our father is."

"That's kind of crazy."

"I know." She picked up her plate of food from the patio table and brought it onto her lap. Poking a Dutch-oven potato with her fork, she said, "I get not letting a guy into your life because he's dangerous or something. Like, if he had raped her or abused her, then he obviously shouldn't be in the picture. But she never made it sound like anything like that happened. She just says she made a huge mistake and then ends the conversation."

I furrowed my brow, trying to figure out why her mom

didn't just tell her. Even if she didn't want the guy in her girls' lives, she could at least tell them who their biological father was. At least give them some details.

After chewing her bite of food, Ava said, "I don't know. Part of me just wishes she'd told me he died in a car accident or something. Because then I could stop looking at every tall, middle-aged guy with light brown hair and wonder if he was my dad."

"Have you ever suspected anyone?"

"In second grade I thought for a little while that my friend Sarah's dad could possibly be my dad too, since I thought I looked kind of like him. He'd told me that he and my mom had known each other before I was born—they worked at the same store the summer my mom would have gotten pregnant with Elyse and me. But when I asked my mom if she'd ever had a crush on him, she just laughed and said he'd tried asking her out a couple of times, but she always said no because working with someone you date would be so awkward if you broke up. So I figured he probably wasn't my dad after all. Plus, I later found out that my friend and all of her siblings got some sort of strong genetic traits from him that Elyse and I would have gotten if we'd been his, and so I dropped him from my list of possible dads."

"Do you still have a list of possible dads going?" I asked.

"Not anymore."

I picked up my plate to finish my steak and potatoes that probably could use another trip inside the microwave. "I used to do something similar."

She narrowed her eyes. "You had a list of possible dads?"

"Not, like, officially," I said. "But yeah, I was the little orphan kid who went up to every gringo with blue eyes that I met and asked him if he was my daddy."

"Oh, that's so sad," Ava said. But then a slight smile lifted her cheeks and she said, "I bet that made for some awkward encounters. I wonder how many guys you met were worried you might actually be theirs. Or how many wives never trusted their husbands to go out for a guys' weekend again after having a cute little orphan ask them if they were theirs."

I smiled, liking that she was able to bring some humor back into the conversation. "I only remember a handful of wives smacking their husbands after seeing the sense of dread come over them as they tried to figure out if I could actually be theirs."

"Were there a lot of orphans with gringo fathers running around then?"

"So many that they actually had to outlaw adoptions from other countries because it was such a huge problem back in the day."

"Really?" Ava's eyes went wide.

"Yes. The reason my family owns so many orphanages down there is because there are, like, five hundred thousand kids with stories like mine. I was just one of the lucky ones."

"CURFEW IS AT TEN, RIGHT?" Carter asked me while he loaded our dishes into one of the stainless-steel dishwashers they had in their massive kitchen.

"Yeah," I said. "Ten o'clock is when all the lights are supposed to go out."

Was he hinting that he might want to hang out a little longer? Because even though our dinner conversation hadn't exactly made for the most cheerful meal I'd ever had, I felt somehow closer to him because of it. And if he was offering me a chance to spend more time with him, I was so on board with it.

I knew it must have been hard to tell me about his past, since Carter didn't exactly strike me as the type of guy who was an open book or wore his heart on his sleeve. But I appreciated him telling me because it was nice to know more of why he was the way he was.

It solved the little mystery of why he'd reacted so strongly when he thought I was throwing away my food at the barbecue. Having lived with such hunger would probably make me a little territorial over food as well.

It also gave me some insight into why he was so meticulous with his planner. Having had so much instability in his early life, knowing what to expect during his day or week probably made him feel more secure and in control of what was going on in his life.

"Well," Carter said as he closed the dishwasher door and dried his hands with a towel. "If you're not in too big of a hurry to get back to the school, I was thinking it might be fun to watch a movie or something to end the evening on a lighter note."

"You sure you don't want me to tell you about all the phone calls Elyse and I eavesdropped on to try to figure out who our dad might be?" I asked. "Or list all the daddy-daughter activities I stayed home from because my mom just didn't look that great in a suit?" I shot him a challenging look. "Because I know how competitive you are about sob stories, I think I might need to tell you a few more of mine so you can know you're not the only kid who had it rough growing up."

"As fun as that sounds..." Carter chuckled, and I liked the way his eyes lit up when he laughed. I liked the dark and brooding vibe he usually put out, but there was just something about the lighter, more carefree version of him that I was addicted to. "I kind of think I might be more in the mood for a movie."

"Okay, fine." I made a show of looking disappointed that he hadn't taken me up on my offer. "But I get to pick the movie, okay?"

"As long as it isn't something sad like *The Fault in Our*

Stars or *A Walk to Remember*, then I guess I'll let you pick this time."

"How did you know those were the exact movies I was thinking of?"

"I'm just good at reading people."

Carter led me back upstairs to the theater room Cambrielle had shown me during her house tour, and we picked *Megamind* since we wanted a good laugh. While Carter got it ready to go, I excused myself to use the bathroom.

In the guest bathroom that was across from Carter's bedroom, I searched the cupboards for some mouthwash— you know, because I was dedicated to oral hygiene, not because I was hoping I might have an excuse to kiss Carter.

Okay, so maybe I wanted to be ready just in case.

And luck must be on my side because I found a small bottle of mouthwash in the cupboard beneath the sink. I gave myself a nice swish and then hurried back to the theater room.

When I made it back, the movie was paused on the opening scene. Carter was sitting on one end of a long couch, his seat in the reclined position all ready to watch the show.

There were several other couches in the room that I could choose from if I wanted to really spread out, but since I wasn't a complete idiot, I sat on the other end of Carter's couch.

I was just trying to get comfortable when Carter looked over at me and asked, "You're going to sit all the way over there?"

"It seemed like a good-enough spot," I said with a shrug,

pretending like I wanted to sit with a full cushion between us. "Why?"

If you asked me to scoot closer, I wouldn't say no.

He pursed his lips together thoughtfully. "I guess I was just thinking that there might be a better option, that's all." He shrugged.

Deciding to play dumb for a second, I pointed to the couch behind us. "Is the view better from there?"

He looked over his shoulder at the leather couch.

"That's a pretty comfortable spot," he said. "But that's not the seat I was thinking of."

"No?" I made a show of looking around and then pointed to the recliner on the other side of him. "Is that the best spot?"

He shook his head. "No."

"Hmmm..." I tapped my chin as if I was really thinking hard about the best place to sit among the many options. "I bet you probably think the floor in front of the couches is actually the best place to watch a movie from. Probably reminds you of your days at the orphanage when you sat on the dirt floors and made your own movies in your head while Señorita Celeste read books to you."

Carter's jaw dropped, and his blue eyes went so wide I worried my attempt at a joke may have just backfired big time.

"Did you really just go there?" he asked, like he couldn't believe he'd heard me right.

"Umm...yes?" I said, the muscles in my neck tightening.

And for a split second, I worried he may cancel our movie night and call a butler or security to come up here and haul my sassy butt out the door.

But then his lips quirked up at the corners and he let out

the most boisterous laugh I'd heard from him so far. "Oh Ava," he said, shaking his head as his shoulders shook with laughter. "I think you may be the first person I've ever met who makes fun of orphans."

I scrunched up my nose. "Too far?"

"It's surprisingly refreshing, actually." He shook his head again, the look in his eyes both amused and disbelieving at the same time. "It's kind of nice being able to joke around with you instead of having you be so serious about it. But..." He held up a finger as if about to set me straight. "If you're going to make fun of my orphan status, then you need to at least get your facts right. Señorita Celeste read to me at the childcare. Señorita Silvia was the one who read to us at the orphanage."

"My bad." I held up my hands.

He chuckled again, and I had the feeling that I may never get tired of hearing that sound from him. It was so lighthearted and knowing that I was responsible for his laughter made me giddy.

It made me want to find ways to make him laugh more often.

He drew in a deep breath, signaling that he was getting back to the topic at hand. "Since you're obviously having a difficult time deciphering which seat I think you should take, I'll give you a little hint."

He slipped his left hand between his cushion and the one beside him to lift some sort of lever, making the seat between us recline.

"Oh," I said, pretending like the thought of sitting right next to him had never occurred to me. "So, the middle seat is actually more comfortable than the seat I'm already on?"

"It's the best seat in the whole house as far as I'm concerned." He patted the spot next to him.

But since I wasn't quite done playing games, I slid only about a foot over from where I already was. I was technically on the cushion he'd indicated, but only just barely.

I leaned back, putting my hands behind my head in a relaxed position. I let out an over-exaggerated sigh and said, "You're right. This spot is super comfy. I think I'm going to enjoy watching the movie from here very mu—"

But I didn't get to finish my sentence. Carter slipped one arm behind my back, spreading his hand against my hip, and slid me across the cushion until I was positioned right next to him.

"Sometimes you just have to take matters into your own hands," he said.

And I probably would have had a witty retort for him if I wasn't so distracted by the fact that my entire left side was lighting up like kindling about to catch fire.

He must have noticed that he'd left me speechless because a wicked grin lifted his cheeks before he said, "What do you think? Is this seat any better?"

Since I was barely thinking in one-word syllables, I just nodded my head and said, "Yeah."

Then he pulled me against him so my head rested on his chest, and as the opening scene of *Megamind* came on the screen all I could think of was that this was so much better.

WHEN THE MOVIE ended and the credits started rolling, the last thing I wanted to do was get up from the couch where I'd been cuddled up to Carter for the past hour and a half. It was probably strange that we were two high school seniors who had chosen to watch a cartoon, but it was probably what we'd needed after the heavy conversation on the back patio at dinner.

The movie was lighthearted and fun, and I hadn't laughed so much in a long time.

Carter pressed a button on a silver remote to turn on the overhead lights at the front of the room. Then he picked up a black remote and used it to turn off the screen.

He set the remotes back down, and then he smoothed his hands up and down my arm. In a quiet voice, he said, "I should probably get you back to the school, huh?"

But after listening to his breathing and his heartbeat and basically just basking in the glory of what it was like to be near Carter Hastings for an extended period of time, leaving his side and going back to the school where I'd have to wait until who knows how long to be alone with him again was the last thing I wanted to do.

We hadn't even really done anything besides watch the movie—no kissing, no fooling around—but it was probably the most enjoyable hour and a half that I'd had in a very long time because I'd been able to be near him. And I didn't know what it was, but I just felt better when I was with Carter. He was like a calming presence to my erratic brain, and I was more peaceful and content when I was with him.

Which was crazy, because he was also the same guy who could send my heart racing into overdrive with just a flip of the switch.

I didn't really know what he thought about me or what had been going through his head during the movie—for all I knew, his attention had been on *Megamind* and the character's quest to be the baddest super villain of all time and he hadn't even really noticed my presence at all. But he had to feel something, right?

And so, since I really didn't want to get up from this couch and remove myself from this wonderful bubble of happiness, I burrowed my face into Carter's chest and said, "I fell asleep. I can't go anywhere," in a muffled voice.

Carter chuckled at my lie. But playing along with me, he brushed his fingertips through the hair that had fallen across my cheek, shifted his position so he could see my face better, and whispered, "Are you a sleep talker, Ava? Did you just say something?"

"Yes," I muttered.

I could feel him watching me, and so I tried to keep my expression neutral. I breathed more rhythmically, mimicking a sleeping person because even though it was totally obvious that I was faking, I was now dedicated to the production.

"I really hate to wake you up," Carter whispered, his hot, minty breath warming my forehead. "But you've left me no choice."

Before I could brace myself, his fingers were tickling my sides. I clenched my muscles, resisting the urge to squirm under his tickling touch. But while I was able to keep from twitching for about ten seconds, I could only hold off for so long because the sides of my ribs were the most ticklish part of my body.

"Ugh," I said, squirming away from his tickling fingers and sitting up. "You're so mean. You know that?"

Carter laughed, and for a moment I thought he was going to keep the tickle torture going just for fun. But he stopped and said, "I had to be mean for your own good." He used the button on the side of the couch to move his seat back to the upright position. "And now that you're awake again, I think it's time for me to take you back so you aren't late for curfew. You don't want to get on the headmistress's bad side."

"I really don't care about getting on her bad side."

"That's only because you've never seen her when she's mad. Believe me, she's not a woman you want to mess with."

I considered telling him that I'd take my chances. But since I really didn't know what would happen if I was late for curfew, I used the lever to put my seat back to the upright position as well. "Fine."

Carter held his hand out to help me up. Then he patted the pockets of his jeans as if checking for something. "I must have left my keys in my gym shorts."

We walked down the hall to his bedroom. While he went to dig his shorts from the dirty laundry basket in his closet, I took the opportunity to look around at the things Carter held special enough to display in his room. He had a few knickknacks here and there, and a framed photo of him, Mack, Hunter, and Nash wearing basketball uniforms sat on his desk. Another photo of him and his siblings standing on a yacht with the ocean in the background was beside that one.

In the corner next to the wall with all the constellations on it was a telescope, which made me think that maybe Carter was interested in astronomy.

There was a giant bookshelf along the wall beside his bed with at least a hundred books. There was everything from personal development books to the classics, to biographies, to popular fantasy novels and mysteries, and even a stack of Calvin and Hobbes comic books in one corner.

He even had a row of books in Spanish.

"You have quite the book selection," I commented when he came to stand beside me. Even though there were a few inches of space between us, the electric charge that was always humming under the surface when we were together was there again.

"What can I say? I like reading. You can live a thousand different lives without ever having to leave your room."

"I like that." I glanced up at him briefly, liking once again how tall he felt beside me. "Do you have a favorite genre?"

He shrugged, his elbow brushing against my arm with the movement and sparking my skin to life. "I should probably say that the personal development books or the biographies are my favorite since those help me keep up the scholarly vibe I try to put off." He peeked over at me, a smirk playing at his lips. "But I guess if you were to hook me up to a lie detector machine, I'd have to admit that a really good fantasy, like one from Brandon Sanderson, is actually the kind of book I prefer to get lost in when I'm reading for pleasure."

"Would it be safe to say that when you pulled out that Spanish personal development book during my first dinner at the academy, you were really just trying to impress me?"

He rubbed his neck with his hand, a slight blush showing on his cheeks. "I *was* actually reading that book. But..." He shrugged. "Maybe subconsciously I was trying to let you think I was a serious student who didn't have time for trivial things, like making friends with the pretty new girl at school."

"So you thought I was pretty when you met me?" I arched an eyebrow, liking that he was giving me some insight into his first impression of me.

"Maybe." He shrugged. "But since I had already decided that I wasn't going to waste time on dating this year, I tried to not let myself notice."

"Ah yes. Because girls are such a huge distraction from the more important things, like getting straight A's and reading impressive books while you eat."

"To be fair, I was still nursing my wounded ego after having my ex-girlfriend dump me for a prince."

"And how has your heart been doing the past few weeks?" I put my hand over his chest where his heart was. "Has it gotten any better?"

He covered my hand with his, the warmth of his skin on mine feeling incredible. "Would you believe me if I told you it might just be better than it's ever been?"

When I lifted my gaze to meet his, the intensity in his eyes scorched my insides, because I had the idea that they might be telling me I was part of the reason why.

His gaze fell to my lips, and I instinctively licked them, anticipating what it would be like to kiss him again.

But since I still wasn't sure exactly where his feelings were concerning me, I tried to push those thoughts away.

He broke eye contact and moved toward his desk. After opening the top drawer, he pulled out a familiar contract with my purple handwriting scrawled across the bottom of the piece of paper.

"I have a confession to make," he said.

"You do?" I asked, feeling breathless for some reason at the sight of that contract and the possible reasons for him to bring it out.

"That third rule on my list of demands actually surprised me when we went over it."

"It surprised you?" I narrowed my eyes, not under-standing.

He nodded and leaned against his desk, partially sitting on it. "You see, I never wrote that rule."

"You didn't?"

He shook his head. "It was actually put there as a prank by my conniving little brother."

"Nash put it there?" I gasped, shocked because when we'd gone over it, Carter had not seemed one bit surprised at its existence. He'd played the part of the arrogant jerk so well.

"I kind of panicked there for a minute as I tried to figure out how to respond," he said. "But then I channeled my inner Ian and decided to go with it."

"So you don't really have throngs of girls throwing themselves at you on a daily basis?" I asked. "Was that just you bluffing?"

"It depends on what you define as a throng." And I didn't know if he was trying to channel his inner Ian again, but the smoldering look that he gave me then was totally that of a guy who knew exactly how hot he was.

And I liked it.

I liked a guy with a healthy dose of confidence.

"Well," I said, deciding that if he was going to bring back his whole Haughty Mc-Hot Hot persona, then I should bring back my inner goddess, too. I straightened my shoulders and said, "I guess I probably shouldn't tell you about the dozens of guys I had to turn down this week because I had to keep our fake girlfriend-and-boyfriend thing going."

"Only dozens?" Carter cocked an eyebrow and let his gaze slowly wander all along my body, obviously raking me in.

I held my breath as I waited for him to finish his appraisal of me.

I knew deep down that I shouldn't care what a guy thought of me because I knew that I was awesome on my own and didn't need anyone's approval.

But there was still a huge part of me that wanted Carter to approve of me.

Wanted him to *want me* in the way I very much wanted him.

After he'd finished eyeing me from head to toe and then back up again, he said, "Are you sure it wasn't hundreds? Because I don't think a girl like you comes around more than once in a lifetime."

"You don't?" I breathed, my heart stuttering in my chest.

Did he truly mean it?

Did Carter, this guy who could have any girl he wanted at our entire school, actually see me that way?

But because I was basically fluent in finding the loophole in all compliments directed at me, I said, "You remember I'm an identical twin, right? So, someone like me actually did come around more than once in your lifetime. We came around twice."

Carter chuckled at my logic. Then looking at me with the sincerest expression in his blue eyes, he said in a low voice, "You may have a look-alike, but you, Ava, are one in a million." He traced his thumb across my cheek. "You're entirely and unapologetically yourself, and I kind of love that about you."

Swirls of heat bloomed across my cheek where he caressed it, and I wanted to just live in this moment forever. I wanted to have him touch me like that everywhere.

But instead of continuing to caress my cheek or tangle his fingers in my hair like I wanted him to, he dropped his hand and reached for the contract again.

He held the paper up between us, and for a moment I wondered what he planned to do with it, but then he started tearing it down the middle.

"You're ripping up our contract?" I asked.

He nodded. "My lawyer never got back to me about the loophole, but if it's okay with you, I'd kind of like to get rid of this right now."

"Does this mean you don't care if I show up on time to our tutoring sessions anymore then?" I asked.

He shook his head. "That's not the rule I have an issue with."

"You don't want me to be ready and willing to learn from you?"

He shook his head again, ripping the contract in half once more. "Not that one, either."

"You don't like the part I added?"

"I'm pretty sure I'm already guilty of breaking that little addendum of yours," he said in a soft voice. "I mean, who couldn't help but fall for a girl who is a goddess on earth with the most enchanting personality, charming wit, and captivating eyes?"

I couldn't breathe.

Was he saying he'd fallen for me?

He ripped the contract pieces in half again. After tossing them on to the floor, he sat on the wooden chair beside his desk, reached for my hand and pulled me closer so I was standing between his splayed legs.

"I don't think I can keep up my half of the bargain anymore, Ava," he said. "I know we said we'd only pretend to like and flirt with each other." His thumb rubbed the skin along my knuckles. "And I said that falling for you wouldn't be a temptation in the least, but I'm realizing that I was just lying to myself because falling for you has been the easiest thing I've ever done."

He pulled me even closer to him, so close that I had no other choice but to climb onto his lap. His hands gripped my hips and he leaned forward so our foreheads were touching. As he was looking deeply into my eyes, I knew that falling for Carter was the easiest thing I'd ever done, too.

I hadn't really expected it. Sure, I'd thought he was the

most beautiful-looking human I'd ever laid eyes on the moment I met him, but that had nothing on what I knew about who he was as a person now.

He was a little rough around the edges at times, but he was a good brother, a loving son, a caring friend. An all-around good person. And based on everything I'd seen from him the past few weeks, I also knew he'd make for an amazing boyfriend.

As we stared at each other, both of our breaths coming in short bursts, I knew I needed to tell him how I felt. So I gathered up as much courage as I could—because, let's face it, this moment was what dreams were made of and I really didn't want to mess it up—and said, "You're not the only one who breached the contract. Because I think that I'm falling for you, too."

He searched my eyes for a moment, as if he wasn't sure he'd heard me right. But then he cupped my face in his hands and kissed me. His lips met mine in a long, slow kiss, and I knew from the urgency of his kiss that he'd been wanting this very thing to happen for as long as I had. That kiss in the woods had sparked something real inside us and the longer we tried to ignore it, the stronger the desire became. He cared about me. He wanted me.

The thought that someone like Carter could actually feel those things about me flooded my chest with a lightness I hadn't felt in a very long time—maybe never before.

"I've been thinking about doing this," he mumbled against my lips in between kisses. "Every day for the past two weeks."

"Me too." I sighed.

He slid his hands up and down my back as he kissed me, and it felt incredible. I slipped my hands into his hair, remembering how much he'd liked it the last time I did that. And when he let out a light moan, I couldn't keep the slight smile from taking shape on my lips because I liked that I could do this to him.

"You're trouble, you know that?" he mumbled in between kisses.

"Good trouble, right?" I asked, pulling away for a second to take a much-needed breath.

He nodded and said, "Very good trouble," before he started trailing kisses down my neck.

CARTER

WAS THIS ACTUALLY HAPPENING? Was I actually kissing the most beautiful girl in the world in my room right now?

Because if this was reality, then I must have done something very good in a previous life to deserve a moment like this.

I breathed in Ava's scent as I kissed her neck. She smelled like lavender and pear with a hint of something citrus. I had no idea if it was from her body wash, lotion, perfume, or maybe a mix of all three, but I wanted to breathe in her scent all day and happily get drunk on her.

I'd never been drunk before, never even had a sip of wine from my parents' wine cellar, but I had a feeling that being drunk felt a lot like how I felt kissing Ava—fuzzy and warm and deliriously happy. Happier than I'd been in such a long time. It was as if I hadn't truly known what it was like to be alive until I met this vivacious girl. And the more I was with her, the more I never wanted to be apart.

I explored her neck and jawline, enjoying the erratic way she was breathing and the slightly salty taste of her skin. But as I trailed kisses across her collarbone, I could tell she was anxious for me to find her lips again because she took my face in her hands and directed it back up to hers.

"Just kiss me, Carter," she commanded. "I need your lips on mine now."

I couldn't help but smile because I liked that she wanted me and wanted this kiss as much as I did. Not about to argue with this feisty girl, I obliged. I sucked gently on her bottom lip, lightly flicked my tongue against her cherry-flavored mouth. And when she opened her mouth to mine, I didn't hesitate to explore.

My stomach muscles tightened as our tongues danced together, and when she moaned into the kiss and pressed herself closer to me, all I could think was that I wanted more.

So much more.

I wanted everything.

Her hands slid down my shoulders and arms, and when she squeezed and then explored my chest with her palms, I was thankful that I'd been putting in the extra time in the gym because I wanted her to like what she felt there.

She must have liked what she felt because when she finished exploring the contours of my chest with her hands, she slipped them under the hemline of my T-shirt and slid them along my stomach and lower back, sending electrical jolts coursing through my system.

I moved my hands along her back again, pulled them along her hips and squeezed the tiny bit of softness she had there. My fingers trailed along the sliver of skin above her jeans, and I loved how warm and smooth her skin was.

"This is so crazy," she said breathlessly, pushing her long hair away from her face and pulling it over one shoulder.

"I know." I sighed into her mouth, my heart racing so fast it felt like it might explode.

Our kisses grew deeper and longer, the movement of our hands on each other slowing down, and my whole body ached for her. I wanted more.

I moved my hands down her back, slipping them down along the underside of her thighs. And then bracing the weight of her body in my hands I stood from the chair, carrying her with me and laying her on my bed.

I didn't have plans for anything more than kissing, since I didn't want to rush things, but when she looked up at me with heavy lidded eyes as I lay on the bed beside her, I couldn't help but wonder what it would be like to take things all the way with Ava.

From what she'd said the first time she came to my room, it didn't sound like she'd slept with a guy before. So if we ever took that step, it probably wouldn't be for a long time down the road.

But I liked the idea of experiencing that first with her someday.

Not because I was some hormonal teenager who just wanted to have sex because guys were genetically wired to reproduce—though I was sure my hormones had something to do with it since I was definitely still a guy who noticed that Ava was a woman. But if we ever took that step, it would be because it would be with *her*. It would be special. It would actually mean something.

I shook those thoughts away. Here I was just barely kissing this girl for the second time in my life after only telling her a few seconds ago that I was falling for her, and I was already hoping for months and years ahead together.

It was insane, wasn't it?

But that was the magic of being around Ava Cohen, I guess. She made me want a future like that. A future where I got to spend my days laughing with her, growing into a better person alongside her, and building a lifetime of memories with her.

And when she reached her arms around my shoulders and back and pressed her body against mine until there was barely enough space left for me to breathe, I had a feeling that I might not just be falling for her, I might have already fallen.

29

IS THIS REAL? I wondered as Carter deepened our kiss further, sending my mind off into a frenzy where anything before or after this moment didn't exist anymore. There was only now. Only me and Carter. And only this magical feeling that I knew I would crave for the rest of my life.

I suddenly understood why people could get addicted to drugs or alcohol or sex, because once you experienced such euphoria, you knew just exactly how amazing you could feel and how you would want to suddenly rearrange all of your plans just to get your next fix.

I was in the middle of a kissing session with Carter, but already I was wondering when the next time would be that I could kiss him.

Like, was his schedule already full for the weekend and I would I have to wait several days until I could find myself tangled up in his arms again? Or was he free tomorrow for lunch so I could get a quick fix in the library stacks after scarfing down a bite to eat?

Regardless of how long I had to wait, though, I knew that this needed to happen again. I needed to kiss Carter as often and long as possible.

"We'll probably need to leave in a few minutes so you're not late for curfew," Carter said, briefly breaking the lock he had on my lips.

"I know." I sighed, taking a much-needed deep breath. "But not a second sooner, okay?"

He grinned, his smile reaching his eyes as he said, "Deal."

He started kissing me again, and as he led my lips in the exchange so hot it was turning my mind to goo, his hands crept along the hem of my shirt and smoothed up across the ridges of my ribcage. I'd never had a boy touch my skin there before, never wanted a guy to become so familiar with me until this very moment, but as his fingers ran across the sensitive skin of my stomach, sparks of electricity sizzled all over my core before spreading to my toes.

It felt incredible.

So freaking incredible.

His hand traveled across my hips and along my back. And as my nerve endings reacted and blood flowed to every part that he touched, I wanted to erase every molecule of air that separated us. I wanted there to be no space where we weren't connected.

When he rolled me onto my back and covered my body with his, I instinctively arched into him, needing to feel that contact between our bodies. Carter was all hard, lean muscle, and I reveled in everything that he was. He felt amazing. He smelled amazing. And the fact that he seemed to be as into me as I was into him boggled my mind.

If you were to ask me on that first day of school after he'd had me sign that contract if I'd ever see myself doing anything remotely close to kissing Carter Hastings, I would have laughed in your face. But here we were, making out on his bed less than a month into the school year, and he was suddenly the only guy I ever wanted to do this with for the rest of my life.

I knew that once I was back in my room tonight and separated from this intoxicating feeling, that I'd probably think I was crazy for wanting to give all my firsts to a guy I met in high school—to think about building a life together and eventually having babies together. But my current frame of mind didn't care about logic; it only cared about making sure moments like this kept on happening for the rest of my existence.

It was possible for seventeen-year-olds to fall in love and eventually get their own happily-ever-after, wasn't it? Those kinds of things didn't just happen in books and movies, right?

Of course I wouldn't talk about wanting anything like that with Carter right now, probably wouldn't even mention it to Elyse since most people considered that line of thinking as insane.

But I don't know...falling in love isn't logical, is it?

It wasn't always something that you could control. And while there was still a lot to get to know about Carter and it was too early to know if we had a chance at a long-term relationship, I knew that I at least wanted to keep moving forward with him.

"Carter, are you in there?" Nash's muffled voice sounded on the other side of the door, followed by a quick knock.

Carter groaned at his brother's interruption, looking like he didn't like the idea of cutting our last few minutes together short. But he pulled himself away from the kiss and rolled back so we were simply laying side by side. Then he called out, "Yeah, I'm in here."

I expected Nash to say something more, but he opened the door instead, saying, "Can I talk to you about—"

He stopped in his tracks and his eyes went wide when he realized Carter wasn't alone in here. After getting an awkward look on his face, he turned away and said, "Um, sorry." He grabbed the doorknob and said, "I, um, I'll just come back later." And then he shut the door.

I turned back to Carter worriedly and said, "Are we going to get in trouble?"

But Carter just shook his head before leaning his forehead against mine and saying, "No. I mean, technically you might get in trouble if we don't get you into your room in the next twenty minutes, but *I'm* going to be totally fine."

I ENDED up making it back to my dorm room just before the dorm parents did their nightly check. After telling Elyse everything that had happened, I went to bed and had the best night's sleep that I'd had in a long time.

The next morning, my mom called to tell Elyse and me that she had a client with a dress emergency and she would need to fly to California. After apologizing over the fact that we'd have to postpone our girls' weekend for a few weeks, she promised to make it up to us before hanging up.

As I finished getting ready for the day, I realized that I'd forgotten to ask her once again about her dating Carter's dad in high school. But then I shrugged it off and went about my day, deciding that maybe it would be best to just ask her about it in person when we were able to get together next.

The next days and weeks went by way too fast. My days were spent in school, my nights and weekends spent with Carter. He showed me more of Eden Falls on the weekends and even took me on a hike to see the waterfall the town was named after.

I'd expected a pretty waterfall, but when we'd first turned the bend and I caught my first glimpse of the gorgeous waterfall, it took my breath away with its crisp blue water and the lush vegetation of the surrounding area. It was definitely the kind of ethereal scene that you'd expect to find in the Garden of Eden—like a place from a dream.

The next weekend Carter took me to the stables at his house and I got to ride a horse for the first time. I'd been afraid that I might get bucked off since the extent of my experience with farm animals was when my mom took me and Elyse to a rodeo in Madison Square Garden when we were eight. But Cambrielle's horse, Starlight, had known just what she was supposed to do with a beginner rider like me, and we were friends by the end of the afternoon.

Basically, Carter and I spent as much time as we could together over the next two weeks doing homework, going to football games, hanging out with our friends and his family whom I was growing to like more and more as the weeks went on. Nash and Cambrielle were basically the extra brother and sister that I'd always wanted. And while Mr. Hastings was out of the country on a three-week retreat that he did each year to recalibrate and just unplug from the hectic world of a billionaire CEO, Mrs. Hastings had been so sweet to me and almost made me feel like part of the family, which was kind of nice since my own mom was so busy developing her new line at the moment.

"So, what are we going to do to celebrate your first ever A on a math test?" Carter asked me one Monday after school. We had just finished doing our homework in the library and had gone up to my dorm room to hang out before he headed home.

"I don't know." I set my books on my desk and looked to where he sat on my bed. "I was thinking dinner at the Italian Amigos might be fun."

"I agree." Carter nodded.

"And maybe follow that up with shakes from Charlie's Food Hut." I sat on the bed beside him.

"Their strawberry shakes are your favorite."

I nodded. Then leaning closer to him, with a smirk on my lips, I said, "But first, I think it would only be right that I thank my tutor properly, since without his help I never would have gotten the A in the first place."

Carter's face lit up and a small smile lifted his cheeks. "And how will you be thanking your tutor?"

I leaned closer, looking at his lips, and whispered, "Like this." Then I kissed him. And even though I'd been able to kiss him several times over the past couple of weeks, my body still reacted like it had the first time. Butterflies fluttered in my stomach. And when his lips slowly grazed my bottom lip, coaxing my mouth to part, my stomach muscles clenched followed by a low swooping sensation as I let myself just get lost in this amazing guy whom I got to call my boyfriend.

My actual, *real* boyfriend.

I ran my fingers along his smooth jaw, and he threaded his fingers into the hair at the nape of my neck.

"Maybe we should just stay here," I mumbled after a moment. "I think this might be better than dinner and shakes."

Carter chuckled against my mouth. "Maybe we'll just have to order in."

"Good idea."

He shifted our positions, so he was leaning against the wall at the head of my bed and I was straddling his lap, and then we were kissing again.

We had already previously decided what boundaries we wanted for our physical relationship for now, so I knew I didn't need to worry about Carter pushing me to have sex with him before I was ready—but that didn't mean I couldn't enjoy all the other fun things we could do before the big step.

He smoothed his hands along the outsides of my thighs. As the nerve endings under my skin sparked to life, I was glad that I hadn't changed out of my school uniform yet and into jeans because having his hands on my bare skin there felt amazing.

Carter pulled away from the kiss. "I know you don't like wearing the same kind of clothes every day. But you in this pleated skirt is kind of the sexiest thing I've ever seen." And when he raked in my legs as he moved his hands up and down, the desire in his eyes made my insides feel like they were being scorched by a wildfire. While I knew that Carter didn't just like me for my looks, I kind of loved that this guy who was on a hotness scale all his own found someone like me sexy.

"I'm glad you like it." I took his tie in my hands and started loosening it for him as I spoke. "I was thinking about wearing a pink off-the-shoulder gown to Cambrielle's soirée this weekend, but maybe I'll wear this instead."

"An off-the-shoulder dress?" Carter asked, intrigue filling his blue eyes.

I nodded, fighting a smile as I undid his tie the rest of the way. "An off-the-shoulder *mini* dress."

I'd originally brought the dress to school because Elyse had told me it made my boobs look awesome and I thought it would be fun to wear to a formal dance if I got asked, but now that I knew Carter was more of a leg guy, I figured I should point out the other assets of the dress. I let go of his tie and pointed to a spot a few inches above my knee. "It hits me about here," I said, peeking to see his reaction. "But the slit goes up to here." I moved my finger a few inches higher.

Carter's eyes went wide when I pointed to the spot just a few inches down my thigh. And after seeming to need a moment to respond, he said, "I think I might need to see this dress." He swallowed hard, his Adam's apple bobbing before he added, "Right now."

I shook my head, grinning from ear to ear since I hadn't expected his reaction to be this good. "Sorry, but you're not allowed to see it until the day of the party."

"But that's five days away," he complained. "How about we just call it my early birthday present?"

"But you don't like celebrating your birthday, remember?"

"I changed my mind," he said quickly. "I love celebrating my birthday. In fact, I think it deserves a week-long celebration."

I laughed at his sudden change of opinion all based on the promise of seeing me in a sexy dress, but I really did want to wait to make a grand entrance at the party and watch his mouth drop open when I walked down to him. "Just wait until Saturday."

He sighed. "Fine."

WE ENDED up ordering in dinner after all since it started raining and we didn't feel like going outside. We ate our tacos and salad at the small table in the corner of my room and then cuddled up on my bed to watch the latest murder mystery movie together, alternating between watching it on my laptop and kissing when it got to the slower parts.

The dorm mom, Heather, walked past my room every twenty minutes or so to make sure we were behaving since she knew Carter was in here. But because my room was at the end of the hall and not many other people had a reason to come this far down, it still felt like we had a good amount of privacy for our movie/make-out session.

I was just unbuttoning Carter's shirt when Elyse barged into the room.

I wanted to remind her about the importance of knocking before swinging the door wide open, which was how we warned each other that someone was about to come in and hopefully avoid walking in on a make-out session. But when her jaw dropped at the sight of Carter and me, I figured her shock was probably a good-enough reminder of its own.

"You might want to stop what you're doing," Elyse said when she noticed that Carter's shirt was already halfway unbuttoned, revealing a good amount of his light brown, muscled chest.

"And why would I want to do that?" I asked, because I was pretty sure I'd been doing exactly what I wanted to do right now.

But Carter, being the gentlemanly sort, got himself back to a sitting position and turned around so he could sit up on the end of my bed. "Is something wrong?" he asked, buttoning his shirt up again.

It was then that I noticed Elyse seemed more agitated than usual. She bit her lip and held out the papers she'd brought with her. "I think I figured out who our dad is."

30

AVA

"YOU FOUND OUT WHAT?" I asked, bolting upright and scooting off my bed to stand in front of my sister.

"I didn't want to say anything until I had more information, but ever since I found out that mom and Carter's dad were so close in high school it got me curious about things," Elyse said, her eyes darting to Carter and then back to me. "At first I thought it must have been just a high-school romance that ended when they graduated, but then I started talking to Mrs. Simmons one day because I saw her in some of the photos from the play mom was in and found out that she was in their grade. We got to talking about things and she told me that Mom and Carter's dad were a pretty serious couple in high school and that everyone had been sure they were going to get married someday."

"Mrs. Simmons told you this?" I furrowed my brow, wondering why Elyse hadn't told me anything about this before.

"Yes." Elyse nodded. "Anyway, I was intrigued by this

because Mom never talked about Mr. Hastings at all, or really said anything about high school for that matter. So I asked her to tell me everything she could about their relationship, since Mom has always been so closed up about her past."

"And what did she say?" I asked. "Did she say why they broke up? Or when?"

"I guess they had to break up when they graduated and Mom had to move back to Israel," Elyse said with a shrug. "Mrs. Simmons said she lost touch with Mom after that, but I guess Mr. Hastings took it pretty badly. She said she thinks he even offered to help Mom get her visa renewed and do whatever to make it work between them, but then Grandpa got really sick at the time and so that complicated things."

"I remember Mom saying something about Grandpa having his heart attack and surgeries right about the time she was starting college."

Elyse nodded. "Yes. And since Mr. Hastings had to help run his family business and Mom didn't feel right about leaving her dad, they ended up just having to accept that they couldn't be together at that time."

"Sad," I said, thinking about how I would feel if I was in my mom's shoes.

Carter cleared his throat. "So how does this lead to you figuring out who your dad is?"

Elyse bit her lip, and after drawing in a shaky breath, she said, "Okay, so according to what Mrs. Simmons said, Carter's dad ended up dating around again about a year later when he realized that the long-distance thing with our mom wasn't going to work out. Mrs. Simmons was at Yale with him and remembers him being even more popular with the girls in college than he was in high school."

"Uh-huh." Carter came to stand by my side and waved his hand like he wanted Elyse to get to the point.

"And he must have met his wife Dawn sometime after that," Elyse said, looking at Carter for confirmation.

"I think they met during his last year at college," Carter said, filling in what he knew of his dad's history. "They dated for about a year, but then Dawn's ex-husband tried to come back into the picture and so there was a bunch of drama. She ended up going back to him for a little while since they had Ian together and she wanted to try and make things work for his sake."

"Is that when your dad went to Guatemala?" I asked Carter.

"Yeah," he said. "He thought some manual labor would help him clear his mind." He tilted his head to the side. "And apparently, the fling with my mom was supposed to help with that, too."

I winced because I knew the repercussions that fling had brought to Carter and his family.

"But didn't your dad get back with Dawn shortly after that?" I asked.

Nash had been born about seven months after Carter, so they couldn't have been broken up for too long, could they?

"I think they got back together that summer."

"Do you know when?" Elyse narrowed her eyes.

"I don't know." Carter ran a hand through his hair, which I'd tousled during our make-out session earlier. "I think it could have been around my dad's birthday."

"And when's that?" Elyse asked, the earnest expression

on her face telling me that this information was really important to her for some reason.

"August thirteenth," Carter said, rubbing his forearm.

"What's going on?" I asked Elyse, my heart pounding because it almost seemed like she was trying to make it sound like my boyfriend's dad might be the mystery man who'd gotten our mom pregnant. "Why does any of this even matter?"

Please don't matter.

Please, please *don't let Mr. Hastings be our dad, too.*

I'd wanted to know who my dad was for my whole life—wanted to know who had given me and Elyse half of our genetic makeup. But if it was Mr. Hastings who had gotten my mom pregnant, I didn't want to hear it.

I'd rather not ever find out who my dad was than find out it was the father of the only guy I'd ever wanted to date.

I couldn't accept that Carter might be my brother.

Elyse handed me the papers she'd been holding on to. "These are some of the photos that Mrs. Simmons took from their five-year reunion."

Carter leaned closer to me so we could look at the images printed on the copy paper together. The first sheet of paper showed a twenty-something version of my mom and Carter's dad posing together for the camera, with Mr. Hastings' arm wrapped tightly around my mom's waist and huge smiles on their faces.

The second page had a photo of them sitting at a round table with a few other people from their graduating class. Mom and Mr. Hastings weren't sitting by each other in this photo, but the camera had captured my mom looking across the table at Mr. Hastings with what I could only interpret as a longing expression on her face.

I knew it was longing because it was exactly the way I'd caught Elyse looking at Mack the past several weeks during our group study sessions.

We Cohen women did not hide our feelings very well.

The next paper had a group shot of everyone who had gone to the five-year reunion. It took a moment to find my mom, but after scanning the rows of faces, I spotted her at the end of the middle row surrounded by random people I didn't recognize.

"Is your dad in this?" I swallowed as I looked up at Carter who was also studying the photos, anxiety visible on his handsome face.

The handsome face that couldn't belong to anyone related to me.

Right?

"Yes," he said after a second, pointing to a spot on the top. "He's right there."

"So there's only one photo of them posing together," I said, trying to persuade everyone that it was all just a major coincidence. Elyse was probably just making something out of nothing because she wanted to know who our dad was as much as I did.

But Elyse just nodded toward the papers I held and said, "There's one more."

I switched the papers around so I could look at the last photo Elyse had printed off. In this one, my mom was sandwiched between Mr. Hastings and another guy with brown hair who I didn't recognize and who was the same height as

Carter's dad. Mack's dad was standing on the other side of Mr. Hastings.

My mom may have been standing slightly closer to Mr. Hastings in the last photo, but that didn't necessarily mean that anything was going on between them that night.

"I don't think this proves anything," I said to Elyse, handing the papers back to her. "It just shows that Mom and Carter's dad were at the same party one night. I think you're doing a lot of mental gymnastics to make this work in your mind."

"You think so?" Elyse raised her eyebrows at me, folding her arms. "Then why don't you ask me when this reunion happened?"

"When did it happen?" Carter asked, looking between my sister and me as if trying to figure this puzzle out.

A strange mix of hope and fear swirled in my gut as I waited for my sister to answer.

Elyse pressed her lips together, and only after my palms had begun to sweat did she say, "It was July twenty-ninth."

July twenty-ninth?

Elyse just stared at me with eyes that were identical to mine, waiting for me to piece together the puzzle she had already solved. But when I didn't understand what she was trying to tell me, she added, "It was July twenty-ninth the summer before we were born."

Oh.

That summer...

My whole body went tingly and a heavy feeling filled my chest, because though I'd been searching for this answer for my entire life, I suddenly wanted to un-hear everything that Elyse had just told me.

Even though I'd never been that great at math, based on the fact that Elyse and I had been born two weeks early, if you subtracted nine months from our due date, we would have been conceived around the end of July or beginning of August of the year our mom had turned twenty-three.

Which meant, our mom had likely gotten pregnant the weekend of her high school reunion.

And there was a huge chance that Carter was our half-brother.

31

CARTER

"ARE you trying to say that your mom got pregnant with you at her high school reunion?" I asked Elyse and Ava after they explained to me why July twenty-ninth was such a significant date to them. "Are you saying that based on the fact that our parents dated seriously in high school and then ended up in a few photos together at their high school reunion, it means my dad was the guy who helped her out with that?"

"We're just saying that he's the strongest candidate we've ever found," Elyse said, watching me with wary eyes, like she was worried I might explode if she said the wrong thing.

And I guess she wasn't far off. Because if I was related to the girl I'd just been making out with a few minutes ago—if I was the *brother* of the girl I'd had fantasies about more times than I'd ever admit—I might just punch a hole through the wall.

Or throw up.

I couldn't decide which urge would win out at the moment.

"So you're saying that our parents slept together this night, and that my dad either didn't know about your existence until very recently, or just chose not to take care of you for the past eighteen years because of some reasons we don't know about?"

"I don't know." Elyse raised her hands in the air. "I'm just figuring these things out right now." She sighed. "It's just what makes the most sense. And with your dad's history of sleeping around and making babies he didn't know about...I guess it's not too unbelievable."

Even though she was talking about my dad and not me, it almost felt like she'd slapped me in the face.

"My dad had a fling one time. That doesn't mean he had unprotected sex with every woman he was mildly attracted to."

"I'm not saying he did," Elyse hurried to say. "But don't you think that if they were both single and unattached at the time, it's possible that they could have gotten carried away when they ran into each other again? Especially when they only broke up the first time because of distance and not because they didn't still care about each other?"

"I don't know." I ran a hand through my hair, my breath coming in short bursts as I tried to think of some kind of reasoning that would prove my dad couldn't have slept with their mom that weekend.

But I was coming up blank, because while my dad was a family man now and had eyes only for Dawn, he'd said before that when he got my own mother pregnant, it had been a time in his life when he'd been a lot more careless.

He'd dated a lot of women that year he and Dawn had been broken up because he'd been trying to numb himself from the pain of losing the woman he loved to her ex-husband.

He and Ava's mom had history. And there was no denying that she was a beautiful woman. She had dark hair, brown eyes, and light brown skin, which was exactly my dad's type.

And even though it wasn't something I'd do now that I had Ava, if Sofia had come back to me last summer and tried to hook up, I probably would have been tempted. Because I didn't know Ava back then and therefore wouldn't have known how much better of a connection I could have had with someone else.

Someone else who might be my *sister*.

I glanced at Ava, and when our gazes locked, I saw the same fear I felt pulsing throughout my body mirrored in her eyes.

"I'm going to be sick." Ava clutched her stomach before sitting down on her bed. She leaned forward and rested her head in her hands.

I wanted to comfort her, to rub her back and tell her that things would be okay, but I suddenly didn't know if doing any of that was even appropriate anymore.

Had I just been making out with my sister?

With someone who was related to me just as much as Cambrielle?

I walked to the corner of the room and sat myself down in one of the chairs, resting my head in my hands just as Ava was doing because this was too much.

Elyse sat on the bed beside Ava and rubbed her back in the way I had wanted to a moment ago. And even though Ava and I weren't thrilled by the prospect of being related, I realized that for Elyse at least, this was probably exciting news. Because for her, she finally solved the mystery she'd been wondering about for years.

This wasn't a bad thing for her. She had no reasons for not wanting my dad to be her father. He was a good guy. She'd seen what a good father he was to me and my siblings, so having him as her father probably was an appealing idea. He was a billionaire. A family man.

He wasn't some creep who had abandoned her mom.

He'd just been the guy who hadn't known about them, just like he hadn't known about me for the first eight years of my life.

Sure, it wasn't a great look for Joel Hastings to have spread his seed so much when he was in his early twenties. But at least with Ava and Elyse's mom, he'd been in love with her at one point. So it wasn't a random fling.

There was still the question of why their mom wouldn't have told him about them, but maybe she had her reasons.

The room was silent for a while as everyone seemed to be processing everything, but then Elyse said, "It does make sense though, right? I mean, Carter's dad did seem really interested in us when we met. He was asking us all sorts of questions, wasn't he? Asking us about our mom and what grade we were in."

Ava turned her head to look at her sister, and when I saw her eyes rimmed with red, it tore at my heart because I didn't want to see her crying. She sighed and said, "I don't know anything right now. I just know that I don't know what I'm going to do when everyone finds out that I've been dating my brother for the past three weeks."

She shifted her gaze to mine, and when our eyes locked, I felt nauseous with dread.

This was going to be a nightmare.

I'd thought that having everyone know Sofia dumped me for a prince was humiliating. But how much worse was it going to be when everyone found out that Ava and I had to break up because we were siblings?

It was going to be a massacre.

32

CARTER

"IS it possible that it could have been anyone else at the reunion?" Ava asked a while later. "What about Mack's dad? He's in the photos from the reunion, too. And from all the other photos I've seen of them in high school, he was good friends with Mom back then, too."

"Do you think that's possible?" Elyse looked at me earnestly, as if I'd have some extra insights into the past that I wasn't around for.

But I shook my head and said, "Mack's birthday is in February. So his mom would have already been expecting him at the time. I'm not sure when Mr. and Mrs. Aarden got married or anything like that, but I'm sure they were together and Dr. Aarden wouldn't have cheated on his wife."

Especially since that was around the time they found out about her first brain tumor. He wouldn't have cheated on Mack's mom when they were going through all of that.

"What about the other guy in that last photo?" Ava asked, seeming to perk up at the possibility of someone besides my dad being her father. "She seemed pretty comfortable with him in the photos."

When Ava stood to grab the papers she'd dropped on the ground earlier, I went to stand next to her to see what the guy looked like again.

I studied the guy with narrowed eyes. I didn't recognize him at all, but he did have a similar hair color as the girls. And if their mom had told them they'd gotten their height from their biological father, this guy was tall enough to match that description.

"Is he in the other photos?" I asked, taking the papers from Ava.

She leaned closer to scan the images with me, and I hated that my body still reacted to her closeness. I forced myself not to think about it; instead, I focused on looking for the guy in the group photo.

"There he is," Ava said, pointing to the same area where my dad and Mack's dad were standing at the top.

"Okay, so he was probably at least friends with my dad and Dr. Aarden if he was by them in several photos," I said as I pulled the group photo up to the top of the stack. I narrowed my eyes as I looked carefully at the people sitting around the table with my dad and Mrs. Cohen. Sure enough, Mr. Aarden was on one side of Mrs. Cohen, and this mystery guy was sitting right on her other side.

Ava and I looked at each other. As if thinking the same thing as me, she said, "Any ideas on how we can find out some info about this guy?"

"I don't know. We could always call your mom and just ask her, right?" I suggested. To me, it seemed like the best way to get answers.

"She's at a really fancy charity ball in New York tonight where they're auctioning off a few of her dresses," Ava said. "She won't answer her phone while she's there."

"Well, we can't call my dad, either, since he's still unreachable for a few days," I said.

But there was someone else who might be able to help us. Someone else who had been in all of the photos from that night, someone who might know who this mystery guy was and what might have gone down at the reunion.

"I think it's time I take you to see Mack's shack," I said. "Maybe Dr. Aarden can help us."

IT WAS STILL RAINING when Ava, Elyse, and I drove up to Mack's house in my truck. It was already eight-thirty at night and more than likely, Dr. Aarden was already in bed since he had brain surgeries that started early in the mornings. But I continued driving toward the modern-style mansion where I'd spent thousands of hours hanging out at with my best friend.

"So this is Mack's shack?" Ava asked as the second biggest house in Eden Falls came into view. She pressed her forehead against the passenger window, her mouth open as she took in the massive house that was lit up by spotlights placed throughout the beautifully landscaped property.

"This is it." I pulled around the curved driveway and parked my truck in front of the path that led to the huge front door. "Ready to go?" I glanced at Ava beside me and then at Elyse who sat behind her.

"Ready," they said together.

All three of us climbed out immediately, eager to solve this mystery. I wasn't exactly sure where Elyse stood with the whole idea of my dad being their father and me being their brother, but from how quickly Ava walked up the cement path under her sister's umbrella, I got the feeling that Ava was just as anxious as I was to prove that my dad couldn't be her father.

We could only hope that was what Dr. Aarden would help us figure out.

Under the protection of the front porch, we closed our umbrellas and propped them beside the rocking chair close to the front door. Then with my heart in my throat, I knocked.

Mack opened the door about thirty seconds later. When he saw us, he stepped back, obviously not expecting us at his house this late. "Hey, guys." He blinked his dark-brown eyes a few times. "What are you doing here?"

I cleared my throat. "We're, uh..." I scratched at a spot behind my ear, not sure I really wanted to tell Mack why we were here. Then I said, "We were hoping to talk to your dad. Is he around?"

"Oh, yeah." Mack stepped back to let us inside and then glanced behind him. "Let me go find him. I think he and my mom were just watching *Finding Your Soulmate*. He'll probably be happy to get out of watching it."

I chuckled at the thought of Dr. Aarden watching the reality dating show with Mrs. Aarden. It was weird to picture a neurosurgeon watching a show where a guy dated thirty different women at once, but I guess it really shouldn't surprise me too much. Dr. Aarden was the kind of husband who would do anything for his wife—even before her cancer came back, he'd done things like that for her.

We only had to wait about a minute before Dr. Aarden appeared in the entryway, wearing a white V-neck shirt and gray sweatpants.

"Hey, Carter." He smiled when he saw me. "Mack says you and your friends needed to talk to me." He glanced at the twins with a curious expression. "Hi, I'm Mack's dad, Brendon Aarden." He held out his hand to Elyse and Ava. "I'm not sure we've met before."

Elyse shook his hand first. "I'm Elyse," she said.

"And I'm Ava." Ava did the same. "We just started going to school with Mack this year."

"It's nice to meet you," Dr. Aarden said to the twins. Then hooking his thumb over his shoulder, he said, "Would you like to sit down?"

"Sure, that would be great," Ava said.

We followed Dr. Aarden into the great room just off the entryway. He took a seat on one couch and the twins and I squished together on the couch across from him.

"So, what can I do for you three?" Dr. Aarden asked, leaning his tall frame against the couch. He'd played basketball in college and had been drafted to play for the NBA, but after Mrs. Aarden was diagnosed with her first brain tumor when she was pregnant with Mack, Dr. Aarden rethought his career choices and ended up going to medical school. He'd been doing his residency at a hospital in New Haven when I first came to Eden Falls and was now one of the best neurosurgeons in the world.

"We were hoping you could help us figure something out," I said, deciding to just jump right into it since it was getting late and I knew he probably had an early morning. "You see, my friends have been trying to solve a puzzle and we were wondering if you might have some of the answers they're looking for."

"Okay." Dr. Aarden ran his thumb and index finger across his chin. "So, what is this puzzle that you're trying to solve?"

I looked at Ava and Elyse, figuring it was best for one of them to take over.

Ava gave me a quick nod and then turned back to Mack's dad. She said, "This is probably going to sound pretty strange, but for the past several years, my sister and I have been on a sort of quest to figure out who our biological father is. We've never had a lot of info to go by since our mom hasn't ever told us very much, but we've been able to find a few clues here and there and have an idea that our father could have been someone she went to the academy with."

"Okay." Dr. Aarden frowned, not seeming to understand how he played a role in helping them yet. "Is your mom someone I would know? I went to the academy, but that was a long, long time ago."

Elyse nodded. "Yes, our mom's name is Miriam Cohen."

"Miriam Cohen?" Dr. Aarden's eyes went wide, and he sat up straighter, leaning forward. "Your mom is Miriam?"

Ava and Elyse glanced at each other, a look of excitement in their eyes at the prospect of Mack's father remembering their mother.

"We found some old photos of our mom with you and your wife and Carter's dad when we were going through some of the old yearbooks at the school," Ava continued.

"And so we figured that she was friends with you guys back then."

"Yes, we were good friends. She and my wife were actually really close back then."

"Yeah?" Elyse asked, her eyes brightening.

"If my wife wasn't already in bed resting, I'd bring her out to meet you, but she hasn't been feeling well lately so..." he drifted off, and I couldn't help but notice the look of grief in his golden-brown eyes.

Whenever I asked Mack about how his mom's health was doing—how the experimental treatments were coming—he made it sound like things were looking up for his mom. But that one look from Dr. Aarden told me that maybe things weren't going as well as they'd hoped. Maybe Mack was acting more optimistic than he felt because it was better than the reality of things.

"Oh, you don't need to get her," Ava said. "In fact, the only thing we really needed tonight was to see if you knew the name of the guy in this photo with you." Ava handed him the paper Elyse had shown us earlier with the photo of Dr. Aarden, my dad, Ms. Cohen, and the random guy we hoped was their father.

Dr. Aarden frowned as he studied the photo. "That's Billy Monaco," he said. "He graduated with us, but we were never really close in high school."

"You weren't?" Ava asked, her lips pouting with disappointment.

Dr. Aarden shook his head and handed the paper back to Ava. "I remember him being really friendly that night, talking to everyone like we'd been the best of friends back in high school, but he was kind of a weird dude."

"He was weird?" Elyse asked, her voice shaking slightly. "Like, weird enough that my mom might have a reason to block him from her life?"

Oh.

I caught onto Elyse's train of thought. Was it possible this Billy Monaco guy was dangerous? And that their mom had never talked about him or involved him in their lives because he was unfit to be around them?

But then Dr. Aarden said, "I don't know if she'd need to do anything like that." He glanced between the three of us confusedly. "What exactly are you three trying to get at here?"

The girls looked at each other, seeming to have some sort of twin telepathic conversation. But when they didn't say anything, I said, "Do you think it's possible that Billy could have convinced their mom to sleep with him at all that night?"

"What?" Dr. Aarden's eyebrows shot up. "Why in the world would you ask me a question like that?"

"I'm sorry," Ava apologized for me. "Carter isn't trying to be inappropriate. It's just that Elyse and I figured out that we could have been conceived around the time of our mom's five-year reunion, and so we're just trying to narrow down our list of suspects to hopefully figure out who our biological father is. Our mom hasn't been very forthcoming with any details and tries to avoid the topic every time we bring it up, so we were hoping that by doing a little digging around of our own we might solve the mystery."

But Dr. Aarden didn't seem to be listening to anything Ava was saying because he just stared at the coffee table between us with a serious expression on his face.

"Dr. Aarden?" Ava asked when he didn't say anything after a moment.

"You're Miriam's actual daughters?" He looked up. And this time, he seemed to study the twins' faces more carefully. As if he was trying to see some sort of resemblance between the girls and their mother. He gave his head a slight shake and then asked, "And did you say you were Mack's age?"

"We didn't say," Elyse answered. "But yes, I guess from what Carter tells us, we're a couple of months younger than your son."

Mr. Aarden just stared at the twins, like he couldn't believe what he was seeing. Then under his breath, I thought I heard him say, "I was told she'd had a miscarriage."

And with those words, something was triggered in my brain.

Something that I hadn't thought of since hearing my dad's conversation in his office a few weeks ago.

My dad had accused a woman for lying about a miscarriage. He told her that he'd done the math, which led him to the conclusion that she'd lied to him about losing her pregnancy. One of the last things I'd heard him ask the person on the other end of the line was 'if the girls knew.'

And from the past few minutes I could only assume that he'd been asking Miriam Cohen if her twin daughters—her beautiful twin daughters, Ava and Elyse—had known that he was their father.

Even though I hadn't heard her answer on the other end of the line, didn't know if she'd even given him an answer, *I* knew the answer to his question.

The answer was no.

Her daughters had not known who their father was.
Until today.

33

AVA

AFTER EXPLAINING TO ELYSE, Carter, and me about how he'd heard my mom was pregnant but had thought she'd had a miscarriage because that was what she'd told everyone, Dr. Aarden left the room, saying he needed to make a few phone calls.

"Who do you think he's calling?" Elyse asked Carter when Dr. Aarden disappeared into what looked like an office just down the hall from the great room we'd been sitting in for the past ten minutes.

"You want my honest guess?" Carter asked, a wary look in his blue eyes.

"Yes," I said, though from his foreboding expression I wasn't sure that I really did want to know. I had a sinking feeling it was the exact answer we'd been hoping to disprove by coming here.

Carter sighed. "I would bet that he's calling my dad right now."

"I-is your dad back to a place where he has service?" I

asked. Carter had told me before that his dad had planned to fly back home in time for Cambrielle's party but wouldn't be in contact with anyone until then.

"He doesn't have his cell phone turned on—just has it with him in case of an emergency. But Dawn has the number for the house that he's staying at, so I'm guessing that if Dr. Aarden can't get ahold of my dad on his cell, he'll call Dawn for the info."

"So do you think he's our dad then?" Elyse asked, a look of hope in her golden-brown eyes.

She had never minded the idea of Carter's dad being our father in the first place, so none of this was bad news to her.

It was just really inconvenient for me and Carter and our feelings for each other.

Carter blew out a low breath before saying, "I think there's a strong chance that he is."

We walked out to Carter's truck. On the drive back to the school through the rain-covered streets of Eden Falls, Carter told Elyse and me about the phone conversation he'd overheard his dad having the day after he'd first met Elyse and me. And even though Carter hadn't heard very much, he'd heard enough that I was suddenly more scared than ever that Carter and I were related.

I knew I should be happy for Elyse and myself.

Happy that after seventeen years of longing and searching, we'd finally found our dad. And it wasn't just any random guy but Mr. Hastings. A guy who—even though I'd only been around him briefly—I knew was a really great man. The kind of dad most girls would dream of having. He was successful, he took amazing care of his family, and he had a great relationship with each of his children, as far as I could tell.

We'd basically hit the jackpot where biological fathers were concerned. And not just that, we'd have Cambrielle and Nash who already felt like family to me as our brother and sister.

It was the kind of situation that I'd dreamed of having my whole life. The picture-perfect family. The amazing house. The answers I'd been searching for.

I should be ecstatic at the chance of being Joel Hastings' daughter—an heir of the seventh richest man in the United States.

But I couldn't be happy about it right now, because if I was his daughter and if Cambrielle and Nash were my new brother and sister, then it meant that Carter was also my brother. And while I knew he was a great brother to his siblings and would be a great brother to Elyse as well, I didn't want him to be *my* brother.

I didn't want to share even an ounce of his father's DNA. Because if I did, then everything I'd felt for him over the past few weeks would no longer be a beautiful and magical thing.

It would be twisted and disgusting and actually illegal.

Marrying your half-brother may have been acceptable a few centuries ago—back in the day when kings married their own sisters to maintain a higher quality of noble blood in the royal family. And sure, Zeus might have been able to marry his sister Hera because he was the most powerful of the Greek gods.

But that wasn't how things worked in twenty-first century America.

Brothers and sisters did not have romantic relationships

with each other. They didn't fall in love and date and kiss and eventually get married. They didn't have babies and build dream homes together and live happily ever after.

That kind of thing was just simply not done.

It made me feel icky inside just thinking about it.

I'd just been making out in my dorm room with my *brother!* I'd just been unbuttoning his shirt and letting my hands explore his chest and arms, and get my fingers tangled in his hair. I'd let him run his hands along my arms and back and lay his strong body on top of mine, let our tongues dance together in a way that made my belly swirl with heat. I'd let him kiss me until my lips were swollen and his five o'clock shadow chaffed at my sensitive skin.

I'd fantasized about having a future where he was the first person I talked to in the morning, and the last person I saw before I closed my eyes to sleep at night.

I'd thought about building a life with Carter after high school, having him by my side through all the big and little events of our lives, the twists and turns, the good times and the bad.

I just hadn't imagined that I'd be doing those things as his sister.

But now that the path of my life was shifting in front of my eyes, I saw the years stretching ahead of me. Instead of being the bride at his wedding, I'd be the bridesmaid. Instead of having his babies, I'd be sitting in the waiting room with the rest of the family as we waited for Carter to come out with a huge smile on his face to tell us that his wife—his wife who wasn't me—had given birth to a beautiful baby girl or boy.

I'd get to hold his babies and watch them as they grew

from children and into adults, but they wouldn't be mine. They'd be someone else's. They'd belong to some lucky girl who got to have everything I wanted because her mom hadn't kept a huge secret from her her whole life.

If my mom had just told me the truth from the very beginning, then I would have met Carter years ago and I would have known from the start that he was off-limits. I never would have thought of him as anything but an older brother from the first day he came here from Guatemala.

I would have thought his bright blue eyes looked beautiful against his tan skin. I would have been intrigued to get to know this human who'd had a very different upbringing than me.

But I never would have looked at him with the longing I've felt for him ever since the first day we met, because I would have known from the start that he was my brother.

While lots of other girls would get crushes on him, I never would have been tempted by his exotically handsome good looks because the rules for our relationship would have been set from the beginning.

I wouldn't be dealing with these confusing feelings swirling around inside of me every time I looked at him, like I did right now.

Yes, even now when I *knew* that we were related, I still wanted to find an excuse to ignore the facts and find myself in his arms again. To have just one final moment where I could soak everything up and know it had to mean goodbye.

But I couldn't have that.

Couldn't even let him know that I wanted one last moment with him.

Because it was twisted.

It was forbidden.

It was *wrong*.

The city passed in a rainy blur as we drove through the small town, and I barely registered where we were until Carter pulled his truck to a stop on the front drive of the academy.

"I'm going to head inside," Elyse said from the backseat, as if sensing I needed a moment alone with Carter before heading up to our room. "I'll see you in a little bit."

"I'll be up soon," I said.

Carter and I sat in silence as we watched Elyse walk up the steps leading to the school, her umbrella protecting her from the rain. And even after she disappeared inside, we still didn't speak right away.

A full two minutes passed with just the sound of our breathing and the rain hitting the windshield before Carter cleared his throat and said, "Interesting day, huh?"

I glanced sideways to peek at him. When our gazes locked, his sad eyes told me he felt as hopeless as I did.

I drew in a long, shaky breath and released it slowly through pursed lips before I said, "Yeah. Interesting day."

What else was there to say?

Nothing.

I had nothing to say because talking about tonight would just make it all the more real.

And I didn't want any of it to be real.

We sat there for another minute, and I just watched the windshield wipers wipe the rain away in a rhythmic motion. But since it was getting late and I knew we both had classes early in the morning, I finally moved to unbuckle my seatbelt. "I guess I better get inside."

Carter nodded, his Adam's apple bobbing as he swallowed. "I-I'll walk you to the door."

I knew I should just walk up the steps by myself and get used to the reality where Carter didn't do gentlemanly things for me like opening doors for me and walking me to the school to make sure I got there safely, but I found myself saying, "Thank you."

He grabbed his umbrella from where he'd stored it between his seat and the driver's side door. Then he stepped out and walked around the truck to let me out, holding the umbrella up and over my head.

For a moment, he looked like he wanted to offer me his arm but seemed to reconsider a split second later. So we ended up walking side by side with zero contact between our bodies.

"Thanks for walking me to the door," I said to Carter once we were at the top step.

"Of course." He nodded, half of his face lit from the overhead light, the other shadowed in the dark night.

I knew I should go inside and head upstairs—it was getting late and I was exhausted from the emotional evening —but I didn't want to say goodbye yet. I was planning to call my mom when I got inside and ask her to finally give me the answers I deserved to have for the past seventeen years. But I knew that once she confirmed everything we'd discovered, it would just make this nightmare more real.

And I didn't want it to be totally real just quite yet.

Carter didn't seem to be in a hurry to leave, either, because he just stood there, watching me, studying my face like he was committing this last night together to his memory.

"I hate this," I finally said, after we'd just stared at each other for a minute.

"Me too."

He closed his umbrella and set it against the stone wall, and then took my hands to pull me into the little alcove that was protected from the rain.

He sighed, still holding my hands, rubbing his thumbs across my knuckles. "I wish we could go back to a couple of hours ago."

I bit my lip and nodded, a sudden surge of emotion taking over me. I wiped at my eyes and pushed out a low breath, hoping to keep the tears at bay. "I should be happy. I know I should be happy that I may finally have the answers I've always wanted."

"But you're not," Carter finished for me, understanding exactly how I felt without me needing to say the words.

I cast my gaze down at his shoes because looking at his face was hard right now. "I don't want to be your sister." My voice broke. "I don't want any of this."

He sighed and pulled me against his chest, wrapping his arms around me and smoothing his hands up and down my back in a comforting gesture. "I don't want you to be my sister, either," he mumbled into my hair, his hot breath sending chills racing across my shoulders.

We just held each other for a long moment, breathing deeply. I pressed my ear to his chest, listening to his heartbeat that had become a comfort to me over the past few weeks. It was still as steady and as strong as it had been the first time I'd listened to it, but now, instead of making me feel excited, it just made me sad. Because this was probably the last time I'd ever have an excuse to listen to it. Brothers and sisters didn't hug each other like this.

But Carter felt so good. He was just the right height for me to tuck myself under his chin. His narrow waist the perfect size for me to wrap my arms around. His signature cologne just the right combination of clean and woodsy with a subtle citrus overtone.

He smelled like happiness, and maybe a little like love, too.

My heart squeezed with that thought.

Getting over Carter was going to be so hard.

I rubbed my face into his chest, wishing that it would help me wipe away reality.

He sighed again and smoothed one hand down the crown of my head, down my hair, and back up until he cradled the nape of my neck in his hands. He coaxed my face to look up at him. He looked deeply into my eyes, then his gaze traveled to my lips. "I should probably go home," he whispered, the regret in his voice clear as a summer day. He met my eyes again, and after releasing another long breath and squeezing me closer, he mumbled, "This is so hard."

"I know," I said quietly. And then, to keep myself from wanting to kiss him since our faces were only inches away, I stood on my tiptoes and wrapped my arms around his neck to hug him tighter.

He wrapped his arms around my waist again and pulled me with him as he leaned against the stone wall.

We stood like that for another long moment, and it felt like my heart was trying to beat its way into his chest. But then Carter straightened up and slid his hands away from my back and to my hips, signaling that he was really going to leave now.

I released my arms from behind his neck and made myself take a step back, forcing some space between us again.

"Good night, Ava," he said, tucking some hair behind my ear—and even though it was just a simple touch, it still sent sparks racing across my scalp.

"Good night, Carter," I said.

He stepped out of the alcove, actually about to leave me for real. After opening his umbrella and holding it over his head, he turned back toward me one last time. With a shrug, he said, "Just think—you may have finally found your dad after all these years. It's what you've always wanted, right?"

He didn't wait for me to respond, though. He just started down the steps and headed to his truck whose engine was still running. And as I watched him, I couldn't help but think that the universe was really cruel. Because it turned out that finding what I always thought I wanted was making me give up what I actually did want: Carter.

ELYSE and I tried video-calling our mom, but it immediately went to voicemail.

"Try again," I told my sister. The charity ball should have ended by now, and unless she had suddenly morphed into the early bird that she'd never been before, she should be awake.

Elyse pressed the button to call our mom again, but just like before, we only got her voicemail.

Was she avoiding us?

I grabbed my phone from where I'd dropped it on my bed when I came in and called her from there. But just like the previous two calls from Elyse's phone, this one ended with my mom's voicemail as well.

"Do you think she's still at the ball?" Elyse asked when I tried calling a fourth time with the same result.

"I don't know," I said. And since I was feeling majorly bitter at the moment, I added, "She's probably already heard from Carter's dad or something and is scrambling for what to do now that her secret is out."

"Probably." Elyse sat on her bed with a sigh.

I was considering calling Mom a fifth time, but just as I was about to press the button to dial her number a text came through from her.

> Mom: Sorry. Can't talk right now.

Can't talk, my eye.

"Did she just message you?" Elyse asked, noticing I was typing a response back to our mother.

"Yep." I enunciated the p at the end of the word with a pop.

Elyse came over to sit by me so she could watch the conversation I was having with our mom.

> Me: Since you seem to be busy, I'm just going to cut to the chase. Has our dad been hiding in Eden Falls this whole time?

I sent the message through, my heart pounding in my temples. My text went from *delivered* to *read*, and Elyse and I just waited...

And waited...

And waited for her to respond.

I held my breath as the conversation dots showed on her side of the messaging screen.

But then the dots disappeared.

"She's probably scrambling right now," I said to Elyse.

The dots reappeared again. I sat up straighter,

wondering if she was finally going to tell us the truth for once in our life.

A text came through a moment later.

> Mom: I'll explain everything this weekend.

She'll explain everything this weekend?

She'd had seventeen freaking years to explain things to us. She could tell us right now.

But before I could text that to her, she sent us another text.

> Mom: I'll tell you everything soon. Until then, please don't go around asking more people questions.

What? Did she actually have the gall to tell us to stop trying to find the answers on our own, after basically leaving us with no other option but to figure it out ourselves since she was never open about the truth?

My hands shook and rage coursed through me as I typed my response.

> Me: Are you serious right now? Don't ask questions? This is my life, Mom. I freaking deserve to know who my father is. Elyse and I both deserve to know who gave us half of our DNA! You don't get to decide everything!

I was fuming! Who the heck did she think she was to still keep this from us? I had tried to give her the benefit of the doubt. To believe that she had her reasons and that maybe she was right to keep us from him and him from us.

But if Mr. Hastings was our dad?

If that kind man who I'd only ever heard good things about since moving to this town was my dad, then maybe my mom was actually in the wrong. Maybe I'd been raised by a deranged woman without even knowing it.

My phone vibrated with a text.

> Mom: Just give me some time to figure this all out. You'll have your answers soon enough.

> Me: You've had 18 freaking years to figure this crap out, Mom. Elyse and I deserve answers.

I rubbed a hand across my forehead, feeling the stress inside me building and building.

Elyse and I watched my phone's screen for the next few minutes, waiting for our mom to respond. But after five minutes passed and no messages came through, I tossed my phone on the pillow and threw myself back against my mattress. I yelled out, "You suck, Mom."

35

AVA

I WENT to bed after crying angry, frustrated tears into my pillow for a while. But instead of finding sleep, my mind just ran on an endless loop of worrying about Carter being my brother, worrying about how everyone at school was going to react when they found out about it, and then worrying about how everything was going to work.

Would my mom finally fess up to everything? Would Mr. Hastings request a DNA test? What would Mrs. Hastings do? Would Cambrielle and Nash be excited? Would Elyse and I have to leave the school dorm and move in with the Hastings family since we were related?

Where would Elyse and I sleep? Would it be in the same wing as the rest of the Hastings kids? Or would we be put on the other side of the house because they knew Carter and I had a complicated relationship and would need some space to figure things out?

Or would our mom take us out of the school and away

from Eden Falls because she really didn't want us to have any kind of association with Mr. Hastings?

Needless to say, I didn't sleep well Monday night because my brain just wanted to worry about all the possible scenarios that might arise from this.

Elyse and I agreed before we went down to breakfast the next morning that we wouldn't tell anyone about what we'd discovered the night before. We didn't have any for-sure answers yet, and so until we did, we didn't want to trigger any of the gossip mills at the school.

When I sat next to Carter during math, I asked him if he'd heard anything from his dad. He shook his head and said, "Nothing yet."

I released a long sigh, not sure how I felt about his dad staying silent just like my mom. As long as I didn't know for sure, there was still hope that this was all just a huge misunderstanding. That my dad could still be some random one-night stand and it didn't happen on my mom's high school reunion night. There was still hope that I wasn't in love with my half-brother.

But being in limbo wasn't exactly that great, either, because I couldn't fully relax. As long as everything was still up in the air, I couldn't really make plans for what to do next.

Carter cleared his throat, bringing me back to the present. "I, um, I should probably let you know that I'm not going to be able to make it to our tutoring session after school today."

"You're not?" I looked up at him, my chest sinking a little.

He nodded. "I had some things come up."

I studied his face, trying to figure out if he was just

making up excuses for why he couldn't spend time alone with me today, when so far this year he'd never had anything interfere with our tutoring sessions. Was this his way of breaking things off?

Was sitting at the same table with me disgusting to him now?

He was sitting as far as he could from me. Whereas over the past few weeks, we couldn't seem to sit close enough during math, with our thighs glued together and our fingers entangled under the table so we could hold hands while Mrs. Simmons taught in the front of the room.

Carter must have noticed that I'd just realized how he was hugging the other end of the table because he sent me an apologetic look.

But he didn't move to scoot closer, either.

I pressed my lips together and nodded slowly before saying, "I'll see if Elyse can work with me after school."

She had taken Statistics the year before and was in Calculus right now, but she was smart enough that she'd probably remember the material and could help me if I needed it.

I ENDED up not needing much assistance from Elyse with my math homework, so I took that as a good sign that maybe I was finally understanding this math thing for once in my life. If tutoring me was too difficult for Carter to bear from here on out, maybe I would be fine math-wise and not need his help anymore.

Or maybe the school could assign me someone new. A girl this time, so I wouldn't be at risk of falling in love with another math tutor who might be related to me, since apparently, I had bad luck with that.

Carter didn't show up to our Thursday tutoring session, either. He didn't give me a heads up or anything about it this time. He simply just didn't show up, and I ended up waiting in the library for a full hour after my texts to him had gone unanswered.

When we had our regularly scheduled study session with everyone that evening, Carter didn't show again. He usually came to our Thursday night study sessions, so I could only assume his absence had something to do with me.

"Do you know where Carter is tonight?" I asked Cambrielle as we worked on our AP Biology assignment. Even though Cambrielle was a grade below us all, she was another Hastings family genius and was taking a lot of the AP classes that everyone else did this year.

"I think he's hanging out with Mack and Hunter tonight." she said with a shrug. "Mack's mom hasn't been doing so well this week, and I think he needed some time to blow off steam."

So maybe he wasn't avoiding me? But this was the first time I'd heard anything about Mrs. Aarden being sick.

I frowned. "What's going on with Mack's mom?"

Cambrielle shifted in her seat, an uncomfortable expression crossing her face before she said, "She has cancer."

"What?" I couldn't keep from asking as a feeling of shock flooded me.

I looked at Elyse who seemed just as surprised by this

fact. I knew I'd been living in my own little bubble with Carter ever since school started, but was I really that bad of a friend to not even notice that anything was going on with Mack?

He always seemed so upbeat most of the time—always the first guy to crack a joke when we were hanging out.

I never would have guessed that he had anything going on that was bothering him aside from the regular things a teenage guy worried about.

Cambrielle seemed to realize that this was the first I'd ever heard of it, so she explained, "His mom had a brain tumor a long time ago, like before I was born. They were able to remove it back then and she was really healthy for a long time. But they found another one this summer, and this one is harder to treat."

"So...is she dying then?" I asked, my stomach and chest feeling with dread.

Wasn't Mack's dad, like, a neurosurgeon or something?

Scarlett, who had looked up from her studying, set her pencil down on her notebook and said, "Mack doesn't really like to talk about it. I think he's been hoping that if he doesn't talk about it, then it'll make it so it's not as real. But yeah, it's not good." Scarlett swallowed, eyeing Cambrielle briefly for confirmation. "I think the doctors say that she'll be lucky if she makes it to Thanksgiving."

Oh no.

Tears instantly pricked at my eyes as I thought about what that meant for Mack. I looked across the table to Elyse and saw she had tears in her eyes as well.

"I wish I'd known," I said, wiping at my eyes with the sleeve of my jacket.

Cambrielle let out a shaky breath, looking torn up about the subject herself. "It's been rough on Mack."

As I watched her try to keep her lips from trembling with emotion, I realized that she could be having a hard time with this as well. She was next-door neighbors to the Aardens. Their dads were best friends. She was probably a lot closer to Mack and his family than the rest of us.

And now that I thought about it, she and Mack did seem to have a special sort of relationship. Mack was always teasing her and her brothers about taking her out on dates to Eden Falls version of "make-out point."

But was it possible there was something going on behind the scenes that no one had picked up on?

Because for all of the flirting Mack did at school—even flirting with Elyse and me on occasion—I had yet to see him go on a date.

But then again, dating was probably the last thing a person wanted to focus on when he was worried about seeing his mom at Christmas.

Oh Mack. My heart hurt for him just thinking about it.

Cambrielle blew out another long breath before forcing a smile and saying, "Anyway, that's where all the guys are tonight. I'm just hoping the soirée this weekend will help cheer everyone up a little."

Right.

The soirée.

As in, the party where I had hoped to flirt and dance with Carter all night.

The party where I would now be forced to watch him hold other girls from school in his arms instead as he led them around the dance floor.

Suddenly, the soirée didn't sound like so much fun anymore.

If I didn't know how much work Cambrielle and her mom had put into planning it, I'd probably look for an excuse not to go. But since she might just be calling me sister in the near future, I should probably try to not start things off on the wrong foot—even though it was going to be complete torture to see how amazing Carter looked in his suit and know I could never touch him the way I wanted to ever again.

"Did you still want all of us to come over early to get ready together?" Elyse asked Cambrielle, jumping on the subject change.

"Yes." Cambrielle's eyes lit up, seeming grateful for the opportunity to discuss something other than Mack and his situation. "I'm just dying for you all to see my dress."

"Did you end up going with the purple one you showed me last week?" Elyse asked.

Cambrielle nodded. "We just got it back from the tailor this week and it's going to be epic."

They continued chatting about all the plans Cambrielle had made for the evening. And though Elyse seemed more than excited for the party our possible half-sister had planned, I only half-listened as they discussed the decorations and the live string quartet Cambrielle and her mom had secured for the event.

Who knew, maybe everything would be all cleared up by the party and there would be some other explanation for who my biological father was that had nothing to do with Mr. Hastings or anyone else in Eden Falls. Maybe the party would be one of the highlights of my senior year, and I'd get to dance the night away with Carter and laugh over the hysteria of the past few days.

But I'd learned a long time ago to not get my hopes up too high where the truth about my father was concerned, so I'd just be holding my breath until then.

36

CARTER

I SUCCESSFULLY AVOIDED SEEING Ava for the rest of the school week, aside from the few classes we had together. I didn't go to any of our after-school study sessions —chickening out on tutoring her and instead opting to study on my own or hang out with Mack instead. During lunch, instead of eating with the crew at our usual table, I went to a chess club meeting on Wednesday and a math club meeting on Thursday—even though I wasn't actually planning to participate in either one of those clubs this year. On Friday, I offered to take Mack to lunch at Charlie's Food Hut because their burgers were his favorite and he looked like he could use a break from everything after his mom had another bad seizure.

Then on Friday night, instead of going to the football game with everyone else, I opted to stay behind and hang out with Dawn. Talking to Mack about his mom made me feel sentimental about my own mothers. And even though my biological mom wasn't here anymore and the thirteenth anniversary of the last day I'd seen her was coming up on Monday, Dawn had been an amazing mom to me for almost a decade now. So I wanted to show her how much I appreciated her treating me like her own flesh and blood and try to do something special just for her.

Since my dad was still out of town until the next day, I asked her to go on a mother/son date night. We had a good time eating dinner at her favorite restaurant in town and watched her favorite movie—*The Proposal*—in the comfy living room.

I was able to keep the conversation on her work, the books she'd been reading, and the podcasts she'd been listening to lately, since she was the one to get me into personal development in the first place. But when the movie ended and she was washing the big popcorn bowl we'd shared, before calling it a night, she looked at me with concern etched in her green eyes and asked, "Is everything okay, Carter? You've seemed a little off the past few days."

"I'm okay," I said, hoping I sounded convincing enough that she wouldn't press me.

But since Dawn was never one to just let things go, she narrowed her eyes and said, "I've missed seeing Ava around this week." She rinsed the soapy bubbles off the stainless-steel bowl. "You two seemed to be getting along really well. Did something happen?"

I leaned against the counter beside her and shoved my hands into the pockets of my sweatpants as I tried to figure out how to answer her question. I didn't want to say that Ava and I had broken up, since we hadn't really done that. I also didn't want to say anything about why things were so up in the air between us, since I had no idea if Mr. Aarden had gotten hold of my dad, or if my dad had said anything to Dawn yet. So I simply settled with, "We're just taking a little break right now."

"Is there anything I can do to help?" Dawn asked, setting the bowl on a towel to dry. "Anything you'd like advice on?"

"No." I shook my head and looked down at my bare feet for a moment before meeting her worried brown eyes again. "We just needed to cool things a little, that's all."

Dawn studied my face, looking like she wasn't quite sure she believed me, but then she patted my arm and said, "Well, I hope we'll be seeing more of her again soon. It was nice seeing you so happy again."

I nodded, swallowing hard because Dawn was right. I'd been really happy with Ava—possibly the happiest I'd ever been in my life because she was the first person with whom I could truly be myself.

But instead of admitting any of that, I simply said, "I'm sure she'll be back again soon."

I just hoped it was as my girlfriend and not because she was my sister.

37

AVA

ELYSE and I still hadn't heard anything from our mom by the time the soirée rolled around on Saturday night. She'd said she'd explain everything this weekend, but so far all we'd gotten was radio silence.

It honestly wouldn't surprise me if she'd just jumped on a plane and headed to Paris so she wouldn't have to face this situation. I had that little faith in her at the moment.

Since there was nothing I could do besides move forward as best I could, I headed over to the Hastings' estate with my sister and Scarlett and tried to mentally prepare myself for the evening ahead.

"I know it's probably a little over the top," Cambrielle said with excitement in her bright blue eyes as she led us up the stairs to her bedroom where we'd be getting ready for the party. "But my mom and I hired a glam squad to help us get ready for tonight."

"A what squad?" Elyse asked when we made it to the top of the landing.

"A glam squad," Cambrielle repeated. "Meaning, we have people here to help us with our hair and makeup."

"Really?" Elyse asked, sounding more excited than expected since she wasn't as into dressing up as I was.

Cambrielle nodded. "They're setting everything up in my room already."

And that seemed to be all the explanation Elyse and Scarlett needed to pick up their pace and hurry down the hall toward Cambrielle's room with her.

As they curved around a corner, I slowed my pace to come to a stop in front of the family portrait I'd looked at my first day in the Hastings' house. But this time, instead of admiring their clothes and the contented vibe the family exuded, I focused on the face of Mr. Hastings.

I looked at his blond hair. His high cheekbones. His aqua-blue eyes that matched the rest of his children's eyes. I tried to see something in his face or his expression that would remind me of what I saw every time I looked in the mirror or in the face of my identical twin sister. But aside from him having a similar hairline and coloring and being tall, I didn't see anything that would necessarily persuade me to think we were related.

But maybe that was because I didn't *want* to see any similarities in this man and myself.

I sighed, looking at the rest of the family who was smiling down at me. They did seem like a happy family. I knew they weren't perfect, since no family was, but as I studied them, I did feel my heart softening to the idea of being one of them. I had always wanted to have both a mom and a dad who loved me. Wanted brothers and even another sister, too. I could probably be very happy as a member of this family someday...once I got over Carter, that is.

Even though it was just a photograph, Carter's eyes seemed to see straight into me, and it almost felt as if the real Carter was looking at me.

Was it crazy that I wanted to be a part of Carter's family, but also be his girlfriend?

To wish for a world where I could have the kind of guy I'd always dreamed of falling in love with want me back, but also be part of his family at the same time.

I guess that was how it ended up working for most people. When you married a person, you married into their family.

The universe just wanted to make things more complicated for me than it did for the typical teen girl.

I was just giving my possible family one last glance before heading down the hall to Cambrielle's room when a door down the hall opened and Carter stepped out, looking halfway dressed for the evening.

He wore his gray suit pants and black socks. His white button-up shirt was on but still currently unbuttoned, and he held two ties in his hands—one navy, the other pink—almost like he'd been on his way to ask someone which tie he should wear for tonight.

His hair was still tousled in the way that I loved, and I had the urge to run my fingers through it just to see if it was as soft as I remembered. Or if it too had changed this week like his apparent feelings for me had.

He shut his bedroom door and finally noticed me when he started walking down the hall in my direction.

"Oh h-hi," he said, startling a little as he took in my

appearance, apparently not expecting to see me this early for the party.

"Hi," I said, tucking some hair behind my ear, suddenly feeling shy after not seeing much of him this week.

"Hi," he said again. But then, after staring blankly at me for a second, he gave his head a quick shake and said, "I was just going to ask Cambrielle which tie she thought would look better for tonight. But since you're here..." He held up the ties in his hands, the opening in his dress shirt widening with the movement and revealing enough of his muscular chest to distract me for a second. "M-maybe you could help instead since you have such an eye for fashion."

"Sure." I set my dress bag and shoes on the floor. "I-I can try to help."

He stepped closer, and only when he noticed my gaze raking in his exposed, tanned chest did he seem to realize that he'd left his room without buttoning his shirt.

"Sorry," he said, his cheeks flushing as he looked down at his all-too-defined eight-pack abs. "I forgot what I looked like."

"I-it's okay," I said, meeting his gaze through my lashes. And before I could stop myself, I added, "Your hands are full. Do you want me help you with that?"

"With my shirt?" he asked, his voice sounding slightly higher than it usually did.

I nodded. "Yeah."

I was probably a glutton for punishment for wanting an excuse to stand close to Carter for a few seconds even though he'd been avoiding me all week, but my body craved his nearness.

Craved the chance to touch him for even just a few

seconds, especially since he'd been hugging the other end of the table in our math class all week.

And buttoning his shirt was innocent enough, right?

He'd been about to go to Cambrielle for help, hadn't he? So me helping him with this couldn't be too taboo, could it?

Not that it would make me not want to do it if it was.

I stepped closer, close enough that I caught a faint whiff of his familiar cologne, and started buttoning his shirt from the bottom.

My hands shook slightly as I took the freshly pressed cotton in my fingers, my stomach fluttering with butterflies as I breathed him in. But I managed to slowly button each one on my way up, my fingers only grazing across his warm skin and making his stomach muscles twitch a few times.

"Thanks for your help in making me more appropriate," he whispered into my hair, leaning closer as I worked on the button at the top of his collar.

Goosebumps raced across my skin from the warmth of his breath, but I forced my expression to remain neutral as I met his blue-eyed gaze. "Of course."

The button hooked through the hole at the top easily, and even though I wanted to smooth my hands down his chest, wanted to have an excuse to touch him longer, I forced myself to take a step back, clasping my hands behind me for good measure.

He studied my face for a moment, probably noting the flush of my cheeks, the shyness of my gaze, and every other physical sign of my attraction for him. But then, seeming to remember that we weren't supposed to notice things like that about each other anymore, he cleared his throat. He held the two ties up again and asked in a soft voice, "Which one do you think I should wear tonight?"

I studied the ties, comparing the two colors against his skin tone and eyes. The navy blue would look nice, very professional and appropriate for any occasion. But since I liked a little pop of color and the pink actually looked really good next to his tan skin, I said, "I'd go with the pink if I were you."

"Yeah?" he asked.

"That's my favorite, anyway. But if you like the blue better it would look great, too."

"Pink is good," he said.

And as if to show that the decision was made, he looped the pink tie around his neck.

I bent down to pick up my things on the floor, deciding I should probably go to Cambrielle's room now even though all I wanted to do was find a reason to stay and talk to Carter since this was the longest we'd been alone in what seemed like forever.

I wanted to ask him why he'd been treating me like a pariah all week. Why he'd skipped out on our tutoring session when I still needed his help.

"Is that the dress you were talking about?" Carter pointed to the dress bag when I looped it over my arm.

I looked at the black bag, remembering how I'd teased him just a few days ago about how high the slit hit on my thigh. "This is it." My cheeks burned a little because there was still a huge part of me that hoped Carter would like how I looked in it tonight.

He looked at the bag again. It seemed like he wanted to say something about the dress, or maybe something else about tonight, but then he gave his head a small shake and said, "I'm sure there'll be a lot of guys dying to dance with you when they see you tonight."

And there it was.

Other guys...

As in: Not. Him.

My vision blurred as the pain of that thought rushed over me.

We were really over, weren't we?

Carter swallowed and lifted his eyes to mine. Just as I feared, there was a finality in his expression that made me feel cold all over.

This was him saying goodbye.

This was him saying we were over and any thoughts I might have entertained about us being together were just me being foolish.

When he'd avoided seeing me all week, when he barely talked to me at school, I'd known that he was probably putting distance between us because things were just awkward with us not knowing what the future held.

But maybe...maybe he just hadn't cared about me in the same way I'd cared for him after all. Maybe saying goodbye to what we'd been wasn't any harder to him than the simple flip of a switch to turn his feelings off.

Maybe once he found out that we could be related, he'd been able to think through his attraction for me and decide that none of it had mattered in the first place.

I didn't know which hurt worse: the possibility that Carter had never cared for me like I'd thought and it had all been just something I'd exaggerated in my head, or that he had cared but was able to turn it off and move on in a matter of a few days.

I'd been told growing up that love was always somewhat unrequited. That even when a couple was married, one partner's feelings were usually stronger than the other's.

But I'd thought that Carter and I could have been the exception. That maybe our love for each other was equal.

But from the stony way he was looking at me as he practically told me to dance with and date other guys, I knew I must have been wrong. Maybe I really had cared about him more than he'd cared for me.

Maybe moving on was as easy for him as turning the page in a book and starting the next chapter of his life with someone else.

And because I never wanted to be seen as the one left wanting in whatever situation I was in, I lifted my chin and straightened my shoulders like I had that day in the Italian Amigos when he'd told me that falling in love with me wouldn't be an issue. I said, "I guess it's a good thing I brought my best dancing heels because I intend to dance with as many cute guys as I can tonight to make up for lost time."

His eyes tightened as my words hung in the air between us, and for a second, I regretted saying them. But then he said, "Then I'll try not to get in the way of all those cute guys for you tonight." He stepped to the side and gestured for me to continue down the hall to Cambrielle's room. "I hope you enjoy the party, Ava."

I nodded. "I hope you enjoy it too, Carter."

And before the tears stinging at the back of my eyes

could show themselves to Carter, I walked to Cambrielle's room and fervently hoped I could make it through the night.

38

CARTER

I SHOULD JUST LEAVE, I told myself as I stood near the refreshment table in my family's grand ballroom in the west wing of the house, glaring at Mack and Ava as they danced to the orchestra arrangement of Justin Bieber's song "Anyone."

When I'd told Ava that all the guys at school would be dying to dance with her tonight once they saw her in her dress, I hadn't meant for her to take that sentence as a challenge. But here we were, an hour and a half into the night and she'd already danced with at least five guys from the football team, three guys from the wrestling team, and was now currently dancing with my best friend who was the star player for the basketball team.

Did she have a thing for jocks? Or was it just tall guys with strong jawlines and big muscles?

Either she did, or all the guys who fit that description were just conveniently drawn to her.

Drawn to her tonight when I wasn't allowed to touch her.

But boy, did I want to touch her. When she'd come down the stairs with my sister and her friends at her side, I had to work hard to keep my jaw from dropping. Because even though I knew Ava was gorgeous, and she'd teased me about how amazing she was going to look in her dress tonight, I somehow hadn't been prepared for the sight.

I rubbed my jaw, still watching her. Even after seeing her dance with guy after guy all night, I still couldn't get over how beautiful she looked tonight. Her hair was pulled back in an elegant side swept updo, showing off the long curve of her neck and the dips of her collarbone. Her pink dress looked like it had been made for her—knowing that her mom was a famous fashion designer, it probably was actually made just for Ava. The sweetheart, off-the shoulder neckline also did nothing to help with my jealousy. Because let's face it, the girl knew just the right cut to wear in order to have every teenage guy within a two-hundred-yard radius turning their heads to stare at her.

And that hemline? Well, let's just say that if I hadn't already been a leg guy, the way Ava's legs looked in the skirt and heels would have definitely converted me.

I closed my eyes and tried to shake away the carnal urges rising up in me as I raked her appearance in.

She might be your sister.

But when I opened my eyes again, I knew it would take actually hearing those words from my dad or her mom to really convince my hormones of that. Because right now, she did not *look* like my sister. Right now, she looked like the girl who had starred in every single dream of mine from the past week.

Well...longer than that, since yeah, I'd dreamed about her before it was forbidden, too.

I pressed my lips together, remembering how her cherry lip balm had tasted the last time I'd kissed her. How was it possible that a person could have so much power over my emotions?

I'd been determined not to get mixed up with a member of the opposite sex when the school year started, but I should have known the second Ava walked into the weight room that first day and my heart did a little flip-flop in my chest that my plans were worthless against the force that was Ava Cohen. Because she was not a mere human. No. She'd been right on the money when she'd written up her little addendum to my contract. She was a *goddess* and only a Titan would be able to resist falling hopelessly and irrevocably in love with her.

Yes, I knew it was crazy that I'd fallen so hard and so fast for a girl I'd only met a month and a half ago, but love didn't care about things like logic—or how closely you may or may not be related to a person. It was controlled by some intangible force that I was powerless to resist.

I took another sip from my water as I watched Ava smile at something Mack said to her. And even though I knew the only reason Mack had asked her to dance in the first place was because I'd asked him to step in after Tayden Archibald's hand kept sliding farther and farther down Ava's back until he was almost squeezing her butt and making her look uncomfortable, I still couldn't watch them without wanting to punch my own best friend in the face.

Because he was making Ava smile. He was making her

laugh. And he was holding her in the way that I should have been holding her tonight.

I crushed the plastic cup in my hand and tossed it in the trash can beside me, knowing I should probably head upstairs before I did something I regretted—something like ripping Ava away from the next guy she danced with and telling her I was the only guy she was ever supposed to dance with, especially when she looked the way she did.

We'd joked about her dress being my early birthday present. And for the first time in thirteen years, I wanted to cash in on the special perks that the birthday boy usually got.

I wanted a "let's forget about reality for the night" card, so we could go back in time to a week ago when I didn't know what was coming for us.

I checked the time on my watch. My dad should have been here before the party started.

Was he just hiding out somewhere?

Had he decided to prolong his trip so he wouldn't have to face everyone and explain to Dawn how he'd fathered twins the month before they got back together?

Almost as if on cue though, through one of the ballroom windows that looked into the main part of the house, I saw the door from the garage open. A second later my dad walked through it wearing shorts and a teal T-shirt, his usual uniform for long flights home.

I expected him to bring in his luggage behind him, but instead, he held the door open for someone to follow him inside. Mr. Aarden walked through the door wearing a white polo shirt and dress pants. Following close behind him was a petite woman in a black designer dress suit who I'd only seen in photographs from decades earlier.

Ava's mom.

My dad briefly glanced through the windows to the party, looking for a moment like he'd rather be in here dancing with Dawn instead of facing the conversation Mr. Aarden was probably forcing him to have with Ava's mom.

But instead of coming inside, he gestured for his guests to continue down the hall that led to his office. And with one last longing glance at the party, he followed the friends from his past inside the room where I'd overheard that implicating call from over a month ago and shut the door.

WHEN I FINISHED my dance with Mack, I decided it was time to take a break for a few minutes. I'd been standing in my heels for the better part of an hour and my feet were killing me.

When Carter had said that I'd have guys lining up to dance with me tonight, I'd decided to make his words true. And so, after flirting with several of the cutest and buffest guys at the party during dinner, I made sure to smile and wave flirtatiously at one of them each time the live string quartet started playing a slow song. Sure enough, one of them would eventually leave the huddle of guys standing around the outer edge of the Hastings' ballroom and come and ask me to dance.

Was I interested in dating any of these guys after tonight? Not really. But it was all about quantity and not quality at this point.

But even though I had more chemistry with a stick of gum than I did with any of the guys I'd danced with—aside from Mack since he'd at least made me laugh—the soirée hadn't been the total bomb I'd feared it might be. Sure, it wasn't the romantic evening I'd planned on having when I'd originally thought Carter and I would be attending as a couple, but the ambiance was magical—Cambrielle, her mom, and the event planner had really outdone themselves with the decor and food.

And even though most of the evening was spent with Carter glaring at me from across the room, I did manage to have an okay time hanging out with my friends in our fancy dresses and looking amazing—thanks to the professional hair and makeup team that had pampered us before the party started.

I looked up at the high ceiling above me as I drank my water. The event planners had hung black strips with dangling silver stars across the ceiling. String lights were strung in-between the rows of stars to mimic a beautiful starlit sky glittering above the chandeliers. The edges of the room had silver and white trees with lanterns and strings of white blossoms hanging from the branches, making it feel like I'd been transported to a fairytale castle where I would wait to find my own happily-ever-after with a prince.

It was breathtaking.

Just like a scene from a movie.

Only in this movie, when the princess was in the middle of falling in love with the prince, she failed to realize that she'd also made the tragic mistake of falling for her brother.

What kind of writer would be deranged enough to write a story like that?

I sighed as I glanced around, looking for a place to sit among the fairytale trees so I could kick off my heels and rest my feet for a few minutes. I found Elyse sitting next to Nash who wore the old-fashioned suit and cravat he'd talked about wearing tonight. I was just about to head in their direction when Carter suddenly appeared at my side and tapped on my shoulder, saying, "My dad just went into his office with your mom and Dr. Aarden."

"My mom's here?" My hand went to my throat, and I felt the blood draining out of my face. "With your dad?"

Carter nodded, his gaze looking out the big windows that showed the main part of the house. "They just went into his office."

Oh no.

I let out a low breath. "You think this is it?" I asked.

Carter's jaw was clenched, and I couldn't help but think he looked as anxious as I felt. "I think we'll find out what's been going on very soon."

The last thing I wanted to do was face the music and find out the truth, but I said, "I'll tell Elyse."

Carter nodded. "That's probably a good idea."

I took two steps toward my sister and Nash before Carter's hand gripped my arm, stopping me.

I turned to face him, wondering what he'd have to say after speaking so little to me and glaring at me all night.

"What?" I asked, my heart in my throat.

He looked at his hand on my arm briefly before stepping closer, close enough that his chest brushed against my shoulder. He said, "I'm probably not going to be able to say this after tonight, but..." His words trailed off and he searched my face for a few heart-pounding seconds before swallowing and saying, "But you look really beautiful tonight. And..." He sighed and looked at the trees behind me before meeting my gaze again. "And I wish it could have been me with you on the dance floor."

When I searched his eyes, the sincerity in them completely melted the ice that had frozen around my heart during the past two hours.

I pressed my lips together, trying to figure out how I should respond to his admission. And before I could think better of it, I found myself saying, "I wish I could have danced with you, too."

At least once.

Just one last memory like that would have been nice to have before the whole world found out that I'd fallen in love with the one guy at school I could never have.

"WHAT ARE they doing in Mr. Hastings' office?" I said to Elyse, but mostly to myself as I sat on the chair beside her, my legs bouncing as I waited for our mom to come out.

It had been over thirty minutes since Carter told me that he'd seen my mom go in there with his dad and Dr. Aarden. She wouldn't have slipped out another door without saying anything to us, would she?

"I'm sure they'll be done soon," Elyse said, putting a hand on my leg like she was trying to stop me from bouncing out of my seat. "They probably just have a lot to talk about."

"Well, I wish they'd just get it over with already," I said. "Just rip off the Band-aid." I sighed and pushed myself off the chair, needing to walk around because just sitting here was going to make me crazy.

I paced back and forth in front of my sister as the string quartet played the song "In My Blood/Swan Lake" by The Piano Guys. It was an angsty song, and it was the perfect theme song for my current mood.

I walked to one of the ballroom's columns and then turned on my toe to pace back in the opposite direction. I'd never really paced before, but I had so much pent-up tension in my body that I finally understood why stressed-out people did it.

When I made it to the refreshment table, I turned around and headed back the way I'd come again. I went back and forth about six times, but on the seventh time, Elyse stood and pulled on my arm, saying, "Everyone is starting to look at you." She looked pointedly behind me at the dance floor. When I turned to see what she was talking about, there were indeed several sets of eyes staring at me.

One of those sets belonging to Carter.

He was standing on the opposite end of the room, leaning against the wall with his legs crossed in front of him.

What was he thinking right now?

Was he fine with all of this?

He'd said he wanted to dance with me tonight. That he thought I was beautiful. But was he as bothered by our predicament as I was?

I couldn't tell, because from this view, he seemed completely fine. Like it was just another fancy ball at the Hastings' estate to him.

Ugh.

How could he be okay with all of this?

How was he not pacing the floor and feeling like his heart was being ripped out of his chest and stomped on by our parents?

"I need some air," I said, turning back to my sister.

"Do you want me to come with you?" she asked, the look

in her golden-brown eyes telling me she was worried I might just be on the verge of insanity.

"I'll be fine. I'll just be a few minutes."

"Okay," she said, watching me carefully, like she thought that if she said anything else she might break me. "I'll text you if Mom comes out."

"I left my phone upstairs," I said. This dress didn't exactly have pockets. "I'll probably just go to the bathroom and then come back."

I left the ballroom, noticing Carter stepping away from the wall when he saw me through the windows, as if he was considering coming after me. But Nash gripped his brother's arm and said something that seemed to make Carter rethink his pursuit. I hurried down the hall to use the bathroom near the conservatory where Carter had taught me a few constellations one night.

I took care of business quickly and then looked at myself in the mirror. I tried to give myself a little pep talk as I adjusted my dress and washed my hands in the sink.

Everything will be fine, I told my reflection. *Carter might not be the guy for you, but you'll have a dad and a stepmom and three new brothers and a sister. It might not be happening in the way you chose, but it will still be pretty great. You may not get to have the relationship you had with Carter when you started out, but at least he'll still be in your life.*

I continued giving myself the best inspirational speech I could think of. The kind where I told myself that everything was happening for a reason. And even though it didn't seem like this was happening for my own good, one day I'd look back on this time and laugh at myself for thinking that being with Carter was the best path for my life when really, something else that I didn't know about yet was going to actually be the thing that gave my life the meaning and fulfillment that I'd always wanted.

I channeled my inner Oprah. I made up my own graduation speech. I repeated all the inspirational quotes that came to my mind as I tried to convince myself that being related to Carter was actually what I wanted.

But after quoting guru after guru for about three minutes straight, I still didn't feel any better.

Because I wasn't at that future point in my life where this would all make sense yet. I didn't have the hindsight that I'd have in twenty years.

I was still in the here and now. And inconveniently for me, in the here and now, my heart still raced every time I stood close to Carter. My nerve endings still burst to life with the slightest touch from the tall guy with dirty-blond hair and bright blue eyes that I wasn't supposed to fall in love with.

As I kept trying to visualize a future where I was happy and smiling as I watched Carter stand next to his faceless bride in front of all our family and friends, all I could picture was the way he'd glared at me from across the room tonight as I danced with other guys.

Was that how it was actually going to be for us from here on out? Was he going to treat me like a pariah from now on because we'd had a normal high school relationship before we knew we were related?

Were all our future family dinners going to be him just scowling at me across the table and making me wish that I'd never been anything more than an acquaintance before we found out the truth?

The years stretched out ahead of me. Years where I'd walk in a room and he'd instantly leave. Years where I would be at Cambrielle's wedding or Nash's Broadway show and Carter and his future girlfriend or wife sat on the opposite end of the aisle because he couldn't bear to be within ten feet of me.

Years where we would barely say two words to each other because he knew I'd once cared for him in a very unsisterly-like way and he was disgusted that it had ever happened in the first place.

I dropped my head forward and closed my eyes as I tried to push those images away.

I didn't want that to be my future.

I didn't want that to be *our* future.

I turned off the water, dried my hands on one of the fluffy white hand towels on the rack, and left the bathroom. But instead of heading back to the ballroom, I turned left and went into the conservatory at the very end of the hall. The room was dark, but it had a glass roof where one could look up at the night sky above.

The mid-October night was clear, not a cloud to be seen —just a full moon and stars that twinkled like diamonds against the inky-black sky. I was looking for the Big Dipper, the only constellation I could remember right now, when footsteps sounded behind me.

I twirled around to see who had found me. It took me a moment, but once the dark figure was about ten feet away, I realized it was Carter.

He stepped closer, and when his face was illuminated by the moonlight streaming through the glass roof above, I saw a look in his eyes that I'd never seen before.

They were wild.

He looked wild.

His shirt was haphazardly tucked into his slacks, his tie loose around his neck, his hair mussed.

When he came closer, my heart thumped against my ribcage. And when he took another step forward, it didn't just thump, it crashed against my ribs like it wanted to jump out of my chest and into him.

Into his chest to be with the only other heart that had matched its beat so perfectly.

And when I looked at his face again, for the first time since meeting him, I wasn't completely sure I was safe.

Not unsafe in the sense that I should fear for my life or anything, but unsafe because this guy who always followed the rules and kept himself and his actions carefully controlled might just be as on edge as I felt.

"I found you," he said, his voice low and husky.

"You found me," I replied.

My eyes darted back and forth between his, trying to figure out what he meant to do now that he was here. I couldn't sense exactly what he was planning, but the feral look in his eyes told me that I should probably tell him to leave. I should tell him that it wasn't a good idea for us to be alone when we were both on edge like this, that we needed to take time for our feelings for each other to morph into something more appropriate.

But I couldn't force the words out of my mouth because my heart just wasn't in them.

My heart was already somewhere else.

With him.

It had left my body without my permission and was now

burrowing itself away so deep inside him that it would have to be dug out piece by piece before it could be sewn back together and returned to me.

And suddenly, the part of me that had been hurting all week—the part that I knew was irrational and sensitive—started asking, "Why have you been avoiding me?" My voice broke. "Why have you been skipping all of our tutoring sessions? Why have you been glaring at me all night like you can't stand to see me anymore?" My chest heaved as the pain from the past few days poured out with my questions. "Why have you been acting like I'm some sort of infectious disease that you can't put enough space between us? Is this how it's going to be from now on? Can we not even be friends?" I looked up at him, desperation tearing through my body as the words flooded out of me. "If we're related, are you just never going to talk to me ever again? Are you just going to ignore me for the rest of my life?"

By the time I was able to stop vomiting words all over him, I had so much pent-up frustration coursing through me that I could probably light the whole strip of Las Vegas with the barely restrained energy.

Carter just stared at me with his chest rising and falling rapidly, his hands flexing at his sides as if trying to calm himself after I'd assaulted him with my words. But then he shook his head and in a too quiet voice, he said, "Do you think I like this?" he asked, stepping closer. "Do you think I like it that I can't look at you without wanting you? Do you think I like that when you walked down the stairs tonight and I saw you in your dress, all I could think about was how much I wanted to just take you away from here so I could hold you and touch you and kiss you until we both forgot who we really might be to each other?"

I took a step back, feeling hot all over, not expecting the intensity of his words.

"What do you want me to say?" He took my hands in his. "I. Can't. Stop. Thinking about you." He enunciated each word, each admission pumping blood back into my heart. "I mean, I have dreams about you, Ava." He glanced to the side and bit his lip. Then he looked down at his shoes.

"I—" he started. "I wanted to keep tutoring you. I wanted for us to still be friends and hang out with everyone like it's normal." He flicked his cool blue eyes back up to mine and said in a husky voice, "But I'm too attracted to you. I'm so freaking attracted to you Ava, it's insane." He sighed heavily. "And I mean, I know we can't be together. It's perverted. It's wrong. But..." He sighed again. "I don't know if I can control myself when I'm around you."

His shoulders drooped, as if he felt defeated admitting all these things to me. And as everything he'd just said sunk in, it felt like lightning striking me right in the heart.

Like lighting striking his heart and mine at the same time because they were one.

He looked down again, rubbing his thumbs across my knuckles, sending electric waves coursing up the veins in my arms.

When he spoke again, his voice was quieter—just a whisper that I could barely hear over the music drifting to us from the ballroom in the background. "And I'm sorry." He leaned his forehead against mine. "I should have told you I couldn't make it on Thursday. I should have warned you that I needed space—that as much as I want to spend every single waking minute with you, I can't. I can't tutor you anymore. I can't be your friend right now. Not when I'm trying to come to terms with being your brother."

I didn't realize I'd been holding my breath through his speech until my lungs felt like they were going to collapse as they screamed out for oxygen. I sucked in a deep breath, filling my lungs with much-needed air, hoping it would clear my head which had become fuzzier and fuzzier the longer Carter spoke.

He hasn't turned off his feelings. He doesn't hate me.

He'd only been trying to come to grips with our possible new reality and putting the necessary space between us so we didn't do something we'd later regret.

Which meant, I should probably leave.

Right now.

"I should go back to the party," I said, knowing that if I stayed here with Carter for much longer, we both might actually give in to our feelings and do something we couldn't take back. "Elyse is probably wondering where I am."

Carter's jaw flexed and he gave a slight nod. "Okay."

But neither one of us made a move to leave. We just stood there, face to face, his hands still holding mine, our foreheads still pressed together, our breaths still mingling, our hearts still racing.

I was working up the nerve to really leave him, to go back to the soirée like a good girl and wait for my mom to come and tell my sister and me that Mr. Hastings was the father she'd kept us from our whole lives when Carter spoke up.

"This might be selfish of me, but I basically just bared my whole soul to you. Just told you a lot of things that I'll probably kick myself for admitting to as soon as we leave this room. But..." He swallowed. "I can't help but wonder if you felt any of that at all this week."

Did he really not know?

Could he really not tell just how hard this was for me, too?

But I guess I hadn't told him, had I? In fact, I'd just danced with a dozen other guys, flaunting it in his face.

Since this was probably the last chance I'd have to tell him how I felt before we officially heard the truth from our parents' mouths, I whispered, "Being with you is all I can think about, too."

"It is?" His chest expanded, like he actually had thought my feelings for him could disappear in the span of just a week.

"Of course," I said, reaching up to caress his high cheekbone with my thumb one last time. "I've been dreading tonight because while I knew the party would be amazing, I knew I'd still hate it because I couldn't spend it with you."

"It's been a pretty bad night," Carter admitted, leaning his cheek into my hand. "I was actually fighting the urge to punch my best friend in the face because I was so jealous he got to dance with you when I couldn't."

I couldn't help the half-smile that lifted my lips. Even though violence wasn't something I'd usually condone, it was nice to know Carter felt so strongly about me.

Carter returned my smile, and it was a welcome sight after the glares he'd been shooting me all night.

After a few seconds where the world seemed to disappear and we got lost in each other's eyes, Carter said, "Don't you want just one last moment?" He took my bare shoulders in his hands, running his thumbs across my collarbones. "Don't you want just one last time to be together?"

My stomach tilted inside me as I thought about what he was saying. And while turning him down was the last thing I wanted to do, I made myself shake my head and say, "We can't. It would be wrong."

His brow furrowed and he searched my eyes. "But is it really?" he asked. "Because what I feel for you doesn't *feel* wrong."

When he slipped his hands over my shoulders and down my back to rest at my waist, I had to agree. Being like this with Carter didn't feel wrong. It felt like exactly what I wanted to do.

But we couldn't act on our feelings.

We couldn't steal one last moment from fate, could we?

And so, since one of us needed to stay here in reality, I said, "Do you know how bad it'll be if it comes out that we're related and we still acted like this?" I pressed my lips together. "This is the twenty-first century. People go to jail for having relationships like this."

I expected Carter to nod. To accept what I was saying as the truth. But instead of agreeing to my logic, Carter just bent closer and whispered into my face with his minty breath, "I don't care."

What?

I shook my head, not believing I was the one who had to talk about the rules when he'd been the poster boy for rule-following a month ago. "I looked it up, Carter," I said. "You can go to jail for up to five years for this."

"I. Don't. Care," he said more firmly, his towering height

and muscular physique more intimidating than it had been a moment before.

"Carter..." I braced my hands on his chest, needing him to see reason. "It's *illegal*. There's no future where we can be together."

"It's illegal if we *know* that we're related and we break the rules anyway." He gripped my waist tighter and pulled me impossibly closer. "But your mom still hasn't told you. And my dad certainly hasn't said anything to me. As of now, the only evidence we really have are a few photos that place them together at the scene of the crime."

"But that's just a technicality."

"No one has to know." He leaned his mouth close to my ear. "It can be our little secret. Our last goodbye."

"But Carter..." I sighed, feeling my resolve wilting like a dahlia that had seen too much sun.

Because even though I knew I shouldn't, I wanted to do exactly what Carter was saying.

I wanted to have one last memory before everything was taken away from us.

"Just one last night," he whispered, his hot breath on my neck. "One last moment to remember what might have been if the universe was kind."

My heart felt like it was going to pound right out of my chest. Because until my mom confirmed my worst nightmare, I couldn't get in trouble for feeling the way I did, could I?

And so, even though the logical part of my brain knew I shouldn't, I gave him the slightest nod.

Carter cradled my head in his hand and whispered, "I love you, Ava. Even if everything changes after tonight, I just want you to know that I love you—not as a brother, but as a mere mortal man who fell under the spell of a goddess."

A tear escaped my eye because I knew this was a goodbye. It was the last time I'd ever be able to admit my true feelings for him. So I whispered, "I love you too, Carter."

His lips descended on mine then, and as he led our mouths in a slow and passionate kiss, I felt my heart ripping apart inside me. It slowly unraveled like a ribbon, because this kiss was not a promise of more good things to come. It wasn't like any of our previous kisses that burst with the excitement and anticipation of a future we could have together.

No. This was the kiss of death—the death of all my hopes and dreams where Carter and me and the future I still selfishly wanted were concerned.

His arms slid more firmly around my waist and he pulled me against him. He was solid and strong, but even though he was both of those things, he was also mortal and vulnerable to the same overwhelming feelings I was susceptible to.

In other words, he was human. Imperfect and only able to be tempted so far before he inevitably fell.

We were both falling.

I wondered if this was how Adam and Eve felt in the Garden of Eden. To know that the consequences of their actions would affect them for the rest of their lives, but to still fall to the temptation standing right before them because not giving in was worse than forever living without.

Eve offered Adam the forbidden fruit, and not wanting to be without his other half, the woman born from his rib, he tasted the fruit and exiled himself to an eternity where he could no longer live in the beautiful, lush garden—the only home he'd ever known.

It made me wonder about the person who had named Eden Falls. Had they somehow known that this town, this little paradise, had something brimming in the air? Something unseen that made its inhabitants act out in ways they normally wouldn't?

Was that what had happened to my mom? Had she come back to Eden Falls and gotten caught up in its spell only to wake up the next morning and realize too late that she'd done something she hadn't really meant to? Something she couldn't continue?

Carter's hands flattened against my back, and when he flicked his tongue along my lips, I opened my mouth to his. If I was already falling to temptation, I might as well make the most of it.

I knotted my hands in his hair as tears trickled down my cheeks, telling him with my kiss all the things I'd never be able to speak aloud after we were torn apart: *I love you, Carter. I love you, and I don't care that I shouldn't. I don't care that loving you like this is wrong because loving you makes me feel more alive than not.*

41

CARTER

I SLIPPED my hands up Ava's back, tangled my fingers in her hair, and let myself memorize everything about how she felt in my arms as we kissed. Because if things went the way we feared tonight, the only time I'd be kissing her again would be in my dreams.

So this needed to be a goodbye kiss. It was one last opportunity to reveal how we truly felt before we were forced to lock away our feelings for the rest of our lives. This was most likely the last chance I'd be allowed to fully appreciate this beautiful creature who had wiggled her way into my heart over the past six weeks.

But even though I'd asked Ava for just one last stolen kiss, I knew deep in my core that this would never be enough.

I would still crave to be with her every second for the rest of my life. These moments alone with her were the times where I felt most alive—most like the person I was supposed to be—the most like my true self.

She might be my sister, I tried to tell myself as I pulled her closer when I should have been pushing her away. *My own flesh and blood.*

But I might as well have been speaking a foreign language because those words meant nothing to me.

Absolutely nothing.

I trailed kisses across her jawline, burrowed my face into the curve of her neck, and breathed in her intoxicating scent as I smoothed my hands up her sides and tried to brand it into my memory.

Because this would be the last time I'd ever be able to touch her like this again, when I could still claim to not really *know* anything romantic between us was forbidden.

I knew I should probably be disgusted with myself for even thinking it, but if I wasn't worried about the repercussions for her, I knew I would gladly kiss her again.

Kiss her every day until my lips were swollen and her delicate skin was chaffed, and they would have to literally lock me behind bars to get me to stop.

I squeezed my eyes shut.

I was going to have to move out of the country and put an ocean between us to keep myself from acting irrationally.

I was just trying to figure out a way to ask her to run away with me when a loud gasp sounded behind us.

Ava's hands, which had been sliding up my back the moment before went still, and she took a sharp intake of breath when she saw who had walked in on us.

I turned my head over my shoulder, to see who'd caught us, and found Ava's look-alike.

Elyse.

And though it was dark and I couldn't see everything

clearly, I could tell from the way she stood with her hand to her chest and her mouth hanging open that she was shocked.

Shocked that Ava and I would be entangled in each other's arms this way when we knew the possibility of who we might be to each other.

I closed my eyes and drew in a deep breath. I didn't want to release Ava yet—because I could hold her in my arms forever and still never get enough—but I forced myself to let her go and stepped away.

"So..." Ava said to her sister as she readjusted her dress until it rested over her hips more comfortably. "I guess you saw that."

"Yeah," Elyse said, still seeming shocked. "I-I did."

I blew out a long breath because I really didn't know how I could explain any of this in a way to make us look good in front of Elyse—like we hadn't just been kissing each other when we knew it was highly possible we were related.

Ava didn't seem to want to say anything about it either, so we just waited for Elyse to explain her reason for coming here.

"So, um," Elyse said after realizing we weren't going to address the big, fat elephant in the room. "Mom just texted me to say that she's here and that she's ready to talk to us in Mr. Hastings' office."

42

———

AVA

WHEN ELYSE and I walked into Mr. Hastings' office a few minutes later, I expected to find our mom with Mr. Hastings and Mr. Aarden. Instead, we walked in to find only her sitting on one of the brown leather chairs.

"Hi girls." She stood up and moved to hug us.

I wasn't exactly sure I wanted to hug this woman who had been ignoring my calls and texts all week, so when she opened her arms for me after hugging Elyse, I just gave her a sort of side hug.

A flash of pain crossed her face after my rejection, but she replaced it with a wary smile. She gestured to a leather sofa against the wall, saying, "Go ahead and take a seat."

I sat next to my sister, set my hands in my lap, and waited expectantly for my mom to explain herself.

"So," she said, drawing in a deep breath. "I guess we all probably know why I'm here, so I'll just get right down to what I have to say to you two." Her brown eyes looked sorrowful. "And well, I guess it's pretty obvious to all of us that we probably should have had this conversation a long time ago."

You think?

I considered saying that out loud and putting up a big stink about how she was about seventeen and a half years too late for this conversation, but since she was actually finally promising answers, I kept my mouth shut.

She smoothed her hands along her black pencil skirt and sighed. "I'm not exactly sure how to start this, so I'll go back to the beginning and hope it explains why I made the choices that I did concerning you two and your biological father."

"If you're going to tell us about how you and Mr. Hastings dated in high school, we already figured that out," I told her, wanting to just cut to the chase. I didn't need a long drawn-out explanation about how they'd been in love at one time and all that crap.

Just give me the details, woman.

"Okay," my mom said, seeming a bit surprised at the mention of her previous relationship with Carter's dad. "Does that mean you also know that before I started dating Joel, there was also a short time when I dated Brendon?"

"Brendon?" I furrowed my brow, not knowing who Brendon was or what he might have to do with this story.

"Oh, um," my mom said. "You might know of him as Dr. Aarden? He has a son your age named Mack."

Still frowning, I glanced at Elyse, curious if she understood where our mom was going with this, but she looked just as confused as I felt.

Mom cleared her throat. "Okay, so Brendon and I dated for just a short time in high school during the fall of our junior year. It was nothing big, just a few dates here and there that fizzled out before it could get too serious. He went on to date my best friend at the time, Brianna, and I got to know his best friend Joel better during our production of *Romeo and Juliet.*"

Elyse and I nodded, this information fitting with what Mrs. Simmons had told Elyse.

"Anyway," my mom said. "Joel and I dated for the next year and a half and grew quite close during that time. But when we graduated and I had to move back to Israel because my student visa was about to expire, we had no choice but to try to move on."

"Did you keep in contact after that?" Elyse asked, clearly more interested in the details than I was since all I was here for was the moment when she told us he was our long-lost dad.

Mom nodded, seeming encouraged that at least one of her daughters was being pleasant to her. "We emailed every week for the first year or so, but after we realized that a long-distance relationship wasn't going to work out, we decided to just end things for real and tried to move on with people in our same zip code."

"That makes sense," Elyse said.

Mom continued, "I basically lost contact with all of my friends from the academy after that and just went on living life, helping take care of your grandfather and getting my degree. As you know, I was able to move back to New York after graduating and started working toward becoming a citizen. Then about five years after my high school graduation, I received an email announcing a class reunion. Since I thought it might be fun to catch up with everyone from the old days, I got myself a cute dress and drove the few hours to attend."

I flexed my hands into fists, my heart rate increasing as I realized she was finally getting close to the part of the story I'd been waiting my whole life to hear.

Mom crossed one of her legs over the other as if trying to get comfortable for what she had to say next. "The reunion was held at one of the hotels in Eden Falls, so I checked myself into a room there. When it came time for it to start, I headed down to the conference room where it was being held and nervously waited to see if any of my friends had come. My friend Cortney was there." Mom met our gazes. "I think she actually teaches math at the academy. Her married name is Cortney Simmons."

"She's my Statistics teacher," I said.

Mom nodded. "So I hung out with Cortney for a little while and asked her to give me an update on all of the latest Eden Falls gossip. She told me that both Joel and Brendon were planning to come and that they were both single, if I was interested in reviving an old fling." She shook her head and cleared her throat. "I'll admit that the idea of rekindling something with Joel did spark some interest in me since here we were, both single and available, but when he showed up, I soon realized that nothing would be happening there because while he was friendly and courteous, he was not open to flirting with me like old times."

"So you and Joel—Mr. Hastings—" I corrected myself. "—didn't rekindle anything that night?" I asked, feeling more confused than ever.

Mom shook her head. "I later found out that he'd been trying to get back with the woman that he's actually married to now, and so he wasn't interested in going down memory lane with me."

I frowned for a moment as I tried to make sense of what she was saying. If she hadn't hooked up with Mr. Hastings that night, then why was she telling us about her high school reunion in the first place?

Why even talk about Mr. Hastings at all?

And since I was tired of beating around the bush, I blurted out, "So is Mr. Hastings our dad or not?"

"What?" Mom put a hand to her chest. "No. Of course not." She shook her head. "Is that what you thought?"

"Well, yeah," I said, like it should have been obvious. I gestured at the room around us. "We're in his office right now and you did come here to talk to him. Isn't that why we're here?"

"No, honey." Mom leaned forward and put her hand on my knee. "Joel Hastings is not your father. I don't know what led you to believe that he was, but it's not him."

It wasn't?

Mr. Hastings wasn't my dad?

Carter's dad wasn't my dad?

It took a moment for the words to sink in, but when they did, I suddenly felt lightheaded.

Carter's dad wasn't my dad.

Which meant that Carter wasn't my brother.

We weren't related.

Which meant that Carter and I could actually be together.

I hadn't fallen in love with my brother.

I needed to tell him. I needed to tell him that our worst nightmare had just been a huge misunderstanding.

I was about to stand up to go and tell him the good news when Elyse brought me back to the present by asking our mom, "So if Mr. Hastings isn't our dad, then who is? Is it another guy from the reunion? Billy?" Elyse looked at me for confirmation that she was remembering the name Dr. Aarden had given us correctly. "Is it a guy named Billy Monaco?"

I didn't know what I expected my mom to do when she heard Elyse's question, but I certainly hadn't expected for her to laugh. Laugh so hysterically that I worried about her sanity.

"You thought Billy Monaco was your father?" she asked.

Elyse and I looked at each other, not seeing how this was funny.

"Who else would it be?" Elyse asked.

Mom sobered up and after drawing in a calming breath, she said, "Okay, so I..." She smoothed her hands along her skirt again, like her palms were suddenly sweaty. "I'm not sure how you even know who Billy Monaco is, but let me first assure you that no, he's definitely not your father. He was hanging around Joel during the reunion because he was trying to sell Joel some kind of business idea and thought it was his chance to do so. But well, I guess I'll just come out and say it. Your father is Brendon." She cleared her throat and looked at both Elyse and me carefully. "Dr. Aarden is your father."

What?

"H-how?" I asked, pulling my head back.

"How?" Mom asked, her voice rising an octave—like she thought I was expecting her to explain the birds and the bees again.

I shook my head. "How could Mack's dad be our dad? Wasn't he married to Mack's mom at the time?"

Mom's features darkened. "Brendon and Brianna were not married at the time, no."

"But Mack is older than us," I said as if it proved that his parents had been together.

"Yes, he is." Mom looked down at the carpeted floor for a moment. "Like I said earlier, at the time of the reunion, Brendon was single. He and Brianna had been together ever since high school and were very serious, but then just a couple of weeks before the reunion, Brianna broke up with him out of the blue and told him she didn't want to see or talk to him anymore. She basically just cut things off with him cold turkey without any warning signs or any real explanation for why she had a sudden change of heart."

"Did he know she was pregnant with Mack?" Elyse asked.

"He didn't."

"Did *she* know she was pregnant with Mack?" I asked.

Mom shook her head. "I don't think so. He was actually born a couple of months prematurely because of some complications, so I don't think she knew about the pregnancy yet herself."

Interesting.

"Anyway," Mom continued. "Brendon wasn't exactly in the best headspace the night of the reunion after having his heart broken a couple of weeks before. And I was pretty bummed that Joel wasn't interested in rekindling anything with me. So we both kind of commiserated together and ended up getting wrapped up in our own little bubble that night."

"And then you slept together?" I asked, knowing that my mom was trying to find a delicate way to put it.

Mom nodded. "Yes. I had a little more to drink that night than I usually did, and so when everyone was leaving, I suggested we take things upstairs to my room and then..." Her cheeks colored, obviously embarrassed to admit all of this to her daughters. "Even though Brendon and I hadn't dated for long in high school, and we'd ended up dating each other's best friends for far longer, we always did have great chemistry. There was always a little spark brimming under the surface between us."

"So you had sex and you got pregnant, and then what?" I asked, impatient for her to get to the part where she *didn't* tell us who our dad was for the last seventeen years.

"Ava," Elyse chided me for my bluntness.

But I just shrugged and said, "I'm just trying to hurry things along."

Mom swallowed. "Okay, so yes, that's basically what happened." She readjusted her legs, crossing the left over the right this time. "Anyway, I went home the next day and didn't hear from Brendon for several weeks. We hadn't necessarily planned on dating since I lived in Ridgewater and he had just been drafted to the NBA. I didn't think anything was up until about a month after the reunion when I realized that my period was late. I tried not to panic, since I was on the pill and was usually pretty good about remembering to take it. But then a few more days passed and my period still hadn't shown up. I took a pregnancy test and found out I was expecting.

"I was pretty scared since I was a single woman and knew how my dad would react when he found out. He'd been supplementing my income when I first moved to the U.S., so I didn't exactly have the greatest job to provide for me and a baby when he cut me off. But I knew it had to be Brendon's baby because he was the only person I'd slept with since my previous boyfriend six months before. I figured that while it would probably be a pretty awkward conversation to have, he'd step up to the plate and at least help me co-parent, even if we weren't going to get married or anything like that."

My mom paused for a moment, and it was then that I noticed a shift in her demeanor. Up to this point, she'd been able to tell her history in a very matter-of-fact manner, but now there was something different in her eyes. An anxiety or fear as she relived the memory from what I now realized must have been a pretty scary time in her life.

And I suddenly felt really bad for how I'd been so rude to her so far tonight.

She'd only been a few years older than I was now. And I knew that it couldn't have been easy to raise Elyse and me alone. Couldn't have been easy telling her strict father that she'd gotten pregnant without a husband, and eventually being shunned because his black and white beliefs didn't make room for what he saw as a huge mistake—a huge sin—on her part.

Suddenly, she looked so alone in that chair across from us all by herself, and I couldn't bear to let her tell the rest of her story while thinking I hated her.

I reached over and tugged on her hand and made room for her to sit on the couch between Elyse and me. We wrapped our arms around her as she continued to tell us a story that must have been so hard for her to live through that it had taken her our whole lives to tell us about.

"Sorry, girls," she whispered as she was nestled between us, kissing us both on the heads. "Sorry it's taken me so long to tell you this."

I rubbed her arm and leaned my head against her shoulder, tears brimming in my own eyes. "It's okay."

And suddenly, it *was* okay. Because even though not knowing who my dad was for all these years had been painful for me, at least I'd had my mom. At least she and Elyse had always been there for me.

No one had been there for my mother.

Mom let out a shaky breath. "It took me a while to get up the nerve to call Brendon and tell him everything. I was probably eight weeks along when I finally dialed his number. I was so nervous that when he first answered the phone, I just skipped through all the small talk and basically blurted out that I was pregnant and it was his, and that I didn't want to have an abortion if he was even thinking about suggesting it.

"He was quiet for a long time after that, and I was worried he may have actually hung up on me, but then he finally said okay and that we would figure this out. He then told me that he had gotten back with Brianna and they were planning to get married since they were expecting a baby as well."

My mom chewed on her bottom lip, then she solemnly said, "And then he told me that Brianna had been diagnosed with a brain tumor and it was why she'd broken up with him before, because she was freaking out about everything and not knowing how to undergo treatments while she was pregnant."

"I'd heard she was sick," I whispered, remembering what

Cambrielle and Scarlett had told me about Mack's mom and how the tumor had come back.

Mom nodded. "Anyway, we didn't really make any plans for how he would be involved with *my* baby since his whole life had basically just exploded on him the week before. Me being pregnant would just add even more to his already heavy plate."

"But we were still his babies," Elyse said, a hint of bitterness in her tone. "Just as much his as Mack is."

"I know." Mom patted Elyse's knee. "I know." She drew in another shaky breath as if gearing up for the next part of her story. "After our initial phone call, I didn't get back in touch with him for a couple of weeks. I wanted to give him time to breathe and get used to the idea. When I was about ten weeks along, I went to the doctor to make sure everything was fine with the pregnancy. I'd had some spotting, so they did an ultrasound. That was when we found out I wasn't having just one baby, but two."

"So now Mr. Aarden had three babies on the way. And a fiancée with a terminal illness," I said, thinking I had an idea of where this story may be going.

Mom nodded. "I waited a few days to call Brendon and tell him the exciting and terrifying news. But he didn't answer my calls. I figured he was probably just overwhelmed with the cancer treatments for Brianna and the two babies he knew about. After another week of unanswered calls, I left him a message explaining that we were expecting twins instead of the one baby, and that I hoped he'd get back to me when he could.

"When I didn't hear anything for another week, I decided to give Joel a call to see if he knew what was going on and how I could get in contact with Brendon. He told me that Brendon had been checked into the hospital for a little while because he was in a really bad place and his family was worried about him being a danger to himself. I could tell that Joel was trying not to say that me having twins was responsible for any of Brendon's troubles, but I knew that it was. And..." Mom pressed her lips together. With a shrug, she said, "It was getting pretty obvious that Brendon was in no place to help me or my babies out, so after hanging up with Joel, I decided to text Brendon that I'd had a miscarriage and that he didn't need to worry about my babies after all.

"He got out of the hospital a week later and called me after getting my message. He told me he was sorry for my loss. He said he knew it was probably really hard on me, but I could tell he was relieved to have one less fire to deal with during that time."

"So you just had us on your own and cut off all contact with your past because you couldn't let anyone find out the truth?" Elyse guessed.

"I didn't know what else to do. I'd claimed you two had died before you were born." She held her hands out at her sides in a helpless gesture. "And yeah, the first few years sucked. They were so hard. But then..." She reached her arms around our shoulders and pulled us against her. "Then things got easier. You two were more self-sufficient and...I guess I just loved you so much and thought you were both so perfect that I didn't want to take a chance of telling Brendon the truth. I didn't want to risk having him reject you all over again. I just couldn't do it."

"You think he'd have turned us away if you'd told him?" I

lifted my head from her shoulder and studied her face. "We heard he was in here with you and Mr. Hastings earlier. Is he not going to accept us?"

I knew he was in the middle of another crisis right now. His wife's health was as bad or worse than it had been all those years before.

But my mom said, "No, you don't need to worry about that. I talked to him, and while he was pretty shocked on Monday when you walked into his house looking for answers, he does want to be a part of your life."

We were quiet for a little while, all lost in our own thoughts. But after a minute or two, Elyse said, "I do have one more question for you, Mom." She lifted her head from our mom's shoulder and pulled away so she could look at her better. "If you were so determined to cut off everyone from your past to protect your secret, why did you send Ava and me to school here? Didn't you know it was super likely that we'd run into someone from your past who would put two and two together?"

"I knew it was a possibility." Mom nodded slowly. "And while it scared me to death to know that my secret might come to light and there could be a lot of repercussions because of it, I knew you deserved to know the truth. I really didn't like keeping such a huge secret from you two." She looked at Elyse and then at me. "And though I knew it would probably come out sooner than later, I had no idea how everyone would take it. Obviously, I did freak out a little when Brendon called me Monday night to tell me that my two beautiful daughters had shown up at his house to ask him questions about their dad. But I knew that it was for the best and that everyone deserved to know the truth."

"So he called you and not Mr. Hastings?" I asked.

"Yes." She nodded. "He said he should have known you were his from the moment you stepped into his house because you looked so much like his sister, and the chances of me getting pregnant with twins twice was super slim. But since he'd believed my miscarriage story, he didn't put two and two together until he found out how old you were."

"Well, I guess I'm glad you were daring enough to send us here for school," I said.

My mom nodded and pulled Elyse and me against her sides again. "I'm glad I did, too."

43

AVA

DR. AARDEN—BRENDON—MY *dad* came into the room a few minutes later.

"Hi," he said, ducking his head down nervously as he looked at Elyse and me. "It's, uh, it's good to meet you two again." He seemed to study both my sister and me, like he was trying to figure out how to tell us apart. "I remember your names, but you may need to forgive me for not knowing who is who right away. Which one of you is Ava? And which is Elyse?"

"I'm Ava." I stepped forward. Not knowing what else to do, I held out my hand for him to shake.

He looked at it for a second before taking it in his and saying, "It's very good to meet you again, Ava." And when our hands touched, I felt an immediate sense of calm come over me.

It could have all been in my head because since when did shaking hands with a forty-year-old guy make me feel anything? But it did feel almost like the energy of the universe was trying to tell me this guy was really my dad. This guy standing in front of me was the person I'd been wondering about my entire life.

He felt like home.

He narrowed his eyes and looked down at our hands, and it made me wonder if he felt it, too. The rightness of this moment. Like the universe had actually been conspiring for things to turn out exactly the way they had.

Afterwards, he shook Elyse's hand next, seeming to study her with curiosity as well as she introduced herself. Then we all just stood there staring at each other for a long time, taking everything in. Mack's dad—*my* dad—suggested we sit down and talk.

I shook my head as Elyse and I sat together, realizing it was going to take some time to adjust to calling this near stranger our dad.

Dr. Aarden sat on the leather chair across from us since my mom had moved to a chair in the corner—letting us have our moment with him while still being there for support if we needed her.

He cleared his throat and looked at us with his golden-brown eyes that matched mine and Elyse's almost exactly—so perfectly that I probably should have noticed the similarity the first time we'd met.

His hair was slightly lighter than mine but had the same texture, fine but thick. And from how tall he seemed when we'd stood in front of him a second ago, I knew that I must have gotten my tall genetics from this man because he was at least six-foot six, maybe a little taller even.

I was sure I'd be spending a lot of time over the next weeks, months, and years studying this man, trying to decipher all the similarities between myself and him. But for now, I would try to focus on being present in the moment and getting to know a little more about him.

He cleared his throat to speak first, leaning slightly forward over his long legs. "So, I'm not exactly sure how to maneuver this new situation that we're all finding ourselves in, but before we get very far into our conversation tonight, I first want to apologize for not being there for you two for the past seventeen and a half years." He cleared his throat again. "Not being there for you three, actually."

He glanced briefly at my mom. "And I guess your mom probably told you about everything that was going on back when she was pregnant and..." He tugged on the collar of his white polo shirt. "I just want you to know how sorry I am that I failed you all back then. I really am." He looked down at his hands, clasping and unclasping them, then back at us. "I'm actually really ashamed that I basically just let your mom disappear from my life. If I'd been a better man and actually tried to follow up with her on the miscarriage story, if I'd been man enough to try to comfort her or something like a decent human would, I might have been able to see what was really going on. Then the last seventeen years would have looked very different for all of you."

"Don't blame yourself for believing me, Brendon," my mom said. "You did just what I hoped you would, so if it's anyone's fault, it's mine."

He shook his head. "Regardless of what happened in the past and the ways we could have handled it better, the fact is that we can't go back in time and fix things. But we can do better now. We can try to move forward." He paused for a moment before adding, "So if you're open to the idea, I would love to spend the next several months while you girls are at the academy getting to know both of you better. And then of course, hopefully continue to move forward from there."

"You would?" Elyse asked, and when I looked at my sister, the raw emotion—the hopefulness in her expression—hit my soul deep. Because I wanted the same thing.

"Of course." Mr. Aarden nodded as he took in the openness of Elyse's expression. "Of course I'd love to get to know everything about you." He moved his gaze to me. "Both of you."

And we all must have gotten caught up in the same overwhelming emotion because we all stood up at the same time. When Mr. Aarden held his arms open to us, Elyse and I didn't hesitate to go to him. He set his strong arms around our shoulders and pulled us close, and it just felt...right.

It felt right to finally hug my dad.

I leaned my head against his solid chest and looked at my sister across from me with tears in my eyes. And when our gazes locked, her eyes had tears in them, too. Because we'd finally found our dad.

And he was a good man.

He wanted to get to know us. He wanted to love us.

That was all we'd ever wanted.

To have a dad who wanted and loved us.

A sniffling noise sounded from the corner—Mom was all watery-eyed as well.

Elyse and I went to hug her next. After we all had a good, happy cry together, we sat down again to make plans for how we would move forward from here.

Mr. Aarden told us about what was going on in his life right then. While his wife, Brianna, knew that he'd slept with our mom after the reunion because he'd told her about it a long time ago, she would still be surprised to find out about Elyse and me.

She was in a delicate condition right now. The tumor was causing more and more issues. "But I know you deserve to have a dad and I want to see what it's like to have daughters—two beautiful daughters," he said. "I'm planning to tell Brianna about everything tomorrow, and then see if we can arrange a time for you two to come over in the next week so all of us can get to know each other better."

"Does Mack know about us yet?" Elyse asked.

And it was then that I realized that not only were we gaining a dad and a stepmother, but we would also have a brother.

A brother who I had liked from the instant I met him because of his charismatic personality.

"I was waiting to talk to all of you first," Mr. Aarden said. "But I'm planning to tell him tomorrow."

"Okay, cool," Elyse said.

I watched Elyse release an anxious breath, and I realized what must be going through her head. Because even though she hadn't acted on it at all, she'd had a crush on Mack since we first came to Eden Falls.

So instead of it being me, *she* was going to be the sister who'd had complicated feelings for our brother.

Life was fun, wasn't it?

But thankfully, for her and Mack's sake at least, she'd never acted on her feelings.

And of course I would keep it a secret. I of all people understood what kind of trouble could come from not knowing who you may or may not be related to when you came to the world of Eden Falls Academy, where the people were as beautiful and intriguing as the scenery around us.

After exchanging numbers with our father so we could be in touch, we all left Mr. Hastings' office a little bit different than we'd been when we'd entered. We walked past the ballroom just as the clock was striking midnight. When I peeked through the windows and listened to the sounds coming from inside, I realized that everyone was singing "Happy Birthday" to Carter.

He was standing just a few feet away from the windows, a huge birthday cake with eighteen tall candles flickering in the dimly lit room. He must have noticed our movement from the corner of his eyes, because after everyone finished singing to him and he had blown out the candles, his eyes locked with mine and he mouthed something like, "Are you okay?"

I nodded and sent him a small smile before mouthing back, "I will be."

He nodded to let me know that he understood. And then he pointed to Dr. Aarden who was walking a few feet ahead of me and mouthed, "Is that your dad?"

I smiled and nodded, tears springing to my eyes because I was so relieved and hopeful about how things had turned out.

When Carter seemed to realize that he was officially off the hook for being my brother, his shoulders relaxed and he mouthed, "I love you."

"I love you, too," I whispered back even though he couldn't hear me through the window and above the excited chatter in the ballroom.

His family surrounded him then, everyone wanting to

give the birthday boy a hug. I slipped my hand in my mom's and went with her and Elyse back to my mom's hotel suite, so we could spend some much-needed mother/daughter time together.

Now that I wasn't on the verge of going crazy because I'd fallen in love with my brother, Carter and I could catch up on everything tomorrow.

Because now we actually had time.

44

———

AVA

ELYSE and I spent the next morning and afternoon with our mom talking about the past as well as everything going on in our lives right now. After that, Mom dropped Elyse off at the school and then offered to drive me to Carter's house so I could tell him everything. I also needed to give him the birthday present I'd ordered him a few weeks ago when we'd first started officially dating.

"Does Carter know you're coming over?" Mom asked as we drove through the small town of Eden Falls.

"Not yet," I said. "I was planning to surprise him, but maybe I should make sure he's actually home before you drop me off on his front porch."

"That's probably a good idea."

I pulled out my phone and texted Carter to give him a heads up.

> Me: I know you don't like celebrating your birthday, but if you aren't in the middle of something right now, I'd love to come over and give you your October 17th Day gift.

His text came through a minute later, as if he'd been waiting for mine.

> Carter: October 17th Day? Hmm, I didn't realize that was a special holiday.

I smiled.

> Me: Well, since "Carter's Birthday" is a forbidden phrase around your house, I figured I'd just start calling it October 17th Day.

> Carter: Thanks for clearing that up. I'm going to hurry and write that in my bullet journal so it's properly noted.

Oh Carter.

That bullet journal might just be a little too important in his life.

But I kind of loved it. Loved that Carter had his own little quirks that made him who he was.

When I didn't respond immediately, another text from Carter came through.

> Carter: So are you coming over? Because I kind of want to see what you got me for my birthday.

> Carter: Aside from that amazing dress you wore last night, that is.

I laughed. How had I not known it was possible to like someone so much?

> Me: My mom is dropping me off on her way out of town. I'll be there in a few minutes.

WHEN MY MOM and I pulled up, Carter was waiting for me on the front porch of his home with a huge smile on his face.

"So this is Joel's boy?" my mom asked after taking Carter's appearance in. "He's quite handsome, isn't he?"

"He is." I smiled at my mom as I lifted the manilla envelope with Carter's gift on my lap. "And he knows it, too."

Mom let out a hearty laugh, her brown eyes smiling. "It must be a Hastings' family trait, because Joel always knew how good-looking he was, too."

We were quiet for a second as my mom seemed to remember something from the past.

I wondered if she was remembering the good times with Carter's dad, or maybe even my father Brendon. But since Carter was waiting and my mom wanted to get back to Ridgewater before dark, I sighed and said, "Well, I better get going."

Mom nodded, her faraway gaze focusing back on me. "You don't want to keep that boy waiting. From what you told me last night, it sounds like you might have a lot to talk about."

"Yes." I chuckled. "I think making sure he knows the story

behind how he's not my brother might be one of the first topics of discussion."

"Oh dear." Mom shook her head. "I really did make a mess of things for you, didn't I?"

I shrugged, deciding to let her off the hook since being mad about things wasn't going to help anything. "It's okay. At least it's all straightened out now."

Sure, I might have made out with Carter when I thought he was possibly my brother, which most people would be embarrassed about. But at the same time, Carter had thought I might be his sister, so at least we knew we were both a similar kind of crazy about each other.

I leaned over the center console and hugged my mom. "I'll see you at Thanksgiving. Have a safe drive home."

"I will. I'll see you soon." She pulled away from the embrace and looked pointedly at me. "Just make sure you actually do some studying with that handsome math tutor of yours, okay? Even though things have been crazy, I still expect you to keep your grades up."

I grinned. "I'll see what I can do."

I climbed out of the car and waved goodbye to my mom. Then I walked over to the boy who was still patiently waiting for me on his porch steps, looking better than a human should have a right to look.

"Hey," he said when I came to stand in front of him, his hands shoved in the pockets of his light blue jeans.

"Hey," I said back, feeling a little more shy around him than usual.

"Do you want to sit?" He gestured at the porch swing they had on the side of the house. "Or would you rather go inside?"

I looked up at the sky. It was actually a really nice day for this late in October. We wouldn't have too many more days like this, so I said, "The porch swing is perfect."

He slipped his hand in mine, intertwining our fingers together, and led me to the swing.

I looked at our hands for a second, loving that we could do this again without feeling like we were breaking some sort of law.

"So, I'm guessing you realized that since Dr. Aarden is my dad, it means we aren't brother and sister after all?" I asked, looking up at his handsome face and liking how petite I felt beside his tall frame.

"Yes. You might say I'm pretty good at putting two and two together." He gave me a soft smile and squeezed my hand.

"Well, that's good," I said. "Hopefully, it was good news."

He chuckled as we sat on the swing together. "Yes, let's just say it was *very* good news."

"You didn't want two extra sisters?" I made a show of looking offended as I angled my body toward him. "You worried we'd become your dad's new favorite kids?"

Carter laughed again, and I liked the way it sounded—a happy, free-spirited sound that made me feel light inside. "I already know Cambrielle is his favorite, so that's not exactly what I was worried about."

I smiled. "Well, I'm glad I'm not your sister, either. Cambrielle and Nash—and probably Ian—all sound like a blast to be related to, but I'm pretty sure I would hate to be related to you."

"That's good. Because the feeling is mutual."

We just looked at each other for a moment with smiles on our faces as the world seemed to right itself around us.

Carter's gaze went to the manilla envelope in my hand. "What do you have in there? Another contract for us to sign?"

I shook my head. "I think we already discovered that we're too good at ignoring those." I held the envelope out to him. "But this is for you."

"My October seventeenth gift?" He arched an eyebrow as he took it from me.

"Yes," I said. "Kind of, at least. I know you aren't big on celebrating this day, but I hope you'll be okay with this."

He slid his finger under the seal, opening the envelope, and then pulled out a certificate from the International Star Registry.

"You named a star after me?" Carter guessed, looking at the piece of paper with the company's logo printed on it.

"Just read it," I said, my palms feeling sweaty as I waited for him to take a closer look at what I'd done.

I knew he was into astronomy and so it seemed like something he would be into, but I'd also taken a slight risk that I wasn't sure he'd like.

He narrowed his gaze as he read the old-fashioned calligraphy, and when his eyes stopped on the name of the star, he looked up at me with surprise in his blue eyes. "You named the star after my mom?" He swallowed, a sudden range of emotions showing on his face. "You named it Astrid?"

I nodded, my heart racing as I hoped it was a good surprise and not a bad one. "I just know how much she means to you and how this time of year is difficult for you because of what happened, and I don't know..." I shrugged, still unable to discern from the look in his eyes if he liked it or hated what I'd done. "I guess I thought it might be nice to name a star after her, so that you could think of her every time you looked at the stars and know that she's looking down on you and watching out for you."

He was quiet as he studied the certificate again. As he ran his fingers across his mother's name and the coordinates of her star, tears started pooling in his eyes.

"Is this okay?" I asked him, suddenly nervous that I might have just brought up more pain for him instead of comfort. "Because I also thought about getting you a T-shirt with the words 'Haughty Mc-Hot Hot' on it, if you think that would be better. Or even just take you out for dinner, if you prefer that. Or—"

Carter touched my arm to stop my nervous rambling. He looked me straight in the eyes and said, "I love it." He ran his hand up my arm and squeezed it. "This is perfect, Ava."

"Really?" I looked up at him carefully, still needing reassurance.

"Yes." He nodded, and the sincerity in his gaze told me that he was speaking the truth. He pulled me against him. "This is the best gift you could have given me," he whispered into my hair.

I wrapped my arms around his torso. "Well, I'm glad you like it."

CARTER and I went inside to eat dinner with his family a little later. I didn't know if any of them knew about why

Carter and I had cooled things off last week—if they knew why we hadn't danced a single dance at Cambrielle's amazing party. But if they did know anything about the angst we'd created for ourselves based on several assumptions, they didn't say anything about it.

We sat around the large wooden table in their formal dining room, eating a delicious pot roast and mashed potatoes that Mr. and Mrs. Hastings had made themselves since it was their chef's day off. Cambrielle and Nash asked their dad all about his latest trip to South America, and then everyone else caught Mr. Hastings up on what they'd been up to in his absence.

Carter held my hand under the table as we all talked and laughed. While there was a huge part of me that would love to become a part of this amazing family someday, I was grateful that it wouldn't be happening in the way that I'd feared just the day before.

"Want to go to the conservatory and look for that star?" Carter whispered against my ear after everyone had finished helping clean up dinner together. "I think it might be dark enough now to see it."

"I'd love to." I dried my hands on a dish towel. Carter pulled me down the long hall past the garage, past the ballroom, and then down to the room made of glass where Carter and I had not so honorably made-out like it was the last thing we'd ever get to do in our lifetime.

"I think this might be one of my favorite rooms in the house now," Carter said as he turned back to me with a wicked smile on his lips.

"You like rooms that remind you of the kind of forbidden moments that could send a person to jail if they got caught?"

He chuckled as he reached for the door. "Forbidden romance does make things more exciting, right? I mean, that contract Nash tampered with certainly forbade us from any sort of relationship and yet, here we are now. Proof that forbidding something only makes you get more creative in making it actually happen."

"That's one way to look at it," I said, my smile broadening. "I suppose I never would have come up with the idea for our little charade if I'd thought anything would actually come from it."

Carter shut the door behind us to block out the light from the hall. If not for the metal frames that held the large panes of glass in place, it almost felt like we had just stepped outside on to a patio in the dark night—a patio that was climate-controlled and filled with beautiful ornate furniture.

Carter pulled me toward the huge telescope near the far wall, and after typing the coordinates to his mom's star into an app on his phone, he moved the telescope to the far corner of the room and got to work locating it through the eyepiece.

As he fiddled with the telescope settings to get it just right, I took him in. He really was a work of art. I knew he wasn't perfect, but I couldn't think of a single thing that I didn't like about him. He was such a good-hearted person.

And even if he wasn't the most social person, never the life of the party, he was a great friend to those he cared about. I felt safe enough to be myself around him, which was something I'd never fully been able to do around anyone besides my mom and Elyse. And it felt amazing. To be liked not just despite all of my quirks and little idiosyncrasies but because of them. He liked me for me.

"I think I found it." Carter looked up from the telescope with a smile on his face and waved me over. "Come see."

I stepped closer, and when I looked through the eyepiece, I saw a beautiful star winking at me in the dark sky, glowing slightly brighter than the other stars surrounding it.

"It's so pretty," I said, taking in the beautiful creation of the universe.

I looked at it for a moment longer and then walked up to Carter who was leaning against the side table where he'd kissed me the evening before.

He held his arms open for me. I gladly went into his embrace, and we held each other for a little while as I listened to his steady heartbeat.

"Thank you again for the birthday present," Carter said in a soft voice against my hair. "I think this might be my favorite birthday yet."

"So it's your birthday now?" I lifted my head to look at him. "Have you finally decided to allow the people who love you to celebrate the day you graced the earth with your amazing presence?"

"I guess you're helping me warm up to the idea a little." He smoothed his fingers through my hair, angling my head back slightly as if positioning me for a kiss. "There's just something else that I'd like for my birthday."

"Yeah?" I arched an eyebrow, curious what else this boy who had the world at his feet could want.

He leaned his face closer, his lips hovering just over mine, and then whispered, "You, Ava. The only thing I want is you."

And since being claimed by Carter was exactly what I

wanted, I smiled and whispered against his lips, "I'm already yours."

I pressed my lips to his and got lost in the moment with the amazing person whom I'd no longer call my math tutor, my fake boyfriend, or even my possible brother. No, the only thing I'd be calling him from now on was *mine*.

EPILOGUE
CAMBRIELLE

"CAMBRIELLE," Ava called my name from one of the couches in the common room after school one day. "Can you please explain to your brother why dressing up like sumo wrestlers for Halloween is a terrible idea?"

I looked over from where I'd been making my afternoon tea at the little kitchenette in our house's common room at the school. Carter and Ava were cuddled up together on a long couch, scrolling through various images of couples wearing coordinating outfits for Halloween. The school's Halloween dance was coming up in less than two weeks, and apparently, since Ava and Carter were officially boyfriend and girlfriend now, they wanted to broadcast their love to the whole school by wearing matching costumes.

It was actually nice to see my brother so happy with Ava. She was fun and they brought out the best in each other, but I really could do with slightly less PDA from the happy couple.

Not that they were in everyone's face with it. I'd actually

only caught them kissing once, but I guess it was more that seeing them so happy together just reminded me of how single I was.

How single I'd always been since the closest I'd ever been to getting asked out on a date was when Mack teased my brothers that he was going to take me to the falls in his truck.

But yeah, that was never going to happen. While Mack and I might have an interesting relationship—one that involved him sleeping on the trundle bed in my room a few times during the first week of school while his parents visited a hospital in New York—it was purely platonic.

Mack had only shown up at my balcony doors after I'd heard him sleepwalking past my open window the previous two nights and told him to just hang out in my room so I could stop chasing him through the woods.

And even though my brothers would freak out if they knew their friend had stayed with me those few nights instead of telling them about his nighttime wanderings, they really had nothing to worry about.

Mack had always been obvious about who he wanted to date, and it had never been the little sister of his best friends. Not in a serious way, at least.

I stepped up behind the couch where Ava and Carter were sitting to take a closer look at the image Carter must have suggested. Sure enough, there was a photo of a college-aged guy and girl wearing inflatable sumo wrestler suits on Carter's iPad.

"What's wrong with those costumes?" I asked Ava after taking a small sip from my tea. "I think they're actually pretty great."

It was, of course, a huge lie. I would never be caught dead in such a horrendous-looking thing. But I couldn't resist teasing her a little.

Carter lifted his arm from Ava's shoulders to give me a fist bump of solidarity before Ava turned around to face me with her mouth hanging open. "You can't be serious, Cambrielle," she said. "I-I've seen your closet and know that there's no way you'd be caught dead wearing an outfit like this."

It was like she was a psychic.

But since I was committed to the act, I stirred my tea and said, "I don't know. I think the peachy-tan skin tone of the suits would really complement your eyes and cheekbones." Yeah, not sure how it would complement cheekbones, but I was making things up as I went. "Plus, it might be a good way to test out how shallow Carter is. I mean, what better way to find out if your love is true than to see if you'll stick with each other when you put on a few hundred pounds?"

"Yeah, no." Ava swiped her finger across the screen to move the sumo-wrestler image out of view. "Half of the reason why I'm dating Carter is because his hotness makes me look hotter. I'd much rather have him show it off than hide it."

Carter chuckled. "Are you saying that if I got fat, you wouldn't like me anymore?"

"Maybe." Ava shot him a sideways glance, her eyebrows wiggling in a challenge.

Carter's jaw dropped, and I wondered if I might need to leave them alone to rethink their relationship.

But then Ava laughed and said, "I'm totally kidding. Yes, your muscles and pretty face are a nice bonus. A very nice bonus." She eyed him flirtatiously. "But if you suddenly got a dad bod and looked like Quasimodo, I *think* I'd still like you."

"You think?" Carter arched his eyebrow. *"You think?"* He leaned closer and started tickling her. "How can you say that after all we've been through?"

Ava giggled and squealed as she tried to get away from him. And even though it was kind of annoying how much they liked each other, they were also super cute together and I was totally jealous of their happiness.

"What's going on in here?" Mack's voice sounded behind us, startling me enough that my tea sloshed a few drops over the brim of my mug.

I quickly licked off the droplets before they could drip onto the rug. Then I looked up at Mack who was a full foot taller than me and said, "Carter and Ava are testing how shallow each of them are."

"And who's winning so far?" Mack asked.

"It's hard to tell," I said.

Ava was now lying on the couch with Carter pinning her in place with his legs as he continued to tickle the sides of her ribs.

As we watched them, Mack lifted my mug from my hands and took a sip. "Mmmm," he said, smacking his lips together. "That's really good. What is it?"

It took me a moment to respond because I hadn't expected him to do that. But once I regained my wits, I took my mug back from him and said, "It's blueberry green tea with a splash of chocolate creamer."

"Nice," he said.

I took another sip from my mug, trying not to think about

the fact that Mack's lips had just been on it. "Have you decided what you're wearing to the Halloween dance?"

"Not yet." He shrugged his broad shoulders. "Haven't really thought that far ahead."

"Yeah, probably not your top priority right now, huh?"

For a brief second, I considered suggesting that we wear the sumo wrestler costumes if Ava and Carter decided not to use them, but since it would be weird to suggest we dress alike, I stopped myself.

Plus, I had already been working on a special costume for the occasion—something that I was hoping would help me finally get on Ben Barnett's radar.

Mack glanced at his watch and sighed. "It's five-thirty. I guess I better head home to help my dad make dinner."

"Yeah?" I asked, feeling a little disappointed that he was leaving already.

He nodded. "We're having the twins over for the first time tonight, so he and my mom want everything to be perfect."

The news about the twins being Mack's half-sisters had been buzzing around the school all week. I knew that Mack had been slightly interested in Ava and Elyse when they'd first come to the school, so I was sure it was a little weird for him to find out he was related to them. Well, actually pretty shocking since it had come completely from left field. But yesterday, while studying for a biology test, when I asked him how he felt about it, he seemed okay with it. He said it was the least of his worries right now, anyway.

Which was why I asked my next question.

"Is your mom out of bed today, then?" I asked, hating that it was a question that even needed to be asked. His mom was the same age as my mom. She shouldn't be spending most of her days in bed when she was barely over forty.

But Mack nodded and said, "Yeah. She's feeling a little better today." He sighed. After glancing at Carter and Ava who had finally stopped their tickling session and were back to looking at possible costume options, he spoke in a low voice, "They're going to New York again next week. I think they were planning to ask your parents if I could stay at your place—with permission this time. So you won't have to worry about me sleepwalking outside your window in the middle of the night."

Even though I knew it meant nothing—that Mack would only be staying at my house because he hated to sleep alone when his mom was getting her treatments—my heart still raced a little at the thought of him sleeping nearby again.

But I tried to keep my face neutral because having feelings for Mack was not something I should ever entertain. So, in as unaffected of a voice as I could manage, I said, "Hopefully you'll sleep better this time."

And hopefully his sleepwalking episodes would stop so my brothers wouldn't find out the real reason why I now kept a men's deodorant and extra toothbrush in my bathroom.

WANT to read a **bonus epilogue** from Carter's point of view set five years in the future? Snag it here: https://Book Hip.com/QTJZSZX

Read Cambrielle and Mack's story next!

Everyone has three lives. A public life, a private life, and a secret life.

Read The Facade here: https://www.judycorry.com/the-facade

Join my Newsletter: https://subscribepage.com/judycorry

Join the Corry Crew on Facebook: https://www.facebook.com/groups/judycorrycrew/

Follow me on Instagram: @authorjudycorry

ENJOY THIS SNEAK PEEK OF THE FACADE

CAMBRIELLE

"Have you guys decided what you're dressing up as for the Halloween dance?" my friend Scarlett, a senior with auburn hair and high cheekbones, asked Elyse and me when we joined her and her best friend Hunter at the table in the great hall for lunch.

"I'm not sure," Elyse said with a shrug. "Usually, Ava and I plan our costumes together, but since she and Carter are coordinating this year, I'm not sure what I'm doing."

Ava and Elyse were identical twins who had just come to Eden Falls Academy at the beginning of the school year. They had caused quite the stir when they first arrived, catching most of the guys' attention at our private school since they were new and gorgeous. But things had settled down a bit now that we were almost two months into the school year and Ava had paired off with my older brother Carter.

"Any ideas what you'd like to dress up as? A character

from a movie, or something else?" I asked Elyse, hoping to be helpful.

"I was thinking about going as Elizabeth Swan from *Pirates of the Caribbean* or maybe even Cher from *Clueless*."

"You would make the perfect Elizabeth Swan." Scarlett's eyes widened with excitement. "You have the perfect bone structure to pull off the Keira Knightley look."

"You think so?" Elyse asked, her cheeks coloring slightly as Scarlett and I looked at her.

"You would look so good," I agreed with Scarlett. "Were you thinking of wearing one of the fancy gowns? Or the pirate clothes?"

"One of the gowns," Elyse said. "My mom has a dress she designed that would be perfect for it." Elyse and Ava's mom was a famous fashion designer, and so of course she would have the hookups for something like that.

"Dang, you're going to look so good. All the guys will be asking you to dance all night," Scarlett said, her tone envious. "Don't you think so, Hunter?" She glanced at Hunter who was, as usual, reading something on his phone.

When he didn't respond, Scarlett nudged him with her elbow.

"Uh, what did you say?" Hunter asked, finally looking up from his phone.

Scarlett eyed Hunter somewhat impatiently and said, "I was saying that Elyse dressing up like Elizabeth Swan is like every guy's fantasy."

"Oh..." Hunter narrowed his green eyes and seemed to take in Elyse's long, brown hair and olive-complected skin for a moment, as if picturing her in eighteenth-century clothes. With a shrug, he said, "I guess I can see it."

And then, he immediately went back to reading whatever he had up on his phone screen.

Scarlett cast our aloof friend a wary glance, like she wasn't sure what to think about how distracted he'd been all year. But then she shrugged and turned her brown-eyed gaze to me. "What about you, Cambrielle? Have you picked your costume yet?"

"I just got the last piece of it yesterday," I said, unable to keep a smile from lifting my lips as I thought about the costume I'd been working on for weeks. Dressing up was one of my favorite things to do, so of course Halloween was one of my favorite holidays.

"And what are you going to be?" Elyse asked.

My smile turned mischievous. "It's a secret."

"It's a secret?" Scarlett asked, her eyes brimming with intrigue just as I'd hoped. "And why is that?"

I shrugged. "I just want to surprise everyone."

Which was true. I did want to keep the Kelana costume my mom and I had been pulling pieces together for over the past few weeks a secret. Kelana being the main character from my favorite romantic fantasy movie.

Though, what would have been even more true was to say that I wanted to surprise a *specific* person with my costume. That person being the super-hot and amazing Ben Barnett.

Ben was in the grade above me—a senior like most of my friends—and I'd had a crush on him ever since last spring when he led the boys' soccer team to the state championships.

There was just something about a guy who could handle

a ball and lead his team to victory that was super attractive to me.

But since I was painfully awkward around guys I liked, I'd never dared do anything about my crush—in fact, I hadn't even said a single word to him since the school year started. I didn't go up to high school gods like Ben.

But I had a plan. I was going to channel my inner Kelana at the Halloween dance and under the disguise of my glittery, pink masquerade mask, faerie-queen makeup, and beautiful one-of-a-kind dress, I was going to finally ask him to dance.

And if the dance went well, I was going to ask him out.

Sure, asking Ben out before I revealed my true identity probably wasn't the greatest plan, but it was all about baby steps at this point. I mean, he would be graduating at the end of the year, and since we were already in the last week of October, there wasn't a whole lot of time left for me to get up the nerve to make something happen.

And if my plan totally bombed and I completely humiliated myself in front of Ben, no one would be the wiser because no one would know it was me.

"Will you give us any hints about your costume?" Elyse asked, searching my face with her golden-brown eyes. "Is it a real person, or maybe a character from a movie?"

I shook my head. "Sorry, but this secret is going to remain locked down tight until we're at the party. I'm not even letting Carter or Nash know."

Carter and Nash were my older brothers who also attended our school.

"Well, aren't you mysterious," Scarlett said.

I shrugged. "I guess so."

Elyse seemed to realize that I wasn't going to give any hints because she turned to Scarlett and asked her what she was planning to dress up as.

Scarlett poked at her salad with her fork. "I'm trying to convince Hunter here to dress up like an astronaut so I can be the pretty alien he finds on Mars." She bumped her shoulder against his. "But so far he's pretty set on not dressing up."

Hunter glanced over at his best friend with a smirk on his lips and said, "When I'm already dressed as the coolest person in the room, why would I dress up like anything else?"

"Why indeed?" Scarlett shook her head, a slight smile lifting her lips at Hunter's cocky statement. But when Hunter went back to looking at his phone, she glanced at Elyse and me and said, "I'll keep working on him."

The rest of our friends joined us at the table with their lunch trays, so we made room for them. My older brother Carter and his girlfriend, Ava—who was Elyse's identical twin—sat on the side where Scarlett and Hunter were.

Carter's best friend Mack, who was also our next-door neighbor, slipped into the spot on my left. And Elyse scooted closer to me to make room for my other brother Nash.

That's right, my brothers and I actually chose to sit at the same table during lunch because we got along, strangely enough.

Now how did I come to have *two* brothers who were both seniors but not twins, despite the fact that they shared the same dirty-blond hair and aqua-blue eyes?

Well, that's a long story, but basically, we all had the same dad—the famous billionaire businessman Joel Hastings

—but while Nash and I were full-blooded siblings born a year apart, my dad got Carter's mom pregnant a few months before he married my mom, so Carter was only seven months older than Nash.

Yep, my dad wasn't just good at making money in his early twenties. He was also accomplished at producing heirs as well.

So my dad had three kids all born within a year and a half of each other in addition to being the stepfather to my oldest brother, Ian, who came from my mom's first marriage.

Things were crazy when we were younger, and my parents had to hire a full-time nanny to help with all the chaos my brothers and I created. But we were all best friends now, and I knew that when Nash and Carter graduated at the end of the year, leaving me all alone for my senior year, I was going to miss them.

I was going to miss all my friends actually, since yep, you guessed it, they were all seniors and I was the only junior among us.

"So I was just asking Cambrielle and Elyse what they were going to wear to the Halloween dance," Scarlett said once everyone had gotten themselves situated around the table. "What are the rest of you planning to dress up like?"

"I was thinking that I'd probably just go as myself," Mack's deep voice sounded from beside me. "I mean, why dress up when I could just go as the coolest person I know?"

"Hey, that's what I said," Hunter said with a smile, slipping his phone into his pocket now that the rest of the crew had joined us.

"Great minds." Mack held out a hand to give Hunter a fist bump across the table.

Hunter bumped his fist against Mack's knuckles. Bemused, I just shook my head, because while I loved my brothers' best friends, they did have a certain arrogance to them.

Though, I guess I couldn't really blame them. They were all basically the princes of Eden Falls Academy—popular, confident, and belonged to the nation's wealthiest families. And while I was definitely not attracted to my brothers— because *ew*—I'd be lying if I didn't admit that Hunter and Mack were super cute.

So cute that when we were all in middle school, I'd totally had a huge crush on Mack.

I'd gotten over that crush eventually, and moved on to liking other guys like Ben, of course. But yeah, Mack, Hunter, and my brothers did have most of the female population at our school crushing on them.

And yes, they knew it, too.

It must be nice knowing so many people wanted you.

Nash cleared his throat, bringing me back to the present as he answered Scarlett's question. "I was planning to go as the Phantom."

"Really?" Elyse turned to my brother with a smile on her glossy pink lips. *"The Phantom of the Opera?"*

Nash nodded. "I figured I might as well start getting into character early since I'll be playing him soon."

Nash and Elyse were both big into the theater program at our school, and while the auditions for the winter musical weren't for several weeks, Nash was basically a shoo-in for the male lead. He'd already played bigger roles in last year's musicals—not the lead yet since the drama teacher Miss Crawley liked to fill those with seniors when possible. But only something crazy would keep Nash from winning the part of the Phantom. And I was pretty sure Elyse had a good shot at getting the part of Christine.

As for me, I was still trying to decide if I wanted to audition to be one of the dancers. So far, I'd only worked as a crew member because unlike my brother who was a spotlight hog, I preferred to keep attention away from myself. But I did miss dancing, and since there would be other dancers on the stage with me, I figured it might be time for me to pull out my ballet shoes again.

"Did you already say what you're going as, Cambrielle?" Mack asked from beside me, breaking me from my thoughts.

"Oh, um." I licked my lips. "It's a secret."

"Really?" Mack raised a dark eyebrow, his brown eyes filling with intrigue the same way Scarlett's had earlier. "And why's that?"

Because I need anonymity in order to put myself out there.

"Just for fun," I said instead. "I figure I'd keep everyone on their toes. Not all of us can go as ourselves like you apparently are."

"And you're sure you can't tell me?" He cocked his head to the side. "You already know I'm great at keeping secrets."

And when he winked, my cheeks burned because I knew exactly which secret he was referring to.

He must have noticed my blush because a wicked grin slipped onto his lips. In a low voice next to my ear, he whispered, "Which reminds me. Have you gotten your room all ready for me to stay in tonight?"

My eyes widened and I almost gasped out loud before I

caught myself. "What?" I glanced around the table to make sure no one heard what he said.

Thankfully, everyone was looking at Carter and Ava as Ava told them all about the costumes they were considering.

"I'm kidding." Mack chuckled, apparently loving my reaction. "I already know I'm staying in Ian's room. Your dad obviously doesn't know that I already spent a few nights in your room last month."

"And we're going to keep it that way." I gave him a warning look before making sure our friends—and most importantly, my brothers—were still paying us no attention.

"Should I be offended that you want to keep me your dirty little secret?" Mack whispered in my ear, making chills race from my neck and down my whole body.

I shivered uncontrollably and whispered back, "Since my dad and brothers would kill you if they ever caught wind of that, then yes, I'm pretty sure I'll be taking that secret to the grave."

Mack pouted. "That's no fun."

I raised an eyebrow. "Well, since I'd like to see you graduate instead of have you come to an untimely death because my family found out, I think it's fine to not be fun."

Not that anything scandalous had happened those few nights he'd slept in my room. Sadly for me, the only times I'd ever been kissed had happened during a game of Spin the Bottle.

What had actually happened was that Mack started sleepwalking again when his parents went to New York for the first round of special treatments for his mom's brain tumor. I had found him asleep on the bank of my family's pond one morning when I'd taken my horse out for a sunrise ride.

When I'd gone up to him to ask why he was sleeping there, he had tried to play it off—pretend like he'd just gone on an early morning swim with the fish but got tired afterwards. But I had overheard Mrs. Aarden telling my mom about Mack's sleepwalking episodes since her diagnosis, so I knew better than to believe him.

And when I heard footsteps on the path outside my open balcony window the next night, I hurried down to help him before he could end up in the pond again.

When it happened a third night and he still wouldn't ask my brothers or anyone else for help, I decided to sneak him up into my bedroom so that if he had another episode, I could catch him when he first got up instead of having to chase him through the woods between our houses.

He came to my room the rest of that week, climbing up the tree by my balcony just after my parents and brothers had gone to bed for the night. And starting out in my room had apparently done the trick because he ended up not sleepwalking any of the nights he stayed on the trundle bed beside me—maybe his subconscious knew he had help close by and he was safe.

And so even though my family probably would have freaked out if they'd known I had a seventeen-year-old guy— one I'd had a major crush on at one point—sleeping just a few feet away from me at night, I was glad that he'd at least trusted me to help him when he wouldn't tell my brothers.

"What time are you coming over, anyway?" I asked Mack as he wolfed down some of his teriyaki chicken.

He swallowed his bite of food and wiped his mouth with

a napkin before saying, "They're heading out after my dad gets off work, so I'll probably be there before dinner."

There was a hint of anxiety in his eyes at the mention of his parents leaving. And I hated seeing it because I hated that his family was even dealing with this. Dealing with the possibility of his mom not being here to watch him graduate.

Whenever I saw the fear in Mack's eyes, I wanted to give him a hug and tell him that everything would be okay. But since he didn't seem to ever want to bring attention to what was going on in his personal life—always preferring to make everyone laugh instead of talking about his family's crisis—I just gave him what I hoped was an understanding smile and said, "Well, my mom and Marie planned to have your favorite pork burritos for dinner, so we'll keep you well fed while your parents are in New York.

Want to find out what happens next? Read The Facade here: https://www.judycorry.com/the-facade

ALSO BY JUDY CORRY

Eden Falls Academy Series:

The Charade (Ava and Carter)

The Facade (Cambrielle and Mack)

The Ruse (Elyse and Asher)

The Confidant (Scarlett and Hunter)

The Confession (Kiara and Nash)

Kings of Eden Falls:

Hide Away With You (Addie and Evan)

Say You Remember Me (Maddie and Ian)

Wish You Were Mine (Lucy and Owen)

Rich and Famous Series:

Assisting My Brother's Best Friend (Kate and Drew)

Hollywood and Ivy (Ivy and Justin)

Her Football Star Ex (Emerson and Vincent)

Friend Zone to End Zone (Arianna and Cole)

Stolen Kisses from a Rock Star (Maya and Landon)

Ridgewater High Series:

When We Began (Cassie and Liam)

Meet Me There (Ashlyn and Luke)

Don't Forget Me (Eliana and Jess)

It Was Always You (Lexi and Noah)

My Second Chance (Juliette and Easton)

My Mistletoe Mix-Up (Raven and Logan)

Forever Yours (Alyssa and Jace)

<u>Standalones:</u>

Protect My Heart (Emma and Arie)

Kissing The Boy Next Door (Lauren and Wes)

ABOUT THE AUTHOR

Judy Corry is the Amazon Top 12 and *USA Today* Bestselling Author of Contemporary and YA Romance. She writes romance because she can't get enough of the feeling of falling in love. She's known for writing heart-pounding kisses, endearing characters, and hard-won happily ever afters.

She lives in Southern Utah with the boy who took her to Prom, their four awesome kids, two dogs and a cat. She's addicted to love stories, dark chocolate and chai lattes.